LOCAL TRIBES

Thomas Hansen Hickenbottom

authorHOUSE®

AuthorHouse™
1663 Liberty Drive
Bloomington, IN 47403
www.authorhouse.com
Phone: 1-800-839-8640

First published by AuthorHouse   5/16/2011

ISBN: 978-1-4520-4367-8 (e)
ISBN: 978-1-4520-4366-1 (sc)
ISBN: 978-1-4520-4365-4 (hc)

Library of Congress Control Number: 2010909252

Printed in the United States of America

This book is printed on acid-free paper.

Cover image of the author courtesy of Donald "Chic" Van Selus.

ACKNOWLEDGEMENTS

The members of the Santa Cruz surfing and commercial and stream-fishing cultures from the late nineteen-sixties, who provided valuable historical information into the formation of this book.

US Representative Mike Honda's Washington, D.C. office for accurate personal interviews with World War Two survivors of the Bataan Death March and for Representative Honda's on-going work in trying to get reparations for American veterans imprisoned by the Japanese in World War Two who were forced into slave labor in the factories of Japan.

The United States Coast Guard Auxiliary of Monterey, California.

World War Two and Korean War veterans who shared personal experiences at the Palo Alto Veterans Administration Hospital.

Bill Dianda of Quality Automotive.

Susan Allison, David Compton and Shari Thompson for clear editorial direction.

PROLOGUE

Santa Cruz, fall of '66.
After Korea, during the spawning of Nam.
Before all the L.A, Berkeley and New Yorkers.
Before the yuppies and techies hit town.
Before the valley invasion.
And before all the UCSC "politically correct" insurgents.

It was still twenty-five cent burgers, "crusin' the loop," late night drags at "four lanes" and beehive hairdos. It was the "Grove" dances on Friday and Saturday nights with music from the Tikis, Corny and the Corvettes and the White Lady. It was massive steelhead, salmon and albacore runs, and uncrowded surf.

The fishing fleet no longer berthed alongside the wharf or in davits on top. The new small craft harbor opened a few years earlier and most workboats opted for berths there.
In winter huge northerly swells spawned by vicious storms in the Gulf of Alaska jacked up steep, pitching waves with a brutal frenzy at Steamer Lane. And only a brave few ever paddled out to challenge them.

The commercial fishers still hung out at the wharf coffee shop in the predawn hours, getting pumped up on caffeine and bragging about who would haul in the biggest catch of the day.

And the kids.
Wild and insatiable with hot salt water running through their veins.
Marco was one of those.

Marco spun the nine-six O'neill Intruder surfboard towards shore and pulled hard as the last wave in the set approached, a grinding nine footer. The wave swept in, felt its way along the reef, peaked up at the point and began to hollow out. Marco buried his arms deep in the wave's face, pulling the surfboard down into the steep mass of ocean energy. He leaped to his feet, pointing the nose of the board downward into the hollowness, jamming a hard turn at the bottom of the watery void as the wave hammered the reef.

The board tracked high up in the heart of the wave as it hollowed out even more, then picked up speed as it hit the shallower reef along the cove. Marco took four quick steps toward the nose and squatted down inside the tube, as he raced to the inner section. Inching closer to the nose, he drove the Intruder at top speed.

The wave opened up even more, becoming a long, concave pipeline of energy. Marco held his breath as he entered the final bowl and forced the board down to the very bottom of the wave. He feared it was so steep it would cause the tail and fin to slip out. Pushing harder, he squatted with head lowered and arms outstretched in front, charging into the green/gray tube as the wave lined up the full length of the beach. The wall of water pitched over him and he was locked inside. As the thick lip descended, he dove off the nose to escape the heavy pummeling. The wave exploded on the shore with a thrashing, pounding roar, pushing a churning mixture of foam, sand and kelp shards up against the shale cliff. Marco dove under it all, then surfaced as a seabird glided overhead.

He stood up in the waist-deep frigid water, pulling his drenched baggy swimsuit up into his long-sleeved wetsuit jacket. The skin on his bare legs tightened in the freezing ocean.

As he waded to shore through the sandy foam, he thought about how strange it was; moments ago the entire cove was awash in raging swells, and now an almost eerie calm descended. That's the way it always was for a surfer: one moment you're racing along, adrenaline surging, using all your skill to ride the natural energy without being consumed by it; then you find yourself sitting quietly atop your board in still water, wanting to experience the stoke of it again.

The Intruder lay forty yards down the beach, fin up, in a mound of tangled kelp, with only a few minor scratches on the rails and bottom. A small spotted seal barked at Marco as it cruised just outside the surf zone. He wondered if it would join the others on Seal Rock by "the Lane" after dark or find refuge in a more secluded rock-nest on the Westside. He smiled as the seal turned and swam through the orange-glazed ocean.

His bare legs began to shiver as November wind turned on-shore. Bits of kelp and sand stuck to the hair on his shins. Goosebumps rose on his thighs and lower back. He zipped up his wetsuit jacket tightly at the neck and snapped the crotch flap together over his " baggies." Another set approached on the horizon as the sun cast a gold hue on the ocean's mottled skin. Bulbous dark clouds began to gather high above.

It had rained hard for three days and let up just long enough for the sea to glass off for two hours. Marco was the only one to paddle out during the calm and knew the conditions wouldn't be stable for long.

That's the way it always was. He was either there when it was happening or he missed it, one of the unwritten laws of surfing. The conditions during storm season could change radically within the briefest period of time. It could be bumpy and choppy one moment, then smooth out and form a glassy skin the next. Only those who were closely aligned with the sea knew that truth. It was almost a kinetic thing, an inner knowing he'd acquired after years of living by the ocean.

Marco was becoming a true devotee of riding " the Cove." It was his passion, his quest, and everything else in life paled in importance. He checked out the conditions several times a day, even during storms to see if it was surfable. He'd just scored again with the perfect surf, the beautiful moment, while everyone else in the world was doing something else.

He was stoked the 1966 north swell season was now pumping in constant waves. The warmer surface water from the hot days of summer had disappeared. Marco switched from a wearing a sleeveless vest to a full wet suit jacket. By January the water temperature would become freezing, when offshore winds blew from the chilly valleys and frost-covered foothills.

Marco wrestled the twenty-eight pound Intruder up the side of the cliff. He cautiously climbed the slick, drenched shale, pulling up the heavy board ever so carefully. His feet turned purple and felt numb from the intense cold. The ocean was probably fifty degrees or so, the air temp around forty-five, with a side-shore wind against his wet, bare legs, turning to a penetrating freeze. He watched another eight-wave set roll through and pictured himself inside each tube as they curled into the shore break. The wind rose in strength, causing the waves to "mush out," losing their perfect shape, becoming lines of choppy water unfit for riding.

He clutched some ice plant tendrils, ascending ever so slowly, at last lifting himself and the board onto the top of the muddy cliff. As he stood shaking in the freeze he felt almost like a guardian of the place, he and the other members of the "Cove crew." It was their break and no one else was welcome. Locals only, man.

Gravel from the road stung the bottoms of his tender, frozen feet as he trudged along West Cliff Drive with the board under arm. He turned down Almar Street toward Oxford Way. His cold fingers stung from gripping the fiberglass rails of the board. He dodged pods dropping from eucalyptus trees as he made it past the Mitchell's house.

The "Cove" was named after them, Mitchell's Cove, because the Mitchell brothers had surfed there during the fifties and lived only a block away. They also opened the very first local surf shop in 1956.

That was back in the balsawood era Marco reminisced, before the "foamies," when boards made out of glued-up balsawood planks were 9'6" to 11'2" in length and weighed between thirty-five and forty pounds. He knew that the shaper, Johnny Rice, had to hone each wood board down with a drawknife and block plane. He was glad that era was long gone and loved his new O'neill foam board. It was so much lighter and way more maneuverable in the waves.

As he trudged down the wet street, he pictured the spring of '57 when he first started surfing, right at the end of " the wood era" at Cowell's Beach. Back then, he had to borrow boards from the older surfers, "grubs," they were called. He'd paddle out at Cowell's Cove, near the beach, and perfect his moves after many a wipe out in the numbing water. He'd only last about forty minutes or so without a wetsuit, but nobody had wetsuits then. After a few freezing dumps in the water, he'd paddle in and try to warm up next to a blazing driftwood fire. Those memories made his legs shiver.

He turned the muddy corner onto Oxford Way and set the Intruder down on the smooth gravel in front of the white two-story house. Light raindrops ran down his cheek. He pulled off the wetsuit jacket, hosed the salt water from it quickly and hung it to drip-dry over the swing on the porch. Then he turned the hose on himself, quickly rinsing off. It was cold as hell, but beat having his body covered with an itchy, salty crust all night long. He wasn't allowed to use the warm indoor shower or rather agreed to not use it. That way he didn't have to pay any utilities. Every now and then though, when no one was around he'd sneak one.

Inside his little room, the sun porch, his "baggies" plopped to the floor. Marco stood next to a small electric heater and cranked it up full blast. He shivered. Wiping wet cornstarch from his arms, he watched the red-hot strips of the heater blast on and off in the darkness and listened to the fan as it pumped out heat. Marco used either cornstarch or baby powder to get his arms to slide into his stiff rubber suit jacket. Cornstarch was the best; it was cheaper than baby powder and who wanted to smell like a baby's ass in the water anyhow. He slid into some levis, a white tee shirt and donned his dark green O'Neill team jacket. He tapped his numb feet against the wood floor. They itched, tingled and burned, turning deep red from purple as sensations returned. Rubbing them briskly brought back the natural skin tone, although they still throbbed.

He fired up a Camel, inhaled and slowly stopped shivering. As he lay back on his narrow, canvas cot, he thought about his dad's recent death and his mom's reaction. Things had gotten too hard for him to live in that house anymore, the house of his youth, the house of death. He just couldn't hack it with her night crying ... the drinking ... and her mood swings. He tried to stick around and help her out, but it was too much to handle and he felt pretty burned out being there.

To get some space from it all, he moved into the sun porch of the Lang and Jenks' house. He didn't have to pay rent, just mow the back lawn and help out with the chores. The Lang and Jenks' kids lived there alone. The Lang brothers' dad married the Jenks' kids' mom, then split town a month later, leaving his two boys with his new wife. Six weeks later, she left suddenly with some new guy for the east coast, leaving all the kids "temporarily" as she put it, promising to send some money soon.

A siren wailed in the dark distance. It faded into a receding drone, reminding Marco of last month when the ambulance took his dad to the Sister's Hospital on West Cliff Drive. A sick feeling pinged in his gut as he remembered that night ...

"*Marco... get up... your father... help me...*" *His mother, Marie, padded back down the hall in her bathrobe, with Marco, half-dazed, in tow. A plastic crucifix and some framed photos crashed on the thin, carpeted floor as they groped along* the wall. His dad, Louie, lay quivering on his stomach in the corner of the bedroom. " Turn 'im over," she yelled. "Quick."

They rolled him onto his back. Marie stuck her fingers in his mouth. " He bit his tongue again." The doorbell rang. " Let 'em in." Marie pointed to the door.

Marco flicked on the hall light. Two orderlies burst in with a litter.

" In there," he pointed towards the bedroom. Moments later, they hustled Louie outside into the foggy night. Marie hurriedly changed into some clothes. They slid the litter into the back of a waiting ambulance. " I'll go, you stay," Marie sobbed, then climbed in the back as the double doors slammed shut. They disappeared seconds later, as a group of neighbors gathered just outside the waist-high, redwood fence next to the persimmon tree and camellias. Marco could hear them mumbling in Italian and English, gesturing towards the house.

Marco shut the door, killed the lights and peeked through the blinds as the neighbors dispersed. He slunk down the hallway to the little living room and sprawled on the couch, staring at patterns on the wall from streetlight slipping through lace curtains. He breathed short and shallow breaths. He waited for the phone to ring, and imagined his dad being hooked up to tubes in the hospital.

Marco picked up the black and white photo from the floor of his dad's boat, " the Three M's," studying it carefully in the low light. Louie was waving with a stogie in hand at whoever was taking the picture. Marco knew it had to be another local fisher. In the photo, Louie had the outriggers out and was trolling for albacore about fifty or so miles outside the bay, in what fisherman called, " the blue water." That meant you were way outside the influence of the bay, running off the coastal shelf of the continent, in the warmer Japanese current, where the albacore migrated.

Louie always felt at home out there. It was a place where a man could be alone with nature and his thoughts, away from " the petty bullshit in town," as he called it.

" Once you've worked on the water," Louie always told Marco, " you'll never wanna work on land again."

He'd often tell Marco about what it was like "out there," at sun up, when the "albies" were running in great schools, and hitting all the lures at once. "My god," he'd say, "what glory when we'd pull in next to the wharf with the hold filled with albacore and unload them, already cleaned and ready to sell." He loved to set the autopilot for the bay, light up a smoke and butcher the guts and skin off the fish, carving perfect foot and a half long fillets. He'd sing and toss the innards into the air while gulls squawked and dove for the free lunch, as "the Three M's" rose and swished with each swell. And then he'd have a swig or two of wine or whiskey or whatever. Louie told Marco he'd teach him how to "fool the albies" after he graduated from high school. He didn't want to take him out so far from land until he " became a man."

On weekends in late spring and during summer vacation, Marco remembered helping out, washing down the decks and cleaning fish during salmon season. He'd go out with his dad for the salmon troll because they weren't usually very far off shore. Louie taught him how to steer the Three M's with the swells hitting the boat from all directions, and just last summer showed him the way to set a course using the compass. Marco already knew how to set the various lines from the outriggers and gain the right speed for trolling.

But albacore was an entirely different matter, and Marie would never allow Marco to go. He reflected on all the fights they'd had about it. She'd been around commercial fishermen for long enough to know how quickly things could change when they were way off shore. She'd heard all the stories at the family parties, when the men sat around and chewed on cigars and sipped homemade red wine, while the women peeled garlic, cooked pasta and gossiped. From behind the boiling pots of steaming water, she'd listen to the tales of engine troubles and VHF troubles and sudden squalls and even a few episodes of boats disappearing altogether. The Coast Guard might reach them in time, if their radio worked, but if things got critical and they were stranded, they were just way out of luck. It was Davey Jones they'd be having they're next drink with.

And then there was the time when Louie lost the small finger on his left hand. He was winching up crab pots in a squall while the Three M's rocked side to side in the heaving swells. His hand got snagged in some frayed line and was sucked into the steel rollers of the winch. He jerked it out before the entire hand was sheared, but the tough nylon rope cinched down hard on the finger, tearing it off at the lower knuckle. He quickly wrapped it up in a greasy rag, taped it to the next finger as a splint and continued to pull in the pots. It was a good catch that day he said, but he had to leave a little bit of himself there in trade, " a little chum fer the crabs," he'd laugh. He stayed out for a few more hours, re-baiting the pots one last time before heading in. He had to hit the whiskey a little earlier that day.

Once ashore, he drove home. Marco recalled Marie unwrapping the wound, crying and screaming at him for not going to the doctor right away. She bundled up the hand in her apron and sped him to Sisters Hospital, just above the wharf, in his old Willys pickup, grinding gears each time she shifted. Marco rode in the bed of the truck, witnessing it all.

The doc sewed up the jagged tear as best he could, put him on morphine and antibiotics and told him to not use the hand for three weeks. Louie gave him a fifty-dollar bill and nine live crabs in a burlap sack in trade for the doc's handy work. *And three days later when the pain and throbbing started to ease up a bit, Louie headed back out the bay with the tide for the fishing grounds, cranked up on morphine. Since then, he was nicknamed," Stub," by his fellow fisherman. Marco loved the way his dad would always gesture with a stogie or cig in the mangled hand as he told the tale at parties.*

Marie couldn't stand to think of losing her only son at sea during albacore season, not if she had anything to say about it, which she always did. It didn't matter how much Marco begged or kissed up, the answer was always, "No."

Marco set the photo down on the coffee table and rolled up in a blue wool navy blanket on the couch. Hours passed, the phone never stirred and before he realized it, he'd fallen into a dream world of jagged images...

Returning from the flashback, Marco found himself on the cold sun porch, feeling the warmth finally returning to his feet. He knelt down and pulled out his black tennis shoes and stained white socks. A small piece of skin had shorn off the bottom of his left foot, stinging as sensations returned. He hadn't noticed it before in the numbing cold. He must've sliced it on the reef after diving under that last wave or cut it on the rough pavement walking home.

He wedged the Camel butt into the hard soil of a shriveled asparagus fern in the red pot next to his cot. The streetlight blinked on, illuminating beaded rain drops on the three picture windows of his room. A frog belched under the porch and a cat hissed. Drops hit the windows forming tiny watery veins, which trickled down the glass. A minute later the windows were awash in pounding rain. A mosquito buzzed as he knelt to tie his black tennis shoes; he smashed the bloodsucker against his neck, crushing it against his skin. Marco lit a white candle and another smoke, sat back against his bed, and stared at the flickering gold light. As it darted back and forth in the drafty room, he sucked a few deep drags and followed the wavy shadows on the sidewall. The heater blasted on and off. He tried to fight off images in his mind of the night his dad died, only three days after the ambulance took him away. He couldn't hold them back, and they busted through clear and intense...

That very afternoon Marco had paddled out at "the Cove" without a wetsuit just before going to the hospital. The waves were puny, broken up, with a slight wind bump on the surface. Light fog hung a few yards above. He stroked out to the usual take off spot just outside the point, sat up, with bare legs dangling in the cold water. The horizon was a mish mash of bright fog and deepening gray. He heard blackbirds chirp in the lone cypress atop the cliff. Occasional seabirds cruised the shallow inner waters with hungry bellies. A gull tore at black mussels on the kelp-coated rocks of the inner reef, and a family of pipers skittered at the water's edge, occasionally stooping to peck for burrowing sand crabs. Marco's head pounded as he tried not to think about his dad lying in the hospital, hooked up to plastic tubes and monitors, going in and out of consciousness.

With eyes closed, he tried to concentrate on the natural sounds, the sounds that in the past always brought him peace: the slapping of the waves on the beach, his breath as it gathered and left his body, and the distant, muted barking of seals and seabirds.

A German shepherd growled on the beach, chasing a gull with a broken wing. The gull lumbered along, dragging the fan of feathers behind, then let out a high-pitched squawk as the dog crunched into its abdomen. The shrieking wail shocked Marco out of his trance. The dog shook the gull's carcass back and forth wildly in his mouth, feathers scattering on the wet sand. Marco's gut wrenched. He felt like vomiting.

He slid off his board into the frigid sea. A freezing blast jolted his senses as he surfaced and flung his arms across the deck of the Intruder. The cold shock zapped his mind and nerves. His inner torment dissipated for a few moments and he felt renewed and released from it all. The ocean had done its job again. But the cold became too intense. Out of survival instinct, he dragged himself atop the board and began to shake uncontrollably. As the shivering subsided, Marco headed to shore, the freeze sliding up his arms with each stroke. He shuffled through the glazed sand and strained up the cliff to his '55 Chevy. The memory of changing into his clothes and driving to Sisters Hospital was lost in a melee of disjoined thoughts and emotions.

Parking the white sedan near the rear entrance to the hospital, he wiped the drying salt from his short hair and face, entered the double rear doors, and paced down the hall. The wooden floor creaked and a light bulb flickered in one of the overhead lamps. An orderly was mopping out an empty room. A pile of stained bedding lay next to the wall by a janitor's cart. The smell of ammonia hung in the hallway.

The thick wood door to his dad's room creaked open. His mom sat in silence, as Marco pulled a chair up to the foot of the bed.

" Where you been?" his mom snapped. Her anger masked the fear that now flashed in her dark eyes.

" In the water...."

"How couldya go surfin' ata time like this?"

" Needed some time ta think."

"Think! Whattaya mean think? You never think 'bout no one but you," she sobbed.

8

Marco felt a rage rising inside. He wanted to yell and tell her how important it was for him to be in the water, how nature helped him keep his cool, but he didn't. Instead, he clenched his teeth.

Louie lay comatose, just as Marco thought he'd be. The whole thing was such an insult to his dad, especially the way Louie hated doctors and hospitals. Marco remembered Louie telling him about getting stiffed by two "valley" doctors he'd taken out on a salmon charter. After a day trolling, they hadn't caught one fish. "Some days they just don't bite, they get spooked or something," Louie had told them, but they still didn't pay. Louie never took out doctors again. He could've taken them to court, but he didn't. Louie always felt that a man's word was good enough for him, and when a man broke his word, the rest of his life was destined to fail. He told Marco to never forget that.

He knew his dad would've much rather gone down in a storm at sea, or any other way than this, being kept alive through IV's and drugs in some smelly hospital bed.

The door opened. Dr. Johnson came in, a tall, lanky man, in a three piece, grey bell-bottomed suit with glasses. Marco thought he looked more like a businessman.

He pulled down his stethoscope, listened to Louie's chest and shook his head, "Damn strong heart, Mrs. D'Giorgio."

Just what an asshole doctor would say, Marco thought.

The doctor held Louie's wrist to check his pulse. Louie suddenly gasped for air. His tongue was still wrapped in gauze.

"Doctor!" Marie was livid.

"Dammit." The doc ran to the door and yelled for the nurse.

Louie sat up in bed and mumbled something in Italian, staring at Marco. His eyes were half shut and watery.

Marco stood up, grabbing for him, "What? What'd you say, dad? "

Louie's eyes opened all the way; he tried to speak and reach for Marco but fell back onto the pillow. Marie bawled out of control. The doctor ran back in and caught her as her legs buckled. "Nurse...nurse," he yelled, "now!"

Marco stood transfixed. He watched his dad take one last long breath and collapse. The muscles in his face relaxed, and his eyes had a peaceful, far away look, as if he were watching dawn sunlight flicker over a school of albacore as they broke the surface of a shimmering sea.

The light grew brilliant in the room. Marco felt dizzy, detached from his body, as if he were slowly drifting a few feet above his mom, not in physical form at all. He shook his head, fighting for composure. Marie was hysterical on the floor in the doctor's arms. A nurse ran in, helping to hoist her to an armchair.

"*Goddamit.*" *Marco bolted from the room, down the hallway. An overhead light blinked like a strobe. A young nun clad in black habit leaned on a push broom against the wall. Marco heard the muffled sound of an accordion playing on a radio in the kitchen. He pushed aside a cart of empty dinner trays and burst through the rear doors.*

Hours later, he couldn't recall the drive back to the Cove, nor how long he'd passed out in the small cave there. When he came to, he was hunched-up against a driftwood log. Outside, a light rain had coated the beach, creating a glossy hue in the bright half moon. He was peering out a dark tunnel into a strange, glistening dreamscape. He heard his own breath as it gathered and left his lungs. He felt his heart beat, then smacked his lips and swallowed. He stroked his calves and stretched. Then it came back… dad's final breath, the hospital and running for the door. It was still a mystery how he got to the cave. He sort of recalled driving there, but it was all a jumble of bizarre thoughts and emotions…

A loud backfire jolted Marco out of the past. He stood up in his room, looked out the sun porch window, as an old Plymouth sedan pulled in front of the house. Gina got out and slammed the door. She clomped up the steps in her high heels, nearly slipping, holding her hand overhead to block the rain.

"Marco… you here?" She pushed the glass door and walked in. Wiping rain from her face, she stared at him for a few seconds. "So… how come you haven't called me in two weeks, or answered the notes I left here?" Her voice was broken up, and he could tell she'd been drinking.

"I… I got a lot on my mind." He was still half-dazed from the vivid flashback.

"Yeah, me too, like what the hell's goin' on?" She leaned against the closed door.

"I've missed you, godammit."

"Yeah?"

She moved closer to him, staring into his eyes, "What's happened to you? Last time on the cliffs you said you loved me. I thought you meant it."

Marco took a deep breath and sighed, "I gotta lot on my mind."

"I'm sure you do. I mean, I know you do…but I guess I'm not one of them.

"Look, it's been a little rough…"

She moved away from him and began to pace, "Rough huh? Well, buddy, what do you think I've been doin'? Awake at night waiting for you to call, wondering what the hell's goin' on." She composed herself a moment, turned, gazed at his broad shoulders and thick chest filling out his tight t-shirt and gave him a seductive smile. "Look, why don't we go out tonight… down to the Grove. The Chocolate Watchband's playin'; our favorite band, right? We could dance, have some fun."

Marco stared at her. The last thing he felt like doing was dancing. He wanted to tell her how he was feeling, how confused he was since his dad's death, that it had nothing to do with her, but the words just wouldn't come.

"Well…?" she looked into his eyes and saw he was far away. "Haven't you anything to say?" She leaned against the picture window with rain splattering the glass. Marco glanced at her and for a moment. She seemed a stranger, a beautiful, olive-skinned stranger with long brown hair, in a tight light blue dress that parted above her knees. He just stared with reddening eyes. "Well, damn you, I'm tired of your silent shit. I thought you really loved me. Was all that just bullshit?" Tears welled up. "All you wanna be is some big surf shit. That's all you care about anymore."

"I…I…" Words wouldn't come. Images of his dad's death still reeled in his mind. He stared at her with a tortured look.

Gina sobbed and bolted for the open doorway. "So, you've got nuthin' more to say, huh? After eight months this is the way it is, huh? Well, fuck you. I'm not waitin' roun'no more. Fuck you and your stinkin' seaweed…."

She sobbed louder, as she ran to the Plymouth and slammed the door. Marco stared through the blurry windows as her car peeled out in the wet gravel.

"Jeesus Christ," he murmured. He didn't know whether to scream or cry or what. What the hell just happened? He wasn't sure. He switched on the porch light, went out, and stared into the rain as it showered down on him. He brushed the rain off the Intruder, and slid it in next to the cot and wall. His breath fell shallow and erratic.

Marco turned on his red plastic transistor radio and listened to a song by that new British group, The Rolling Stones. He wiped the sweat and rain from his face and short-cropped hair, lit a smoke and sat back against the wall, watching rivulets streak down the windows. So, she's going to the Grove, huh.

He reminisced about the times he and Gina would go down to" the Grove," the Coconut Grove, on Main Beach next to the casino at the boardwalk. They'd dance and meet up with other Westsiders. He liked to go hear the hot local bands, the *Tiki's* and *Corny and the Corvettes*. She liked the bands from " over the hill," like the *E-Types* and the *Syndicate of*

Sound. " Better to dance to," she'd argue. They both liked the *Chocolate Watchband* and rarely missed a show. Afterwards they'd stroll along Main Beach, sipping wine or beer, and go make out on the sand in the cave next to Cowells Beach.

Shit, why'd he treat her that way? Why couldn't he just tell her how he was feeling, but in his family a lot of things were hoed under the soil. Dad and mom never talked things out. There was always a lot of silence in the house, unless they were shouting at each other. Why couldn't she just understand how he felt? Oh sure, things had been pretty weird between them since his dad's death, but before that it was hot, real hot.

Pictures filled his mind of how they used to make out wildly at the Skyview Drive-in Theater in Louie's old Willys pickup on weekend nights. He'd deep tongue her and run his hands all over. He loved her smooth skin and Chanel perfume. Chanel Number Five mixed with sweat. They'd moan and pant and get really excited, but they'd never gone all the way yet. He'd finger her a little in her wet spot through her panties. She'd rub him through his levis. Their bodies raged for release, but both of them had Catholic chastity and original sin stuffed down their throats since they were little kids. His dad's advice on birth control also echoed in his mind, " Keep that pecker in yer pants till after yer married." But they both knew that soon they were going to cross the line into heaven.

They even talked about getting married and having some kids and living in a little house by the beach. Marco would fish on his dad's boat and she would be a mom. Marco began to wonder if it was completely over now or if she'd come back. He rubbed his forehead, sighed again and heard the fog buoy moan on the bay.

He sat back on his cot, leaned against the wall and watched the rain blast the window, then let up. He fired another smoke and felt the nicotine rush as his eyes reddened.

Rain continued to thump the glass. Marco slid into his sleeping bag and listened to the soft splattering on the gravel outside, as he drifted off, totally spent. The electric heater flared on and off. Muted sounds from the transistor radio played into the night. And whatever was going on outside at the Grove or anywhere else faded in a silent dreamy mist.

The front door opened. Someone pounded on the sun porch door. "Marco?" It was Jeremy Lang. He was four years younger than Marco, a member of " the Cove crew," who lived in the house upstairs with the rest of the tribe. "Marco, get up."

Marco stretched and sat up. The candle was still flickering. The dark blue wax had pooled and dripped on the floor. He wasn't sure how long he'd slept, two hours, maybe three.

" Yeah, yeah... just a minute." Marco unlocked the door.

" Marc' you gotta come quick."

" What?"

" It's Gina, she's with some valley jerk off." Jeremy helped himself to one of Marco's smokes and wiped the rain from his glasses." We were all at the Grove and she was pretty drunk."

Marco stared at the rain-splattered window and yawned. Yellow bay leaves had stuck to it. He watched Jeremy take a long drag, as he wiped his glasses again. " Gina and the guy took off... headed down the beach, towards the pier. The val was holding her up as they walked. Saw 'em from the window."

Marco remained silent as the reality of the moment sunk in.

" Ain't cha gonna do nothin'?"

" Gimme the smokes." He lit one." Okay, let's go." He realized he should've never let her take off the way she did. It was a huge mistake. He picked up a belt and wrapped it around his fist. " Hate those fuckin'vals. Can't surf worth a shit and always get in our way."

Jeremy chimed in," Yeah, and they wear surf clothes and bleach their hair, tryin' ta look cool, even though they don't live anywhere near the ocean. Phony baloney."

Marco jolted fully awake. If some val was with Gina, he was going to

13

kick his ass. He kept railing against valley surfers. " Just like a turkey would. Struttin' around the valley with big tail feathers. Straight-off Adolphs, that's what they are. All they do is ride the white water." Marco was fuming. "Ain't no way a valley turkey's gonna be with my chick."

" Right on, bro."

Marco smacked the wall with his belted fist, " C'mon."

Jeremy blew out the candle.

The front door closed slowly, automatically. They flicked their smokes onto the pavement, and as Marco's Chevy sped down the street toward the beach, the scent of candle wax filled the tiny porch. It was time for some valley maggot to pay the piper. His ass was grass and Marco was going to be the lawn mower.

Marco slid his white sedan into a parking place next to the Dream Inn, a two-story cement hotel in front of Cowell's Beach, next to the wharf.

A light mist fell on the beach as Marco and Jeremy stared into the darkness.

"I can't see a damn thing," Jeremy whispered.

" Let's check it out."

They shuffled through the wet sand toward the end of the beach. A seagull took flight, squawking in protest, as they rounded the shale cliff next to Cowells Cove.

" Nothin' here," Jeremy announced, as they reached the shallow cave in the cliff. That was the secret spot Marco and Gina used for make-out sessions. " Hey, maybe they're under the wharf... outta the rain."

"C'mon." They struggled through the mushy wet packed sand, nearly stumbling over slick seaweed clumps. As they approached the pier, sand filtered into Marco's tennis shoes. He could smell the thick layer of tar on the pilings. Something cold and sickening bit at his gut.

" You hear that," Jere asked.

" Hear what? "

" Listen."

They cocked their heads and listened as their breathing slowed in the hollows of their chests. From the dark forest of pilings underneath the wharf came muffled sobbing.

" Up there." Marco pointed to a spot where the pier's water main attached to a nest of other pipes on the sand. Jeremy flicked on a small flashlight. The weak beam slid in and out of the darkness, vaguely illuminating the sand and rough wooden braces with rusting metal bolts, casting a pale yellow hue on every object it touched.

" Holy shit." Jeremy gasped.

Gina lay curled up on the sand, her dress pulled up, puking and sobbing at the same time. Marco stood there in shock watching her writhe. She squinted as the flashlight beam caught her eyes. " Help me...please." Jeremy lifted her into sitting position.

" Jere...Jeremy...it's you...oh thank God," she whimpered. " Oh, God..." she retched up more, rolled over on the sand choking for air.

Marco saw her bra and panties in a clump. " What the hell's this?" He held them up, waving them at her.

" He...he forced me." She cried then choked. Marco's shock turned quickly to rage. His fists and teeth clenched. He screamed. Two pigeons bolted from the darkness. Feathers wafted down as one grazed its wing against a piling. " I just wanted some attention...from you."

" Oh, I'd say you got some attention!"

" Well, you weren't giving me any." She turned and gagged then leaned on her arms and cried.

" Godammit," Marco stuttered. " Get'er outta here... take the car... take'er home."

" No... not home," she moaned. "Not to mom's...to Nicci's." She continued to sob louder then caught her breath and turned to Marco. " He took me you bastard... and where were you?" She bent over, dry heaved and began to pass out.

" Marc, whatta we gonna do?" Jeremy held her up again, got her to her knees.

" Get'er outta here!"

They pulled her up, cradling her under each arm. The stench of red wine, puke, sweat, wet sand and body fluids followed them to the car. They stretched her limp form across the back seat, jamming her against the locked door.

" Take'er to 'er sister's. Then go home. I'll meet ya later."

" But..."

" Just do it dammit."

" Whatta 'bout you?

" I'm goin' after the val."

" Hey bro', he's probably long gone by now. You don't even know what he looks like." Marco's eyes reddened. He started to punch his fists together. " He was wearing a red jacket and had bleached hair. That's all I remember."

" I'll find 'im."

Jeremy saw the hate and disgust in Marco's eyes. " Okay... okay, bro."

The Chevy skidded around the corner down Beach Street, disappearing in the mist. Marco paced the beach through the wharf pilings toward the river mouth, a quarter mile east. The tall pole lights lining Beach Street cast long bright fingers across the rain-glazed beach. Seals barked under the wharf. All else was quiet except for the rhythmic pounding of the shore break as he walked the low tide line. He'd find the bastard, one way or another and when he did he'd kick his ass. Kick it good.

A light mist gathered as he made his way along the dark beachfront. Lights from the wharf created sparkling, undulating patterns on the glassy surface of the night sea, as swells rose and dipped towards shore. An occasional gull bleated. Walking along the beach edge, hearing the ocean sounds and night gulls was somewhat calming. He was still pissed as hell, but cooling off. As Marco approached the bubbling San Lorenzo River which sliced Santa Cruz in half, he could hear the surf pounding on the wide sandbar which formed every year during rainy winters.

He sat down and began to compose himself. His breath slowed and heart stopped racing. His mind radically shifted in and out with wild speculations. Why had things gotten so far out of control so fast? Maybe he wasn't supposed to be with Gina after all. But he really loved her, loved her deeply. Why couldn't he have said something reassuring to her, before she barged out of his room? Told her how he really felt.

Now he sure wasn't the first guy to do it with her like he thought he'd be. It was going to be a sacred thing between them; they'd talked about it before. She wasn't a virgin anymore that's for sure. Maybe she wasn't supposed to be the mother of his kids. He could never do it with her now anyway ever since the valley guy beat him to it. Once word got around that a val got to her first, he'd be the laughing stock of the local surf scene. That wouldn't do. He'd always be second now, and to some valley dick. Maybe she really loved doing it with the val. Maybe she was the one who picked him up and had it all planned. Now that he found her under the wharf, was she just pretending about it all being the val's fault? A big black lab ran from the darkness over to him, panting loudly.

" Get outta here," Marco grabbed a driftwood stick and pitched it into the water. The lab chased it, picked it out and ran down the beach, huffing. Marco peered out into the gathering fog, watching a wave unfold along the bar, but it was just too thick to see anything. He remembered hearing that it was right there at the river mouth, that the first surfers ever rode a wave on the mainland. Three Hawaiian princes had paddled out there when they were visiting California, some Hawaiian guys with names no one could pronounce. Santa Cruz became known as "Surf City," ever since. The princes said that surfing would never catch on in Santa Cruz because the water was way too cold. Yeah, right. Wetsuits changed all that. But Marco understood why some Hawaiians used to warm water might say that.

A chilly blast of onshore wind brought with it a sudden shower drenching Marco. From across the wide beach, he saw someone limping under the edge of the boardwalk. Was it the val? He stood and ran across the soaked sand towards the boardwalk, feeling the adrenaline rage through him. He was so ready to punch the guy's lights out. He caught his breath and hurried along under the rim of the boardwalk, shielding himself from the rain. It started to really pound as he approached the Ferris wheel. He ducked under the wooden pathway to escape the pelting water. No sign of the val. He was pumped up to beat the shit out of the guy. He picked up a metal trashcan and heaved it against a wooden piling that supported the stairs to the boardwalk, screaming, "You fuckin' shithead. Where are you?" The dented can bounced off the piling and rolled to a stop. It sounded like a metal drum as cold rain pummeled it. Maybe Jeremy was right; the valley scumbag was long gone.

The smell of wood smoke wafted from farther in. A small fire reflected among the thick timbers, which shored up the main planking of the boardwalk. Some bum must've had a camp earlier and since vacated it. He got down on all fours and made it over to the little blaze. The heat felt soothing against his wet clothes and face, as his eyes adjusted to the subdued light. He tossed on a couple of sticks from a pile next to the fire.

Exhausted, Marco leaned back against a rough timber, staring up at the under belly of the boardwalk. He thought back to when he was a little kid, before he started board surfing, around nineteen fifty-six. He and his buddies, the Lindsay brothers and Eddie, would body surf and mat surf at the river mouth and at Cowells Cove. They'd sometimes scout underneath the boardwalk for pocket change that tourists dropped through the planks from above. One time they even found a gold ring and another time a twenty-dollar bill. During Easter week in fifty-seven, they discovered a small peephole into the girls' bathroom directly below the roller coaster. They'd take turns learning about female anatomy and laugh afterwards, comparing specimens. Marco smiled as he recalled those innocent times when life wasn't so complicated and intense.

"Jus' make yersef' at home," a gravelly voice called from the darkness behind him. Marco turned so quickly, his face brushed against a splintered post, grazing him on the left ear.

" Aw, don't sweat it none," the voice went on, " there's plenty a' room."

From out of the blackness appeared a bent over, balding, bony and ravaged-looking man. He had a bundle of dry driftwood under arm. " Don't fret none." He tossed the sticks next to the little blaze and sat down. " Got caught out in da wash, huh?"

Marco hunched down and placed his hand around a stout short stick.

"Name's Pigeon, what's yeren?" He fussed with the driftwood, selecting a few choice pieces for the fire. " Ya see, ya gotta find the driest ones ta throw on first. Otherwise you'll stink up wit smoke." He gave Marco a half snarl, showing various missing teeth, surrounded by a dirty, short, gray beard. " Whatsha doin' here this time a night?"

" Lookin' for somebody," Marco replied carefully scanning Pigeon. Tattoos marked both his arms up to the elbows. He had a twitch as he talked.

"Ain't nobody roun' here 'cept ol' Pigeon." He sat back and surveyed Marco with hazy, light blue eyes that seemed to scatter from place to place without focusing on any one spot. "You live roun' here?"

" Yeah." Marco kept staring at the man's hands. They quivered constantly.

" Betcha gotta nice warm place ta sleep at night," Pigeon added, as he placed another stick on the fire.

" Sort of. " Marco thought he heard sarcasm.

" Looky here bud, you better warm up a bit and shove off. I ain't used ta no comp'ny from the likes a you."

" Sure, I'll be going now." Marco picked up on the man's sudden shift in tone.

" Hey, go ahead an get a good heat on ya. I ain't sayin' go yet." Pigeon would never turn a man away from a hot fire, even if he didn't like him. He'd been there a lot before, himself. It was one of the hobo's unspoken understandings. The same way with food; you always gave half of what you had, even if it was just a can of tuna or a slice of bread.

" Okay," Marco still shivered a bit and the heat felt good.

" Yer a bit outta sorts, ain't ya?"

" A little."

" Shit kid, you ain't seen nuthin'." Pigeon pulled a small bottle of Tokay wine from his brown wool trench coat, unscrewed the lid and took a pull.

19

He had a French knife in the other pocket, just in case of trouble. " Have some." He handed it to Marco.

" Nah." Marco took another look at Pigeon's toothless grin and smelled his rank breath." No thanks." In the subdued firelight, he saw a wide scar, which dropped from Pigeon' s right ear to his lips, a bayonet slice.

" Yer a pussy ain't ya. A guy offers ya a drink an' ya ain't tak'n it." That was another hobo rule. You always shared your liquor, and the recipient always took it. It was a matter of respect.

Marco thought maybe the rain wasn't so cold outside after all.

" I seen tons a pussies like you. Back in Ko-rea. Usually got the shit blown outta they selves." He took another big pull and coughed. " Never got me though, the sunsabitches. Tried like hell, too." He rubbed the scar on his neck. " Layed 'em wide open I did." He snickered, remembering a grim time during the assault on Outpost Harry.

" Jus' like field dressin' a big buck. Ya start at their ass an' slice up to the ribs." He stared at Marco with wild eyes. "Doin' the same ta yer kind in Nam right now… little pussies, just like you."

Pigeon turned to stoke the fire. Marco ducked behind a piling and crawled blindly toward the open beach, tearing a hole in his levis when he scraped his knee on a rock. He heard wild cackling and coughing fade away in the darkness as he reached the beach, stood up and ran hard towards the wharf as rain smacked him.

He made it under the wharf as thunder boomed. Breath steamed around his face. He bent over and grabbed his gut, sweat and rain falling to the moist sand. He'd had a sharp pang in his stomach from time to time ever since his dad's death. The cold rang through him again, his jeans, shoes and jacket soaked through. The nightlights from the Dream Inn cast long, flickering beams towards him in the downpour. The lights from the hotel seemed like spotlights from Nazi concentration camps in World War Two movies, the ones used to spot runaway prisoners. He was starting to feel like one, or at least like someone who wanted to be somewhere else. What was he doing shivering like a wet rat under the wharf at god knows what hour?

Staring blindly at the hotel, he flashed back to nineteen sixty, when the Dream Inn was being built. He and his westside friends would kick out windows, steal construction tools and set fire to piles of lumber stored inside. Hey, who the hell wanted a huge cement block hotel overlooking their beach. It would steal the afternoon sun and cast shadows where they liked to lie on the sand. And what about all the tourists? They'd pay big money to stay there and gawk down on them. More vals in their territory.

Mooring lights from boats bobbed in the mist off shore. He thought about spending the night on the *Three M's*. He could use the skiff nested in a rack on the public landing to row out to his dad's boat, moored just to leeside of the wharf. The *Three M's* would be stocked with lots of canned food, drinking water, extra wool clothes and foul weather gear. He could fire up the little cook stove in the cabin, pull out a bottle of his dad's VO and be set for the rest of the night. He would inherit the boat anyway once his dad's estate was settled. It was all in Louie's will, agreed upon years before when he was just a kid. Fathers always passed on their boats to their sons. That's the way it was for generations he thought, since the beginning of time, when there were just fish and fishermen, fathers and sons.

The foghorn moaned on the mile buoy. A car's headlights cruised slowly down Beach Hill and pulled into the parking lot next to the Dream Inn. Oh no, probably the cops. Who else would be stalking around that time of night? This was all he needed, to be harassed by the cops about why he was out so late.

The headlights angled right at the wharf, causing weird shadows and irregular patterns in the misty air. A flashlight beam briefly illumined the beach. The rain cleared. Small streams of water, which constantly flowed off the wharf during storms, now gave way to alternating splatters.

As he watched from his hiding place, Marco saw the single beam approaching, gaining in intensity as it flashed wildly through the pilings. He didn't want anything to do with the cops, especially since they popped him and Jeremy a few months back for stealing some fishing gear from the United Cigar Store on Pacific Avenue. He was released to Louie who was in tight with all the cops. Louie would donate and cook salmon for the annual sheriffs and policeman's barbecue. They sent Jeremy to "Juvie," Juvenille Hall, for two days but then released him, as it was his first offense. Marco knew he was definitely on their shit list, and they warned him that if they ever caught him doing anything illegal again, they'd throw the book at him. He crouched getting ready to spring into the darkness back down toward the river mouth, rain or no rain.

" Marc, you there?" It was Jeremy.

"You prick. Ya scared the shit outta me." Marco stood, brushing the sand from his jeans.

" Thought you were a cop." His split knee throbbed.

They both chuckled uneasily.

"Been lookin' for ya, man. Drove all the way down ta "the mouth" and back again. Got out an' yelled for ya all up an down the boardwalk, too."

Marco took a couple of deep breaths.

"You find the val?"

"The val... no." He thought back to that toothless smirk of Pigeon's. "Didn't find nobody."

"Didn't think ya would. Not in this rain."

They thumped through the hard-packed, wet sand toward Marco's Chevy. "What about Gina?"

"Took her to Nicci's like you said. She was wasted, man. Didn't throw up in the car though. Dry heaved a bunch. Me and Nicci got her inside, then I split."

Marco started to feel the jab in his gut again. As they reached the Chevy, Jeremy asked, "Want me ta drive?"

"It's my car ain't it?"

"Sure, bro, I just thought..."

"You didn't think nuthin'. And how many times have I told ya ta never leave her runnin' when you're not in 'er! "

"Sorry, man, thought you'd want the heater on."

They got in. "You got any smokes or did you smoke alla mine?"

"Right there, man, over the visor, where they always are."

Marco picked up on the nevousness in Jeremy's voice. He pushed in the lighter, pulled a Camel from the pack and lit it. He took a long drag and exhaled quickly, rubbing his eyes. "Look Jere, sorry." The warm blast from the heater did feel good on his frozen legs and chest.

His friend gazed at him cautiously. "Hey... it's cool, man... forget it."

"Naw really... thanks for comin' an' gettin' me." He reached over and gave Jeremy a solid pat on the chest. "Shit man, you an' me's brothers. You wanna drive?"

"Nah, go ahead."

"Ya sure, hey, why don't ya?"

"I been drivin' all night."

"Okay, anytime ya want to though, okay?" They smiled at each other. "Hey watch this." Marco backed the sedan up, cranked it around the corner, slipped it in first and stomped on the gas hard. The four-barreled Hollie carb sucked gas down into the throat of the 327, V-8. The Chevy took off sideways fishtailing into a straight line, peeling rubber halfway up Beach Hill. Marco and Jeremy both hooted as they flashed past the Dream Inn, running the stop sign at the corner of Bay and West Cliff.

"Hey man, ain't you afraid a the cops?" Jeremy asked, as they gained speed along the cliffs.

" Fuck the cops," Marco yelled, as they roared through the stop sign at Pelton Street. " They ain't never gonna catch us, never."

Jeremy held on tight to the seat as the sedan sped around the turn by the lighthouse. Marco slowed as they approached the corner at Almar. " Ya know what Jere, I hope the swell's pumpin' tomorrow. Gotta feelin' it will be. Feel like ridin' some real grinders at the Cove."

" Me too," Jeremy added with some reluctance. " Me, too, bro."

They opened the front door to the house and went in.

" See ya in the morn. Get me up early."

" Yeah... see ya then."

Jeremy wiped off his glasses and climbed the dark stairway to his room. Marco slid out of his soaked clothes and into his down bag on the cot. He shivered as he reached over and rested his palm on the rail of the Intruder. He felt the thin, egg-shaped rail and smooth fiberglass covering. The warmth returned slowly. He stopped shivering and stared a long time at the muted streetlight through the rain-pelted window. He pulled up the hood on the sleeping bag and could smell his naked body. It stunk. He placed his hand over his nose and blew into his palm. His breath was wild.

As rain streaked down the picture windows, casting fluid shadows against the wall, he wondered if the waves would be firing off at dawn. Shit, it was early morning already, just after midnight anyway. Images of grinding tubes at the Cove at dawn nursed Marco into unconsciousness his deep snoring echoed across the room.

Dawn light slid over Loma Prieta, the highest peak in the Santa Cruz mountain chain, showering its rays on the bumpy surface of Monterey Bay and Surf City. Seals stirred on the catwalks under the wharf and sea birds nesting among the pilings ruffled their wings after the cold, wet night. Sandpipers huddled in an angry pack against the shale cliffs of the Cove, upset they weren't able to pick for crabs with the intense waves sweeping the shoreline.

Knuckles tapped lightly on the sun porch door." Hey Marco... get up." Jeremy tapped louder. Marc'... the Cove's up."

Marco stood atop a high cliff above a dark pit. The wind blew hard against his face. From the black hollows of the pit he heard a sound like distant thunder. It was moving closer, changing in tone as it neared. Was it big waves pounding the shore? It got louder. Was it a train roaring at him? A sudden tremendous explosion of light. Then the sound of wind blowing through leaves." Marco, help me." It was the voice of a child, a girl's voice. " Marco, please." Then silence. A scowling face appeared with searing blue eyes and a toothless grin. Blood trickled from its nostrils. Sobbing laughter morphed into an intense, cryptic scream which echoed over and over as if rattling inside a giant steel pipe. Marco awoke shaking. He sat up, short of breath as Jeremy entered his room.

" Surf's happening, bro." Jeremy was already in his wetsuit jacket and trunks. " Abe and Willy are suitin' up right now." Marco wiped sweat from his cheeks. " You okay, man?"

"Yeah, cool... had a weird dream."

" C'mon man, the Cove's on fire."

" Whattaya mean?"

" Saw it before dawn, six to eight feet, bro, c'mon."

Marco pulled on his wet baggies." Bitchen. " The cold, soggy swimsuit shocked his crotch and thighs.

" Yeah, I called D.J. too. He's on his way."

"Cool." Marco slid the Intruder from behind the cot. "Thanks for wakin' me." He dusted the sleeves of the damp wetsuit jacket with cornstarch. It was another cold blast against his skin but his body heat would soon warm the inner layer of jacket.

They hustled along Almar Street towards West Cliff, dodging mud puddles and gravel. Marco was stoked heading for the surf after such a strange damn night. Nothing like a few great waves to ease the weird memories of Gina and that twisted fucker under the boardwalk.

"I'm tellin'ya Marc', its some of the best waves we've had all season."

" I hope so, Jere, I hope so."

"You'll see. I saw a big set break from around the point. Big hollow tubes. And we'll be the first ones out… like we always are."

" Yep. Just you and me bro."

"Just you an'me." Jeremy was happy to hear Marco feeling no grief or at least showing none. He knew a lot was going on inside but Marco never showed how he really felt about anything. " Man, I can't even count how many times we've scored like this."

"Yeah." Marco thought about how Jeremy was always there for him and always looked up to him. And all the epic sessions they've had at the Cove. "You're the best, Jere."

"No, you are. Hey you're the king of the Cove bro! I'll never forget that big wave you got from way outside and rode it all the way to Fingerbowl. You were in the tube for at least ten seconds."

" Hmm." The king. Marco wasn't feeling like the king of anything. He was forcing thoughts of Gina and his dad out of his mind, trying to stay focused on the potential for great waves.

As they descended the dirt and shale cliff, a set rolled in, every wave peeling off in perfect form along the Cove.

Marco exclaimed." Bitchen' bro, we're the first ones here."

" Knew we would be."

They set their boards down and waxed up with parafin. The beach smelled like rotting kelp and wet sand, a nearly sickening stench. An exposed, broken sewer pipe ran out from the beach into the line up. Jeremy once stepped on it during a wipe out at the inner bowl section. He was out for two weeks with eight stitches on his left foot and on heavy antibiotics.

Marco was first to hit the water, pulling toward the point. He had to paddle on his stomach. The slice on his knee hurt too much for knee paddling but he sure as hell wasn't going to let a small thing like that keep him from getting some hot waves. He was feeling better with every stroke. Jeremy followed quickly behind and caught up as they rose over the first two waves of a set.

" I think we can take off… outside the point …on the bigger set … waves." Marco sputtered as they stroked farther.

" I dunno, bro. That bowl at the point looks pretty nasty." Jeremy stopped paddling sat up on his board, catching his breath. He decided to hang out at the take off spot just inside the point.

Marco pumped further out beyond the point and sat atop his board awaiting the next set. He scanned the reefs further to the north where the big waves would form up first then shift toward the outside point where he sat. Glad as hell to be back in the water, he thought, away from all the crap coming down on land. And Gina, what a goddam mess she was. Screwin' a val and pretending he took advantage of her. He forced her to do it. Right. He forced her to get drunk and leave the Grove with him too, right. And he forced her to walk with him down the beach and take off her pants and bra and put them in a neat little pile, right. What a bunch of bullshit. She was guilty as sin. The more he thought about it the clearer everything became. He was a chump to think about it any other way.

He turned toward the cliff and saw three guys in wetsuit jackets with boards climb down the cliff: Abe, Willy, and D.J. Marco could tell by their boards. Everybody had different boards. Different sizes, different shapes and some even had colored pigment. Abe's was clear with a wide balsa stringer running down the center, made by Johnny Rice. Willy's was a blue-railed Yount, while D.J's was a see-through yellow, three stringer, Haut Signature model.

Abe was eighteen, just graduated from high school, too, and wanted to be a classical guitarist. Willy, Abe's brother was fifteen, same as Jeremy and still a sophomore at Santa Cruz High. Kind of wild and crazy, he loved to fight and surf more than anything. D. J, a senior in high school was the son of a famous local sculptor. He lived on the next block Alta Street, a stone's throw from where all the others lived. Marco was stoked to see all the crew together again for some bitchen waves.

A set humped up on the horizon. Marco watched as they hit the reefs a few hundred yards north. Four big swells swooped into the outside reefs, elongated and began to reel into the Cove. Realizing that the fourth wave was the biggest so far, Marco let the first three go by.

Jeremy rode the second wave and was paddling back out as Marco dropped down the face of the fourth. He made a sharp turn at the bottom, set his rail high in the wave and took a few quick steps forward, crouching near the nose of his board. He was driving it at full speed. The wave hollowed out as he entered the rear of the section at the point. Marco "back-doored" it and was riding completely inside the tube.

He heard the group on the shore hooting and whistling while he sped toward the inner section, just as his fin grabbed a clump of kelp. He flew off the nose as the thick lip slammed down. It knocked the wind out of him, impaling him on the rocky inside reef. Surfacing, he gasped for air and took a fast breath going under the next wave as it crashed down. White water pushed him all the way into the beach in a melee of churning sand and foam. Abe and D.J. ran over to him.

"Hey man... that was an all-time tube!" D.J. yelled as he helped Marco to his feet. "Knocked the wind outta ya, huh?"

Marco coughed wildly for a few seconds, finally getting his breath back. He nodded and gagged, spitting up salt water.

"Better take it easy for awhile."

Abe pulled Marco's board over to him. "Fin's busted, Marc." He set it down next to him. "Cracked along the base." He ran his finger along where the fin attached to the underside of the board. "Lucky it didn't snap off."

"Prob'ly hit the reef or the pipe,' D.J. added. "Tough luck."

They all watched as Jeremy sliced along a nice six- footer and pulled over the back just before it closed out on the shore. Willy made it out, spun around quickly and was on the next one, hooting in the curl as it covered him for a second in the inner bowl.

"Hey man, I'm on it," D.J. added chuckling. "Guess there'll be one less guy out, too."

Abe nodded. They both laughed and rushed into the water, paddling out between sets. Marco sat on the Intruder and watched as the guys rode wave after wave. It just didn't seem fair. Why did he have to just watch it all and not take part? Well, he did set the pace with that one tube ride. Nobody since had gotten one that big or that good.

The November sun beat down on his wetsuit and bare legs, warming him a bit. Marco rubbed his legs briskly. They didn't seem as cold anymore although they still shook.

Empty waves rolled through the Cove as the crew paddled back towards "outside point." Marco imagined himself slicing along inside the tube of one. Should he run back to the house and get his other O'Neill team board? He wasn't sure. The Intruder was definitely his board of choice for the Cove with more of a point-break shape. It was a lot faster than his other beach break model, which was more of a nose-riding, "hot dog" board for smaller waves.

Marco stared at the horizon between sets. It heaved up and down like undulating corduroy. No boats at all. Not even big container vessels. Just too rough. On days when it was calm, the horizon had a ruler edge to it with no movement at all. It sucked not to be out with the boys on such a righteous day, but he'd had a lot of days just like this one to himself. He figured he was way ahead of everyone in the tally of total great waves. And there was going to be the big pre-contest party tonight, too.

The Wharf Rats Surf Club from Capitola always held a "major rager" before a big contest, and this coming weekend was going to be the Northern California Championships. He figured he'd go back to the house, hose off and see if there was any work at his uncle's burger joint. He could use the bucks to score some brews for the party.

Marco climbed back up the cliff and watched one more set reel into the Cove with all his pals having a blast. The tide was sucking out, revealing rocks along the inner cove. As he walked along Almar Street, steam rose from the pavement. The rich scent of wet eucalyptus flavored the chilly offshore breeze. The skin on his legs tightened as goose bumps poked through, as if he was covered with coarse, flesh-colored sandpaper.

Marco leaned the Intruder against the porch handrail. He'd have to get it over to Bumpsy's house, for repair. " Bumpsy," was a surf photographer and big wave rider who made his rent money by patching boards. The Cove crew called him, "Bumpsy" because he had huge surf bumps, calcium deposits caused by knee paddling on both his feet. They were so large he had to loosen the laces on his tennis shoes around them in order to get them to fit. Patching jobs were plentiful for him. The rocky shoreline of the Westside was pure murder on boards even though they were all covered with two layers of ten-ounce fiberglass.

A note was pinned to his door. He unfolded and read it.

Marco,

> *Your mom called. Said it was important for you to go over and get your mail. Said two men were looking for you. She sounded worried.*

> *- Karie*

The last thing he wanted to do was go home. Or see his mom. He'd avoided her for over a month, even though he'd driven past several times. It didn't feel like home anymore. Surfing was all he wanted to do. Surf and be alone. The cut on his knee burned as salt water dried in it. He hosed off, slid into dry clothes and drove down Oxford Way towards his mom's.

Marco unlatched the waist-high picket gate to his mom's house, hesitating a moment. The front yard used to be a picture of beauty. Once, roses formed neat lines around the perimeter of the white, ship-lapped house laced with camellias and chest-high ferns. Abalone shells and chunks of driftwood bordered clumps of annuals. A neatly trimmed lawn had carpeted the areas between the flowers. And of course garlic, parsley, Swiss chard, zucchini and tomato plants were interspersed everywhere next to a small patch of dirt where basilico plants thrived in the full sun during summer. A cement birdbath hid silently in the shadows of the porch, directly under the hanging fuscia baskets. But now, the roses hadn't been pruned, weeds popped up everywhere and the lawn needed moving. Even the hummingbird feeders were dry.

In the corner, by the fence, stood the persimmon tree. Marco had buried all the family's cats and dogs under that tree. He knew persimmon trees went back at least four generations in his family ever since his great grandfather came over from Switzerland in 1870, to fish in central California. He was from the Italian part of Switzerland, a little village in the lake country near the border. Marco heard that even though his grandfather was from farming stock, he always wanted to fish, to live on the coast, and moving to " the new country" offered a change.

Marie would always say to Marco," We ain't no damn Italians, we're Swiss and Portuguese." Whatever that meant. In the past they ate pasta, fish and grew most of their own vegetables. And whenever they had company over all the adults drank homemade red wine and nibbled on French bread with anchovies or pesto or red sauce, persimmon cookies and biscotti, too. Swiss or Portuguese or Italian, it all seemed the same to Marco.

The wooden steps squeaked as he climbed to the porch landing. His finger was poised on the brass knocker, when he heard talking inside. He moved his ear close to the panes in door.

" I always liked you, Marie." It was a man's voice.

" I've always liked you too, Vince."

He heard his mom's voice, some laughing, then silence. Christ, she's with some guy in there. Dad's one month gone and she's already screwing around. Rage surged through him. Should he bolt out of there or what? He uncovered the hide-a-key from under a red brick next to one of the flowerpots and slid it into the lock. The door opened without a sound. At least the hinges were still well oiled.

Marco smelled garlic, olive oil and oregano. The hallway was dark except for some diffused light showing faintly on the wall. He crept down the thin, brown carpet to his former bedroom. Marie would always put his mail on the desk in there. The hall light reflected faintly on pictures hanging on the wall.

Once inside the small, sun-faded white bedroom he gazed quietly at the photographs: he and his sister holding prayer books and rosaries on the day of their first communion just before she died; a faded black and white of Louie and Marie on their wedding day outside a little chapel in L.A; the *Three M's* cruising the bay somewhere with Louie waving out the cabin window; Louie and his brother, Uncle Joe, both with cigars and broad smiles, holding up two huge salmon; Marie sitting in a chair with both Marco and baby Mary on opposite knees; Louie in his white Navy uniform leaning on the steel rail of a ship with his cap pulled down on one side of his brow; and five small color shots of various cats and dogs.

An antique chiming clock, which came from Marie's family when they first emigrated from Portugal, rang eight times on the mantle in the living room. An orange tabby appeared from the hallway and circled Marco's legs purring loudly. Marco bent down as the cat lay on its back. He rubbed her soft belly. " Good girl, Lucky." The cat closed her eyes and purred louder. Marco stood, feeling a little dizzy. He had to lean against the wall for a few seconds. Lucky bolted away into the kitchen hallway.

A note on the desk told him Marie had gone to the store and for him to wait there. It was two days old. Two white envelopes were addressed to him on the table. One had the seal of the Selective Service System on it. The other was from the Federal Marshall's office. The first was dated October 1st, over a month ago, an *"ORDER TO REPORT FOR INDUCTION."* It was from the President of the United States.

"*Mr. Marco Luigi D'Giorgio,*

You are hereby ordered for induction into the Armed Forces of the United States, and to report at the Greyhound Bus terminal, 425 Front Street, Santa Cruz, California, on October 30th, 1966, at 8:00 AM, for forwarding to an Armed Forces Induction Station." October 30th, that was the day after his nineteenth birthday. He read on; "*Willful failure to report at the place and hour of the day named with this Order subjects the violator to fine and imprisonment...*" Today's November 9th. He missed the appointment, not that he would've showed up anyway. He tossed the Order on the carpet and opened the letter from the Federal Marshalls.

"*Mr. Marco Luigi D'Giorgio:*

You failed to report for your pre-induction physical examination on October 30th, as ordered by the United States Selective Service System. This is a violation of section FS 1213 of the United States Selective Service Act.

Therefore, you are now hereby ordered to report to the United States Army Induction Station at Oakland, California, for immediate induction into the United States Army. Failure to do so is a federal offense, punishable by a mandatory five-year sentence in the United States Federal Penitentiary at Fort Levenworth, Kansas.

You have seven days to appear at the Oakland Induction Center upon receipt of this letter or face criminal charges. Failure to comply with this order within seven days will result in a bench warrant issued against you. The Federal Marshall's Office will then be notified to take you into their custody. You will then begin your five-year sentence for violation of the Federal Selective Service Act, FS1213.

If you have any questions or to arrange transportation to the Armed Forces Induction Station you are advised to call...

The rest was a blur. Holy shit, drafted. He tossed it on the carpet, too. The Army. Prison. Sure as hell don't want to go to either. His stomach burned. He felt like he might puke. Sweat bubbled on his face. His eyes glazed and heart raced. He sat down on the bed. He heard footsteps in the hall. The front door opened. "Well, Marie, you know you can call me any time."

"I know..."

"I'll come right over. I'm just down the street."

"Thanks, Vince."

"Hey no problem. No problem at all."

"And thanks for the romaine and broccoli and herbs."

"Hey, Marie,' he chuckled. "Lots where that came from. Just let me know... garden's full."

She closed the door softly and peeked out the curtain as the stooped-over, white-haired man left the yard. She smiled when he turned and waved by the gate, then watched him limp along the fence holding onto his red suspenders, a sweat-stained fedora atop his head.

Marie went into the kitchen, rinsed the dirt from the roots of the romaine and herbs then sat them on a paper towel. She poured another glass of red wine and took a sip. Leaning on the table she surveyed a picture of her and Louie and the two kids all dressed up for Easter Mass when the kids were five and three. She took another swig and began to whimper.

Marco crept along the hallway toward the front door dislodging a dusty plastic crucifix on the wall. It fell to the carpet with a chattering thud. Marie heard it from the kitchen.

" Someone there?" she called cautiously. She turned and saw Marco craning around the door. " Marco." He tried to open it but she'd dead bolted it from the inside. She set the glass down and hurried over to him. " Son, where you been?"

Busted. She stood close to him, barely five feet tall. Her short, grey-tipped hair was messy and uncombed. Her eyes sparkled. Marco wasn't sure if it was tears or a wine induced glow from her tryst. She ran her left hand through her hair. Her lipstick was smeared.

" I got my own place."

"Where?"

" Over by the Cove."

" I found the phone number on a piece of paper in your room and called it." So glad yer home."

" Not for long."

" I could use yer help here."

Looked like she had plenty of help. " Who was that guy?"

" Oh, Vince, uh, Mr. Galli, from down the street. You know him."

"Yeah…" Vince was one of old guys who dug around in his garden all day with a few of the other old guard. They were all retired for many years and mostly hung out in Vince's garage telling lies to each other. Marco knew a few were fishermen, one was a carpenter, a sheriff and another was a butcher. Louie always called them, " the bullshitter's club."

"He's been coming by. See how I'm doin'. He's a nice man."

Nice man all right. Dad's been gone a little over a month and the neighborhood widowers are already stalking the place. " Got your message… about the mail."

"Marco, two men came by looking for ya. What've ya done this time?"

" Nuthin'."

" They were askin' all kindsa questions."

" What'd ya tell 'em? "

" Nuthin', nuthin' at all. Said I didn't know where ya were, that you were gone. Gone for awhile."

" Who were they? "

" Government men, gave me a card."

Marco followed her into the kitchen. An empty wine glass sat on the low coffee table in the living room with a half plate of persimmon cookies. The smell of garlic and oregano rose from a cast iron pan on the gas stove. The smell reminded Marco of the fried chicken his mom used to cook. She'd first toss it in a paper bag with flour and herbs and fry it up with garlic in olive oil until it was gold and crispy.

On the counter next to the stove was a cookie jar shaped like a fat, laughing priest in a brown robe with the words, " Thou shalt not steal." Marie quickly set her wine glass in the sink.

" Here," she handed Marco a business card.

He read the name on the gold-embossed card, " Frank Stevens, Federal Marshall." It had the seal of the United States government stamped on it, San Jose office. Valley pigs, he thought.

" What's it all about? " Marie leaned on the table.

"This." Marco pulled out the folded up letter from his jeans, "Goddam draft notice. Missed my physical. Now they're after my ass."

" No." Marie was stunned. " Whatcha gonna do? "

" Get the hell outta here."

" Whattaya mean, 'out of here,' this house...what? "

"I don't know what I mean." He opened up the refrigerator and nervously looked inside like he always did as a kid when he first got home after school.

" Ya hungry, I fix ya some fish."

" I don't want no fish, mom." She looked at him like she wasn't quite sure who he was anymore.

" Why ya lookin' at me like that? "

" Like what? "

He didn't say anything, just felt a mixture of rage and uncertainty.

" Son, listen, if yer country calls, ya gotta go defend it like yer dad did."

" You don't know what the hell yer talkin' 'bout."

She began to whimper more. " Ya owe it to yer country son. Yer dad

35

was a Navy man. He served in the war. Ya know he did." Marco rubbed his head and eyes. " Son, maybe it's time ya grow up, be a man."

" What?" He couldn't believe what she was saying

" Ya can't just surf and get inta trouble yer whole life. If yer father was here…"

" What the hell do you know what he'd do?' She was trembling . He continued.

" This ain't no goddam world war. It's a buncha shit. You saw what happened to Mikey over there. He came back all messed up. So did Johnny Boy."

She thought about her nephew, Mike, "Mikey," who returned with major wounds and in a wheelchair. All he did now was stare blankly at the walls with a weird smile on his face, slobber and piss in his pants. And her sister's son, John, "Johnny Boy," they called him. He was a Marine over there. After his discharge, he beat the crap out of an innocent Asian kid who just happened to be sitting on a bus bench in front of the wharf across from Beach Liquors. Two fishermen pulled him off as he was kicking the kid in the back of the head down in the gutter. They forced Johnny Boy into their pick up and trucked him home. Tears welled in her eyes.

" Then ya might go ta prison."

"Bullshit. Ain't no way I'm goin' over there. I ain't gonna end up like Lenny either."

Marco thought about Lenny. "Lenny the Bull," his second cousin who spent a year and a half in " the big house," San Quentin, for laying into a couple of cops outside " the Grove" one night. He told Marco he was drunk and pissed off about losing five hundred in cash in a card game, money he made on an albacore run that morning. He broke one cop's jaw and knocked the other out cold. He split town and got popped in Santa Barbara when he tried to get on a deep-sea boat headed for Mexico.

The cops put out an APB on Lenny and sent it to all the harbormasters up and down the coast. After his parole Marco saw him at a family salmon barbecue. "The Bull" told him about the butt wackers and weirdos in prison and he swore he'd never go back to such a place again no matter what.

Marco stared at a large, rectangular color print of a wave breaking on an abandoned beach hanging over the mantle in the living room. Louie and Marco picked it up at a Native Sons of Italy rummage sale. It hung there for as long as Marco could remember. He pictured himself standing on the beach in the print with the Intruder under his arm.

" I'm outta here." Marco turned and bolted for the door, leaving it wide open.

Through the open door Marie saw the Chevy back out the driveway. She hobbled down the hall, sat at the table, looked at the photo of the family together at Easter and bawled, her face in her hands. She reached over, pulled her rosary beads from the drawer, took a drink and began to pray.

Marco punched it around the corner tires screeching. He drove along West Cliff thinking about all the fights his mom and dad had in that house. He heard it all at night when they thought he was asleep: the arguments in their bedroom about wearing a rubber or not, all the yelling and door slamming.

No wonder dad would go stay on the boat for days at a time. Maybe he wasn't just out on long fishing trips. Maybe dad was just trying to get the hell away from her, just like he was now.

Subdued sunlight scattered across the tops of the wind blown, choppy waves that swept into the Cove. The onshore breeze and high tide pushed a jagged line of flotsam and foam ashore. Two seals bobbed over a set and pulled against the rising tide as Marco's '55 Chevy jerked into the dirt lot overlooking the Cove, mud splattering the bottom third of the white sedan. The engine block hissed and steam seeped from under the hood. Marco got out and stood staring at the choppy waves as the chill bit through his team jacket. He flicked a smoldering butt off the cliff. It tumbled end over end to the wet shale. The Cove crew had split the scene.

Mom's lost it. Never going back over there. Can't even talk to her. Got no clue. No clue at all. "You gotta serve yer country like your dad did." Was she living on a different planet or what? Go to Vietnam and come back like "Johnny Boy?" Or maybe not come back at all? Or how about a little time in the federal pen with all the poop shooters licking their chops? Thanks, but no thanks.

Time to figure out an escape plan. A new life somewhere. A place to surf and fish and get out of town for a while. Maybe not forever, just until the war was over. Whenever that might be. Not sure what dad would say. He went. He didn't split town. He always said, " We ain't speakin' Kraut or Japanese here are we?" But that war was way different. Those veterans were real heroes and a lot of them died for a noble cause: to save the world from the Nazis. It was tough and brutal and the effect on those soldiers was obvious. He knew some of his uncles never got over it. They were " shell shocked" and really spaced out.

As he stared out on the wind-chopped sea he remembered the story about how Uncle Gus had survived the Bataan Death March after being captured in the Phillipines, transported on a Jap "hell ship," the *Coral Maru*, where POW's were stacked like canned squid in the hold of the ship. He was forced into slave labor just east of Hirohata, Japan, where he fired furnaces for the Seitetsu Steel Company sixteen hours a day with constant beatings. He was so thin and emaciated when he finally got home that no one recognized him. Now he just sits on a bench on the wharf during the daytime and sometimes talks to fish crates and nets. He feeds seagulls with stale bread and throws fish guts to the seals under the wharf. Every time Marco saw him it gave him the creeps.

World War Two was only over for twenty years and lots of vets were still stinging from war wounds, both physical and mental. And a lot of them still hated the Krauts and could 'never again trust a Jap,' especially military who were stationed at Pearl Harbor. He'd overhear them talk about their war experiences at the Dawn Fishers Café or during the Veterans Day celebration on the wharf.

The picture of the sunset on Marie's mantle came to mind. Why not go to someplace a lot warmer like Mexico with great surf and fishing, away from the States? Maybe the Feds would just forget about him in time. He pulled up his collar, got back in the Chevy and drove towards his place on Oxford Way. It was time for a serious pow wow with the boys.

A bevy of surfboards lined the porch rail of the Oxford Way house. Another note hung on his door, this one from Jeremy. The Cove crew were all down at Cowells Beach hanging out by the Surf Shop. Marco didn't feel like going.

The Surf Shop was located directly under the Dream Inn on the cement sidewalk that skirted the beach. Marco called it "the cavern." It was a long cement room without much light coming in. Boards and wetsuits could be rented there, usually by tourists staying at the hotel.

During the summer months Marco always made extra bucks as a surf instructor there. It was also a good place to hustle tourist chicks. They'd line the beach in their bikinis trying to get that "California tan" before returning to their inland homes. Marco would show them a good time, take them for paddles or give them surf lessons and maybe even score a date for the dances at the Grove. They always had plenty of money to blow, which was another big plus for the local guys. But in the late fall and winter the pickings were usually pretty sparse. Marco and the crew would try to con some older guy or wino to buy them some brewskis and then head back down to Cowells Cove for a beer bust. He figured that must be what the boys were up to. Marco didn't feel like drinking. Besides, he was on call to work at uncle Joe's hamburger joint.

He left a note telling the guys to meet up at six at the house for an important meeting and went inside to use the phone.

Karen, "Karie," was in the kitchen sitting at the table with papers spread out. She was staring at the pile of bills, biting her nails and eating a bowl of oatmeal with no milk.

" Hey sis, what's hap'nin?" She looked up.

" Oh, Marco." She stood up wiping toast crumbs from her light green, wool sweater. "Look at all these."

He rubbed her shoulders as she sighed. A kettle steamed on the two-burner, gas stove. The linoleum floor was cracked and down to bare wood in spots. A small refrigerator hummed constantly in the corner.

"Want some oatmeal? Help yourself." She was a pretty girl with long curly brown hair, held back with a barrette. Her blue eyes shone in the subdued light from a small table lamp.

" Wish Willy and Abe could get some work. I'm doin' all I can cleaning houses after school… and on weekends."

" Where's yer mom? Thought she was sendin' ya money every month."

" In Florida for a while. Something about a guy named Fred who owns a trucking business."

" Florida, huh, when's she coming back?"

"I… I dunno… hasn't called in weeks." Her eyes reddened slightly. " I wish she'd call."

" Can't ya call her?"

" Don't know where she is exactly. Abe took the last message from 'er. Didn't write down any phone number."

" She'll prob'ly call soon." Marco wasn't sure how convincing he was. He just couldn't think of anything else appropriate to say. " What about Abe and Willy's dad?"

She was obviously getting pissed and Marco was sorry he brought it up. " That bastard hasn't sent money for over a month now. The last two hundred he sent's going for bills."

Marco was feeling like a heel for upsetting her." Hey, it'll all work out, don't sweat it. Something'll happen."

" Yeah, what? Think it's just gonna fall outta the sky?"

" No… uh, I dunno…" There was a strained silence for few seconds. The air between them seemed thick and cold. " I just came in ta use the phone."

" It isn't long distance is it?"

" Nah, just callin' work. My uncle's place."

" Ask him if he can get Willy or Abe a job there."

" I'm only part time. They don't really need nobody."

" Ask him anyway. You never know when someone might quit." She cleared her throat. "Ya know Marco, I know we had a deal you could stay here for just doin' chores, but things are changing. I may ask you to pay something from now on, maybe fifty a month. You're the only one with a job and I don't ask you for much around here."

" Uh huh, well, I guess so…I mean I thought we had a deal tradin' for work."

" Yeah, that's right, we did, but I just can't do it anymore. I love you Marco. You're like family. You know you are, but I'm not asking for much, just fifty bucks to help out." She paused, sensing the rift between them. " Okay, how 'bout thirty bucks, a dollar a day? Otherwise I might have to rent out your room." She was embarrassed but Marco could tell she was desperate.

" Sure, hey it's cool. I get paid on the fifteenth. Can I give ya half then?" He didn't want to seem like he was just sponging off her and he loved living so close to the Cove.

"That'd be great, thank you Marco." She gave him a big hug. She was holding back tears. Marco knew it was hard for her to ask for the money.

" Hey I'll bring some burgers and stuff home with me for everybody on days I work."

"Thank you Marco." She was barely able to hold back the tears.

" And I'll ask my uncle if there's any more work... for Willy and Abe. Or maybe he might know other guys who're hiring."

" Thank you." She disappeared in the downstairs bathroom. Marco knew she was crying.

He slinked into the dark study picked up the rotary and dialed, using the soft light from the side window. It rang five times.

" Hello, Cruz 'N' Eat, how can we serve ya?" It was his uncle.

" Uncle Joe, it's me."

" Hey Marco, how ya doin' boy?'"

" I gotta problem."

" Don't tell me yer not comin' in? We gonna be busy as hell."

" No, it ain't that..."

" Good, come on down an' we'll talk. I gotta go. Got deliveries coming in. You can slice fries 'till we need ya on the grill."

" Yeah, okay." The phone clicked, then hummed on the other end. Marco slid out the rear door. He didn't want to face Karie again. The lawn was soggy and stained the sides of his black tennies as he hoofed around the side.

The hanging mist cleared somewhat as he drove the cliffs. He dropped the Intruder in "Bumpsy's" back yard with a note attached. Hopefully he could get it patched soon, maybe by the weekend. It would have to sit for a while though to dry out. He'd call over there later to make his plea. He'd just have to ride his other team board until then. As he cruised the cliffs toward work he watched the swells rise up and move east as they swooped into the bay.

The Lane was firing off about twelve feet with twenty or so guys out. He smiled as he thought about how glad he was to have the Cove as his home break now, away from the crowds. Cowells had twice as many in the water, about four to five foot but the swell was hitting perfectly. He saw a nice six wave set form up and peel into the inner cove. He pulled down the sun visor as a blast of bright sunlight flashed into his eyes. A pack of Camels fell onto the dash. He pushed in the lighter and fired one up. The storm was letting up, at least for a while anyway, and last night's memories were fading a bit with every drag on the smoke. He pulled into a parking place near the back door of the Cruz N Eat as the nicotine flooded his brain.

The Cruz 'N' Eat was located on the corner of Soquel and Ocean Streets, one of the busiest intersections in town. A giant v-shaped, neon sign advertised burgers for twenty-five cents, fries for fifteen and shakes for thirty. All the traffic from "the valley" had to venture right past it on the way to the beach and boardwalk.

After a long beach day in Santa Cruz, hungry tourists could always grab a few burgers and drinks before going back over the hill to that smog basin of roaches, San Jose. It was more than convenient. They'd just drive up to the joint, place their orders at the window and within minutes could be careening back over Highway Seventeen with a bag full of grub. If they happened to find a "red star" on their receipt the whole meal was free, a little marketing idea of uncle Joe's. One in every three hundred orders was a winner. On a bustling Saturday or Sunday afternoon as many as three or four were likely to appear.

Marco opened the rear screen door to the smell of grease. The hood on the grill caught a lot of it but the sticky stuff always got on everything anyway, tracked around on the workers' shoes. Marco slipped a white apron around his waist and donned a paper orange and blue, sailor-styled hat with the words "Cruz 'N' Eat" on both sides. Uncle Joe met him as he was rounding the walk-in freezer.

"Marco, Marco," he yelled in his robust voice, slapping him on the shoulder.

"Take these patties out front."

Marco hauled the steel cart of fresh ground meat into the kitchen, and placed them in a stainless steel refrigerator behind the grill. The Cruz 'N' Eat ground their own patties and hand sliced all the fries. And a little venison might get ground in as a filler if Uncle Joe was lucky with the 30.06 during deer season.

"Hey Marco, what's up?" Leo, a short, chubby teen, flipped a dozen or so burgers on the grill. "Didn't know you were on today."

"Yeah, he wanted me here to do fries first."

"Cool, see ya in a bit.'" Leo slid the burgers onto waiting buns already spread with "Secret Surf Sauce" and pickles. Customers could buy small bottles of the sauce to use at home. It consisted of three parts ketchup, one part mustard with a shake of garlic powder. Uncle Joe advertised it as their secret blend. A picture of Marco slashing a stylish cutback adorned the label with the lighthouse in the background.

Leo had already grill-toasted the buns; that was another Cruz'N' Eat signature. There was a big sign on the wall behind the grill that stated, "*If your bun isn't toasted, we'll eat your buns!*" "Order up." He pushed the batch of steaming burgers forward to Edie, a cute brunette with a bubble hairdo. She constantly chewed bubble gum and blew bubbles at the register. People thought she resembled Annette Funicello, the movie star who acted with Frankie Avalon in the Hollywood beach-films. Joe thought that was a plus having her work the takeout window.

"Startin' to pick up," Leo announced, as he wiped the sweat from under his cap, then slapped down ten more patties and buns on the grill.

Marco returned to the back office where Joe counted all the money and did his ordering of supplies. He was on the phone. "Look, I ordered the French rolls same time I did the buns. Where the hell are they? ... need them before noon... look, that's yer problem... just get 'em over here." He slammed down the phone swearing something in Italian. "Aw the sunsabitches never get it right." He motioned Marco to sit down.

"That's what ya get for doin' business with cousins. You always come last." He leaned back on a swivel chair and stared at Marco. "So, how's yer mom?"

"Okay... I guess."

"Look Marc', don' bullshit uncle Joe." Marco sat up and cleared his throat. Joe continued. "I heard she's not doin' good, heard she's on the sauce too...yer aunt Cat saw her in Graff's Market."

Marco cleared his throat and changed the subject. "I got a problem."

Joe sat up in the chair and lit a cigar." I remember when you was jus' born. I was in the waitin' room. Did you know that?"

"No... no I didn't."

"Thatsa right. Even held ya up before yer dad did. He was a mess. No sleep fer days, just in from two crappy days of trolling." He took a few quick puffs on the cigar. "Hard on yer mom, ya know. Had ta cut'er open ta get

46

ya out. In for over a week. You stayed with Kat and me till she got out. Ya took the bottle right away."

Marco always did get along great with Joe. He seemed to understand him better than his own parents. Joe always came to his little league games and helped him buy his first surfboard.

" Katherine never could have kids, shoulda seen the way she cradled ya." He leaned back again and puffed away. " So whattaya need, a full time job?'

" Naw...that ain't it." Marco sat up straight, fidgeting with his apron. "I got drafted." His eyes glazed and he felt the shooting pain in his gut.

" Drafted?" Joe crushed out the stogie on the side of his desk. " Jessuskeyrist." They stood up and embraced. The hat flew off Marco's head.

" It's worse than that...."

"Worse? Whattaya mean, worse?"

Marco stood there rubbing his eyes with his apron relaying the whole story about how he didn't report and the how Feds were on his trail for evasion.

"Sit down. Look son, I gotta tell ya something." Joe leaned back in the swivel chair, fired up a Marlboro and took a long drag. "You know yer dad was in the Navy." Marco nodded. "Well, back then everybody was goin' in, ya know, ta fight Hitler an' Mussolini an'the Japs." He leaned forward and looked Marco directly in the eyes. "But I didn't go... had asthma an' a bad back from workin' in the carpenters union... they didn't want me... not even fer a desk job... was pissed as hell for awhile." He cleared his throat and spat into the wastebasket. " But ya know what, then they started comin' back... the dead ones. Two a my good pals from high school got it at Normandy... then a few more from Guadalcanal, an ya know what? After awhile I was glad as hell I didn't go." He took a big breath and leaned over close to Marco. " Then I helped out yer mom a lot when Louie was overseas." Joe cleared his throat. " You better really think things out."

Disjoined images flashed through Marco at the speed of light...Gina under the wharf... old Pigeon's yellowed tooth grin... the picture above his mom's mantle...Louie in the hospital...waves breaking at the Cove... He tried to stand up feeling light-headed. His knees buckled and he fell over onto the desk.

He opened his eyes when Joe put a wet towel on his brow. The room was cast in a bubble of pulsating light. "It's okay... you'll be okay." Marco sat back in the chair staring at the erratic shapes in the ceiling plaster. "Jus' be quiet awhile." Joe squatted next to him and stared with compassionate eyes. "I'm gonna help ya." He coughed and choked for a few seconds. "Getcha outta this mess... don't worry 'bout nuthin.'" Joe's face faded in and out of focus, then into clarity. " It's gonna be okay."

"I wanna sit up."

" Okay... let's try it slow."

Marco sat up in the chair in a half-dream state. That's it; it was a just a dream. He'd soon wake up on his cot in the sun porch and all this wouldn't be real, just a weird-ass dream.

" Want some water? I'll get ya some water." Joe left and quietly closed the door.

Marco blinked a few times. It wasn't a dream. It was all real, too real. He returned to full consciousness. He scanned his levis and tennies and shirt not quite sure who he was. He saw his reflection in the glass desktop and it all came back: Marco the surfer, Marco the draft evader, Marco the outlaw. He stood up, the lightness gone, feeling totally back in his body.

Joe returned holding an orange, waxed cup with water and ice. "Here you go." He held it out. Marco took it and sipped. "You sure you're okay? Want me ta call the doc?"

Marco shook his head. "Nah, I'm cool."

"When was the last time ya ate somethin'?"

"I dunno, yesterday I guess."

"I knew it. Ya need ta eat, yer too damn weak. I'll get ya somethin'." Joe sat back behind the desk. "I know a lawyer in San Jose, a friend a the family's. Used ta come over and fish for salmon with Louie. I'll give'm a call." He motioned Marco to sit back down, picked up the phone and fumbled with a steel address book, which flipped open after he pressed a button. He dialed the number and scanned the room as if not wanting to make direct eye contact. "Yeah... tell him it's Joe D'Giorgio... yeah, D'Giorgio, in Santa Cruz... I see, uh huh... uh huh... you tell him I got some salmon... that's right, salmon." He held his hand over the receiver and whispered to Marco, "That otta do it. That bastard never turns down salmon." Marco smiled and Joe smiled back, then a few seconds later,

"Yeah, Gordon, how ya doin' over there...uh huh, busy here too... yeah, I need yer advice on somethin'... right, a little fam'ly matter... uh huh ... yeah, I gotta bunch a thick fillets in the walk-in right now...nah, this time a year they're frozen...fresh frozen... tonight... well, sure I guess we could... you an' Marge... yeah, that'll work...eight a clock then."

Marco listened as Uncle Joe briefly explained the situation to the lawyer.

Joe wasn't like the rest of his other "uncles." Joe hated pasta and red wine and hardly ever ate fish, barbequed salmon occasionally if it was marinated. He always got seasick on the boat and only went to help out Louie when he was in a pinch. Marco smiled when he remembered Louie announcing at parties, "You sure as shit ain't no damn Italian. All ya like is porterhouses and sippin' whiskey. Christ, ya probably don't even like ta fuck." That would really piss off Marie and she'd always get in Louie's face about it. She'd point to the crucifix on the wall and and shake her finger at him. "Sometimes I can't even believe we're brothers." Everybody would laugh out loud. Then Louie and Joe would clink their glasses and laugh too. Of course Joe's was whiskey and Louie's was Dago red. Marco watched Joe gesture with his hands as he talked to the lawyer and liked the way he joked and laughed. Joe set the phone on its cradle.

" Okay, here's the deal. He's gonna make a few calls an' come over for dinner tonight, him an' his wife. He says fer you ta lay low fer awhile. So call me tomorrow."

Marco smiled and almost laughed." Thanks... thanks."

"Oh, he said ya better not drive yer car. Feds prob'ly got yer number from DMV. They'll be lookin' for it." Joe stood up, opened the desk drawer, pulled out two one hundred dollar bills and stuffed them in Marco's jacket. "This is ta tie ya over." Joe gave him a big bear hug. "Ya better get outta here now."

" But, what about work ? "

"Aw, fuck it...I'll call somebody else in. All kinds a guys wanna work."

"But...."

"No buts about it. Hey, wait a minute." Joe left for a moment and returned with a bag. "Here's a couple a steak sandwiches, some fries and a chocolate shake. You gotta eat sumthin'. And get some rest fer god's sake." Joe gave him another hug and kissed him on both cheeks. "Call me in the mornin'... roun' ten... not earlier...now get outta here."

"Okay...okay...." Marco walked out feeling dazed but relieved.

"Hey, take off yer apron." Joe laughed from the office, "'les you wanna go flip some burgers or clean out the grease trap."

Marco dropped it in the dirty laundry bin from habit even though it wasn't used.

Joe leaned back in his chair and thought about the times he'd go over with the wine and do chores for Marie while Louie was overseas and then eventually address her personal needs. He wondered if the wine stain ever came up from the time he was laying it into her by the fireplace, how wet and firm she was. How he always used a rubber except for a couple of times when they just couldn't wait. Hey, he didn't want to be no Kilroy, no way. They finally broke it off a few weeks before Louie came home. Marco was born nine months later. "Jeesuschrist," he mumbled aloud in the empty room.

Marco pushed open the screen door with his shoulder and saw Nicci's purple Plymouth parked a few stalls from his Chevy. What the hell? As he approached, Gina got out. She'd been crying. Marco leaned on the door of his sedan with his hands stuffed in his jacket pockets. She got up real close then stepped back. "Marco, we gotta talk."

"'bout what?"

"You know damn well. Last night… it was all a big mistake."

"Yeah?"

"Of course it was. I was drunk. Didn't know what I was doing. And pissed off at you."

"Oh yeah?"

"Listen God dammit. It wasn't my fault. Can't you see that?"

He thought about how he found her bra and panties folded on the sand. He imagined the val pumping her. "You really piss me off, you know that. I can't trust you at all."

She started to sob. "I love you. I want to be with you, just you."

Marco couldn't hear it. "Yeah, you shoulda thought about that when you were…with him."

She began to sob. "Marco, I'm so sorry."

"Look, I'm done with you. I'm gettin' outta here, way outta here."

"Whattaya mean?" She was stuttering.

"Outta town. Way outta yer life. It's over, get it?" His voice was cracking and he was holding back tears. "You'll never be the mother of my kids."

She held a fist to her mouth to keep from bawling. She climbed into the Plymouth, slamming the door. Marco hopped in the Chevy and gunned it out the parking lot. He shifted into second and punched it just as the light was turning red.

His heart pounded and stomach churned as he fought back tears. Okay, he'd crossed a line he never thought he would, telling Gina to basically fuck off for good. But he had to end it. He yelled and pounded the wheel with his fists as tears fell freely. He had to get hold of himself. He smelled the hot food, reached in the bag and pulled out handfuls of fries, jamming them in his mouth. Marco drove towards the harbor, taking all the side streets. His hands trembled on the greasy steering wheel. Gotta go hide the car.

enny "the Bull's" boat repair yard was nestled at the dead end of Alta Loma Street, a stone's-throw from the harbor. Fisherman could haul out there, scrape and repaint their hulls, do other more involved work or pay Lenny to do it.

Marco drove down the gravel road and unhooked the chain with a white wooden sign hanging from the middle. " *Lennys*" was scrawled freehand across it in red paint. Marco parked in front of the main barn. Three long rows of chicken coops spread eastward past a smaller, graying redwood storage and tool shed. Busted-out wire sprang from the coops, and wood-framed, slat doors hung by rusty hinges. Weeds poked up through the rotted-out coop floor planks. Marco heard the "bucka-ba-cooing" sound from pigeons in cages, hidden from view.

He walked past a high metal hoist used for removing engines. A sloping wooden ramp careened down into a flat area at the upper harbor. An iron winch with thick braided steel cable ran down to the water for hauling up the boats. Half a dozen empty boat trailers lined the gravel area above the ramp, used for moving the vessels to various spots on the property, where they'd be blocked up, dogged down and readied for repair. A rusted-out, faded blue Ford F 350 diesel pickup was parked next to the trailers and used for hauling them around the yard. A scraggly grey cat with gold eyes ran out from under the truck as Marco approached, turned towards him and yowled.

Two Monterey hulls were blocked up, one with a torn keel and the other with the cabin missing, covered with a dark green canvas tarp. A few wooden dinghies were scattered among the weeds and yellow mustard grass. Red five-gallon fuel cans littered the side of the barn next to a fifty-five-gallon barrel of diesel with a red hand crank and black hose. A rusty Dodge pickup and a green and white '55 Chevy station wagon sat in the graveled lot in front of the white, single-storied, ship-lapped house.

Marco heard Lenny rented the house out to three commercial fishermen and lived in the barn. Lenny's mom had died of an aneurism last fall and willed the place to him. Marco and Louie went to the funeral. She and her husband Benny had raised poultry there for decades. Benny was a chicken farmer from the Ozarks who was discharged on the west coast after World War II and never went home. They sold eggs to people and chickens to the local markets. After Lenny's dad was killed in an auto accident, the place went to hell. Louie and Marco tried to help by going out there weekly and trading fish for eggs. Lenny's mom couldn't do all the work herself to keep the place maintained or get good help. She ended up eating most of the chickens, sold a few, then lived off her husband's social security until she died.

A light rain drifted in. Marco slid open the wooden door to the barn. It screeched loudly on its ungreased, rust-pitted steel rollers.

The interior was cast in hard shadows. He smelled kerosene and wood smoke. Diffused light slanted in through smoke-glazed sash windows. Cobwebs hung from thick redwood rafters and post beams. A kerosene lantern sat atop a wooden crate next to a wood stove with a black cast iron skillet on top. A blue-enameled plate chattered on the rim of the skillet as steam squirted out, creating whitish brown streaks down the sides. The top burner of the stove popped and hissed as juices splattered.

"Lenny?" Marco squinted further into the dark hollows of the barn. "Hey, Lenny." He stood listening to the pot simmer as his eyes adjusted to the dark. The lantern's flame swished around inside the charred globe. A door moaned open on the side next to empty horse stalls and a dirty, green John Deere D4 tractor. It looked like it hadn't seen work for decades.

A short, slightly balding figure limped in carrying a steel feed pail. He moved from the shadows into the grey light by a window, setting the pail next to three big paper sacks of pigeon feed. Even from that distance, Marco could make out Lenny's shiny, cratered neck and face as he skulked in and out of the half light. His blue Navy watch cap and wide shoulders clothed in blue dungarees appeared in the lantern's glow. Marco thought he was about as thick as he was wide. Lenny turned the wick up, lifted the hot plate from the skillet with a set of pliers and stirred the broth with a bent soupspoon. Marco thought he looked much older than his thirty-two years.

"Whattaya want here at Lenny's?" He muttered in a gravelly low voice as he peeled off the heavy, dark blue wool sweater.

"Hi Lenny."

Lenny slid a small oak log into the belly of the stove. " Seen ya drive in. Was feedin' the birds."

"I gotta favor ta ask."

Lenny shrugged." I ain't got no money."

"Nah, it ain't that."

"Ain't got no work." He cleared his throat and spit on the ground. "Waitin' fer parts ta come in."

"I'm in a jam, need to hide my car for awhile."

The thick-necked, bulky man turned and looked Marco square in the eyes. Marco shuddered as those tortured, deep-set brown eyes peered through him. "I ain't lookin' fer no trouble roun' here. Don't want no cops comin' roun'."

"It ain't that. It's the Feds."

"The Feds, what the fuck?"

Marco told him the story and how he needed time to figure things out. Lenny pointed to a crate for Marco sit on. He stared into the darkness for a few moments then coughed. "Yer dad came an picked me up from the pen, when I got out. Gave me a deckhand job for awhile… till I got this place." He spat again. "Gave me a break. Nobody else would." He lifted the lid with the pliers again and smelled it. "Hungry? They stop layin' eggs, they go inta the pot."

Marco knew about his dad and Lenny but just sat silent and shook his head. Lenny scooped some stew into a bowl with a tin cup and sat it to cool on a wooden barrel. It did smell kind of smell good but Marco had the two steak sandwiches in the car. He could smell the rosemary and thyme and garlic. He remembered seeing herbs growing on the side of the main house. "Guess ya can keep it here awhile. Pull it inta the white shed in back a the house."

Marco stood up in a hurry. "Thanks, thanks Lenny." He held out his hand. Lenny took it and gripped it tight, holding on, staring into Marco's eyes. "Don' ever let them bastards take ya in. Got it?"

"Yeah."

"I mean it. Ain't nuthin' worse." Lenny squeezed down hard. Marco had the feeling that Lenny could crush all the bones in his hand.

" Yeah… got it." Marco could see that Lenny was thinking something horrible.

His pocked face quivered. He bit down on his lip.

"Now get outta here."

"Sure, sure thing." Marco stumbled toward the door, nearly tripping over a steel toolbox in the shadowy room. He pulled hard to get the heavy slider open.

"Thanks a lot Lenny." He pulled the shrill door shut.

Lenny sat on an overturned half-oak barrel and watched him leave. He picked up the steaming bowl, smelled it and mumbled," Mutha fuckas." He watched the steam rise from the bowl. He pulled a pigeon from the pocket of his dungarees, holding it firm in his left hand, while rubbing its head with his thumb. " An' ta night yer goin' in fer a hot bath too." Lenny snarled and laughed, coughing violently.

Marco moved the sedan into the white shed and shuffled through the high weeds to the gravel road entrance. He wondered when he might be able to drive his car again in daylight. Maybe after things cooled off, then again, maybe never.

He climbed down the muddy path next to main road onto the railroad ditch. Time to hoof it back to the Westside and meet up with the cove crew and talk things out. He was getting ideas about the big escape plan. Time to get the hell out of town. And the sooner the better. He almost slipped on his ass as he made it onto the railroad tracks.

Marco paced the railroad tracks next to the harbor, heading for home, carefully placing his feet on the packed gravel between the ties. The rails were covered with dew and mist, creating a thin layer of rust, which would get ground off when the afternoon Southern Pacific headed southeast from the Lone Star quarry north of town.

Marco reflected on the times during the summer months when he and his buddies would hop the train south under the trestle by Cowells, then jump off when it slowed into the yard by the Watsonville canneries. They'd eat Mexican food at a little local joint where they served cold cervesas to anybody with money, then hitch a ride back to town. It was a fun thing to do on hot, wave-less summer afternoons.

They'd climb into the sand cars and wait for the train to leave the yard in back of the Fun Spot, a small gas station and beach rental place a block from Cowells. They always had to wear sunglasses when hopping the train or the blowing sand from the cars would burn their eyes. Once the train got moving and they were out of sight from the yard bulls, who'd always be checking for bums, they'd climb down between the cars for a better view of the countryside and to get away from the blowing sand. It was a fun adventure, careening past the beaches and surf breaks in the south county.

Marco continued towards the Westside along the rail line from Lenny's. He skirted past a temporary hobo camp half- hidden in a large patch of bramble. An empty gallon wine jug and a mildewed sleeping bag were covered by a soaked piece of flattened cardboard.

Marco thought about how he'd sometimes set a penny on the tracks over by the lagoon on Bay Street after elementary school when he was a kid, then wait for the gravel train to come. It was cool to find the penny all flattened out if he could find it at all once the train spit it off the rails.

He climbed down the wooden stairs at the edge of the San Lorenzo River where the walkway crossed the water along the train trestle to the boardwalk and Beach Street. His stomach grumbled. He gingerly pulled the bag of steak sandwiches from under his coat. They'd probably be still slightly warm from his body heat. He'd wolfed down the shake and fries on the drive to Lenny's from the Cruz 'N Eat. Sitting on a wide steel cross bar of the trestle he began to devour the food. The steak sandwich tasted good, a little soggy, with the bun smashed, but it definitely hit the spot.

Got rid of the car for now, will have to hitch or ride a bike for awhile. That poor damn Lenny. San Quentin sure changed him. Crazy damn guy, just holes up in that barn and feeds his pigeons.

Marco gazed at the bank of the San Lorenzo River and remembered the morning when Louie took him fishing there for the first time.

It was back in fifty-five when he was just eight years old. Louie got him up before dawn, made scrambled eggs with bell pepper, onions, cheddar and linguisa, buttered white toast with strawberry jam and hot chocolate. They had their lines in the river before the sun came up. It was the first day of steelhead season that year, with fish pushing upstream from the river mouth to spawn. It was a nippy November morning. Marco's fingers stung holding the cold pole and steel Langley spinning reel. Louie spied a fat hen swimming along the bank. She was probably loaded with roe. He asked the other fishermen to pull their lines out so Marco could try to catch her. As the hen swam over Marco's bait, Louie yelled, " pull up, pull up.' Marco jerked the rod skyward, setting the hook in the fish's gills. " Reel in, reel in." Marco reeled the fish to the surface. Louie reached down and plucked her out. The guys along the bank cheered and whistled.

A game warden saw all the action and climbed down the cliff to inspect the catch. Marco was standing over the fish as the warden approached.

" Where'd you hook that fish, son?"

In unison four of the guys next to him yelled, " In the mouth."

The Warden just shook his head and walked way as laughter erupted along the riverbank. Marco later learned it was illegal to snag a fish anywhere on the body. It had to be hooked in the mouth.

That morning was one of the special moments of his life; he and his ol' man together. It was a rite of passage, catching your first fish with your dad.

Unwrapping the second sandwich, he stared out at the wharf in the graying mist. No boats would be moored there anymore, at least not after the first big north swell of the season. The *Three M's* was the only craft still there. Marco knew all the other fishing boats now had berths in the new small craft harbor or down in Moss Landing. He thought about the days before the harbor when the fleet moored on the lee side of the wharf. The party boats, those chartered for a day's fishing trip, tied up at the various landings along the wharf. Marco missed those days when the wharf was the real hub for local fishers.

He used to love riding his new red, three-speed Schwinn down to the wharf. He'd wait in the Dawn Fishers Cafe with a mug of hot chocolate until he saw the *Three M's* coming in. He knew all the waitresses there and they always made him special hot chocolate. They would load his mug up with steaming milk, real chocolate syrup and a mountain of whipped cream. The rest of the customers got the hot water and dry mix.

One by one the fleet would arrive from the outer waters, tie up next to the wharf and unload their daily catches. The fish would be hoisted up in iced wooden crates from the holds on the boats. Marco and some of the other local boys would clean them in stainless steel sinks atop the wharf. The guts and heads would then splatter down under the wharf into the hungry mouths of seals and gulls. Marco could make ten to twenty bucks a day cleaning fish for those who chartered out but didn't want to do the dirty work themselves.

He'd hose the slime and guts off the decks and flush out the ice boxes onboard the *Three M's* while Louie would sell his catch to one of the fish markets on the pier or sometimes right off the boat to anyone who happened to be there with cash. Then dad would drive him home in the old Willys pick up with greenbacks in hand, singing songs together.

Steak sauce oozed from the French roll dripping onto Marco's green team jacket.

"Dammit." He dabbed at it with his finger but it splattered his name just below the O'neill emblem. He'd have to wash it before the next contest. Gotta look the part he thought, be proud to be a team member. Who was he kidding? He'd never be able to show his face at the contest. The Feds'd be there to nab him once they figured out his M.O.

He gazed at the wharf again as the mist thinned, reminiscing further. He used to go spear fishing under there. He and his buddies either dropped down the steps to the old busted up Nichols boat landing or climbed down a ladder near the end of the wharf onto the maze of catwalks. They bought the green, five pronged, barbed, spearheads at United Cigar Store on Pacific Avenue. After Marco bought the spearhead he'd have to get a pole to attach it to. He'd climb over a neighbor's fence at night and steal an eight to ten foot redwood beanpole from one of the old Italian guy's gardens.

United Cigar was the local freshwater fisherman's hang out. Every afternoon guys would drift in, smoke cigars and compare notes about the day's fishing in the local river and streams. They'd compare stories about different holes in the San Lorenzo, Branciforte Creek or Soquel Creek: what bait or lure or fly was most successful and how big the catches were. Louie was like a fishing god to all the boys who hung out there. He'd wow them with stories of big catches on the bay. Marco loved being there with him. A long line of magazine racks lined the wall of the store and Marco would sneak looks at the girlie mags. They stocked the hottest reels and poles, too.

The catwalks under the pier were used by the wharf maintenance crew for shoring up pilings damaged by big swells during the winter surf season. They also became sleeping platforms for seals. With spear in hand Marco would stalk the pilings, staring intently into the rising and falling swells for the flash of a perch as it turned sideways as waves passed. The pile perches would hover next to the tarred pilings nibbling on barnacles. His favorite technique was to scrape off barnacles with the spearhead under water and wait for a fat perch to show up. Marco kept the head of the spear underwater and jabbed quickly when the fish flashed. He learned that if he tried to throw it from above water the perch would bolt away from the sound of the spear breaking the surface.

Other times Marco would rip off long bamboo stalks from a large clump by the side of Wessendorf and Thal's Mortuary, down by the Civic Auditorium to use as snagging poles. He'd pedal off with the one to two inch thick poles in hand and head for the wharf, then attach some thirty-pound monofilament line with a treble hook and snag for smelt along the catwalks. The guys at Staggo's Fish Market always gave him a two-pound empty tin can to put his catch in. On good days he'd emerge with the can full of smelt, then sell them back to the guys at the same market and make enough to buy a burger and chocolate shake from the little grill next to the aquarium. He'd chomp on the burger and watch the fish in the aquarium window. They had a baby seal in a tank too, "Snorky." Marco always wondered if Snorky wouldn't be happier living under the wharf with the other seals, but they did feed him fresh fish all day long. On great days Marco would even have smelt left to take home for Marie to fry up for dinner. Those memories seemed like some lost life he could never return to, not with all the crap going on now.

Marco switched position on the steel trestle beam as the fog became dense again blocking his view of the wharf. The fog was weird that way. It might come in and go out all day long. Some days it would stop close to the ocean's edge blocking out the beach or maybe hover out on the bay all day. Occasionally, it would envelope the entire town for weeks.

Realizing how wasted he still was, he leaned back against the beam watching the onshore mist envelope the trestle. The car was safely stashed at Lenny's. The cops couldn't ID him driving around town anymore and it was over with Gina, too. It was weird running into her at the Cruz N Eat, but he was glad to have it over and done with. The thought of the val putting it to her made his stomach tighten. No loose ends. Good bye and good luck. And it felt good to have a full stomach. The steak sandwiches did their job.

The out-going river water mixing with the oncoming tidal push made a comforting, sloshing sound along the banks and beach. He pulled up the collar around his neck. His eyelids dropped. Marco heard the invisible shore break as a distant, mellow thumping sound which lulled him slowly into sleep...water... *the flowing water... the peaceful sound of water...*

A chill bit into his back. He awoke slowly with a deep yawn. How long had he been out? Hard to say, thirty minutes, maybe an hour. Nah, couldn't have been an hour. The beach mist had cleared and the shore break pounded louder.

Jumping down from the cross beam, he hobbled over the trestle bridge towards the boardwalk. Once across the river he'd be back on the Westside. He leaned over the handrail trying to spot steelhead in the river below. Way too murky from the rain runoff.

He reflected on earlier years when he and his beach pals used to swing into the river from a heavy rope that hung down from the under side of the trestle. They'd run along the river's edge, jump up on the rope and see who could swing out the farthest. Last summer some out of town kid dove off the trestle and broke his neck. He didn't die but couldn't move from the neck down. Stupid valley idiot.

Marco climbed over the eight foot high, locked redwood entrance gate to the Boardwalk with a " *Keep Out*" sign attached. He plunked down on the pavement and paced along the wide walkway of the empty amusement park next to the seawall. It felt eerie being there alone. Pools of rain reflected the grey sky. The Boardwalk was always closed down and empty in the late fall. The tourists were long gone by mid September or early October. Marco loved it then, when the locals could have the town all to themselves again without the traffic and beach crowds.

He thought about how it was on a typical summer evening. Thousands of out-of-towners converged there: whining kids demanding ice cream cones, cotton candy, and soft drinks, much to the irritation of their parents; adults swilling beers and chowing down on corn dogs and burgers with a never-ending supply of money disappearing from their wallets and purses; preteens in small groups hooted it up on the rides. People watchers adorned the many benches along the route. Older teens on the make-out patrol and even a few drunken idiots looking for fights. Screams could be heard over a mile away as riders lurched down the first vertical drop of the Big Dipper rollercoaster.

Vals would make the drive to the beach to escape the intense summer heat in the Santa Clara Valley. It might be a hundred degrees over the hill and fifty at the beach under a dense fog. Some of the worst weather of the year in town was in the summer but that never stopped the tourists from coming. People from far away would save up all year to come to town for a week of what they thought would be the perfect beach vacation, only to find a shroud of dense mist. Local surf club guys would wear their club jackets to the Boardwalk in hopes of scoring drunken valley chicks.

But by November all the spilled sodas and sticky crap on the pavement were washed clean by the fall rains. Marco still saw a patchwork of black, ground-in gum and sun-baked, red-stained splotches from candy apples. He figured there must be tens of thousands of squished black gum spots on the cement.

Marco heard only his shuffling footsteps as he moved along the silent, towering rides. He stopped in front of the Fun House, its entrance a giant clown's mouth tourists had to pass through to enter. Weird mirrors distorted figures once they got inside. Dozens of high-pressure holes adorned the floor. Some guy out of sight would blast on the air when a babe in a skirt walked over them. Marco's favorite was the giant wooden slide where he'd sit on burlap sacks and slide down. He'd always get kicked out for trying to stand up and surf down on the sacks instead of merely sitting like the rest of the riders did.

He felt for smokes in his jacket pocket, pulling out a smashed pack with two thin Camels. Matches soaked, damn. He saw his reflection in a rain-stained dark window: wet, short brown hair with sad, intense greenish eyes and wide nose; wide shoulders stuffed inside a tight fitting, dark green jacket with black competition stripe, O'Neill logo and his name embroidered underneath.

Pulling his collar up and slinking against the walls of the buildings, he stayed under the over-hanging roofs as thick dew dropped off. He stopped in front of the Turnover Pie Shop and remembered back as kid when he was just getting into the waves.

Back in '57, he was ten and couldn't even afford a mat for mat surfing. He took a burlap potato sack and stuck an inner tube inside to use as a mat. It wasn't quite the same as a real surf mat but it got him into the shore break at Cowells and the river mouth in the early mornings on weekends. On his way back home he'd walk along the warmer pavement of the Boardwalk so his feet wouldn't freeze. Some mornings Bill the pie man would see him coming and give him a piece of hot apple pie with cinnamon sauce or some hot chocolate for free. Then the rest of the walk home, up Beach Hill and down Bay Street lugging the inner tube sack, didn't seem so bad.

He moved past Art's Hot Dog Stand, the Balloon Dart game and stopped in front of The Plunge, the famous indoor pool directly adjacent the beach. Marco gazed up at the huge, carved, wooden bust of King Neptune at its entrance. He learned to swim there when he was six years old from one of the lifeguards at Cowells who taught swimming lessons after hours. Louie would pay with salmon steaks, which the lifeguard relished. Marco loved the Plunge, especially watching people dive off the three-meter board. The pool water was half fresh/half salt water, pumped in from a pipe that went out across Main Beach into the ocean. They kept it a nice warm temperature, too.

The pool was lined with statues of naked women with flowing hair that wrapped around and covered their boobs. They carried vases of cascading water, which dumped into a toddler's area only a couple of feet deep. Marco was bummed when the Plunge was forced to shut down due to cracks in the pool caused by the pressure of the shifting sands beneath it. Last season during a period of big surf and high tides the waves actually washed Main Beach away, then flooded into the building wrecking the men's shower room leaving the pool strewn with sand. The drains and filters got all screwed up. A month or so later, some valley dope got his finger stuck in one of the drains and drowned. That was the last straw. The Boardwalk's insurance company made them shut the place down. Marco heard they were going to cement it over and put in a miniature golf course. What a waste.

The surf was booming on the beach. The swell was beginning to pump in. Every other set was rising in size and intensity. Hadn't seen it like that all season. Must be some real kick ass storm up in the northern Pacific sending these bombs down here. Coming up fast. Really gnawing at the beach.

But Marco knew the surf conditions could change radically in the winter. Last season he was out at the Lane on a slightly overhead day when it jumped up quick. Within an hour it had risen ten to twelve feet. By the time he caught his last wave that day it was way overhead and Third Reef was showing.

The waves were moving quickly through the wharf, definitely a strong northwest swell. Big lines sweeping in. He fumbled for his smokes as a set rolled in, each wave licking the bottom of the wharf, then remembered he didn't have dry matches. His heart began to race with thoughts of riding some big ones.

He paced past Marini's cigar and salt water taffy shop, past the bazooka gun shooting gallery and into the rear door of the casino. Even in the winter when the rest of the Boardwalk was closed the casino or " penny arcade," was always open. Marco could play nickel pinball, use the rifle shooting gallery or play penny soccer. There were the peak-machines too. One was called "Fan Dancer." He'd put in a penny look in thinking he'd was going to see some naked babe dancing behind a fan, when really it was just a stupid fan moving back and forth.

Marco hoofed over to Freddy or "Reddy," as they called him, a kid with curly red hair he knew from the beach. Reddy walked around with his hands in a blue change apron, giving out nickels for paper money.

" Reddy, got any matches?"

" Hey Marco, what's up?"

" Need some matches."

" C'mon over here,"

Reddy and Marco went behind a glass case where prizes were kept for tickets received from the arcade games. Reddy squatted behind the case handing Marco two books of matches. " Hey take this, too." He stuck his hand into the case and came up with a monkey-on-a-stick toy. Reddy pushed the sticks together in his palm. The monkey flipped over with a back somersault. " Try it. It's the favorite around here. If you flip it just right, the monkey's head gets caught in his own ass."

Marco took the toy. " Yeah, thanks." He walked out the west entrance leading to the wharf and tossed the monkey in a trashcan. Head up his own ass, that's Reddy all right. Marco lit a flattened Camel and sucked it deep. Tasted good. Damn good. Heading toward the wharf and Cowells he watched a few more big sets swing in under the wharf. There was way too much West in this swell to surf anywhere on the Westside. The waves would swing away from the sandbars elongating into giant unmakable sections.

A well-formed peak rose up and peeled off left from the middle of

Main Beach. Casino's, holy shit, Casino's was breaking. Casino's was a near-mythical surf break that only formed on huge days when the swell was directly from the northwest.

Marco first heard about it back in the late fifties when the older surfers congregated around driftwood fires at Cowells Cove. That was back in the days before wetsuits when they had to wear sleeveless wool pullovers in the water or nothing at all. Even when wet, the wool kept them warm. Sooner rather than later Marco's feet would freeze up, turn purple and lose all feeling. He'd stumble off his board, swim in through forty-eight degree water and run for the beach fire as his nuts sucked up into the warmer areas of his crotch.

Marco knew that a couple of the older surfers had ridden Casino's in nineteen fifty-seven, a decade ago on balsa boards. And no one had seen it break since. Marco wasn't even sure if the story was true or not. He watched another set move in. The first three waves closed out but the last two formed perfect lefts peeling off into the wharf, about eighty or ninety yards offshore, then exploding on the sand. They looked about twelve feet high maybe bigger if you were paddling over the face of one. Shit. The Intruder was over at Bumpsy's for repair and his other O'Neill team board and wetsuit were stashed at the Oxford Street house. Marco imagined himself gliding down the face of one of those big left-handers. O'Neill rental shop, he'd go there. He flipped the butt onto the sand and ran towards the Dream Inn.

Marco stopped to catch his breath in front of The Dog House, where often he'd bought a foot long hot dog for fifty cents with fries. The place was called, "Sis's" by the local beach crowd because the owner was a nice Italian lady called " Sis." She and her husband, Leo, ran the place.

Marco peered across the parking lot over the sand, to under the Dream Inn. Clay, the kid who manned the rental shop, was just sliding the glass door shut to the entrance. Marco yelled and waved his arms. Clay looked over. Marco ran past Olivard's Fish Market and the Ideal Restaurant at the entrance to the wharf and jumped down onto the sand. " Clay…wait."

Out of breath, he trudged over the hard packed wet beach to the shop.

"Clay, I need to borrow a board…and a suit."

" What?"

" Yeah…Casino's…I wanna ride Casino's."

" Casino's? You're crazy. Surf's gettin'outta control. O'Neill just called and told me to close the shop. Afraid it might flood. Told me to get the hell outta here."

"Look man, I'm on the team, you know that. O'Neill wouldn't care."

"Bullshit. It'd be my ass if anything happened to a rental board. It's too big out there. The Lane's closed out. Third Reef's breakin' and the whole damn beach is bein' sucked out."

"C'mon man, I'll take full responsibility. Look, gimme a board and suit for just one hour, for just one wave."

Clay could see the excitement and passion in Marco's eyes. "I dunno."

"Look man, I'll give ya two quarts a beer tonight. Come by the house. We're gonna go to a party. You can go with us."

"I dunno."

"C'mom bro. I'm gonna go ride one wave at Casino's. This is the chance of a lifetime. Can you dig that? Just one wave and I'll tell everybody you gave me the board I did it on."

Clay smoothed out his scraggly mustache and looked at the horizon. It rose and fell as far as he could see with white water and foam churning. "You sure about this."

"Never more sure a anything in my life. C'mon."

"Aw man... two quarts you said?" Clay thought about how he was itching to get some beer for his hot date that night.

"Ya got 'em."

"Okay, just one wave."

"Ya got my word."

"Sure as shit hope so." Clay slid open the door to the rental shop, "the cavern." Marco hustled to the wet suit rack and pulled a jacket off. "Here, gimme that." He handed Clay the rubber jacket and as he sprinkled cornstarch down the sleeves, Marco checked out the boards.

"There's not much here. The best one's probably the red, ten foot Intruder."

Marco picked it up and held it under his arm. It felt a little wider than his team board but it was thin and in decent shape, not too many dings, plus it was an Intruder. He figured it probably weighed about twenty-eight pounds or so. The weight of the board would be an advantage for dropping down the face of the bigger waves. And the extra length would add acceleration once he got it up to its full planing speed. "Beggars can't be choosers. I'll take it." It was half a foot longer than his usual board but would be a better paddler. He'd be able to catch waves easier with it and scratch over the bigger sets if he had to clear the impact zone in a hurry.

Clay added, "Ain't no swimsuits here. They went over to the Forty-First Avenue shop last weekend."

" I'll havta wear my boxers I guess. I'll just snap up the crotch flap."

They both laughed an uneasy laugh. Clay watched with concerned silence as Marco stripped down and slid into the rubber jacket. He slid open the door and helped Marco pull the ten-footer outside.

They edged toward the wharf together as the massive shore break pummeled the sand. The mist was dissipating, giving way to a diffused late afternoon clearing. The sky on the undulating horizon was beginning to show red and gold.

" You sure about this? Sun'll be goin' down soon."

" Got it all figured. I'll go off from the landing between sets so I don't have to paddle out from the beach. I'll wait fer the next set, paddle inta position, then nab the best formed one and come in."

It all sounded real easy Clay thought, maybe too easy. But if anyone could pull it off he knew Marco could; Marco, one of the top surfers in northern California. Marco, the O'neill team rider. He'd be the only one to try and ride Casino's Reef in recent history. It was the stuff legends were made of and Clay would be part of that legend. And the fact that he did it on an O'neill board would be good for business. Clay imagined the board hanging from the ceiling of the shop with the words, " *Marco's Casino Board* " inscribed on it. The incident might even be mentioned in Surfer Magazine and O'Neill's might even do a special marketing of the board, make a few minor design changes and call it the "Casino Model." All of which Clay would be praised for.

As they walked onto the pier people began to gather. Cars pulled up and parked. Someone was actually going out on such a giant day? He must be crazy. Who'd even think about going near the ocean today? It was way out of control. Other surfers, guys with boards on their cars pulled in and parked along Beach Street. The word had spread fast. Someone was going for it.

Marco paced slowly out on the wharf, eyes scanning the swells as they pushed through the pilings and swung towards the beach. He gauged where the big sets were forming. It was still the last couple of waves in each set that had the best shape, the bigger ones. He sat the long red board down on a bench and watched as a few more sets ripped through the pilings, turned and unleashed their energy as off shore spray blew off their tops. Clay was silent. It was suddenly not a time for words, only for deep introspection and planning. Precise planning.

Marco took a couple of deep breaths. "It's time, man." He picked up the board and quickly descended the wooden steps of the old Nichols boat landing. The steps were wet and cold from swells flooding over them.

Marco carefully scanned through the pilings and jumped on the board atop a smaller swell as it moved through. He didn't hear Clay yell, " Good luck, bro," as he pumped hard for what he thought was the take off spot. The current coming through the pier was strong and pushed him quickly away from the wharf. He realized that the rip was trying to flush him east toward the river mouth. He stroked hard against it to keep from being swept down. He was far off the beach just west of the casino.

The first wave of the next set rumbled through. Marco could hear it rip at the pilings as it swept along. He pulled hard over it and realized he was out of position and drifting down the beach. He gave it everything to get back to the take off spot, his muscles burning as he sprinted hard against the powerful rip.

The next wave was way too lined up without a definite peak. Marco went over it as another rose up behind. He pulled hard, hard, hard and harder to stay in position. He knew he had to either take off on something soon or be swept eastward in the brutal current. But this wave had no peak either. It would be suicide to try and ride it. He'd end up beat to a pulp and maybe even dinner for crabs on the bottom. He went over it as tears began to form. His stomach muscles started to cramp from the hard pulling.

Wave four. Bigger than the others with a definite peak, but could he get exactly in the right spot to take off? He had to. Adrenaline surged through him. He knew this was it. No turning back. He screamed a cryptic yell like a man does when he knows he has only one chance for survival. He felt a combination of intense fear coupled with a clearness of sight he never knew before. He swung the ten-footer shoreward and paddled like a man possessed. The wave peaked up, a steep wall of water sucking skyward.

Marco took a deep breath, pulling fiercely. The board penetrated the wave's skin, dropping downward. He stood up, squatted, grabbed the rail and pulled the board down the vertical face. It hollowed out so much he thought the board might slip sideways. He pulled harder on the rail. It sliced a gash in the elongating wall of water, streaking at full speed toward the wharf and shore. He shuffled toward the nose pushing the Intruder at its maximun speed, setting the rail high in the heart of the wave.

He heard a thunderous explosion as the peak peeled off and broke behind him. No way was he going to look back. He didn't want to know what it looked like, no way. He was gliding along on instinct only, statue-like, mesmerized by the bright moment. The wave lined up further, hooking full bore towards the wharf and beach, looking impossible to ride for much longer. Marco took a few steps back and buried the tail and rail hard up into the face. The board sliced up and over the top of the swell as it unleashed all its power on the sandy reef. Marco launched over the top with the plume of spray and dove under for a second. When he surfaced he realized the wave he rode was the last one in the set. He climbed on the board and stroked with all his remaining energy for the beach.

He made it just forty yards offshore as the next set roared in. The first wave of the set broke quite a ways out. Marco slid to the very back of the board and held onto the rails in the prone position as ten feet of surging white water and foam pushed him towards the beach. He kept the nose of the Intruder up and bounced along in the churning water. He plowed onto the beach in a melee of foam and sand.

Marco stood up, clutched the nose of the board and dragged it up onto the hard packed sand away from the next oncoming surge. He spit out sand and salt water and wiped his reddened eyes. The beach was littered with clumps of kelp and driftwood. He waded through a long shallow lake of seawater and foam formed by the surging ocean. A large crowd of onlookers hovered along the sidewalk. Marco didn't want to deal with them. He cradled the board under arm making his way under the wharf, back towards the rental shop. From atop the wharf Clay hooted, pumping his right arm in the air. " Fuckin' unreal bro, you did it! "

Marco nodded, not quite completely realizing the full thrust of what he'd achieved. Seemed like just a few minutes in the water. No big deal. Just went out and rode one wave. One very big, lined up, sucked out, reeling off, down the line wave. The adrenaline began to dissipate and more normal feelings returned. His bare legs shivered. His fingers hurt from carrying the ten-footer under arm and his feet began to numb out.

He looked back as another set rolled through the wharf and saw a piling dislodge as a swell rammed it. The thundering roar as the wave smashed the beach made his eyes blink. He felt a shiver climb his back, raising goose bumps underneath his wetsuit jacket. He realized how insane he must look, standing there at sunset in his underwear, unshaven, trembling, holding a long red surfboard.

He pushed through the wharf, turned and headed the short distance to the rental shop. A crowd was gathering. Clay had already opened the door to the shop and was waiting with a towel. Jeremy and Willy were there too. " Yeah, Marco, you ripped it," Willy yelled.

People started to clap and hoot. Marco raised his hand and shook his fist, " Get the fuck outta here, alla you."

Willy, Clay and Jeremy looked at each other cautiously, trying to figure out Marco's intentions. Willy yelled at the crowd. " Yeah, get movin'… now." He shoved a few guys. " Leave'm alone." The crowd fractured and filtered back towards the wharf and Main Street where most had parked.

Willy, Jeremy and Clay were silent as Marco slid the Intruder inside the shop and climbed inside. He shivered hard. Clay tossed him the towel.

" Fuckin'-A." Marco whispered as he dried off and pulled on his clothes. It took a few minutes of fidgeting to tie his tennies. His fingers were stiff and frozen. The other guys hovered outside mumbling in a huddle.

The door slid open. " Anybody got a smoke?" Marco emerged from the cavern. Willy dug into his shirt pocket. " Nah, I don't want one a yer filters. I want a real smoke."

" Here ya go." Clay was a non-filter man too and handed him a Lucky. They smoked and watched as a grueling set formed outside the wharf, turned and swooped shoreward.

" Shit, look at the size of that set." Willy snorted. The waves crashed the wharf and sent spray and foam up onto the top, enveloping a parked car. " Man this is unreal!"

" I'll bet the beach is gonna totally wash out at high tide," Jeremy added.

" They'll probably close down the wharf soon." Clay said, as he dragged on his cig. " I'm closing the shop and getting outta here. I may have to come back and sand bag. Gotta call O'Neill about it."

" There's nuthin' ta worry 'bout till the tide comes back in," Marco said. " Then all hell's gonna break loose. Don't forget ta come by for those two quarts."

" What time?"

" I dunno, how 'bout aroun' six-thirty? "

" I'll be there." Clay locked up. " See you guys after six."

The guys smoked in a huddle watching sand peel off the beach with every receding, savage wave. Kelp patches and driftwood slammed the shore with the oncoming surge. White water flooded the entire beach, churning up logs, trashcans and anything else in its path. The wooden lifeguard tower leaned over, hovered for two waves then plopped on its side, busting up further with every wave. The two poles from the volleyball court stuck up like twisted metal masts from a sunken ship. Everything else churned in the wild melee.

Willy, Marco and Jeremy piled in Willy's old black Buick.

" That was one bitchin' ride, Marc." Willy cranked up the motor. It turned over slow but finally caught. " For a guy in his undies, anyway." They all laughed. The Buick lurched up Beach Hill and screeched to a halt at the stop sign at Bay St. "Gonna party tonight, celebrate your ride and see if we can hustle some babes at the Wharf Rats' party."

Marco sat silently watching the surf along the cliffs as they drove around the lighthouse heading for their pad. Willy and Jeremy argued about who was the better local board shaper, Jim Foley, Mike Winterburn, Joel Woods or Tom Hoye at O'Neills or Doug Haut, Johnny Rice or George Olson. They agreed that Foley, Winterburn and Rice had the most experience but Woods was coming up fast. Olsen's boards had nice shapes but tended to have heavier glass jobs. Haut had been in business for himself for only one year but was making some hot new designs, especially his signature model. Phil Lingman was creating some nice shapes at Scofield Surfboards too.

Jeremy added there were also a few garage shapers who didn't have full on businesses but made decent boards too: Mark Angell, Dave Sweet, and the Benson Brothers. If you got a shaped blank from one of them you had to transport it carefully over to someone who'd then laminate and finish it off, which was a hassle. If you took all the trouble to go that route you could save around fifty bucks on the overall cost.

None of that mattered to Marco. He simply ordered what he wanted and got it free because he was a sponsored team member. He could even walk into the display shop and pull a new board right off the racks if he wanted.

The sun was nearly down when the old Buick glided into the dirt pull out atop the Cove. "Why don't ya guys leave me off here. I'll meet up with ya at the house."

"Okay, Marc, see ya in a bit." Willy pulled out and sputtered off.

The sun was setting when Marco plopped down in the ice plant atop the bluff over-looking the Cove. The onshore wind blew lines of ripples across the faces of the big swells. They crashed down outside the point, then as a torrent of white water plunged onto the beach, ripping at the shale cliffs.

An orange sun slowly dropped behind the bumpy horizon. The sky close to the ocean's edge faded from yellow to fiery pink as the deepening blue curtain descended from above. Marco watched as the raging ocean swept the kelp and sand into the offshore rip, carrying it southward toward Fingerbowl and It Beach.

The beach now had a winter look instead of the summer look. In the summer the beach was filled with sand and had a steep face graduating down to the shore break. In winter, big swells tore at the sand until it was flat and even with the height of the sea. Then in the spring all the sand would wash back in and be re-deposited. It must've been that way since the beginning of time, Marco thought. Before humans and fisherman and surfers and wars, the constant seasonal ebb and flow of the beach in the eternal currents of the ocean.

And every fall Marco knew when the big waves were going to hit. He was always the first guy out on the first north swell of the season at the Cove. It was a kinetic thing, an inner knowing. He told one of the older surfers his feelings once and the guy said, " Aw, it's just all that dago fishing blood in your veins." It was probably true.

He learned a lot about the weather and moods of the ocean from being out on the boat with his dad. And Louie always seemed to know where the fish would mass on instinct. He rarely came up short and told Marco about times when he'd have dreams about where they'd be biting the next day.

Marco stood up, brushed the weeds and dirt from his jeans as the sun made its final drop. The walk back to his place was filled with disjointed thoughts about his mom, Uncle Joe, Gina and the Feds. And how about that wave at Casino's? People would be talking about it all over town once the word got out. Maybe somebody even got a photo of him from the beach. Who cares, he did it. It was a personal thing. He kept the legend alive and no one would probably ride it again for a decade, maybe never again. He turned down Oxford Way from Almar Street wondering what was going to happen next. And the Wharf Rats party tonight was sure to be a hooter.

Four cars were parked in front of the Oxford Street house: Jeremy's old Rambler station wagon, DJ's faded green Volkswagen van and a blocked-up older Ford coupe with a blown front end which was Jeremy and Karie's mom's. Wherever in hell she was. Clay's yellow VW convertible was parked a few houses down the street. His blonde date was sitting in it alone waiting impatiently.

A new Chevy pickup that belonged to a guy named Deets who was trying to get something going with Karie was across the street. Marco didn't dig him. He didn't surf, was kind of a loud-mouthed "jock" who played football at Santa Cruz High and was three years older than Karie. But he did take her to the grocery store a lot and helped her get around town when Abe couldn't drive her. Abe told her he thought Deets was just trying to get in her pants and to be careful. She told him to mind his own business and that she knew exactly what she was doing. Still, though, the guys were a bit concerned, especially after what had happened to Gina.

The Stones were blasting out, "Tiiiiiime is on my side, yes it is..." on a clock radio as Marco entered the front door. Abe, Willy, Jeremy and Clay were sitting around the kitchen table.

"Marco." Willy yelled above the music." We been waitin' for ya before we pop the brews."

"Hey, turn down the sounds a minute." Marco pulled up a chair and leaned back against the wall. "Where's D.J, his car's out front."

Jeremy muted the radio and leaned on the old Wedgewood cook stove. "Over at his weird uncle's scoring some more brewskis."

"We already gotta case a Coors but we decided a few more sixers would be a good addition," Abe added. Willy opened the refrigerator and passed out the half quarts to everyone.

" You wanna do the honors, Jere? " Clay asked, as he rubbed his eyes under his glasses and smoothed back his 'stache.

" No, you. You're the guy made it all happen."

Clay raised his foaming bottle. " Here's to Marco, brave conqueror of the infamous Casinos Reef. Only man in modern history to ride said reef." Cheers rang out around the table and they all took a swig. " Furthermore, he rode a huge left tube in his boxers without shittin' in 'em!" The gang whooped and laughed louder. Even Marco chuckled at that one. " Down the hatch." They all chugged.

" Yeah, what the fuck," yelled Willy as he threw his can against the wall. It landed near an empty paper bag next to the sink and drain board. Abe and Clay tossed theirs too, both making it into the bag. " Hell of a ride and I was there to see it."

" So was I." Jeremy smiled a coy smile at Marco.

" What were you guys doin' down there, anyway? " Marco asked as he leaned forward in his chair.

" Scorin' the brewski's. Had a wino buy us a case of half quarts at Beach Liquors. We were right across the street when you an' Clay were walkin' out onto the wharf. We yelled but you didn't hear us."

"Saw the whole thing from right in front." Jeremy smiled again at Marco. " Then we hoofed it over to the rental shop when we saw you head back under the wharf."

" And if it wasn't for me, none of it would've happened." Clay took a bow.

"Let's drink to that." Abe suggested and produced another round. They all pulled the pop- tops.

Marco stood up and raised his can. " To Clay. Old pal and former O'Neill employee, who will probably get canned for givin' me the board and wetsuit… just kiddin, bro."

Clay laughed and added, " To Marco, for being crazy enough to try such a stunt. And I wanna see if there's any brown stains on those shorts."

Everybody laughed and took another long pull.

" Go ahead man," Marco added. " They're draining right now across your chair at the shop."

" You bastard." Clay laughed and took another swig.

" Listen you guys, I gotta tell ya all somethin' serious." Marco sat back down. So did everybody else except for Willy who leaned against the humming frig.

" Serious, huh, sounds serious," Abe joked.

"So, what's up pup?" Clay slowly settled back in his chair.

Marco told the story about the draft notice and the Feds going over to his mom's place and hiding his Chevy. Silence filled the room for half a minute.

" That's heavy bro." Willy stammered. " They got my cousin Bruce two months ago, right after his nineteenth birthday too."

Abe picked up a classical guitar and plunked a few bars of "Satisfaction." " Wow Marco, that sucks."

Jeremy was silent.

" I dunno man. I been thinkin'. Thinkin' bout splittin." Marco got up and paced around. Abe struggled with the chords.

" Splittin' to where?" Jeremy broke the silence. "I hearda some guys goin' up to Canada."

" Too fuckin' cold up there. And besides, the surf's probably shitty. I was thinkin' 'bout Mexico."

" Humm..." Jeremy whispered under his breath. "Mexico huh?"

" Yeah, I was thinkin' 'bout maybe Matachen Bay, south a Mazatlan. Member the great waves we got there last year?"

" That was so bitchen'." Willy chimed in. " Water was so warm ya couldn't keep wax on yer board."

"Hey, remember that ride I got all the length of the bay?" Abe added. " It was about a quarter mile long."

" Yeah, we remember," Willy added. "How could we forget. You talked about it all the way home! " Everybody laughed as Abe tried to backhand Willy.

" But Marco got the longest nose ride." Jeremy added.

" And you got the best tube ride." Marco smiled back at him.

" Hey what about the tube I got at the inside section?" Willy boasted, "I thought that was the best tube."

They all bickered and bragged as Marco recalled their ten-day trip down there last winter. Matachen Bay was one of the most classic point breaks on the entire west coast of mainland Mexico. From Santa Cruz it was at least a two-day car ride if you drove day and night. That's the way they did it; two days, day and night with someone always driving while the others slept. That is of course with the help of a little jar of white pills. No stopping except for gas that was the rule.

" Hey man, ain't you afraid of gettin' popped at the border by the Feds?" Willy asked. " Sure as shit they'll be lookin' for draft dodgers."

" Yeah, what about that? " Abe set down the guitar and leaned on his arms on the table.

" I ain't plannin' on drivin'." Marco answered with a sly grin.

" You can't fly. They might be checkin' the airports, too." Abe added.

" Are you thinkin' what I'm thinkin'?" Jeremy chimed in.

" Maybe, what's that?" Marco asked, with a smirk on his face.

" The *Three M's*." Jeremy barked.

" You got it bro, the *Three M's*."

" You mean yer dad's boat?" Willy stood up and leaned against the wall.

" She's mine now and all I gotta do is fill'er full a food an' diesel and hit the high seas."

" Not only would you be a draft dodger, you'd be a pirate, too," Willy laughed.

" That's how I figure it. I could fish and surf and live on the boat."

" But what about the Coast Guard? Won't they be lookin', too?"

" Fuck the Coast Guard. Not if I was twenty or thirty miles off shore when I went across. Shit, my ol' man used to go a lot farther out than that for albacore."

" How'd you live down there?" Abe asked.

" Like I said, fish and surf mostly. I could always charter out to tourists every once in awhile for some bucks."

" I like livin' right here and surfin' the cove," Willy retorted. " I think you just want some company when you run for it."

" Oh yeah, well you'll be nineteen in a few months." Marco looked at Abe, then over to Willy and Jeremy. "And you guys'll be coming up for the draft, too."

" That's bullshit. Me and Jeremy got two more years of high school." Willy yelled.

" Yeah? If you read the papers or listened to the news, you'd think different. They're plannin' ta draft everybody."

"By the time we graduate the whole thing might be over."

" Don't count on it." Marco was getting pissed at Willy for trying to spoil his scheme. " A little planning now could save yer ass later, that's all I'm saying. High school's a buncha crap anyway."

"That's for sure." Willy added.

"Especially for us surfers. We don't fit in." Marco continued. "We're some a the best athletes in school, but the coaches hate us cause we don't play school sports."

"Yeah." Jeremy added, " I got a referral for not suitin' for PE last week. I was just too cold after surfin' the Cove before school."

" Fuck, who wants to go hang out in a smelly locker room when you could be getting' tubed," Willy yelled.

"Lets drink to that," Abe added. They up ended the brews.

The door swung open. D.J. barged in with a large paper bag. They called him " D.J." because he constantly played loud rock music in his van, always changing channels for the best song. " Party's arrived!" The large paper bag with the six packs of Burgie smacked down on the table.

" Hey careful, we don't want the whole thing to be foam." Willy yelled with a laugh.

" Drink up mates they're still cold. Fuckin' guy had us by 'im two sixers as part of the deal."

" Last week it was one sixer."

" Yeah I know, that's what I said to him but hey, we got'em didn't we?"

" Beggers can't be choosers, I guess. " Willy chuckled.

" More like, minors can't be choosers." Abe popped a can of Burgie and sucked on the foam.

DJ saw Marco and slapped him on back." Heard about the ride, Marc. Was it really as hair ball as they said?" DJ winked at him and smiled.

" Don't believe everything you hear." Marco answered as he looked away and walked into the other room.

DJ laughed. " Problem is, knowing you, I believe it."

Willy and D. J. argued about the difference between Burgie and Coors. Abe turned the record player on. As the first few bars of "I can't get no satisfaction" blared out, Jeremy followed Marco with beer in hand.

Marco and Jeremy sat on the old faded red couch. They could see and hear the gang in the kitchen clearly from the dark living room. Willy was telling D.J. about Marco getting drafted, gesturing with both arms as Abe tried to plunk out the chords to " Satisfaction" on the nylon string guitar.

" You really serious about Mexico?" Jeremy asked.

" Damn straight. I know I can make a go of it down there. And besides, there ain't nuthin' for me here anymore, 'cept you guys and the Cove."

" Hmm, does seem like a cool idea, surfin' and fishin' for a while. Not havin' ta wear a wetsuit an' all those bitchen waves."

" Yeah, maybe for a long while. Ya know, it's startin' ta get real crowded around here. The other day there was eighteen guys out at Cowells and a dozen or so at the Lane."

" And the university, too."

The university. Marco knew that Uncle Joe and a lot of other businessmen even went down and tried to fight it when they first wanted to build it. Nobody really wanted it in town. Uncle Joe said it'd really screw up Santa Cruz. Just like it did to Berkeley and Davis. Took over the whole damn town, even the city council." Uncle Joe told me all about it. Drove all the Berkeley locals out and they hate veterans, anything to do with the military. Stopped having parades on Veteran's Day up there. Can you believe that, got no respect for the people who put their asses on the line for freedom, their freedom. " Marco realized he was repeating Uncle Joe's exact words.

" Ya know, my 'ol man was in the army."

"That right?"

" Yeah, World War Two. Somewhere in the Pacific. Mom said he'd never talk about it. He'd just get these real quiet looks on his face every time she'd mention it. Then he'd start drinkin' again." Jeremy sipped his beer and belched. " One night he really flipped out an smacked 'er around with a broom handle. Next day we moved in with gramma, just her and me." Marco listened as Jeremy shuddered a bit. "Never seen 'im since."

" I never knew your ol' man."

" Naw, he split town when I was about five. But I still remember how he used to throw me up in the air an' catch me. He'd make a sound like an airplane and I'd laugh real hard and pee my pants."

Jeremy sat quietly and sipped the Coors wondering where his real dad might be. His mom then married Willy and Abe's dad. They moved into the Oxford Street house when Jeremy's mom inherited it a few months later. And now she was separated again.

Marco stared at the slow revolutions of the ceiling fan blades as they circled half hidden, in and out of the bright light from the kitchen. The light flooded the wooden parlor floor, casting hard shadows. A small table lamp with colored roses painted on the globe shown dimly on the desk by the phone. It was the lamp they always left on all night illuminating the way to the stairs.

An overhead light clicked on at the top of the stairwell. Karie and Deets thumped down, walking right past Marco and Jeremy hidden in the darkness and into the kitchen.

" Turn that music down." Karie was furious. " And where did that beer come from?"

"Hey sis, have a brew." Willy handed her one.

" Dammit, don't you get it?" She turned off the phonogragh. " You guys

76

are really stupid, you know that?" They all stood in silence. "All we need around here is for the cops to come over."

" Hey come on sis, it's Saturday night." Willy chimed.

" I don't care what night it is, you guys are really screwin' up."

" We're just primin' up a bit, that's all." D.J. added.

"Primin' up... primin' up for what...juvie?"

Willy, Abe and D.J. chuckled in unison. Clay finished his beer, grabbed a couple of half quarts and slinked out the front door.

" Hey, sis, cool it. We ain't hurtin' nobody. Were just havin' a little meeting that's all. A meeting of the minds." D. J. up ended his Burgie and tossed it in the sink.

" You mean a meeting of the mindless." Karie stomped over and picked the empty from the sink. "You guys wanna drink, you do it somewhere else."

" Hey this is our house, too." Willy popped another beer.

" Oh yeah, when was the last time you paid any bills."

" I paid the garbage last month."

" That was after they stopped picking it up. Then you went down and paid it."

Jeremy and Marco came in from the darkness. " Let's head on over to the Wharf Rats party now guys," Marco offered." Time ta split the scene."

" Dammit, don't you guys get it. You're all screwin' up big time." She sighed aloud, " We got enough problems without this. Don't you know what would happen if the county found out we were livin' here alone? We'd all go to foster homes."

" Hey, take a chill pill." Willy then turned to Deets. " At least then she'd be on some kinda pill."

D.J. folded up the cardboard lid to the case of Burgie and headed for the door. Abe set the guitar on the table and left. Willy was still arguing with Karie as Marco and Jeremy slid out the back door. As they rounded the house they could hear Willy and Karie hassling inside.

" Don't tell me what to do, you're my step sister, not my mother."

" You are such a jerk. You're probably the main reason your dad left town."

" Why you little bitch..."

Something made of glass smashed on the kitchen floor as Marco and Jeremy rounded the front of the house. They heard Karie scream. A full half quart can busted through the window above the sink. It popped open and fizzed on the porch. Willy ran out front.

"C'mon." He panted, "Let's get the fuck outta here."

They all piled into D.J.'s van. Karie yelled from the porch," You bastard, Willy!"

The Volkswagen sputtered off down the street towards West Cliff Drive.

"What happened man?" Jeremy asked, holding on to his knees as he squatted down in the rear of the van.

"Had to pop 'im," Willy said with a grin. "The jock. Started mouthin' off. Popped 'im good. Hate them fuckin' "jocks." You know, the guys who play football, basketball and baseball. They always parade around in their letterman jackets thinking they're hot shit." Willy took a big gulp, powering down a whole can. "I'd rather surf any day than hang around in a sweaty jock strap."

"Right on bro and hustle chicks on the beach." DJ hooted.

Marco thought about how they'd all cut class to go surf the Cove when it was pumping.

"School sports's is for kooks." Willy was hyped up." Glad I smacked that "jock" good."

Abe handed them all another brew as the van turned past the lighthouse. "Let's cruise the strip," D.J. offered. "Maybe we'll find some chicks to take to the party."

"Right on." Willy agreed and took a long swig. He belched and sang out loudly, "I can't get no … no satisfaction, no, no, no."

Abe, D.J. and Willy sang it again a few times in unison. Marco and Jeremy stared out the two rear windows as a light rain began to fall. Cruise the strip, huh. Every Friday and Saturday night scores of cars filled with teenagers descended on the main streets of Santa Cruz. It was like an addiction or religious rite. They blew in from "the valley," Watsonville and Monterey.

For those in the know, like the cove crew, the local cruise route began on the two-way, two-laned Pacific Avenue, led down Beach Street to the Boardwalk in front of the Grove, then spanned down Ocean Street, past the Cruz 'N' Eat into the parking lot at Taco Tio or A&W Root beer restaurants, only to begin the journey again down Pacific Avenue. It was like a giant, blacktopped loop Marco thought, where everyone who was out looking for action could check out everybody else. Hot-rodders would sometimes peel out from A & W Root Beer down Ocean Street in front of Quality Automotive with tires smoking to see who'd "lay the longest patch."

D.J's van loped down Beach Street along the low-lying road next to the wharf and Main Beach. The bright streetlights became shimmering ponds on the dark, wet pavement. Horns honked and people waved as the cars sped past each other.

Occasionally, Marco heard the squeal of tires, as souped-up older Chevys, new Mustangs, GTO's and custom street rods vied for racing rights which would happen up on the coast highway later that night. The quarter-mile drag races would take place at " four lanes," a spot on the coast highway about three miles north of town after all the parties died out. They'd race for beers or money and even for " pink slips;" if you lost, your car was signed over to the winner.

Marco heard the sound of burning rubber and thought how he might be able to sell his '55 sedan to some hot-rodder for Mexico money. Why have it just sit at Lenny's when it could bring in some good cash? Any hot-rodder would love get their hands on it with its 327 V-8 and Holley carb. They'd just have to drop a Munsi four-speed tranny with a Hurst shifter in her, get a set of American Torque-Thrust II aluminun wheels, seven inch fronts, eight inch rears, a dual-exhaust glass pack muffler and she'd be a mean street rod.

" How 'bout a little icin' on the cake?" D.J. offered, as he winked at Willy seated next to him. He pulled out a thickly packed, hand rolled smoke. " Fire 'er up, bro."

" Yowser." Willy struck a match and sucked on the reefer.

" I just picked up a matchbox this afternoon," D.J. added. " Thought we'd add a new dimension to things." A " matchbox" was a small amount of pot, usually around four dollars worth that could fit in a wooden matchbox.

" What is it? " Jeremy asked, as the odor wafted into the rear of the van. " Smells like burning cloth."

" It's Mary Jane, bro. You know, cannabis sativa."

" What are ya doin' with that stuff?" Marco broke in. "That shit'll fuck you up."

D.J. laughed." That's what 'the man' wants you to think. Ain't nuthin' bad about it. I been tokin' it for weeks now and all it does is make you feel mellow and get the munchies."

" Yeah," Willy added. "Me and D.J. been groovin' with it." He handed it back to D.J. who hit it hard and passed it to Abe.

" Give it a try, bro. It ain't nuthin'."

Abe stared at the smoking joint in his fingers for a few seconds.

" C'mon, Abe, don't be a lightweight," D. J. taunted. " It ain't like cigs, it's mellow man."

Abe, who wasn't about to be overshadowed by his younger brother, held it up and puffed. He exhaled the dense smoke and coughed violently. " Take it." He waved it at Jeremy and he coughed more.

" You sure it's cool," he jestured to D.J.

" 'Course I am," D J smiled. " Hey, my ol' man smokes it every morning."

That's why his sculptures are so weird Marco thought. He knew D.J.'s dad used to have a job as an art teacher but was fired recently. Every time he'd go over to D.J.'s to rouse him for dawn surf sessions, his dad would be " creating art" in his garage studio. He'd see the light shining from under the garage door as he walked past the house to knock on D. J's bedroom window.

Willy and Abe watched Jeremy fill his lungs slowly and blow it out in a steady flow.

" It's smoother than tobacco, kinda funny tasting."

" You'll get used to it. Give it a shot Marc. Anybody who does Camel non-filters like you, will find it real mellow," D.J. preached.

" Naw, not for me." He pushed it aside. " Maybe later."

"I'll take it," Willy jumped in. "Don't waste it on him."

" Whattaya mean by that," Marco challenged.

" Hey, if you don't wanna play, it's okay by me. There's just more for the rest of us... bro." He over stressed the word "bro" as if mocking him.

" Fine by me... bro," Marco replied as the reefer was handed back to Willy. It made the rounds another time. When it came to Jeremy, he took a quick look at Marco's disapproving glance and passed it back forward. Marco sat in silence as the others began to laugh and ramble on about non-sensible things as the drug swarmed their brains. They sounded like babbling idiots, laughing just to be laughing. After a few minutes they settled down.

" We ain't gonna find no chicks in this weather, man. Let's head over to the gig." Willy added, "You do still wanna go to the partay, don't you? " He stared glassy eyed at Marco.

" Yeah," Marco hesitated. "Yeah, I do."

" Yer the big surf star and all. Aren'tcha pals with those guys?"

" Yeah, I am. They're cool guys."

" For Capitola guys." Willy added. "Surf's shitty in Capitola... Crapitola, I mean."

" Hey, they're friends a' mine, okay?"

" Knock it off, Willy." D.J. gave him a " shut your mouth" look.

" Hey, I heard " The Jug Band's" gonna play there." Abe offered, trying to change the subject.

"Yeah." Marco continued, "Two a' the Wharf Rat guys, D.A. and J.B. are in the band."

" Why are they called, ' The Jug Band?" Abe asked.

" It's short for, 'Sunday Matinee Jug Band.' They play the Catalyst on Front Street sometimes," Jeremy added.

" I'll bet the place'll be swarmin' with babes." D.J. raised his eyebrows and smacked his lips.

" Prob'ly," Marco said softly as he thought back to last nights' fiasco with Gina. "Babes." Who was he kidding? Hustling chicks was the last thing on his mind. He just wanted to get away from his real life for a little while and a party seemed like the right place to do it.

" Hey," Abe added, " I bet it'll be a real rager. Those Wharf Rat guys always have the best parties."

Marco listened as they talked about different chicks they'd met at the beach and at parties. His mind was filled with images of Gina under the wharf; her disheveled hair and torn dress and the way she collapsed on the sand.

" Why are they called the Wharf Rats, any way?" Abe asked. " Seems like a real weird name for a surf club."

" This is the way the story goes." D.J. added. " I asked the same question to one of them at the Grove last weekend. One afternoon last winter, one of the guys in the club, J. B, was out on the pier in Capitola during a huge swell. He was watching the big waves slam against the pilings when he saw a rat float out from under the pier on a busted off piece of wood. The wood drifted in towards the beach with the current. A big set loomed in and he was sure the rat was going to eat it in the shore break. Well, just as a wave was about to break on the wood, the rat ran up to the tip of the plank, trying to get out of the way I guess. As the wave picked up the wood, the rat's weight on the end of it caused the plank to glide down the face of the wave. The rat was surfing the wave on the tip of the plank like he was hanging ten with his claws. The wave closed out and pounded the beach hard. J.B. was sure the rat drowned. Then he saw the plank wash up on the beach and get this: the rat was still hanging on. The rat jumped off onto the sand, ran up the beach and disappeared under the Venetian Court. I swear to god, that was the story. So the Capitola guys took it as an omen and named their club the " Wharf Rats."

" No fuckin' way, bro," Willy stammered. " You expect us to believe that? It's total bullshit."

"I dunno," Abe said. " It may've happened. Hey, I heard a lot stranger shit than that."

" You are so stupid if you believe that," returned Willy.

" Hey Marco, how 'bout gettin' us some grub from yer uncle's place? I'm starvin," D.J. begged, as he flipped the radio dial looking for the best song.

" I dunno."

" C'mon man, just a few burgers or somethin'. You didn't have ta pay fer any beer… or gas."

" Yeah bro, that's right," Willy agreed. " We all popped for the case."

Marco didn't want to go back to the Cruz N Eat but the guys had a point and it was on the way to the party. " All right."

The VW sputtered into a parking spot next to the bathroom and pay phone, alongside the burger joint. Marco slid in the back door and returned a few minutes later with two large white bags stuffed with burgers, shakes and fries. Sighs and grunts filled the van as the gang drove down Soquel Avenue toward the little coastal hamlet of Capitola.

" You're a bitchen guy, bro." D.J. nodded to Marco as he tore into a double cheese burger. A glob of surf sauce oozed on his pants as he took a big bite. " Godammit."

Marco listened as they all slopped the burgers down, babbled and rambled on about picking up girls at the party. He munched on a double burger. Going to the party sounded okay at first but now it seemed kinda dumb. They were all getting on his nerves, their idiotic howling and the constant talk about finding chicks. It seemed like a stupid game.

He couldn't fight off images of Gina puking on the beach and crying hysterically. He'd hoped breaking up with her would make him feel better, but the haunting continued. He felt sorry for Gina but could never be with her again, especially since the val had her first. Just one more thing he couldn't deal with. Not now anyway. Maybe never. What the hell. Maybe a few beers at the party would take his mind off things. For awhile anyway.

Thick fog filtered shoreward as the van coasted down the long hill by the wharf in Capitola. The streetlights were hazy dots hanging in the mist. Tired windshield wipers slapped back and forth erratically.

" Where to now?" D.J. called as the van's brakes squealed.

" Think they said on Fanmar somewhere." Marco answered clearing his throat, " at the blonde bomber's place."

" Whose place?" Willy asked.

" The blonde bomber. She's a local beach chick. I think she's goin' with one of the guys in Wharf Rats."

" Where's Fanmar?"

" It's past the theater I think, I dunno."

" Okay. Hey, I mean there ain't that many streets in ' Tola anyway."

They drove down Esplanade Street, which bordered the beachfront and western edge of town. Capitola or 'Tola,' as it was called wasn't actually a town in the normal sense. It was more of a beach village.

On the corner of Esplanade was Ben's Country Store. Next to it was the Edgewater Club, a local drinking hole, nestled between Ben's and Johnson's Skeeball and Arcade which also featured live dance music sometimes on Friday and Saturday nights in a small, adjacent room called "the Bandstand." They drove passed Andy's Arcade, the Cove Bar and Babe's Bandstand. A small merry-go-round leaned on the beachside of the building along the wood-planked boardwalk. Across the street stood the Capitola Hotel, Hennessey's and the Capitola Bowl which housed eight, wooden bowling lanes.

Marco knew that the few locals who lived year round in "Tola" thought of it more as a state of mind. It was one of the most laid- back beach haunts on the entire west coast. The unofficial mayor, if you could call him that, was a tall, skinny guy named Slim. He sported a butch, spiked hairdo and a goatee. He was always drunk on Rainier Ale and every day he would parade down the center of the street in his black and white serape.

They drove through the center of town along the cement seawall and past Mac's Patio and the Capitola Theater.

" Hey man, there's Fanmar." Willy pointed to a small, alley-like street.

" Right on," D.J. said. " Hey Marco, what's the address?"

" I dunno. Look for a green place with two palms out front."

" Over there."

They pulled up to the place. Someone was out front looking under the hood of an old Dodge pickup with a flashlight.

" You sure this is the place?" D.J. asked as the van squealed to a stop.

"That's what I heard."

" You know that guy?"

A skinny freckled-face guy in a red Wharf Rat's jacket looked up from under the raised hood.

" Yeah," Marco said as he peered out the window. "It's Toad."

" Hey, Toad… this where the party's hap'nin?"

" Who's that?" Toad raised the flashlight into the cab of the van. " Hey Marco." He slammed down the rusty hood of the Dodge and came over to the van. " Hey, whattaya doin' in 'Tola? Didn't think you ever left the Westside."

"J. B. told me ta come out for the party."

" It ain't here man. The bomber's sick and the band ain't showin'. It's gonna be out at " the lodge."

" Where?"

" Gimme a ride. I'll show ya."

" Right on." D.J. said. " Hop in."

Toad climbed in the side door with a sleeping bag under arm and slumped down next to Marco.

" What's up with your truck?" Marco asked.

" It's the damn carb or the points or the plugs. I dunno. Won't ever start when it's really foggy."

" Huh," Marco thought, it's always foggy in Capitola, wonder if it ever started.

" You know these guys?" Marco pointed as he introduced the crew.

" Sorta, I seen a few a you out at ' the mouth' the other day. Some a you are in Surf City Surfing Assosciation. I seen ya wearin' your black jackets an' patches. Don't you ride a blue-railed Yount?" he nodded at Willy.

" Yeah." Willy answered.

"Thought so. You got righteously tubed on an outside set wave."

Willy turned to Abe. "See, now maybe you'll believe me about it."

Abe, not to give his little brother any slack added, "You sure it was him, could've been anybody."

" It was him alright." Toad agreed, " Everybody was hootin' it up in the water as he rode by."

Willy raised his fists above his head in a victory salute to himself. " I ruled the mouth that day."

"It was a cool ride, that's for sure,"

" Where's this "lodge" you were talkin' about?" D.J. asked as the van chugged down the street.

" It ain't really a lodge. It's a clearing in the forest. We call it ' the lodge.' It's up Old Mill Road in Aptos."

" Aptos." D.J. said," I never been out there."

" Ain't much to it that's for sure. But it's a great place to party. No one around at all. Tonight we're havin' a Rex an' sex party."

" A what?" Jeremy asked.

" You know, the beer "Rex." It's three bucks a case. We got about eight or ten cases. And there's gonna be lotsa chicks, too. We're all gonna camp out and get down. You guys are welcome. We were thinkin' about askin' you to join our club or be an honorary member or something." He motioned to Marco.

" What?" Jeremy asked surprisingly. " Marco's a Westsider."

"Yeah, you really helped out one of our members, D.A. at the Lane the other day. We heard you quit S.C.S.A. too. We gotta couple a Westside guys in our club. There's Selby, an' Duke, an' Skinner an' Bowersock." Abe handed Toad a beer. He popped it and sucked the foam. "Think about it."

" How'd you help out D.A. at the Lane?" asked Abe.

D.A. was one of the top surfers in Wharf Rats. He did pretty well in the contests and surfed with power and style. Even though he was from Capitola he was well respected by the Cove crew.

" Lost his board on a big wave, too steep, board spun out. Lip hit 'im pretty hard. It was headed for the Blow Hole when it flipped out of the whitewater. I went over an' got it and paddled it back out to 'im."

" He said it was really cool." Toad added, "He was pretty wasted from the pounding."

" Aw, you're such a bitchen guy, Marco." Willy blew him a kiss.

" Fuck off." Marco yelled.

" Hey cool it you two." D.J. tapped Willy on the shoulder with his fist. " We're all goin' to a party, right?"

" Yahoo," Willy yelled." Rex an' sex!"

Abe handed Toad another beer as they drove along Soquel Drive towards Aptos in the south county.

Marco sat back against the cold steel shell of the van as the others talked about the upcoming surf contest next weekend, the Northern California Championships at the Lane. They all agreed that the Point Hookers Surf Club would probably win the club trophy but argued about who the individual winners might be. It was going to be fiercely competitive with all the local clubs entering. The top six individual winners would go on to represent northern California in the U.S. Championships next month at Huntington Beach. Marco was currently rated number five even though it was his first year in the men's division. All the other surfers in his division were at least three to five years older than him.

" You gotta good chance to make it." Toad said to Marco, " long as you don't blow it."

Everybody knew he was referring to the last contest when Marco only made it to the semi-finals. He kept waiting for better waves in his heat and didn't get enough scorable rides when the heat ended.

Marco was still nervous competing against the older, more experienced guys who intimidated him in the water. All of them were the true northern masters with a lot of contest savvy to draw from. He was still learning the ropes and felt like he was living in their shadows. It was one thing to admire them from afar and another thing altogether to be competing against them. He wasn't sure if he was really ready to be in the same arena with the pros.

" Hey man, Marco's got what it takes. We all know that," Jeremy said as he grabbed another beer.

" Yeah, he's hot alright," Willy added, " No doubt about that, at least in the surf."

" What's that supposed ta mean?" Marco was getting really sick of Willy's insults.

" Hey, will you guys knock it off." DJ interjected. "Have another beer or something."

Jeremy reminded them about the ride Marco got at " the Lane" in the last contest when he rode for nearly a quarter mile on his last wave in an early heat. Marco got tubed three different times and pulled off a long nose ride all the way to the point at Cowells. It was the highest score in the contest, a perfect 10. Jeremy then told Toad about the wave he got that afternoon at Casino's.

" No shit." Toad said. "You mean that place Casino's really breaks? Thought it was just a myth."

" You're sitting right next to the guy who rode it…alone… on a borrowed board."

" And in his cute little undies, too.'" Willy flipped his hands and made a face so he looked kind of faggy.

" Knock it off, ass bite." Abe pushed hard against Willy's seat with both legs. "I'd like to see you try and ride it."

" I'm not that stupid."

"Oh yeah, who says?"

The two brothers exchanged a short flurry of insults as the VW pulled to a stop sign on Soquel Drive.

" Turn up this road." Toad pointed to a dirt road inland, over some railroad tracks into a thick redwood forest. "About a mile in. You'll see the cars."

The van slid in behind a newish International pickup. They got out as a chilling wind whipped through the redwoods. D.J. hefted the remainder of the case of beer under arm. Toad clicked on a flashlight and shined it into the bushes." Follow me."

" Man, it's freezin' up here." D.J. complained as they headed up a thin trail into the shadowed forest.

" That's why you gotta keep drinkin'." Willy added. " It numbs you out."

They stepped slowly up the path. The downed oak leaves and redwood mulch were glazed with a slippery coating of goo from the rain and rot. The forest smelled strong of decay. Toad told them that " the lodge" was an ancient Ohlone Indian site. He'd found stone tools there while scrounging around in the leaves for his car keys a few weeks earlier. The Wharf Rats' members all took it to be a good omen, to be carrying on their own sort of tribal ceremonies there.

Toad went on to say that the Ohlones probably gathered acorns there to be processed for food. The Wharf Rats used the site for drunken fertility. And in keeping with the ceremonial spirit, they'd always do what they called a full moon chant and guzzling ritual at midnight.

All revellers who hadn't puked their guts out and passed out by then would chant and sing and chug Rex. Then they'd throw their empties into the darkness and wail a few bars of a blithering non-sensical song at the moon. Of course those fortunate enough to have snared a lovely beach squaw for the evening were hidden away somewhere else in the forest, practicing a more ancient type of ceremony inside a sleeping bag, under a blanket or in a tent.

A fire blazed ahead as the crew made their way into the meadow. The sky had cleared. Stars shone bright above the trees. Smoke from the fire curled around the group and stank of rotten wood. As they approached, Toad let out a hoot. The group turned and began to howl.

" Plunk yer magic twanger, Toadie," one of the Wharf Rats guys yelled. " Arg, arg, arg." Everybody laughed.

" Got some visitors from the Westside." Toad announced as they all crowded around the fire.

" Right on." The president of Wharf Rats said," Welcome to the lodge."

" We brought some brewski's and a little frosting for the cake." D.J. announced. He piled the remainder of the case of Burgie on top the stack of Rex's.

" This is a Rex only party, bro," one of the guys shrieked out of the darkness.

"Just bein' hospitable," D.J. replied. He returned to the circle and pulled a big doob from his jacket pocket. " Anybody care for a little smoke between friends? You know, like the Indians used to?"

That comment got a few grunts and laughs from the group. He lit it up with a cinder from the fire and passed it to the prez. Then he tossed the matchbox and a pack of rolling papers onto a log. " There's more where that came from. Fire at will."

D.J. introduced himself and the rest of the cove crew. " And of course you all know Marco."

Marco wasn't feeling too talkative but added," Good to be here. Thanks for invitin' us."

The prez nodded. "Glad you guys came. Wasn't sure you would."

" We heard about your last party from Willy," Abe said. " Thought we'd check it out."

" It's a long way from the Westside." Toad smiled.

" Cold as shit, too," Jeremy added.

" Just gotta keep the fire a blazin' an yer head a crazin'," one of guys by the fire chimed in.

"Yo, yo, yo,yo..." several of the Rats chanted in unison. Girls laughed and hooted.

The doob made it around a few times and somebody rolled up another. Marco pretended to sip slowly at a Rex but actually found the taste repulsive. Worse than an Oly for sure, kind of like wet cold piss might taste. The talk quickly turned to the upcoming contest. He found it all boring. The same old predictions about who'd win, who'd go to the U.S. Championships and more shit about board designs and recent swells at the best spots.

He decided to go take a leak in the trees. He carefully made his way to a stand of redwoods and nearly tripped over someone in the darkness. He leaned over and smelled the strong stench of puke.

" Watch out goddammit." It was a girl's voice.

Marco bent down and sat her up. He looked back in the distance at the fire and heard an acoustic guitar and the group singing, " I wanna hold your hand, I wanna hold your haaaaand..." Flames reflected off the drooping oaks above them.

" Who are you?" The girl slurred her speech.

" Marco."

" Oh jeesus." She whined then took some deep breaths and burped. " Look, you gotta help me. I wanna get outta here." She stared shaking. " Please. What did you say your name was?" She was becoming slightly more coherent.

" Marco, from the Westside."

" Marco, huh, that's an odd name."

" Yeah, I'm friends with some of the Wharf Rat guys. I surf at the Sewer House sometimes. Sewer House was an inside wave by the Capitola jetty.

" Look Marco, can you drive?"

" Drive?"

"Yeah, you too drunk to drive?"

" Nah, no I'm not."

"Please get me out of here. I'm freezin'."

Marco thought about last night, about Gina and the valley guy. " I dunno."

" Look, I got a car here. Just get me back to "the point," okay?" Marco was cold, too, legs and neck chilled and didn't really care to get all wasted on beer. " We can go to my place. Let me get cleaned up. Then I'll take you to the Westside... please." She groaned and belched loudly. " Feel like crap, don't trust those guys."

She smelled like crap too." Okay, I guess. Wait a minute." Marco went back over and tapped Jeremy on the shoulder. He pulled him aside and told him about the girl.

" Sure, sure Marc," Jeremy smirked. " Maybe you'll get lucky." Jeremy snickered and returned to the fire.

Marco returned to the bushes. She was leaning against an oak. "Oh gawd, my stomach. I hate that Rex. Got a flashlight somewhere. Down there."

Marco squatted and stirred the leaves up with a stick. " Found it." He carefully lifted it making sure there wasn't any puke on it.

They made their way down the slippery path. She stumbled a few times but he held on to her hand, pulling her upright. Her purse swung wildly from one arm. She moaned and coughed having to stop every few yards to get her balance.

The moon shown bright on them as they stood next to her car, a late model Chevelle. She fumbled with her purse and produced the keys." Here you go." She laid them in his hand gently and slowly closed his palm with her other hand and smiled a warm smile.

" Thanks."

They got in. As the engine cranked the radio blasted on. He switched off KDON and turned up the heater.

" Nice car." The Chevelle rolled down the dirt road quietly and smoothly. " Great suspension."

" Just got it. Used to be my mom's. She got a new T-bird."

Marco was impressed. Must have some bucks. " By the way, what's yer name?"

" Oh yeah, sorry. I'm...Vickie."

" Pleased ta meet ya"

" Ditto."

As they wove through the little village of Aptos Vickie leaned against the door window, closing her eyes. The road lights illumed her face from time to time. Marco saw her long blonde hair and tan face. Her head bobbed up and down every few seconds.

" Where's yer place?"

She took a few deep breaths and squinted at him. " What...oh, Thirty-Sixth Avenue. Two houses from the beach, 102." She burped a few times. " Sorry." Her head fell against the door window and she closed her eyes again.

Marco took the back roads along the cliffs into 'Tola and wound his way up the hill above the wharf towards "the point." He drove past the Hook surf spot at Pleasure Point. That's where the Point Hookers got their name. "The point" was short for Pleasure Point. Most people called it that.

Vickie was out cold when he pulled in front of the little white house at 102, 36th. She was scrunched between the seat and door with her mouth wide open. Marco shut down the Chevelle wondering what to do. She was dead to the world. No way was she going to drive him back to the Westside. He couldn't just leave her in the car and take off. She'd freeze her butt off during the night. And he didn't know if her parents were home and if he should ring the doorbell at such a late hour. He didn't want to get her in trouble but couldn't just leave her either. He decided to try and wake her.

" Vickie." He shook her. She didn't respond. He shook her harder and spoke louder. " Vickie, you're home."

She lifted her head from the door window and blinked a few times. She yawned and rubbed her forehead." Huh...?"

" Yer home now."

She opened her eyes as if startled and slid up against the handle. The door whipped open. She fell out into the mud. Marco got out, ran over and picked her up, leaning her against the side of the Chevelle, "Aw, fuck." was all she said.

" I'll get ya inside... you'll be okay." He put her arm over his neck. They limped toward the house.

" Not there." She whimpered. "The cabin... behind the house."

They wove between the front house and garage under an overhanging patio area into a small backyard. Their shoes squished through the soaked grass. Marco felt the cold water ooze into his tennies. He held her upright with one of her arms across the back of his neck. His other arm cradled her under her armpit and across her rib cage. He could tell she wasn't wearing a bra. She'd stumble a little every few seconds and his hand would slide under her right breast. A weak porch light cast a pale yellow glow onto the door and cement steps.

" Under the mat...the key." Vickie was grunting and weaving.

" Can you stand up?" Marco leaned her against the door. " I'll get the key." He turned the lock and tried to support her at the same time.

As the door careened open, they both fell on the carpet. A small nightlight illumined the front room. Marco shut the door and felt his way along a wall until he found the light switch. He flicked it on.

Vickie was down and out on the floor. He located the thermostat and rolled it up to seventy-five. He took a towel from the sink in the adjoining kitchen and gently wiped the crud from her soft face. She looked pretty, even in her screwed up state. A mermaid out of water, he thought. She reeked of beer and puke and rotten leaves, her clothes soaked and stained.

He decided to get her in bed and cover her up. She'd have to clean herself up after she came to the next morning or afternoon or whenever she awoke from her stupor. It probably was the next day already he thought, early the next morning anyway. At least she'd be warm and comfortable, as comfortable as someone could be in her condition.

Marco half carried, half dragged her into the little bedroom then lifted her atop the bed. He pulled the plump white goose down comforter aside and slid her limp body over in the center where she couldn't roll off. She babbled something under her breath, which he couldn't make out, sighed and collapsed. Her green corduroy skirt had crept above her thighs, revealing well-developed, muscular legs. She must be a swimmer or something. Her blonde hair flared out like a wispy fan on the pillow and fell across her shoulder. Her breasts, firm, yet small, peaked up against the soft white angora sweater. Her chest rose and fell silently with each breath. An angel in the rough, he thought.

As he watched her body stretch, rise and fall there in the clean sheets, something inside him began to awaken. His breath came shallow and fast and the juices began to stir. He was surprised to feel the fullness in his jeans, rubbing against his shorts.

He ran his hand along her thighs, barely touching the surface of her skin. Her thin, light-colored hairs rose and stood erect as his palm passed over. His heart pounded. He slid the soft wool sweater above her right breast. Leaning down, he circled the nipple with his tongue, licking gently beneath it. He surrounded it with his full lips, slowly sucking the entire breast gently in his mouth. Unreal. She took a deep breath, mumbled something and faded out again. He moved his nose along her neck, against the soft angora and licked under her chin. She took another long breath, exhaling in his face. The stench of stale beer and puke pushed him back. It made him gag. She smelled like rotten anchovies. Then it hit him. What the hell was he doing? He stood up, covered her with the comforter and left the room. Goddam, she's fine. Smelled like shit though.

He plopped down on a white couch. Images of Gina drunk and puking flowed into his mind. He'd never take advantage of someone in that state. He helped Vickie get home. He felt good about that. He wasn't going to lay it into her like the val did to Gina. So what was the truth anyway? Did the val really force her or did Gina take the lead. It was water under the bridge now anyway. Over and done with between them. But Jesus Christ, just a few days earlier they were still an item. Not such a hot duo like they were before Louie's death, but still a couple. In time it was going to be okay again, he just needed a little more time to morn and everything would be back to normal. Why couldn't she just understand that, instead of getting wasted and humping the val?

And how'd he ever get back to the Westside now? Maybe take Vickie's car. Hey she owed him big time and she said she'd drive him over there anyway. Nah, what if he got stopped by the cops for some reason. He'd be majorly screwed and maybe even arrested for auto theft as well as evasion. Couldn't chance it.

He stared at a poster of John Lennon holding a white dove, with the words: " *Give Peace a Chance*" scrawled beneath it. Peace. What an alien concept; with his dad dead, Gina and the val, the Feds after him… he'd love to give it a chance, but how? He felt as if he were a seal caught in one of his dad's fishing nets, fighting hard to get unwound. The only peace he knew was paddling out at the Cove alone, with waves reeling off from outside the point.

He picked up her leather purse and rifled through it, finding a ten-dollar bill in the wallet. What the hell. She could at least pay for cab fare. No shit, poor little rich girl. Where would she still be if he hadn't gotten her out of there?

He went over to the wall phone and dialed 423-1111, Green Cab. It was an easy number to remember. He was sure they made it that way so any drunk could get a ride home, anytime, anywhere, as long they weren't too out of it to remember how to count.

He heard about it at a party last month. D.J. took a cab home in the middle of the night after he woke up wasted in some strange chick's bed. The dispatcher told Marco it would be about forty-five minutes until they could get there, evidently a big night for drunks.

Marco pulled off a slip of paper from a note pad by the phone and scribed a message:

> *Vickie,*
> *I got you home safe*
> *you're a beautiful girl*
> *- a friend from the Westside*

He pinned it with a thumbtack to the backside of the front door where he was sure she'd see it, dropped the keys to the Chevelle on the oval wooden table in the kitchen and locked the door as he left. He didn't want to wait there. What if Vickie came to and found him there? What would she do?

What if her parents came out to check on her and found him there? Hey, Vickie might not even be her real name either.

He wondered if in the morning or afternoon or whenever she woke up, if she'd even remember who he was, what he looked like, his name or how she got home. What the hell. He helped her, that was what mattered and he even got a little taste of heaven too, not that she'd ever know.

The cold air singed his cheeks and neck. He pulled up the collar on his team jacket and blew hot, steamy air into his fists, cupped his hands and smelled his breath. Not too bad.

He walked down to the corner of 36th and East Cliff Drive, where it overlooked the ocean and stared at the moon on the choppy surface. It flashed around as a jumbled, flickering ball. The stormy swells crackled in the moonlight, erupting from the outer bay waters. All was quiet, except for the sloshing of high tide waves washing over boulders at the base of the cliff. He heard the shrieking of a sewer rat in the corrugated steel pipe that ran under the road. He decided to hoof it along East Cliff Drive, to keep moving, to stay warm, rubbing his thighs.

He watched the broken up swells move into "Inside." Inside Pleasure or "Inside" as it was called was the reef section that was closest to the shore. The waves would first show at two outside reef sections, Sewer Peak and First Peak, depending on the swell direction then swing down through Second Peak into a deep water channel, then reform at "Inside."

Marco reminisced how in the seventh and eighth grades, back in1960, he and Joey would hitchhike with their boards out to " the point" to surf. From the Westside, it was a challenging ordeal, but once they hitched a ride with their heavy boards they'd always find reefs to surf with no one out.

The cold onshore wind stabbed Marco's body as he hiked southward. He stopped under a grove of cypress trees atop a sheer cliff, which overlooked "the Hook." The Hook was a right sliding, rock reef wave, which broke just offshore. It was one of the most popular surf breaks at Pleasure Point. The Point Hookers took their name from the break.

It was also the spot where some of the Point Hookers would roll their broken down cars off the cliff. Some of them drove old cars known as " twenty-five dollar delights." They'd buy them cheap from old men who hadn't driven for years but still had their old sedans in their garages. If they broke down around town, the boys simply took the license plates off and just abandoned them. Of course, nobody ever registered them with the DMV, but they'd take the plates off anyway to protect the old codgers they bought them from. When the cars were on their last legs, they were simply driven to the cliff and rolled off at the Hook.

A couple of the older Pleasure Point surfers told Marco about how they had their own crowd control squad. If any vals dared to be in the water at the Hook when the local boys showed up, the locals would simply send down the "heavies" who would yell " Okay, you guys are out of the water." If they didn't paddle in immediately, one of the heavies would go out and beat the crap out of them. Sometimes they'd even wait until a val made the climb up the steep, muddy path and then kick him in the head, sending the guy flying off the cliff, board in hand. The word got around the valley fast and kept the spot empty for quite awhile.

But times were changing, just like on the Westside. A lot more guys were buying boards and driving over the hill from the valley on weekends. And some were even starting to move into town. The pecking order was still fairly solid but weakening. And a lot of the new members in the Point Hookers were more interested in getting drunk than kicking ass.

Marco learned another valuable technique from one of the older Pleasure Point surfers one hot summer afternoon at Cowell's Beach. As the Grubs sat around and sucked down cold brews on hot summer days, eventually the urge to pee would arise. Rather than make the eighty-yard walk through hot sand to the bathrooms on the wharf, an ingenious plan was invented.

Everyone wore baggies which made it easy to pull them up to the waist from the knees. All the Grubs had to do was sit in an upright position on the sand, usually facing the ocean, spread their legs, pull up their baggies, hang their cocks out at sand level and pee. When they were done, they'd simply slide the suit down on their leg, cover up the wet sand with dry and pop another cold one. The technique became known as " the Pleasure Point method" and was perfected by many a beer swiller during the summer months.

The smoke from his Camel felt warm as Marco sucked it in. He was grateful no one but his crew surfed the Cove yet, but he'd a seen a few cars pull in and check it out while they were in the water. He and his friends would flip them off and yell until they left. They never paddled out, but how much longer would it last until they did.

He further reminisced about the real early years, when respect ruled in the surf. The older, more experienced surfers always had their choice of waves and the younger guys had to " pay their dues" to get in the pecking order. It was a tight-knit group and anyone who wanted respect had to gain it. People always helped each other out in the water, especially in dangerous conditions at the Lane and it was a real friendly scene. It was turning into a more aggressive, dog-eat-dog world with all the crowds and kooks getting in the way and snaking waves.

He turned and began the trudge back to the spot where he told the dispatcher he'd be waiting. The air was freezing on his face and his hands ached.

Headlights approached from around the bend by the grocery store, "Bruce's free store," the local Point surfers called it because they used to rip off so much stuff from it. Marco waved his arms. The cab pulled over. He climbed in. The heater was blasting and the AM radio crackled.

"Where to, kid." He could smell liquor on the cabbie's breath.

"The Wesside man, the Wessside."

Hail pelted the sun porch windows bouncing on the gravel beneath Marco's room. A tabby lunged under the porch hungrily chasing a mouse and a milk truck backfired as it jerked down Oxford Way.

Marco awoke inside his down bag and sunk beneath the top flap. The air was bitter in his room. He reached down blindly and twisted the dial on the electric heater full bore, then retreated into the warmth of the sleeping bag. He listened as hail rattled the windows. No way would he get out of his mummy bag until the room warmed. He pulled his knees closer to his chest and sunk deeper into his cocoon.

He wondered if Vickie was awake yet, if she'd found his note or if that sweet body of hers was still faded out in the ozone. He reminisced about her muscular thighs and firmness. He was glad he got to sample it but felt a little guilty, too. In her condition he could've done anything he wanted and didn't. A tasty little sample wasn't any big deal. She may have even enjoyed it too. He was gentle with her. Hey, what was done was done, no sense feeling weird about it now.

Twenty minutes or so passed as Marco stirred in his dark sack listening to the electric heater pulse on and off. He slid his head out. The warmer air was overtaking the chill. It was safe to emerge. The heater never fully warmed the room but took off enough of the sting until he got dressed.

He swung over and pulled on his clothes in a hurry. His soaked socks and tennies from the night before smelled of wet lawn and forest mud. He flung the wet socks in a corner of the room where the sun blasted through the glass windows, then pulled another white pair from his backpack.

The hail abated. Light broke through fast moving clouds. Standing outside the porch the winter sun blazed against his face. It felt strangely warm for a day in early November, but that's the way it was sometimes in Santa Cruz. The frost could be glazing the front steps at dawn, then by noon it could be in the fifties, maybe even the sixties if he could find a spot out of the wind. A brisk breeze swirled around his cheeks and neck. Probably still around forty-eight or forty-nine.

Marco knew those temperatures well. The ocean was usually in the upper forties or low fifties in the winter. It felt cold and shocking at first as he waded into the frigid water but once he started paddling hard, his body warmed up enough to grab dozens of waves. After that, the ripping freeze took over and he'd be back on the sand in search of a blazing driftwood fire or at least a towel and dry clothes. But if he lost his board early and had to swim in, it was curtains. The worst-case scenario was ditching his board on the real big days if he was ever caught inside the break zone. It was the ultimate insult and meant a long swim in freezing-ass water. Marco rarely lost his board even though he always rode with reckless confidence.

One day last week Marco dropped into a huge wave at the Cove from way around the point riding so for back in the tube he disappeared inside the wave. He then reappeared with his hair still dry. Willy and Abe were huddled next to a beach fire and agreed it was "his style, guts and big balls" which lead to his fame. Jeremy even suggested Marco had a " sixth sense" about wave riding.

Atop the cliff over looking the Cove Marco watched bumpy, head-high, wind-blown swells slosh along the medium tide rocks. The swell had dropped from its giant size the day before into the head-high range. Wasn't really worth riding with all the chop and wind on the faces of the waves. He imagined himself in just the right spot on every wave he saw even if it was stormy and wind blown.

He climbed down the cliff and shuffled quietly along the exposed, wet sand with a wool blanket under arm. Four gulls huddled on a rock in a windless spot by the base of the cliff. The cypress trees on the point churned with sudden gusts. Glossy sunlight shone on kelp patches at the water's edge. Clumps of bubbles and foam washed in from the shore break.

It was still too early to call Uncle Joe to find out what the lawyer from San Jose had to say. He had a few hours to burn with no one around, just the empty beach, the winter sun, the windy surf and recent memories of sweet Vickie.

Marco slinked inside a dry cave that bent about twenty yards into the dense shale. It was the same cave the Cove crew used for full moon initiations. If the crew wanted to invite a new guy into its elite ranks the initiate had to show up at midnight during a big swell, chug a quart of beer and then go ride the cove naked for one wave. They had to ride all the way into the shore break without kicking out and take a dive under as the wave hollowed out on the beach.

Immediately afterwards the initiate would run back to the cave where he'd be treated to more beers while thawing out next to a roaring fire. So far only four had passed the test: DJ, Abe, Willy, and Jeremy. Marco was the head honcho who set the rules for membership. He told the crew that he too had done the same thing on the first night he ever rode the Cove in nineteen sixty-four. It was a total lie but nobody ever questioned him. As he put it, " you either do it and surf here with us, on one of the best point breaks on the coast or be a spineless jellyfish and surf somewhere else."

After the initiate had done the deed he'd receive a nickname by the group around the fire. D.J. was named for his constant listening to rock music; Willy was called, " Wild Will," because of his radical surf style and on-land antics; Abe was nick named, " guts," because he was fearless in the bigger waves. Jeremy was known as " the fish." He got held under for close to a minute when a big wave broke on him and dragged him along the reef. And Marco was simply Marco. They never called each other by their secret nicknames except when they were surfing the Cove together.

The cave was damp and musty smelling. Marco opted to toss the blanket against the cliff in a spot where the wind wasn't a factor and the sun's rays shafted down. He wrapped up in the wool listening to the waves. He propped his neck with both hands and closed his eyes. The rare winter warmth felt good on his face. The rays burrowed deep, deeper and deeper. His mind became a bubble, floating in a warm sea mist. The heat sank further into his core. His breathing was deep and slow. Thoughts raced then disappeared from those last minutes of Louie's death; fishing on the *Three M's*; making out with Gina at the drive in; riding deep in the tube at the Cove. Then they all flushed away in a swirling circle of light.

Slowly ascending above the cliff he was a grain of sand blown into the clouds from the beach. Spinning, spinning farther out above the sea, until he envisioned himself in the distance, a speck on the ocean's skin. He swooped in closer like an all-seeing eye, finally picturing himself with crystalline clarity resting atop the Intruder in brilliant turquoise water.

In the farther distance another image approached, a speck on the bright horizon. A blonde-haired maiden atop a giant sea turtle drifted towards him. She was naked to the waist, with small, firm, wet breasts reflecting the sun in tiny droplets. She looked like Vickie, sort of like Vickie. She moved closer, waving to him, beckoning with a sweet, wide smile. Closer, almost close enough to touch. Her eyes were two blue beams of light. She pushed her breasts up with her hands, licking her bottom lip, then reached down grabbing for Marco's hand. He strained to take it. She moved slightly back. He strained to touch her soft palm but drifted backwards. She reached out with both arms fully outstretched. He lunged at her one more time slipping off the Intruder into the bright water.

Down, he drifted down into the warm depths of the bright sea. As he descended the water became a deeper shade of blue. He needed a breath of air but kept sinking. He struggled with both arms, kicking his legs furiously. He groped for the surface, his lungs straining. He blew out all his air and began to suck seawater into his lungs with violent gulps...

A gull squawked loudly. Marco's eyes fluttered as sweat dripped off his nose and chin. He turned from the flashing sun. The beach appeared green, then purple, swirling around in a shifting void.

He rubbed his eyes, took some long breaths and heard the sound of the waves beating against the shore. He focused on some smooth rocks a few feet away. A small sand crab ran under a clump of kelp. The image of the blonde-haired girl on the sea turtle again engulfed his thoughts. She wanted him and he her. He felt the hardness tighten against his jeans. Still mesmerized by her image he lay back down, closed his eyes again and spread his legs. She was coming back, calling for him, calling him by name. He wanted her to take him away, to take his body.

Unbuttoning his pants, he pushed them to his knees. A hand slowly stroked his arch. It was her hand. He called out to her. He felt her close now; she was lying on him, rubbing her slick body against his. He ran circles along her neck with his tongue. She pulled him against her, opening up wide. She was so wet and firm. He was in her now, in, all the way in, slipping deeper still. Louder the waves, pounding the shore. A bright light came into view. He was going further in, deeper, harder, feeling every atom of her. His body rang with fever.

" Oh god," he screamed. " God, oh god, god..."

Washing against her now, two converging waterfalls cascading into a warm pool from a high rocky cliff. Waters boiling, raging into a single stream. A flash of light. The all-consuming, pulsating light exploding somewhere in bright space. Floating, drifting, drifting, floating. Neither here nor there, yet everywhere... flowing quietly now over smooth pebbles... trickling along, tumbling gently... into a still, silent, clear pond.

A hawk circled the beach, high above the cypress trees. Its sharp eyes surveyed Marco's chest as it rose and fell. Marco's head dropped slightly to the side. The hawk banked to the right, plummeting straight down. A skinny rat was sniffing a piece of rotten kelp on a shale outcrop a few yards from where Marco lay. A scream shrieked from the rat as the hawk's talons ripped into it's back. Marco sat up, bolted awake. He watched the hawk flapping wildly with its squirming prey as it disappeared past the cypress on the point.

He lay back down and adjusted his vision, breath slow and methodical. What a feeling; light and weightless. The sky seemed clearer somehow, the morning warmer and more peaceful. He thought back to the image of the girl on the turtle. In the past he'd fantasized about Gina while pleasuring himself on the beach, lots of times on the beach. But it was over between them. Vickie would be his new dream lover now. He thought about how wonderful she'd just made him feel.

The oncoming tide was surging towards the cliffs covering shallow rocks and waterlogged sticks. Small, wind-blown waves lapped the beach. The swell had dropped fast, almost non-existent now.

He must've been there for over an hour he thought as he retraced his steps along the empty beach. The on-shores blew harder. Kelp flakes tumbled over the sand. Foam blew off the tops of the creamy waves as they unfolded on the beachfront.

He'd go back to the house to his little room, his home, home sweet sun porch. Hey, it was big enough to sleep in and store his board; that was all that mattered. Who needed anything more?

The rays lost their heat, with chill wind finding the back of his neck, as he trudged away from the beach. Funny he thought, how much more uncomfortable he felt the farther away he got from the ocean. His shadow loomed out in front, a dark specter on the wet road as he turned the corner on Oxford Way.

The door to the sunroom was half-open. Must not of closed it tight. His pack's contents were strewn on the floor. The sleeping bag was tossed in a corner. Who the hell had ransacked his room?

Marco pushed open the front door to the main house and went in. Funny, no signs of life. "Karie…you here." The kitchen smelled of stale beer with the bag of empties missing by the stove. A chill wafted in from the broken pane above the sink and glass shards sparkled the linoleum. Where was everybody? He then recalled not seeing any cars in front of the house when he took the walk to the cove. That was strange but he figured the crew must be in their rooms sleeping it off from the night before. And where was Karie? She was always doing laundry or housework on weekend mornings, the early bird that she was. He figured he'd wake Jeremy and find out how it went at the party. As he climbed the stairwell the phone rang. He picked it up. It was Karie. "Marco? Christ, why are you still there?"

"Huh."

"Marco, were you with them?"

"With who?"

She was stuttering, "Goddam it…with the rest of them."

"I been here since late last night, why?"

"You mean you don't know?"

"Know what?"

"The party, the bust. You mean you weren't with them?"

"No, I left early."

"Jesus Marco, you gotta get outta there. A neighbor called the cops and they came last night. They saw the broken glass and found the beer cans, took it as evidence. They know that we're minors living there alone." Marco heard her take a long breath, then sigh. "They took me in. Then all the crap came out about the party you went to. It's on the front page of The

Sentinel for Christ's sake." She started to cry. " Get your stuff and get out now. Marco, the cops know you were living there… Willy's in juvie."

" Juvie?"

"Yeah. Found him in a tent with some young girl…it's all in the paper. Don't know where Abe and DJ and Jeremy are. I'm over at Auntie's. Cops called her and asked her to watch over me, ' to take temporary custody' they called it… otherwise I'd be in juvie, too." There was a silence. "Marco, you there?"

" Yeah, yeah…okay. I'll get out."

"It's all over… Marco. Be careful." Her words were ice as if she had a sense about something she couldn't quite express. " I gotta go."

The phone went dead with an eerie tone. He set it back on the receiver slowly and stared at the shards reflecting sunlight on the floor. Gotta get out quick. Keep cool. Figure things out. The cops must've searched his room during the time he was at the beach just hours ago. What the hell would've happened if he'd been there at the time? Would he be in custody now? Probably. Too close for comfort. They were definitely hot on his trail. Was it the local cops or the Feds? Guess it really didn't matter; they'd both like to nab his ass. He went to the sun porch feeling way violated. The cops threw everything around, upturned the cot and rifled through his pack. He was stunned. He was alone there all night not knowing what had happened. Just sleeping peacefully in his bag while major shit was coming down.

Marco slipped a half carton of smokes in his pack along with his baggies, a hooded sweatshirt, a pair of jeans and a couple cans of pork and beans from the cupboard. He grabbed some candles, a can opener, a pocketknife, a tablespoon, cramming them in his pack. He pushed out the front door, slid the pack on, flipped his wetsuit jacket over his left shoulder and the down bag over his right. He turned one last time to see his once cozy little room, now ransacked. It was good while it lasted, close to the Cove and the tribe.

He pedaled off down Almar on Willy's rusty, one speed Schwinn and turned toward the ocean. Where in hell to go now? Where else? The Cove.

ate afternoon rays crept up the beach towards the cliff as the silver sun smacked against the horizon. A small spotted seal cruised just off shore for reef fish. Candlelight cast wavy patterns on the sandy, light brown walls of the cave. A half opened can of beans hissed among the embers of a small driftwood fire. Marco sat back on his sleeping bag propped up by his pack, staring outside.

The huge surf from the day before had flushed out most of the sand on the beach. Only a narrow strip remained along the base of the cliff. The winter swells always pulled sand off shore until spring when it would be re-deposited again, creating new beaches and new reefs. He thought about how it was an eternal cycle of natural ocean energy moving in and out way before humans existed and would continue until the end of time. The human world seemed insignificant to him when compared to the awesome power of nature.

He'd seen big storms totally wash out beaches. And now over night the waves had gone from mountainous to puny little swells. That was another rule of the surf. It could be giant and classic for days at a time or simply flatten out within a few hours. The ocean was powerful and unpredictable, a lot like life. One day you're ripping on the swells then the next day stomped down hard on the reef. Go figure.

He'd just lay low till tomorrow, let things cool off a little. They'd never find him in the cave. Make a break before dawn for the *Three M's*. Maybe dad's fishermen friends would help him out; give him some diesel, some food, then he'd head south, way south.

He fumbled for matches in his jacket. His hands were shaking. He pulled out the two hundred bucks Uncle Joe gave him. Uncle Joe. Christ, forgot to call him. What'll he think? Can't go back to the house. Might get popped by the cops. Damn. Have to sneak to a pay phone after nightfall.

He flamed a smoke and stared at the choppy sea outside the cave. The orange/gold light of sunset splattered across the churning ocean skin. Gulls glided along the inner waters. Sandpipers ran to and fro as wave surges lapped forward and receded. He smelled the rotting kelp along the base of the cliff.

He loved the sound of the waves. He closed his eyes and listened intently. Every one was different, similar, but different. Was he the only one who knew that? And if he listened long enough, they'd take him away. They'd flush his mind of all other thoughts leaving him with a peaceful feeling. Sometimes he didn't want to reopen his eyes like now, escaping farther away, simply flowing along with the rhythms of the sea. His breathing fell into cadence with the waves. As they receded, he'd breathe in, exhale as they slapped the shore. At times, so engrossed with the process, he'd forget he had a body. He'd be a wisp of foam floating above the shoreline, riding along on an eternal wind current.

The sound of feet slicing through wet sand. "Marco! You in there?" He bolted from his reverie. "Marco…" Jeremy trudged into the cave, panting. "Jeesus, man, glad I found you." Marco sat up straighter, still half dazed. "You okay?"

"Yeah, yeah, just restin." He wasn't quite back in his body yet.

"Shit man, glad I found you. Everything's fucked up."

Marco yawned, then squinted at Jeremy. "Yeah, that's what Karie told me." His vision cleared.

"Karie, where's Karie?"

Marco told him about how he came home and found everything trashed, Karie being at her aunt's and about the cops going through his room while he was gone for a few hours.

"Thought she might be in juvie, with Willy."

"What the hell happened out there last night?"

"The shit hit the fan, that's what. Things were goin' great. Everybody was groovin' and partyin' when the sheriffs came. They busted the whole thing. Willy was in a tent with some young jailbait and slappin' it to her when he got popped. Get this, the chick was the daughter of a Capitola cop. His ass is grass, hauled him away naked."

"Jeezus."

"Yeah, me an' Abe and DJ got away through the forest and had to hike back into Aptos and call a cab. We stayed at DJ's place last night"

"What about DJ's van?"

"DJ's ol' man called the cops and reported it stolen. Told 'em we were there all night."

" But the cops went over to our place and found all the empties and stuff."

"I know, I know. Willy must've blabbed or something."

" No, a neighbor called in. That's what Karie said. They must've heard the glass breaking and all the yelling. "

They both looked out the cave and watched a wind-blown wave break on the beach in the moonlight.

" You wanna stay here with me, tonight?"

" I ain't gotta sleeping bag, I'd freeze."

" How 'bout we sneak back inta the house and get yers. We could go over the back fence. Nobody'd see us. We could grab some more food, head back here."

" Guess so. Not sure I wanna go back to DJ's. Not with the cops huntin"round. Rather be with you anyway."

" Where's Abe an' DJ now?"

"Over at Abe's uncle's place. You know, the guy who bought us the brews."

" We can call 'em from the house, tell 'em our plan."

" Shit Marc, you really think we should cut outta town?"

" Hey, you wanna end up in juvie, too?" Jeremy looked at him with a blank stare. " It's time ta hit the high seas."

" I guess so… hope so."

"Hey man, it'll be an adventure. Just us guys together like it's always been." Marco tried to sound convincing but Jeremy looked at him cautiously. " Don't sweat it bro, it's time ta make quick tracks, just like streakin' through the outside bowl at the Cove. Just make yer track and don't look back." He slapped Jeremy on the shoulder. " C'mon bro, let's go get yer stuff."

They paced through the hard sand to the cliff and began the climb up the moist shale.

" By the way, how'd you know where I was?" Marco reached down with one arm, giving Jere a lift past a sticky section of the cliff, while holding on to an ice plant tendril.

"Snuck in the house. Saw your stuff gone. Came down here an' saw Willy's bike in the weeds, then smelled the smoke from your fire."

Pretty smart. Hell, they were all drawn to the Cove. Where else would a guy go to think things out? Marco's sore knee throbbed as they weaved in and out of the thick bushes and trees along Almar heading for the house, two outlaws stalking the shadows.

Marco and Jeremy pulled out three rotten planks from the fence behind the Oxford house, squeezed through a section under a drooping willow and surveyed the back yard. Marco motioned to slink along the fence. They squatted next to the back porch in a patch of calla lilies, listening for any movement. It was inky-black inside the house.

They crept onto the wooden porch landing. It creaked under their weight, another shoring-up project on Marco's caretaker list. The back door was open wide resting against a shelf of canned goods Karie's grandmother had jarred years before. The house was basically the same as before but now felt cold, empty and rather spooky with a freezing draft. Hard to believe just a day earlier it was thriving with chatter and life. Now, as they entered it seemed more like a dark two-story tomb.

They sat on the sofa in the living room. "Go up and get yer stuff. I gotta make a call. And don't turn on any lights; the neighbors may be watching. Maybe the asshole who called the cops."

Jeremy nodded, felt his way over to the banister and began the slow dark ascent to his room. Marco felt his way along the wall to the little desk where the phone sat. As he reached for the phone he bumped the table lamp. Its hand-painted antique globe tumbled off and shattered on the floor. He froze. Did anybody hear that? His breath stopped and heart raced. Dammit. He fumbled the receiver off and felt the rotary dial. He had to count around each finger hole seven times until he thought he had Uncle Joe's. " Hello," a voice answered on the other end. It didn't sound familiar. " Is Joe there," he asked.

" Joe who? "

He hung up. Crap, wrong number. He tried again, painstakingly counting each hole as he dialed. No answer. He tried again. No answer. Damn. The dial tone blared in his ear as he dropped the phone on its cradle.

What now? Would Uncle Joe think he was flaking-out? He'd have to try later, but when, or how? Once they split from the house they'd never return, too risky. Who knew what was going to happen to the place now that Karie was with her aunt. The anchor was gone from the boat and Marco knew all too well what happened to a boat when it lost its anchor. He slid down the wall and sat on the floor, staring in the darkness.

Jeremy switched on the little night light with a white shell glued to it next his bed. His mom gave it to him last Christmas. He pulled out his sleeping bag from underneath. In the faint light he could see a few of the framed photos on his nightstand. He picked up the one of him and his sister Karie sitting on his mom's lap at someone's wedding party. Karie had long curly hair and a wide grin as if she were about to burst out laughing. He couldn't remember whose wedding it was because he was only six then and Karie four. It was the only picture he had of his mom and sister together.

Where was his mom now? He didn't know, but she looked vibrant and beautiful and young in the photo in her yellow floral-print sundress. He wished she was still around to talk to and share things with, to have Sunday morning cinnamon toast and hot chocolate while they all three snuggled under blankets, watching cartoons on TV. The way a mother and her kids should be. Jeremy slid the photo in his jacket pocket. He pulled his Boy Scout knife and waterproof matches from the drawer. He never cared much for the Scouts but his dad wanted him to try it out. It was the American thing to do, his dad said. He kept a few souvenirs from his time at Camp Pico Blanco one summer when he was eleven. And now dad was gone too, packed up and split town. Jeremy never ever understood why he didn't keep in contact with him. He realized he didn't know very much at all about his dad or what it was like being married to his mom, but he still loved and missed them anyway.

He grabbed a wool shirt, an extra pair of jeans, two pairs of socks and rolled them up in the sleeping bag. He wanted to stay longer, to have a little more time to reflect on everything but couldn't. He had to get the hell out. Who knew when the cops might come back? Carefully descending the dark stairs, he whispered loudly, " Marco, where are you?"

" Here." Marco stood up and leaned against the wall. "Over here. Got everything?"

"Yeah." Jeremy thought about how strange his answer was. He didn't have much: a photo, a sleeping bag and some clothes. That's what his life had come down to.

" Let's check the kitchen." Jeremy found a flashlight in a drawer by the sink and flicked it on. Glass still shone from the linoleum. " Careful you don't step on any." A cold blast funneled in the busted pane above the sink. In the shady, crypt-like silence the refrigerator's constant hum seemed louder than Marco remembered. The beam of light seemed like the sweeping arc from the lighthouse seen from the deck of the *Three M's* as she approached her mooring.

They rifled through the canned goods, settling for some chicken noodle soup, peanut butter and crackers. Marco crammed them in his jacket. They clinked as he snuck through the back door. As Jeremy softly shut the door behind, it latched from the inside. He realized he'd never be back. It created an ominous metallic sound, the sound of a final " good-bye."

They slinked back along the side fence. Marco flashed the light on the crew's board stash piled under the willow. They'd have to come back and liberate them before the cops confiscated them. Jeremy had the same thought as they squeezed through the loose slats and hoofed it out the neighbor's yard to the sidewalk.

"That was weird man," Jeremy said under his breath. "Christ, that used ta be my home."

Marco nodded and thought about how strange it was to be sneaking around like they were. "No shit," was all he could manage.

They sat atop a low-lying cement wall about half a block away.

"Look Marc, I don't think we outta go back to the cave, too damn wet and cold. Why don't we go over to Abe's uncle's and have a pow wow?"

Marco wasn't too keen on going back to the beach either. " But all my stuff's there."

"Yeah, look, why don't you go get it and meet up with us."

"Okay." Marco emptied the canned goods into Jeremy's rolled up bag. " Meet cha in half an hour."

"Right on." As Marco turned and headed for the cove Jeremy pleaded, " An fer Christ's sake, keep yer head down."

Marco nodded and circled the corner. Streetlights blinked on along West Cliff Drive when he reached the dirt parking lot above the Cove. The thick salt air was strong. A thin string of smoke wafted up from below.

He gathered his gear from the cave and climbed carefully up the cliff, stretching up through the wet ice plant and clumps of weeds. He pulled up his collar, mounted the old Schwinn with bag and wetsuit slung on his left shoulder.

He didn't really want to go stay the night at Abe and Willy's uncle's place. The guy was a little strange and had a hot temper when he drank, which was every night. Marco once saw him punch out the plaster in a wall during a tirade with his wife, but he was definitely good for buying them beer, especially if he got to keep a free sixer for doing the deed.

Marco stashed the bike in a juniper hedge next to the house and knocked on the door.

"C'mon in," a loud voice yelled from inside. It was the uncle. Marco pushed inside with his gear in tow. " Looks like your goin' campin' too." Marco nodded. "They're out back. In the garage." The uncle sat on a stuffed chair watching a western on TV. It was "Gunsmoke." He laughed as Marco shuffled past. "That Chester's one funny guy. Never really does shit, just gets in the way." Marco nodded and moved through the kitchen.

The uncle's wife sat at a small table playing cards by herself. She was thin and pretty with straight blonde hair held back in a ponytail. She sipped a beer. A small, pink transistor radio was turned way down. Marco could barely make out a late fifties rock and roll song. He thought it might be the Everly Brothers. She stopped pulling single cards from a deck when Marco came in." Boys are out back." She added. " Sounds like you guys are in a jam."

Marco shook his head, "Not really."

"Hmmm, that's not what the paper says." She pointed to an unfolded paper on the shelf by the sink. " Better watch yer butts."

Marco picked up the *Surf City Sentinel* and read the headlines : *TEEN SEX ORGY BUSTED BY SHERIFFS*. He dropped the paper on the table.

"What a joke."

"Sounds kind of fun to me." She winked at Marco with a coy smile. He pushed out the rear door. The temps were dropping quickly. At least when it rained it wasn't so damn cold, just wet. It was clear and frigid, might even frost by early morning. He opened the door to the garage and went in.

"Hey, Marco," DJ scowled. " Didn't know when we'd see you again."

Marco pulled up a chair in front of a small woodstove next to the workbench. Jeremy and DJ sat on a tattered, plump, dark blue couch. White stuffing and several bent springs popped out along the bottom. Abe picked away at his guitar as usual, sitting on a low stool.

Various hand tools hung from pegs along the wall above the bench. A table saw and radial arm saw were nested in front of the garage door. It smelled like wood dust, glue and paint. A pair of unfinished dressers stood in the middle of the cement slab. One of the drawers was split apart on the bench next to two, long bar clamps and a jar of glue. A calendar with the picture of a moose next to a rushing river somewhere in the wilderness hung above the bench. "*The Sportsman's Shop*" was printed in bold letters across the top. The heat from the stove felt good on Marco's legs and face. Everybody looked drained. "So," Marco answered D.J., "Your ol' man said you guys were with him last night, huh?"

"Yeah, saved our butts. Cops called 'im late last night or early this morning, whatever. Said they impounded my van."

"Uh, huh." Marco rubbed his thighs and listened. The heat from the wood stove felt great, although the place reeked of smoke.

"My ol' man said he guessed it was stolen. They bought the story for now anyway."

"Unless Willy told them different," Jeremy added. "Who knows?"

"Well, least it bought us some time," DJ said. "What the hell happened to you? You disappeared with some Point chick."

Marco told them the story about taking Vickie home and getting in late. Abe just sat quietly and thumped on nylon strings with a tortured look.

"Hey, it was a great party until the cops came," DJ groaned. "More babes showed up and everybody got wasted. Willy was about the third guy with the chick in the tent. I was makin' out with some little bunny from Capitola on a blanket when they came."

"We were lucky to get outta there without gettin' popped." Jeremy added. "Wasn't sure we'd ever make it out of those woods. Some guy from Wharf Rats showed us the way. We barely had enough money to get back home. It's a long ass cab ride from Aptos."

Abe nodded and set the guitar down. "But we're screwed now. The cops ain't gonna believe we were at DJ's. We went home and there was a card from the police department on the door. And Karie was missing. I went in her room and a lot of her clothes were gone. Figured the cops had her, especially with the broken window and glass still all over the floor. Wish she would've cleaned it up."

"So you went over to DJ's?" Marco asked.

"Yeah, it seemed like the best place to go. And DJ's dad's cool. He lied for us." Abe looked at the guitar and sighed.

Marco thought again about how weird it was that he was in the sun porch all night long crashed out in his bag without knowing the house was abandoned. "Look you guys, I gotta plan. We gotta split the scene." They listened as he relayed his idea about heading to San Blas and living off the boat until they could come up with a better plan. "Cause if we don't, they're gonna come down hard on us all." A sobering silence fell across the garage.

The wood stove popped and the tin chimney pipe creaked from the heat, " Like they did on Willy."

Abe groaned as he thought about his brother being in juvie, " Goddamit all."

They sat in silence gazing at Abe. Each had a different vision of what it must be like in a cold cement cell in juvie.

"I'm tellin' ya, we gotta get outta town quick." Marco added, " As soon as we can."

"Hey man, how the hell are we going to make it down there. We ain't even got enough money for food for the trip and how are we all gonna fit on the boat anyway?" DJ was getting choked up.

"You got any better ideas?" Marco retorted. "Whattaya think they're gonna do to you when they find out the truth. You think your ol' man won't be in the shit house too?"

DJ sat back on the couch, stared at the stove and itched his eyebrows. " I don't know man, I don't know."

"You better figure it out quick, bro." Marco added, " cause the cops'll be headed over to yer place real soon."

"I'll bet Willy never told 'em anything." Abe defended his brother.

"Well, who knows? Even if he didn't, they still saw the busted glass and all the empties. Those bastards'll get us on something." Marco wasn't sure if Willy blabbed or what, not that he much cared about him. He was a loud-mouthed jerk most of the time. Still, he wouldn't wish juvie on anybody. " The boat has three bunks on her and someone'll have to be at the wheel all the time. We can trade off and we'll keep the *Three M's* headin' south day and night. We can do it easily. Three guys can sleep while one's awake. Then we'll trade off. That's the way my dad and Paolo used to do it when they'd go on long trips for albacore." The guys sat in silence as Marco railed on. He pulled the two hundred dollar bills from his jeans. " And this will get us started."

"Where'd you get that?" DJ asked.

"From my uncle."

"Nice, but it sure ain't enough to get us all the way to Mexico."

"Hey, we won't need that much on the boat. Just diesel and food and we can fish all the way down. My ol' man has a stove on board too and a little barbeque. Hey, how does barbequed fish and cold beer sound?"

Jeremy giggled nervously.

"You don't even know how much fuel is on board. What about that? " DJ was grilling him hard now.

114

"Hey, my ol' man's always got fuel. Even if she's low we can get more before we leave." Marco wasn't sure there was any fuel but he was giving it his best shot. " This two hundred will buy plenty."

"What about extra money? How we gonna get any more?" Abe was getting interested but there was skepticism in his voice.

"Got about forty in cash," Jeremy added.

"What about you guys?" Marco asked Abe and DJ.

"About twenty," Abe added.

DJ looked upset and confused. "I'm not saying I'm going, okay? I got about one forty at my dad's."

"Hey, that's enough for starters," Marco said cheerfully. "And I got an idea how we can get more, a lot more in just a few minutes."

They all stared at Marco in wonder.

"Oh yeah, how?" DJ said sarcastically. "What are you gonna to do, rob a bank?"

"Not exactly."

"What the fuck're you talkin' about?" DJ was getting more aggravated by the minute.

"I say we borrow it from the vals."

"What?" Abe chimed in. "Whattaya mean, ' borrow' it?"

They sat in total awe as Marco unveiled his plan. They'd go down to the parking lot over looking Cowells Beach where everybody parked to go surfing at the beginners' surf spot. They'd wait until a val climbed down the shale steps and paddled out. Then while one of the crew kept look out, someone would bust in the car and liberate cash from the turkey's wallet. They'd hit as many cars as they could in fifteen minutes or so. Marco would be out in the water keeping watch and diverting the val's attention. Then, when a sign of all clear was given from the cliff, Marco would take a wave to the beach and meet up on the *Three M's*.

"That's insane man. What if we get popped?" DJ was really livid.

"We won't," Marco added. "It'll be short and sweet. They won't even know want hit 'em."

Abe and Jeremy chuckled uneasily. "Yeah, I say we stuff the turkeys," Abe yelled.

"More like skewer them," Marco added quickly. "Then we'll board the *Three M's* and hit the high seas."

"That's a little too wild," DJ retorted, but he definitely felt the momentum swinging to Marco's side.

"Ya got any better ideas, bro? Lets hear 'em," Marco asked.

DJ looked at the faces of his old friends and realized he'd be out in the cold if he didn't go along. He certainly didn't want to be thought of as a valley sympathizer. "No, no I don't."

They all saw the confused, dejected look on his face and realized they were in it together. Dead silence hung in the air.

"Okay then, it's a done deal. I knew you'd be with us, bro." Marco reached over and gave DJ a slap on the shoulder. "It'll be a snap. We'll have a great cruise down south and a new life in Mexico."

"And we'll surf in warm water without wetsuits," Abe professed.

"Yeah. With no cops and no valley kooks taking off in front of us either. Hey, what about our boards, they're still over at the old place?" Jeremy inserted. It sounded strange to him that he called his former home, "the old place."

"We gotta go back there tonight, score 'em and keep 'em over here." Abe was getting bolder now and a little excited. "Before the cops come back."

Marco was stoked to hear Abe getting pumped up. They now had a plan, his plan. And it was all going to be cool. The cove crew all together in Mexico, surfing their brains out, living a free life away from all the crap in Santa Cruz. Except for Willy.

Abe and Jeremy volunteered to go heist the boards after midnight when the neighbors were asleep. Jeremy knew the route through the busted-out fence. They'd take whatever food they could carry, return and hold up in the garage for the night. DJ would go to his place, gather his stuff and either stay there for the night or meet up in the garage with them.

Marco decided to ride the Schwinn along the cliffs to the pay phone by the Lane. He had to talk to Uncle Joe no matter how late it was. Depending on how he felt afterwards, he might even pedal down to the wharf, row out to the *Three M's* and check things out. He could always sleep on board or go back to the garage with Abe and Jeremy.

They left the warm garage, split up and went their own ways. Marco turned the corner and rode towards West Cliff Drive, the bitter night air stinging his cheeks. He peddled fast. His body heat was rising as blood raged through him. He was jacked up, charging into the mist.

The pay phone at the Lane was glazed with a mixture of fog, rain and dew. Marco sat on a tar-coated log that lined the dirt parking lot. Was it too late to call Uncle Joe? Would he be pissed calling this late? What if he was laying it into Aunt Cat and the phone rang? He'd really be pissed. He rubbed his hands and thighs in the freeze. Gotta call him. Gotta find out what the lawyer said. That's what was really important. Uncle Joe would want him to.

He slid a dime into the slot and heard it tinkle into the innards of the metal box. The dial tone blared. He took a long breath and quickly dialed. The connection seemed to take an eternity. Finally it rang. Once, twice, three times, four, five, six. Someone picked up the phone and fumbled with it, "Yeah...who is it?" It was Uncle Joe obviously groggy and drifting somewhere between the dream world and Marco.

"Uncle Joe..."

"Ah shit... Marco... wait a minute...." Marco heard some mumbling on the other end. "I gotta go downstairs... hold on." Marco listened as the waves broke out on the reef and swooshed to shore. A gull screeched and he heard a seal bark. "Okay honey, you can hang up now." A clicking noise went through the line. "Marco my boy, thought you'd never call." He yawned and became more clearheaded. "Where ya been?"

"Layin' low, like you said."

"Uh huh, listen. I got together with Hancock, you know, the attorney. That sunnavabitch can sure put away the salmon...and the gin. Look, he's working on it. Knows a lotta people in the federal courts, but it's gonna take a few days." A few days, that could be an eternity Marco thought. How was he supposed to lay low that long without the cops finding him. "Marco, you there?"

"Yeah, I was jus' thinkin'."

117

" You gotta keep cool till we get this worked out. Where ya stayin?"

"Nowhere really."

"Whatta ya mean?"

Marco told him about the cops and the party and his room being torn up.

" Aw shit, Marco, you weren't in on that were ya? The paper made it sound like a big drug bust and everything."

"I wasn't there. I mean I wasn't there for all that."

Uncle Joe sighed. "You really gotta keep yer cool right now. Don't go doin' any stupid shit… look, sorry, you got any place to hang out for a couple a days?"

Marco thought about the garage where Abe and Jeremy stayed. It didn't seem that inviting, especially with their drunk uncle around. Who knows what the hell might happen if he flipped out on them. "I was thinkin' 'bout stayin' on the boat."

"The boat, huh." Joe imagined it was probably cold and smelly and bleak. "Ain't cha got no where else you could go?"

"Not really."

"Probably stakin' out yer mom's. Okay, guess it'll do for now. Ya gotta lay real low. I'll bring ya some food and more cash tamorrow. After work around ten."

"Okay…thanks a lot."

" Don't sweat it, kid, we'll getcha through this. An' one more thing, don't tell anybody where ya are. You know how things get aroun' in this town."

"Okay, you got it."

"Now I gotta go deal with Caterina. Hates like hell to wake up in the middle a night. Can't get back ta sleep. Guess I'll havta wear her out a little bit." He chuckled to himself. "See ya tamorrow night."

"Bye." The phone went dead, dial tone humming. Marco hung up and sighed. Sounds good, at least for now. Just lay low a bit longer. Uncle Joe would take care of things.

He sat back on the log and pulled up his collar. All his gear was back in the garage but he didn't feel like going back there. He could always get it later or have the guys get it. No big deal.

He sat on the drenched log and lit a smoke. It would help with the cold. He stared into the mist where the waves were breaking, thinking about the Northern California Championships this coming weekend. The now empty cliffs at the Lane would be filled with contestants and onlookers. Photographers and writers would be interviewing the contestants and all the surf shops would have board display booths. Team riders would try to sell boards or get orders from anyone who happened by. It was going to be the biggest surf event of the year. But he'd never be able to take part now. Surely the cops and the Feds would be on the lookout for him once they figured out who he really was. More than anything he wanted to have a shot at the crown, winning it for the cove crew, for his tribe and for his unique style.

"Style" was everything. A lot of guys could get decent waves and ride them well, but Marco was one of the rare few who surfed like an artist, confident and smooth. He'd slip along with the wave in a way that seemed effortless and fluid. His moves flowed with the waves, not jerky and disjoined but as an integral part. He was always in sync with the natural lines of the waves he rode even when he was pushing himself and his board to the limits. He could ride far back in the curl with grace and always emerged without falling off. That's what set him apart from the others.

The Lane was his home turf, sporting the biggest rideable waves in the county. It was one of the crown jewel surf spots in Northern California. Only the true pioneers of the era would dare go out there when it was really pumping.

Marco reflected on how the Lane got its name way back in the early forties, when one of the surfers of the era was hanging out on the beach at Cowells with members of the original Santa Cruz Surfing Club. They were all standing around with hollow boards and solid planks in hand, staring out at the large waves breaking on Third Reef when one of them said, "My god, it's so big it's breaking out in the steamer lanes," referring to the shipping lanes which were used to transport goods up and down the coast. Ever since then, it became known as Steamer Lane or more simply, the Lane.

It was time to find shelter for the night. He watched another set crumble on the wind shattered sea and mounted the bike again. The dewy seat soaked his butt and crotch. He coasted along the cliff at a slower pace, watching the lights from the wharf scatter across the small swells as he aimed towards the pier. The boat. Who would've ever thought it would come down to holing up like an outlaw on the boat. Then a few seconds later it came to him, his dad would.

He pulled in under the thin grove of cypress trees along the edge of the cliff across the street from the Oblates of Saint Joseph's Seminary. It was a place where they trained Catholic priests and held small Sunday masses. He used to have to go to midnight mass there on Christmas Eve with his dad and mom when he was a kid.

The church thing was a waste of time. God never answered any of his prayers and it was a big hassle to keep awake until midnight on Christmas. And it was the only time they ever went to church anyway except for Easter, so why bother? Marco heard uncle Joe once say, " The whole church thing is just about tax-free real estate and mind control."

The "body and blood of Christ" thing really disturbed him. It reminded him of the scary times he'd see previews of coming attractions at the Del Mar Theater when he was a little shaver. He'd show up for a kid's movie or all-day cartoons. Then they'd project a preview of Dracula in a black suit biting on some chick's neck, sucking blood and all.

Marco would run into the lobby until it was over, scared as hell. Sometimes at night afterwards he'd have a hard time getting to sleep and on many occasions leave the light on until dawn, especially during full moons.

Whenever he'd see the black-clothed priest at midnight mass lift up the chalice of wine and say "the blood of Christ," it flashed him back to those early times at the theater. Then he'd always picture the priests as vampires.

They did have pretty good chicken barbeques in the summer at the seminary. Louie always took Marco there for the Festival of Saint Joseph. Louie and other Westside Italians would sit around and get sloshed on red wine and laugh and bullshit all afternoon. Marco loved to eat the homemade cakes and pies that the white-haired widows would donate. They had little game booths too, where he'd pay money to try and win prizes. All the money went to help support the seminary, to breed more vampires.

He thought about the stories he heard from the drunken Indian, "Chief," he was called. Chief was one of the bums who hung out down on the beach by the wharf everyday with a couple of other World War Two and Korean vets. The gremmies would listen to him rant on about how the Spanish soldiers imprisoned the local Indians when they built the Holy Cross Mission on a bluff above downtown. He would yell and sometimes cry about how the padres tortured his forefathers. He claimed he was descended from the local tribe, the Ohlones. He said the tolling of the bells at Holy Cross Mission must've seemed like a screaming demon to the Ohlones, reminding them of the whip and chains they'd face if they were ever caught.

They sat through his stories, acting as if they really cared. They just humored him for a while until he agreed to buy them a couple of six packs across the street at Beach Liquors. Every time the chimes from the Oblates of Saint Josephs would ring, Chief would flinch. Then the boys would slink down to the cave at Cowells Cove and chug the brews.

Catechism in elementary school was real strange, too. The only reason he went was because he got to leave Bay View Elementary School early on Wednesday afternoons. Sometimes he'd cut out on the way back to school and go hang out at the beach. He never learned his prayers very well and had the fewest gold stars in his prayer book of all the kids. He spit on the gravel, watching the lights from the wharf create thin lines atop the black ocean. Sighing, he mounted and rode on along the cliff's edge.

Marco pedaled slowly along West Cliff Drive and stopped at the end of Santa Cruz Street where his mom still lived, the street of his youth. He decided to swing down it.

He coasted past the neighborhood vegetable gardens where the old Italian guys hung out.

Every morning at dawn they'd be out in different gardens along the street. They'd have their coffee, laugh and gesture wildly with their arms. Sometimes they'd yell back and forth down the block. Marie called it, "the Italian telephone." Then by mid-morning after all the garlic and tomato and herb beds were raked, they'd meet up at the retired sheriff's garage for a little homemade wine and a cigar or two. It was strictly a guy's place, no women allowed. They'd often swap stories about this widow or that one and who had the best chance of courting them for a possible brief interlude. That is, if any of them could even still get it up at their ages which was always another wild discussion for speculation. Louie called them, " the bullshitters' club." He rarely joined them, preferring to just hang out on the *Three M's*, but when he did he'd bring over smoked salmon or albacore to snack on.

On Sundays after Mass, the fishermen would spread out their endless nets in the middle of the street from one end to the other, blocking the entire area from traffic. They'd go through the massive web, repairing the holes with a glass of dago red near by.

There'd be fish scales and kelp and dried seal blood in the strands. And the stink. If Marco happened to be home when the on-shore wind was blowing, the rotten stench would drive him out. Sometimes he'd ride his bike quickly across the nets, going down to check out the surf. The pissed-off fisherman would swear at him in Italian and flip him off. But it was fun and he never got caught.

All the while the fisher's wives were in the kitchen gossiping and cooking up the afternoon's meal, usually a fish stew or a red-sauce pasta dish with lots of garlic and fresh herbs. And the young brides would sit out on widow

Theresa's porch with suckling babies on a breast while the unmarried ones would giggle and check out the young, strong sons as they worked the nets with their dads. The older men, too tired or broken down from the long and hard years on the sea, would be sitting in the cellar next to the kegs of home-made wine, telling dirty jokes and lies.

Marco coasted farther down the street dodging moon shadows, which obscured the pavement, stopping in front of his mom's place. It seemed abandoned. The small porch where he used to hang his wetsuit out to dry and stash his bike was uninviting. The hanging potted plants were shriveled up and dying. And the cellar where Louie and Marco's uncles used to make wine was probably more like a crypt. It felt so strange to have lived in that very house all his life and to now feel no attachment to it. He wondered if he would ever see the inside of it again.

His bedroom closet was still filled with a life's amount of treasure: his Little League uniforms and first communion clothes that Marie wanted to save, a bunch of boxes with school papers and projects from when he first started school at Bay View Elementary. And his secret cigar box, with whole sand dollar shells, special bean shooters, a broken, wooden-handled slingshot that he was going to fix someday and a busted fishing reel that used to be his grandpa's. His marble collection in the nightstand, his BB rifle under his bed. They were all collecting dust or mold.

The horn on the mile buoy droned on the bay. Must be a fog bank moving shoreward. The sky above was clearing, stars speckled in the black void and the near-full moon lit up the sides of the houses across the street. Brisk wind blew past him and Marco smelled the salty air. Gotta keep moving, get the blood pumping again.

He turned and began the clip back to the cliffs. He moved the pedals faster, pushing harder. By the time he reached the ocean's edge warmth started to return. His fingers still stung from the cold steel handlebars as the breeze licked them.

He glided down Beach Hill past the Dream Inn, skidding to a stop at the top of the stairs, which led down to the beach. Of course the beach was deserted at that hour. It was coated with dew and rain, a wide carpet of goldish/silver light illumined by the strong floodlights from the hotel. He wished he had his sling shot. He'd pop the stupid lights. They were only there so the hotel customers could peer down at the beach at night from their cushy rooms. It wasn't their beach anyway. Why should he share it with them? They hadn't any real connection to it, just wanted to gawk down from their high balconies on him and his pals as they hung out on the sand.

The carpet of light faded into the cliff by the cove. The two wooden poles that supported the volleyball net during summer months were lying flat on the sand from yesterday's big storm surge. One was dragged down to the beachfront, the other pushed against the cement foundation of the hotel. Marco figured the only reason they weren't washed away completely was the cement footing attached to each of them.

He didn't feel like going out to the wharf, rowing out to the *Three M's* and bedding down right away. He was too awake from the brisk bike ride and decided to walk along the low tide line down to the cove.

He skidded through the wet-packed sand, heard the fog buoy and knew a dense bank of mist hovered somewhere out there even though he couldn't see it from shore. He certainly wanted to be aboard the *Three M's* before the fog made landfall.

A gull took flight as he entered the darker area of the beach just past the shale point at the cove. He was beyond the annoying hotel lights and more comfortable in the moonlight. The broken-up shore break was loud, always louder late at night with the absence of daytime sounds. It had tricked him many times in the past. Some nights when he couldn't sleep in his bed a block away, he'd hear it pound the beach, figuring the surf was big. The next day he'd find it really dinky. It was the pure silence of the night that amplified the sound.

He smelled something unusual. It was pipe smoke, a good-smelling, sweet mixture. Down the beach he saw someone sitting atop a large rock that jutted out a few yards from the cliff. The rock was usually submerged but very much exposed during minus tides.

Marco remembered diving off the rock when he was a young gremmie during summer months when he was still just skim boarding and body surfing. He'd wade out to it, warm up in the sun and eventually take the plunge in the frigid water.

As he drew closer, Marco recognized the figure on the rock. It was Sam. He always smoked a pipe. Sam would swim back and forth along the beach with his red swim cap every day in the summer. He never used a wetsuit when he surfed either. Seeing Sam reminded him of the other Cowell's Beach fixtures too. There was the skinny French lady they all called "alligator woman," because she'd been out in the sun for so many years her skin was hard and brown and full of wrinkles. There was Al, who was thought to be "the emperor of Cowells" because he was always sipping beer and sunning on his backrest everyday. And Les, an older, muscular guy who always tried to get younger girls to do gymnastic moves with him on the beach. He'd hoist them in the air on their stomachs balanced on his legs. Most people thought he was just getting a nice shot of their tight bods.

Sam was a lot older than most of the beach crowd who hung out at Cowells. He was a legend to all the kids at the beach. He started surfing back in the twenties and rode waves in Hawaii with some of the true early masters of the sport like the Kahanamoku brothers, Clarence Maki and Blue Makua. He was tall and regal looking and spoke with great intelligence. His stories of the early days, surfing in Hawaii, always drew a crowd with Marco and the surf kids. They never knew if he was telling the truth or simply making things up. He also boasted to have first surfed the famed Malibu Beach down south with Tom Blake, another West Coast surfing legend.

As Marco drew closer Sam didn't turn to look. "Good evening or rather, good morning."

Marco wondered how he could've possibly seen him. "Hi Sam."

"What could possibly bring you out at this early hour." Sam continued to peer into the horizon.

"I, uh, I couldn't sleep."

"I know the feeling. I couldn't either, never can when the moon's waxing full." He blew some smoke out. "Lovely tonight. You see that?" He pointed to the heavens. "It's the Pleiades and there's Orion and of course Polaris, the north star. And Scorpio is rising in the south."

Marco gazed up but wasn't sure where to look. "Yeah."

Sam puffed a few. "You are certainly a curious young man." Marco wasn't sure what he meant by that. "I've watched you grow you know, ever since you started coming down here, when was it, in Fifty-five? And now you're quite a water man." Sam always watched all the contests at the Lane and knew Marco well from the beach. On big days at the Lane Sam would stand at the point and yell "Outside," as the big sets were forming. Marco would listen closely to him, then gain position for the best wave of each set.

"Thanks." That was quite a compliment coming from him and all.

"And I assume you'll be competing this weekend?" Marco didn't know what to say. How could Sam possibly know anything about what he'd been through in the last twenty-four hours and that he'd never be able to be in this weekend's event. "They'll all be here you know, all the northern greats. And I must say, you've quite a chance to do well." He rubbed his eyes under his wire-rimmed glasses, turned and gazed at Marco. "What, cat got your tongue?"

"Yeah, probably...I dunno."

"You seem a bit out of sorts. Is it the stiff competition? You know, that brings out the best in the truly great athletes. One rises to a challenge. You're younger than the others in your division but you could easily win if you don't psyche yourself out. It's a mental game, too. Just don't let the older masters intimidate you. Don't let them take the best waves of every set. You have just as much right to them." He took a long breath, then continued. "Reminds me of the nineteen twenty-eight Hawaiian championships at Waikiki. I was the lone "haole" out there up against the best South Shore surfers of the day. But I didn't let their stature and fame upset my resolve, and in the end, I took first place. Did the same in thirty-two."

Marco had heard it all before, many times, when Sam would hold court on those late summer afternoons on the beach. He'd go on and on about early surfing history and all the classic rides he'd gotten all over the world. It was a bit repetitious but Marco and his pals would rather sit in the warm sand and listen to his stories than go home and deal with their parents and life away from the beach. "So," Sam summarized, "Take your best shot and who knows, you could end up on top."

"Yeah. Okay, I'll do my best." Marco wondered if he might ask Sam for some advice on what to do. Sam was kind of like a father figure to him and very worldly in his travels and life experiences. He may have another view of things.

"That's the spirit. Now, if you don't mind, I'd like to have a little more alone time with the heavens." Sam tapped out his pipe and fumbled in his jacket for the pouch.

"Sure, sure, I was just about ta leave anyway." So much for that idea.

"Good luck this weekend. I'll be watching."

Marco gazed one more time at the sky but still couldn't make out the Pleiades. Time to get on the *Three M's* and bunk down for the night. Feeling tired finally. Sam's humming faded as Marco marched towards the wharf. His shadow stuck close as he moved through the flood light section of the Dream Inn then disappeared altogether in the darkness on the steps leading up from the beach.

Picking up the Schwinn, he peered offshore. Was that the fogbank coming in or just his eyes playing tricks? The air was definitely starting to feel even wetter than before. His breath steamed. He climbed on the dew-drenched bike, coasting to the wharf's entrance.

Marco's eyes reddened as he cycled onto the tarred, wooden road beams of the pier. The cold darted against his face and neck. The steel handlebars sent a freezing shock through his palms. The bump, bump, bump of the wooden beams on the bike's rims rattled his body. He slowly bucked towards the public landing where the skiff was nested.

He dismounted by two Monterey-hulled fishing boats sitting in davits next to the metal swinging hoist, which raised and lowered the boats into the water. Marco stashed the bike behind a pile of wooden fish crates. The pungent odor from the dried-out fish carcasses made him wince. Lights from the Boardwalk and Beach Street cast long, white and gold ribbons onto the mottled surface of the bay.

The stairs down to the landing were wet and slick, the cold jabbing through the thin soles of his tennies. It felt eerie to descend the dark stairs into the under belly of the wharf. An on-shore breeze ripped along the landing a few feet above water level. Fresh seal and seagull crap spotted the wet timbers of the landing deck. One misstep and he'd surely slip into the freezing ocean. He'd seen many an unlucky fisherman fall and fracture a tailbone, twist an ankle or sprain their wrists on the mucky stuff.

His dad's wooden skiff was dogged down by a chain attached to a piling about head-high secured at both ends for added support. Several other dinghies had been torn away from the racks by the heavy surf the day before. One swung precariously from its bow chain in mid air a few feet above the water. Another was filled with water, bobbing slowly to the surface, and a third was swinging around erratically into the pilings every time a swell passed through. Marco pulled it over next to the landing and tied it off.

He reached up and unhooked the galvanized clip that unlocked the chain to the braces above the *Three M's* skiff. He carefully unwrapped the chain. It was looped three times around the hull. His dad took great pains to secure it during winter months if he had to moor by the wharf. It took a little longer at the end of a hard day's fishing but he never had a problem with it coming loose. Louie knew that a few minutes of extra effort always make a difference when dealing with the sea. That was something he taught Marco at a very early age. Sometimes the surf at the harbor was too nasty to motor through with a sandy shoal at the entrance. Louie preferred mooring at the wharf during those conditions until the swell abated.

Marco slid the red dingy off the landing in between swells. Louie had scribbled the name *"Dago Red,"* on its stern, claiming it was the color of his homemade red wine. Marco climbed down the last few stairs at sea level to access the skiff. They were covered with slick, bright green kelp tendrils and barnacles. The handrail, a thin galvanized pipe, was loose, rusted brown and felt like it might bust off at any moment. He hopped aboard quickly pushing away from the pilings, balancing with both hands on opposite rails. The wooden seat was surprisingly dry. Dry but cold. He pulled the oars from beneath the seat and floated quietly away from the wharf.

The fog buoy blared as his breath steamed. A thick shroud of on-shore mist was enveloping the end of the wharf and would soon blanket the fish markets and restaurants too. Marco knew that within a short time the entire pier would be hidden from view, swallowed up in a curtain of dense fog.

He slipped the oars in their locks and took a few meager pulls. The skiff slid across a bumpy swell and slowed to a stop, bobbing atop the wind-etched surface. The swell moved shoreward creating a dark line as it headed to the beach, the light from the land becoming a deep shadow on the wave's backside.

Marco thought about the times when he and his pals would paddle out to Cowells on Fourth of July nights and watch the fireworks from the water. The beaches would be packed with people but the Cove crew always had the best seats for the display, riding waves from time to time during the fireworks. As they sliced along the waves, bright colors from the sky would flash on the water. The swells would change colors with each explosion.

And a short ways out on the bay, half a dozen fishing boats would tie up together creating a wide, floating raft of revellers. A Navy ship always came into the bay on the Fourth as a sign of respect for all the local veterans. The mayor would go out on the wharf and welcome the seamen to town. The navy guys would hang with the locals and go to the boardwalk for some fun. Whiskey, beer and wine would be free flowing as local fisherman, guys on shore leave, proud veterans and their wives would wave flags and sing songs late into the night. They'd shoot off flare guns from time to time and blow off firecrackers. The seaman would swap t-shirts with their ship's logo on them for local shirts. Guys would wear the shirts around town until next year's event. They'd become collector's items. One fisherman had twelve.

Last year Marco saw the mayor give the ship's captain the key to the city. In exchange, the captain gave the mayor a framed proclamation honoring all the local veterans who served in the military, and there were many. The framed citation would end up being proudly displayed in one of the restaurants on the wharf. But if a big salmon bite was on, Louie and the other fishers would be out before dawn the next morning with their trolling lines in the water.

The *Three M's* listed from side to side slightly as Marco climbed up onto her stern with a line from the skiff in hand. He gripped onto a slippery metal winch and pulled himself up onto the wooden splash rail startling three pelicans huddled on the deck. The seabirds took flight with angry squawks. He tied the skiff off to a cleat and slid onto the deck. It was spotted with bird crap, half-eaten fish carcasses and feathers. Since no one had been out on her to do maintenance work, she had become a floating seabird sanctuary. Marco imagined tired pelicans and gulls using her as a temporary home leaving their remnants behind.

His dad would be really peeved to see her in such disrepair. She was his pride and joy and he'd always keep her in ship shape: lines stowed in clean coils, winches oiled and covered, decks and holds flushed clean. It took all his resolve for Marco to walk along the rail to the cabin without losing it on the slimy deck. He reached behind the fire extinguisher and found the hidden key to the cabin. He fumbled with the lock. It was so salt caked and crusty he couldn't quite get the key all the way in. Now what?

He made his way to the stern again, to a crate covered with several oily burlap sacks next to the lid of the fish hold. The fog was moving in faster, now only several boat lengths away. He felt the wet freeze attack his jacket. Marco uncovered the crate. Inside were big lead weights, trolling hooks, net repair tools, a long, rusty French knife, a pair of rusting pliers, two sets of rubber gloves and a quart can of engine oil. He pulled out the knife and oil and set them on the deck.

He held the tip of the blade against the rim of the can and tapped down on the handle until he made a small slit in the lid. He'd watched Louie do it that exact way many times in the past. He covered everything back up and returned to the cabin door. He held the lock upside down and tried to jiggle some oil into the key crack. The oil dripped clumsily onto his jacket, jeans and tennies, then finally into the key slot. He set the oil atop the cabin and wiped his hand on his jeans keeping the lock upside down as the oil slid into it. The fog swirled around him as he moved the key back and forth in the slot. It sunk all the way in. He gently twisted it side to side, nursing it along. The lock popped open. Marco blew out a long steamy breath. Did it.

He slid open the cabin door and entered to stale, freezing air. It didn't seem much warmer than the walk-in freezer at the Cruz N Eat. He flicked on a little light above the chart shelf. Batteries still had a charge. He reached down and turned on the shut off valve on the line from the propane tank, heard the gas surge into the lines, lit a wooden match and fired up the burners on the stove. He latched the door and wiped the rest of the oil from his hands on a rag he found in an empty coffee can. Pulling a navy-blue wool blanket off one of the bunks, he wrapped up and sat down. The *Three M's* creaked from her stem line as she rose over the little swells. It was amazing she hadn't torn free of her mooring during the big swell the day before.

Marco shivered all over. He couldn't stop. He tried breathing faster. That didn't work. He stood up and huddled closer to the small flames with arms folded across his body. He remembered an old saying from a book he had to read at Mission Hill Junior High about the old West, " Indians make small fires and hover around, white men make big fires and stand back." It never made sense to him then, but he definitely understood the theory now.

As the bluish flames warmed his face and head, he held out his hands and rubbed them together a foot or so above the heat. The warmth slowly started to return, first to his arms and chest, then his thighs. But his feet still froze. He realized his shoes were totally soaked and he'd never thaw if they remained wet. He decided to shut off one burner altogether and turn the other down. The cabin would stay warm with just one on, plus he wouldn't use up as much propane. He slipped out of the tennies and set them on their sides, propped up next to the burner. His socks stuck to the cabin floor. He pulled them off and hung them over a bunk rail.

The fog completely engulfed the boat. Marco saw drops forming on the steaming porthole glass. Before he switched off the chart light, he saw the little photo screwed to the wall of him and Louie on opening day of commercial salmon season many years past. Louie was sitting on a fish box with Marco on his lap. He was holding up a huge salmon with his left arm, the biggest caught that day. The salmon was longer than Marco. Louie and Marco were grinning at each other. He switched off the light.

Marco wrapped up in two wool blankets on the bunk. He prayed his feet would stop throbbing and rubbed them back and forth inside the blanket, moving his toes briskly together. After a while they started to sting less, considering how cold they were. He stopped shivering, tightly wound up in his wool cocoon.

His mind began to fade. What a night. Tomorrow he'd clean things up. Tomorrow he'd start to get her back in ship shape and take stock of things. Tomorrow would begin a new phase of his escape plan. His eyelids closed to the sound of swells sloshing against the hull, the pulling of the mooring lines and the buoy's muffled droning in the dense vapor. Tomorrow...

The nylon stem line groaned and stretched as fog enveloped the boat late in the night. *The Three M's* rose and ducked like a heavy piece of waterlogged driftwood. Wrapped tightly in the blankets Marco's unconscious mind swam wildly with scattered images and scenes.

The picture of Marco and Louie fell to the cabin floor with a loud thud. Marco bolted awake. The luminous hands of the clock read three thirty-three. He sensed the cold, something very cold and wondered if the cabin door had somehow slid open. It was closed. He turned and peered at the stove. The burner was off. How'd that happen? Did the propane tank empty? Colder yet, as if freezing air was piping in from outside.

Something moved in the corner, slow swirling mist, smoke-like yet with no real substance. It dimmed and brightened at the same time. What the hell? Marco felt a piercing chill. It started at his feet, slowly moving up his back and neck. It buzzed the top of his head. He became mesmerized in a dream state. He felt weightless, without a body as if he were just a thought floating around in a frigid dream world.

A faint, raspy voice called to him… " Marcooo… Marcoo…" The swirling mist pulsated brighter and brighter. " Marcooo… Marcoo…" It sounded like someone was whispering in a long pipe. A calm, warm, loving feeling trickled through him. It became familar. He felt it as a boy while sitting on Louie's lap or being hugged: a solid, loving, safe feeling. The swirling mist almost took shape, arm-like whips of smoke reaching out, yet quickly disappearing back into the rolling mist.

" Marcoo…Marcooo…" The garbled voice called, muted, desperate sounding.

The swirling light body dissipated slowly. The muted voice silenced. Marco returned from the ether as the warmth abated. He felt the weight of his body on the bunk and blankets again. He was shivering. Was it from the cold or from the crazy experience?

Then it came to him. As the swirling smoke faded away completely in the dark cabin air he called out. " Dad...dad is it you?" He cried louder. " Dad, come back, come back..." He teared up. Everything in the cabin seemed brighter than before. He could clearly see the instruments and fine details on the cabin door as if it were midday.

Moments later, it started to dim. His eyes readjusted to the dark and details became blurry. The flame was burning on the stove again. He realized it wasn't really cold at all. The cabin windows were steamed from the warm air. He picked up the photo on the floor. The glass wasn't broken on the frame. He stared at it for a few minutes with a blank mind. How the hell could it have unscrewed itself from the wall?

Was dad trying to contact him? Was that a crazy idea or what? It had to have been a dream. Shit like that really didn't happen. It was a dream, just a crazy damn dream.

He lay back down and kept the photo close under the blankets. What was it dad was trying to say to him just before he died in the hospital? He thought back to how Louie tried to talk and gesture seconds before he breathed his last breath. What was that all about? He'd never know now. He'd probably wonder about it all his life.

It was a rough return to dream land. He twisted in the bunk for few minutes wrapping back up in the wool, finally finding a quiet dark harbor to rest in.

Marco's eyes fluttered open. Dawn light illumined the port side cabin wall. Probably around six-thirty or so outside, clear and cold. He felt the swells moving shoreward at a faster pace, sloshing against the hull and knew a brisk on-shore wind was blowing. No boats would be heading out to the fishing grounds until it mellowed.

His stomach grumbled. No food for nearly a day. He didn't feel like rummaging through the boat yet. How about a hardy breakfast on the wharf? The Dawn Fishers Café opened at five every morning, the pre-dawn hangout for the local fishers. They'd be gathering, bullshitting and getting tanked up on coffee.

Marco slid into a pair of wool socks and his dad's rubber work boots. His frozen tennies were totally uninviting. He pulled on Louie's wool, navy-blue watch coat. His team jacket was soaked from the night before. He untied the skiff for the short row to the wharf. The bumpy wind chop slapped the dinghy as he labored against the wind.

He clomped across the wooden planks of the wharf to the café. Silver light cracked through the clouds, casting a bright hue on the wet walkway. It looked like it might rain again any minute. The freezing wind ripped along the sidewalk. On the left side of the long, single story building was a small fish market where people could buy fresh fish unloaded right across the wharf from the boats. The refrigerated glass case and ice barrels were empty. One of the workers would be in around seven to fill the display case and open by eight-thirty or nine.

Marco pulled open the thick glass door to the café and went in. He stood in front of the cash register and surveyed the scene. The local boys were lined up on the stools at the counter as usual. They were gesturing and smoking and laughing and chiding with the waitresses. They never sat in any of the booths. Those were reserved for the paying customers who wanted great views of the bay. The fishers mostly just gulped coffee anyway.

On a typical workday, they'd be heading out before first light. Marco knew no one would be going out until the storm blew through which meant the boys would be amped up on coffee and hanging out longer than usual.

Marco slid into a booth next to the long, picture window facing northwest toward the Lane and West Cliff Drive. The dream still loomed large in his mind. Could dead spirits really visit the living? Weird. It was all too weird to be real. It was nothing more than a crazy dream. Rain rattled the window.

A waitress came over with coffeepot in hand. It was Annie. They were related by marriage somehow but Marco never quite figured out just how. She was in her mid twenties with dark hair rolled up in a bun. She wore thin-framed glasses and had a cute face. "Oh, Marco, it's you. God, for a minute I thought I was seeing things. Thought it was your dad's ghost. He came in every morning you know and always wore that wool jacket." Marco nodded. Dads' ghost huh; that was a weird thing to say, especially after last night.

" What'll it be? I know, hot chocolate. You always used to have hot chocolate with Louie."

" Yeah, sure." She dropped a menu in front of him and went to the steaming coffee bar at the busing station. She walked behind the counter and mumbled something to one of the guys there. He turned and stared at Marco, then all the men turned and gazed at him. Marco crouched down and peeked out the window, not that he could see much, they were covered with condensation. All he saw was his muted reflection. He did look a little like his dad in the coat and all.

A thick-girthed, short, dark-complexted guy stood up and came over. It was Paolo. He helped Louie out quite a bit on the *Three M's*. He was only about five-eight but really strong. He appeared to be about as thick as he was wide. Louie told Marco once that Paolo could hoist up a crab pot with one arm and fling it on deck.

"Marco, how ya doin? Mind if I sit down?" Paolo's curious smile adorned the four-day stubble on his face.

"Sure."

"Jees, I ain't seen ya in a long time. How ya doin' these days?" Paolo had a gentle face with wide, gleaming, brown eyes. Marco could tell he was studying him.

"Okay, I guess."

"Christ Marc, I'm so sorry about yer dad. One hellava guy. We made a lotta money tagether in albacore. Crabs too." He chuckled. "Ya know, I told 'im not ta go out that day he lost his finger. But would he listen? Hell no, had his mind made up to go check his pots, even with a squall coming in. Hellava guy."

Annie brought the mug and set it down. "Here ya are, honey bunny. Just the way you like it." From across the table Marco could smell a combination of coffee, cigarettes, garlic and body odor from Paolo. Marco was amazed at the size of his arms. They were bigger than Marco's thighs. Marco knew he played linebacker at Santa Cruz High in his younger days and made the all-league team back in the fifties. Then it was work on the commercial boats that further developed his girth.

" Hey sweetheart," Paolo said. " You give Marco here a big breakfast and put it on my tab."

"I was going to give it to him myself."

"Nah, put on my tab. Put it on there or I ain't gonna ever tip ya again." Paolo winked at Marco.

"What tip? If you ever left me anything more than a quarter, I'd probably have a heart attack." She gave him a slight tap on the cheek. "You know what they say, 'little tip…little dick!'"

"Why you…" Paolo tried to slap her on the butt as she scurried off. "She wishes it was littler." Paolo winked at Marco. Marco chuckled. He saw Paolo's four gold molars when he smiled. "You eat up and let's have a little talk afterwards. Ya know, well I guess ya don't, during that last big blow I went out and retied the boat. She was swayin' around a bit. It's time ta get her inta Moss Landing fer the season." Marco nervously read the menu. "Tried to getta holda yer mom a few times… to move the boat inta the harbor, but I couldn't get through to 'er." Marco was feeling real nervous and Paolo picked up on it. "Hey get some grub and we'll have a little talk, okay?"

"Okay, sure." Paolo returned to the counter. Marco sipped on the hot mug. Paolo would be a great guy to tell him what he needed to know about running the boat. He knew her well, had done work on the diesel engine and knew exactly what state the *Three M's* was in. He'd gone out with Louie many times on multi-day trips for salmon and albacore. Marco knew Paolo was the last guy to work with Louie before he got sick.

Taking the boat to Moss Landing was a good idea. Under usual winter conditions that is. But his plan was to leave the bay for Mexico, not tie up in a harbor for the winter. But Moss Landing was the harbor in the middle of Monterey Bay where Louie always kept the *Three M's* during the winter months. It was close to the commercial cannery, too, the Santa Cruz Cannery. Marco always wondered why it wasn't called the "Moss Landing Cannery." Louie and his crew sold their huge catches of herring, mackerel, squid and anchovies to them when they were still dragging for fish.

But Louie stopped " dragging a net" right after he got fined heavily for taking illegal fish. He argued it was hard as hell to tell what was in the net at times but the judge didn't buy it. He told Marco he gave up net fishing, fired his crew and decided it was a lot easier to go it alone without the hassles of the Fish and Game wardens on his ass. They were always trying to make life hard for the net men.

Louie then decided to work the boat by himself or with one other guy. That's when Paolo started working with him. And the Fish and Game didn't bug him as much anymore although they'd board him from time to time just to keep tabs on him. Louie felt it was just a way to stick their noses in his business and play games with the commercial guys who were out there working hard every day just to feed their families.

And Moss Landing was more of a "working harbor," Louie called it than the newly opened Santa Cruz harbor. He told Marco that most of the commercial fleet berthed there. In Santa Cruz, he'd say a lot of "yachty types and fair weather sailors" hung out. They were the sailboat crew. Some were world- class, open ocean racers, while others were weekend sailors. And a lot of times yachties and fisherman saw things differently. Louie never cared for their arrogant attitudes and the way they threw money around. One time in the harbor he heard one of the wealthy racers say, " Owning a racing boat and sailing her is like standing in a shower with foul weather gear, being soaked from head to toe, throwing hundred dollar bills out the porthole."

He felt more at home in Moss Landing where "the real watermen" kept their boats. That's where Louie would haul out the boat annually when she needed to have her hull scraped and repainted and do other maintenance work. Work he and Marco did themselves. They were constantly doing chores on the boat to stave off the hard beating from the sea. That's why Louie always said they were called "work boats."

Moving the boat to Moss Landing might not be such a bad idea. It would be away from the heat of the local cops and Feds and would be a great jumping off point for the open ocean down to Mexico. But how would the rest of the crew get there? Unless he told Paolo they were just going along for the ride that day. Nah, he'd have to leave her where she was until they split town.

He'd only need a few more days to put everything together. And in the meantime he'd pick Paolo's brain about all the fine details for the actual trip.

"Okay sugar, what'll it be?" Annie came up from behind.

Marco hadn't even looked at the menu. "Uh, I guess bacon, bacon and eggs scrambled."

"Comes with hash browns and toast. What kinda toast you want, sourdough, white, wheat or rye?"

"White."

"You got it sweetie, be back in a few." She handed the tag to Bayani, "Bay," the Filipino cook who was leaning against the counter listening to one of the fishers blab on about some babe.

Marco blew into the hot cup and watched the steam disappear. He'd hole up on the *Three M's*, go through all the storage areas to see what was aboard and try to figure what they needed for the trip south: how much food to take, how much fuel they'd need, where to stow the boards, etc. Paolo would be the answer to a lot of things. He'd have to get the Intruder back from Bumpsy. It was definitely the board he wanted for the trip. He knew Bumpsy would have it ready by the weekend. Some fiberglass strands and resin was all the board needed to strengthen the crack along the fin.

They'd make a hit on the val's cars on Saturday or Sunday, buy some food and bust out the next morning. Then it was just a few days until they were south of the border. No more cops, Feds, no more draft or vals and no more hassles, just surf and sun and friends; and definitely a lot of cold cervesas and barbecued fish on the beach in Mexico.

Marco recalled tales of the great fishing in Mexico from his uncles. They had to use steel leaders down there because most of the fish had teeth and they were great fighters. He imagined himself casting a spinner off the stern of the *Three M's* while sitting with cold beer in hand between surf sessions at Mexico's many point breaks.

He and the cove crew would simply motor around until they found a point they wanted to ride, drop an anchor and paddle out with absolutely no one around. He knew they'd score tons of empty waves that way, maybe even find a few virgin breaks.

While other Mexico-bound surfers had to drive the crappy, washed-out, washboard roads to get to the beaches, he and the boys could access it all by water. They'd be able to go places and see reef breaks the others couldn't. They would totally rule. Marco imagined himself planted on the nose of the Intruder on a long, green unwinding sand point wave when Annie slid the hot plate of eggs and bacon in front of him.

"Here you go baby cakes," jolting Marco from his daydream. "You need ketsup or hot sauce?"

"Nah, no thanks." The food smelled great. "Thanks a lot."

"My pleasure, treasure." She gave him a wink and scurried off.

The steam rose into Marco's nostrils and his stomach growled. The crunchy bacon was heavenly and the hot buttered toast and homemade blackberry jam made his mouth water. He devoured it fast. Annie brought over another mug of chocolate and looked at the empty plate. Marco had swished out every morsel with the last half slice of toast.

"Damn, that plate's so clean, I can put it right back in the rack. You want more?"

"Nah, I'm just right." He was still hungry but wasn't going to admit it. "It was great."

Annie removed the plate and hustled it into an empty bus tray. She went over to the cash resister as a tallish blonde woman entered and stood next to the register. Annie whispered to her as she unbuttoned her raincoat. They both looked over at Marco, sharing a few more words. Annie set the tag on the glass counter and walked back to the line of loud fisherman. The blonde woman continued to stare at Marco. He saw her from the corner of his eye and wondered who she was. She pulled her coat back on and disappeared out the door. Strange, Marco thought. Why would anybody go back out into the weather so soon?

The rain stopped. Sun poked through the thick cloudbank, casting bright spots on the dark ocean. It often did that at dawn Marco thought, maybe something to do with the temperature change. He wasn't sure, just a guess.

Annie came back over with another plate of food, just like the last one. "Here you go sugar. Paolo told Bay to give you breakfast on him. I guess the order got put in twice. Hope you don't mind," she said with a wink.

"Bitchen," was all Marco could muster. A miracle had just taken place. Maybe there was a god.

He consumed the second plate slower, savoring each bite. He belched under his breath and felt gas forming. He rose to leave, taking the last sip of the hot chocolate, sucking the thick syrup from the bottom. The last swallow was always the best. All the gritty chocolate that hadn't dissolved always pooled at the very bottom of the cup creating a powerful flavor blast.

Paolo stood too as he saw Marco heading for the door. He tapped another guy on the chin with a closed fist." Yeah, that's what you think. It'll never happen, I'd put money on it. Hey, I'm Italian. I say if you can't fuck it or eat it…bury it! " Laughter rose from the group as Paolo left. Another fisherman whispered something aloud to the remaining group, then more laughter.

Marco stared at the candy bars in the glass counter by the register.

"Hey Marc, ya gotta minute?"

Paolo met him at the double glass doors. They exited as a cold blast blew shoreward.

"She's breakin' up for awhile," Paolo said as he looked skyward. " Not supposed ta really blow anymore for a day or so. Maybe a few showers. Fuckin' cold though." They watched the clouds spread apart slightly as the winds pushed against the massive puffs of vapor. "Must be blowin' like hell up there. Should all settle down by this afternoon. Where ya gonna be later?"

"When?"

"I dunno, after two or so."

"Probably on the boat."

"The boat, huh?" Paolo seemed surprised.

"Yeah. I was there last night, got aboard late." Paolo looked at him cautiously, carefully. Marco could see he was trying to figure him out. He knew he could trust him, though. Louie always said, "I'd trust him with my life."

"Ya mean ya ain't stayin' at home?"

Home, where the hell was home. "Haven't been there fer two months."

Paolo's face turned serious. "Look Marc, I don't know what's goin' on, but ya know you can count on me ta help ya out."

"Yeah, I know."

"Good. Look, you sure ya wanna go out ta the boat now? You could come over ta my place. I'm gonna work on some pots. You could hang out by the wood stove and watch TV or somethin'. I'll make us some lunch later. Hey, you like pesto? I gotta big batch in the freezer. And maybe have little glass a vino." Paolo's big smile returned.

The idea of going out to the boat did seem a little foreign, especially after the great breakfast in the warm café but Marco needed to take stock of things. 'Nah, I just wanna go hang out on the boat.'

Just like his ol' man, Paolo thought. "Okay. Look, if ya need to get a holda me just call on the CB, channel six. I always got it on." Even when fishermen were in port or working on gear, they always kept their radios on in case someone on the bay needed help. And when old fishermen were just too tired to go out anymore many of them would sit around in their garages doing little projects, always listening to the crackling CB to hear what was going on with the fleet. "An 'fire that stove up. Gonna be a cold sunnavabitch today."

"Okay."

Marco held out his hand to shake Paolo's. Paolo gave him a big bear hug. That's the way it was done. A handshake was for strangers or businessmen. A hug was for family.

Marco pulled up the collar on the wool coat as Paolo waddled away. He watched him cross the wharf, look down at the skiff, gaze out at the *Three M's* then turn back towards him. "On the boat aroun' three, then?"

Marco nodded. Paolo fired up the rusty Chevy pickup and slowly chugged off the wharf with wooden fish boxes and net floats sliding around in the bed.

The wind gusted as Marco crossed the wharf. He saw a group of Filipinos erecting a canvas tarp from the back of a pickup truck. They pitched it from two vertical wooden poles on the truck bed then lashed it to the handrail on the lee side of the wharf. It would shelter them from the wind and rain as they fished for smelt and perch.

They were Bay's relatives. They fished daily on the wharf all year long in all kinds of weather. Marco heard that some of them were pretty beat up. He'd heard the stories. A few had survived the Manila Massacre back in '45 during the closing months of the war when the Imperial Japanese Army was retreating during the Battle for the Liberation of Manila.

Marco's dad told him that Manila was once thought of as "the Pearl of the Pacific," before it was completely destroyed. When the Japanese troops were leaving the city, they slaughtered between 30,000 and 100,000 civilians. The enemy troops took out their anger and frustration by raping and mutilating the innocent populace. Louie said it was one of the worst atrocities committed by the Japanese during the war and Bay's relatives were deeply traumatized from it. Marco heard the story during the Veteran's Day celebration on the wharf last year.

He recalled hearing that worse destruction was inflicted on Manila than on London by the Germans. The death toll was like the bombings of Hiroshima and Tokyo.

Fishing on the wharf was a reprieve from those harsh memories and also became a mainstay of their diet. There was something peaceful and reassuring about having a line in the water and staring out onto the bay.

Marco saw them sometimes frying up their catches right there atop single burner butane stoves. They'd gut the fish, batter them in cornmeal, crack a few brews and have a picnic.

Marco descended the wet stairs to the boat landing. Spray blew shoreward across the surface of the bay as he rowed away from the wharf. It was a cold, bumpy row, hard to keep a straight line in the onshore breezes. Marco watched the swells move into the beach as wind waves sporadically blew foam across the top of the sea. The skiff pitched and tossed sideways against the swells and wind. His arms and back muscles burned from the intense pulling. He strained with all his might finally bobbing against the low stern of the *Three M's*.

It was tricky boarding in the unsettled sea. He finally grabbed the splash rail and tried to pull himself up. His muscles burned and shook. A swell rose, pushing the skiff against his legs that helped boost him up the last few feet onto the deck. He tied the skiff off the stern with sufficient length so it could swing freely in the wind without hitting the boat.

The *Three M's* rose and fell slowly. She had a wide beam and was a fairly heavy boat for her length, which gave her extra stability in churning seas. She also had a high prow, which helped her slice through heavy seas. Louie could work her in harsher weather than the other day boats. She was the biggest boat of her kind in the local fleet at forty-six feet. Louie'd be the only one out on rough days and could get top price for his catches at the markets on the wharf. The buyers would line up with empty boxes on the landing as the *Three M's* berthed.

Marco checked the stem line running out to the mooring. It was strong and not frayed. Paolo surely must've retied it during the last big storm or it would've showed signs of wear from the intense pulling. The wind eased up a bit. Paolo was probably right about it mellowing out. Weather was one thing fishermen knew a lot about. Their very existence depended on it.

Louie used to get up way before dawn and listen to the weather report on the radio in the kitchen as he drank his first cup of coffee. Marco would toss in his bed as the monotone voice of the radio reporter blared out the forecast. He'd hear the front door shut, the Willy's start up, back out the driveway, then he'd slowly drift back to sleep for a few more hours.

Another big blow in a few days meant another thing... big waves. When it blew hard like that out on the open ocean it created massive swells. They'd sometimes hit the coast during a storm, just before a storm or right after. It was going to get big again soon. Marco could feel it.

He hoped the cove crew would move all the boards and gear down to the boat soon after dark that evening. He'd have to hang for the day on the boat, scope things out and finalize plans for leaving.

Marco returned to the warmer cabin. It felt good after the frigid blast outside. He smelled a hint of diesel down in the bilge and heard the faint sound of water sloshing. He'd have to pump it out when he could. The way to do it would be to fire up the diesel and charge the batteries first, then activate the pumps. He hung up the wool coat, lay back down on the bunk and decided to wait until Paolo came aboard. He'd instruct him exactly how to go about things. Marco had seen his dad do it many times but didn't want to take a chance on screwing anything up. He re-lit the stove and turned the burner down about halfway.

He rolled up in the wool blanket watching the second hand tick around the little clock atop the chart shelf. He stared at the wires in the open fuse box. The coiled cord from the CB radio microphone swayed as the boat slid over swells. A sharp shadow slanted down from the dusty plastic Jesus that stared out the cabin window. Its outstretched arms and palms faced the open ocean.

Marco closed his eyes and listened to the bow line creak and stretch as the *Three M's* rose slowly over the swells. Moments later all he heard was the clicking of the second hand on the clock and the almost silent shifting of water in the bilge. It felt good to have his stomach full of food. His breath slowed and his mind finally gave way to the dark veil of sleep.

The inner bay smoothed out as the on-shore breezes abated. A tiny wind bump scattered across the surface as the waning storm made landfall. Hungry seals swished under the wharf pilings for perch. Sea birds floated in small groupings atop the calming surface, sucking in the lukewarm rays from the clearing sky. The skiff bobbed alongside the heaving *Three M's*, the weight of its submerged tie line pulling toward the boat's hull.

The dinghy thumped against the port side where Marco napped in the tight bunk.

In his deep, quiet, inner-space, Marco heard the bumping. It first sounded like a finger tapping against a window, then seemed more like a fist on a table. As his mind journeyed out from the dark hole, he heard it more clearly, louder. His eyes strained open. He closed them immediately as sunlight flashed through the glazed starboard porthole.

How long had he crashed out? He exhaled and yawned. A stale, humid scent hung in the air. It was warmer at least. He could sit up in the cabin without having the wool blanket wrapped around him. He turned off the burner and cracked the cabin hatch. He felt the humidity lessen as cold, fresh air seeped in.

The clock on the chart table read two fifty-three. Any moment now Paolo was due in. He stood and stretched. It was a totally different world outside with bright sun beaming in. He slid open the cabin door and went out on deck.

Sure enough, clearing skies and semi-smooth ocean but still icy cold. No surprise there. The stubble on his jaw itched. Could sure use a smoke. Peering shoreward he thought about how it would be a lot warmer on the beach where the sun reflected on the sand. The frigid sea absorbed all the solar heat, not that there was much. But even on cold, clear winter days the sand would be a lot warmer if he was lying on it out of the wind.

He'd done that many times in the past when his legs and feet froze from surfing at Cowells. He'd paddle into Cowell's Cove, nestle against the shale cliff out of the wind in the direct sun and pull the warm top sand up around his legs until they stopped shivering. Then he'd either go back out in the water or walk up Beach Hill to his house a few blocks away.

It was always a toss up. He'd be covered with warm sand watching wave after wave peel off. If he walked, he'd have to lug the heavy board all the way home as his cold, bare feet scrunched down on hard pavement. If he paddled back out, it would be the freezing water again but he'd at least get a few more waves. Then he'd climb up the chopped out steps in the shale cliff and end up just a block from home. And because there were always empty waves to ride he'd usually bite the bullet and paddle back out.

He reflected on a couple of years back, when he and Eddie had surfed six foot Cowells alone until the skin on their bare knees blistered from all the endless paddling back to the outside take off spot. They were so tired afterwards they could barely climb the shale steps and had to help each other lift the boards to the top of the cliff.

They stood on the empty dirt parking lot over looking the scene and watched perfect waves line up all the way to the beach without anyone out. Eddie turned to him and said, " You know Marco, someday this is all gonna change." As they both stood there shaking from the cold with stinging knees, it didn't seem like it would ever change. It would always be just a few friends surfing together without any other major life decisions to be made, just waves and friends, no crowds and no worries.

Marco realized Eddie was right on target. It was all changing real fast. Now carloads of vals were beginning to invade the beaches and surf spots and it was getting harder to control the crowds in the water. There were just too many of them. But they were still just kooks, "Straight off Adolfs", without a clue to what was really happening, phony " Bleach Boys" look-alikes."

How bitchen it had been to be a surfer, a counter–culture, free-spirited, ocean devotee from the late fifties balsa era before the Bleach Boys turned everything upside down. They turned surfing into a national symbol of coastal California beach life. Southern California, that is. The Northern surfers hated to be stereotyped into something other than just pure, wave riding pioneers. And besides, the surf was way better in the north. Bigger, more powerful, colder water, more intense and challenging.

The down-southers rarely wore wetsuits and surfed at easy spots like Mailbu, Doheny and Dana. Most of the band members in the Bleach Boys didn't even surf at all. It was all just another L.A. bullshit scheme, just the wet dream of some record producer to capitalize on. They were just SoCal, Hollywood bullshit artists who ruined the sport. The surfing magazines were published in Southern California, too, and always spotlighted the south bay crew. They rarely focused on the north, even though that's where all the real challenging surf was.

Even guys in the Midwest were wearing madras shirts and bleaching out their hair to have what they thought to be "the California surfer look." It made him sick to think about it: how surfing went from an intensely individual form of expression into a designer/commercial scam that the whole damn world could now see and imitate. "Hey, I can see by your outfit that you are a surfer."

And the stupid Hollywood movies like the "Gidget" series. Frankie Avalon and Annette dancing the bop on the beach with real phony surfing scenes. It almost made him puke. But they were national favorites, which helped to turn surfing into a big marketing scam.

It took a lot more resolve to paddle out at the Lane on a big day in freezing-ass, cold water than any of the down-southers could ever imagine. It was character building as hell and if you lost your board it was a long swim in through dangerous conditions. None but the brave need apply.

But it was crowd control at its maximum. Marco and the Westside boys watched with glee as many a souther or val lost their boards and spilled their guts out there. After one nasty wipe out on a big day they'd barely make it to shore, drive away and were never seen again. Some never made it to shore.

Marco loved watching them lose it and yell for help as they washed into the cliffs. If you couldn't handle it, you shouldn't be out there: that was the simple rule. It was no-bullshit surfing at its finest. You could either ride it or you couldn't and if you strayed out where you didn't belong, you paid a big price. But for those who could it was pure heaven, heaven inside a ten-foot tube.

Even on smaller days a lot more guys were starting to go out anyway. Novice kooks getting in the way, doing stupid things that put the locals at risk. Like jumping off their boards when caught inside and diving for the bottom as their thirty pound boards flipped around in the white water potentially hitting surfers who might be paddling out.

Marco nearly got his head gashed open one day when a kook's board hit him. He rolled over under water on his O'Neill team board holding onto the rails hard as the flailing board hit him. It broke three of his fingers and he was out of the surf for three weeks. If he hadn't rolled over, it may have killed him.

And Marco was getting real tired of pushing guys off waves who dropped in on him, running them over and yelling at them. It just wasn't fun any more. He rarely surfed the Lane now except on big days and focused on the Cove with his closest friends. South of the border would be new territory and a whole new bitchen life style.

He spit overboard and watched it float along the hull. It had to be 3 PM by now and no sign of Paolo. Wasn't like him to flake out. Marco then realized he hadn't turned on the CB like Paolo asked him to do. He was the flake, not Paolo.

He went in and stared at the switches and dials and flipped up the toggle he thought turned it on. Nothing. Were the batteries too low or was he not doing it right? He realized how little he actually knew about operating some aspects of the boat. It was months since he was last out with his dad. He fumbled with other dials trying to figure it out.

"Ahoy." He heard a faint voice yell from the wharf. It was Paolo, waving arms over his head. "Ahoy, Marco."

Marco waved back. He untied the skiff and struggled over to the wharf in the choppy water. He guided the little craft next to the ladder by the landing. Paolo was standing there with a big grin, "Permission to come aboard," he boomed. Marco smiled and nodded.

That was something fisherman always asked before they boarded someone's boat, a way of showing respect. It was Marco who was most honored. As Paolo climbed in and sat down, the skiff sunk slightly due to his weight. But Paolo was a seasoned fisherman, used to getting aboard all types of boats in all kinds of weather. He carried a burlap sack and a medium-sized, thin cardboard box, the type used for take-out food at a restaurant.

"Found this on the landing." He held up the box. "Had yer name on it."

As Marco rowed away from the wharf he saw his name printed in big block letters on top of the box. "Who's it from?"

"I uh, I dunno. Smells good though. Maybe some friend a yer dad's."

"Is there a note on it? "

"Nope, nothing, just yer name."

"Go ahead an' open it."

Paulo stuck his big thumb under the flap and popped the lid.

"Sandwiches, tuna sandwiches and an apple and some candy bars. A treasure chest," he chuckled.

"Hmmm." Marco wondered who would've left something for him. Wouldn't be Uncle Joe. He wasn't due out until later that night. Sure as hell wasn't his mom. Strange, very strange.

"Hey gimme the oars." Paolo saw Marco struggling. Marco slid them over. "This is how you do it." Paolo sunk them deep and pulled back with mighty strokes. The dinghy glided quickly away from the landing. Marco was amazed at his strength and skill, obviously a master oarsman. "See...ya dig in deep, pull hard, then ya twist yer wrists an' push 'em forward when they break the water, so they glide flat in the air, until ya bury 'em deep again."

Marco clutched the take-out box as they moved toward the *Three M's*. Maybe it was Annie or somebody at The Dawn Fishers Café. Who knows? He was stoked to have the food.

They slid alongside the *Three M's*, tied off and climbed aboard. The sun was blazing down and it felt warm for November except for the bitter wind. The deck was still sticky from all the bird crap and night dew, semi-dry in sunlit patches. Marco entered the cabin and sat on a bunk. Paolo leaned on the chart table. "So, Marc, what the hell's goin' on? I know somethin's up."

Marco's eyes half-closed. He could sure use a friend, a confidant. Somebody who'd just listen and not judge him. Maybe Paolo was just that guy. Louie always trusted Paolo and Marco knew Paulo had helped his dad out of some tight spots before out at sea and vice versa. He couldn't quite speak as the deep-set emotions he'd stored away were beginning to finally surface. Paolo sensed that. "Hey looky here. It's gonna be okay."

Paolo stood up and bear hugged him. Marco took a big breath and exhaled as tears welled. Paolo sat him back down on the bunk. Marco's eyes burned. He was speechless, shaking, filled with emotion, not knowing where to begin.

"Jeesuskeyrist." Paolo cracked a small latch on a narrow closet door and pulled out a bottle of VO. He knew right where to find it. "Here, take a belt. Yer ol' man kept this 'round fer times just like these. Seen 'im take quite a few pulls from time ta time."

Marco stood up trying to compose himself, whimpering." Shit... goddammit all."

"Hey, it's cool Marc. Take it easy. Sit back down... have a little sip." He looked up at Paolo's huge bulk holding out the bottle. "Ya know what, I'm gonna have one, too." Paolo up ended it and exhaled slowly. "Man, that's the good stuff alright, twelve year old. Yer ol' man always had the good stuff."

Marco struggled for composure, grasping the bottle. He held it up and took a hefty gulp, then realized the last time the bottle had been tipped it was his dad pouring one. Jeesus, having a drink with your dead father.

"Hey, take it slow." Marco handed it back. The broad-shouldered Italian set it on the floor, turned over an empty five gallon bait bucket and sat down. Marco wondered if it was strong enough to hold his weight. "You wanna tell me what the hell's up?"

Marco blew out the hot liquor taste. It warmed up his stomach and throat. It was pretty smooth tasting, not that he was any real judge of hard liquor. He was mostly a cold beer guy. Cold Beer and Camels. "Got any smokes?"

"Don't use 'em. Yer dad smoked Pall Malls. Bet there's a pack er two 'round here somewheres." He got up and searched further in the thin closet. "Whud I tell ya."

He handed Marco a sealed pack of the long non-filters. "Strictly a stogie man, myself. Love havin' one after dinner with a glass a vino. Yer dad got me hooked on 'em."

Marco knew his dad liked them. " Maybe there's some in there, too."

Marco tore off the cellophane with his teeth on the pack as Paolo dug deeper in the closet, coming up with a flat, rectangular, gold and red box. "I'll be goddammed, Roi-Tans."

"Whud I tell ya." Marco mimicked Paolo's last sentence. They both chuckled uneasily.

Paolo pulled one out and lit it on the burner of the stove while Marco fumbled in his pockets for matches. "Allow me." Paolo handed the cigar to Marco, who lit the cig with the burning end.

The cabin filled with grey and blue smoke. They puffed in silence and watched the smoke bend out the door.

"Ya wanna talk now?" Paolo sipped from the bottle and gazed at Marco curiously.

"Ah shit." Marco took another quick sip, wiped his lips on his coat sleeve and sat back against the bunk wondering where he should start, if he should start. "I dunno," was all he could come up with.

Paolo sat there peering deep into Marco's eyes. He could sense the uncertainty and his need to talk, not knowing how. "Just start anywhere."

"I… I'm in some deep shit." He took another belt, a bigger pull this time.

"That right?" Paolo was all ears, sitting back on the five-gallon bucket leaning against the chart table, trying to make Marco feel more comfortable.

The VO gave Marco a warm numb feeling, flooding his senses. His mind floated around inside his head with duller emotions rattling around. Emotions and thoughts he'd kept locked away for weeks, maybe years. His eyes flushed and breath slowed. He took a moment to scan the inside of the cabin, all the gauges, hooks, sinkers and other gear. His eyes watered. "O, o, okay, he, here's, the, the scoop…" He began the story with Gina, then rambled about the Feds, the surf party, the cops, Louie's death. It all came out as disjoined babble mixed with sudden emotional swings and tears.

Paolo nodded from time to time, sucking the stogie and sipping. Christ, he thought, here was Louie's kid on Louie's boat in a terrible mess. Life was weird as hell. But he'd heard a lot of soul-searching and riveting conversations on the boat already between Louie and him. Louie spilling his guts about how much he disliked Marie and being worried about how it would affect Marco if he left her. But he couldn't stand it anymore and went back to the house only to pay the bills and see Marco who wasn't there much anyway. And Marie wasn't screwing him any more, mostly ragging on him whenever he was around. But he'd never divorce her. That was something you never did. The church wouldn't allow it, not that Louie ever went to Mass anymore. But he was married in the church so he'd have to go along with the rules. And everybody would talk and gossip about them. He'd just rarely see her and that was how it would have to be.

Paolo's mind returned to the present. Marco sobbed and talked. The tears were a new thing. Louie never showed those kinds of emotions. World War Two vets always sucked it up. They kept their secrets close to themselves even though he knew they'd probably love to get it all out in the open. It was their war training. You never showed emotion, you go do your goddam job and get on with it. Paolo was too young for Korea and too old for Vietnam and was glad of it. Going to war had to really suck but he had the greatest respect for those who survived it.

Marco ended his dire story with his palms pushing tears to the side of his face. He felt suddenly really strange that he'd unloaded everything on Paolo. Paolo must think he was nuts. He felt stupid and ashamed that he told everything, everything except for his plan to split on the boat. But it did feel good to get it off his chest; the inner turmoil had eased somehow.

The same way the bay glassed off after a storm passed through. He just sat there waiting for Paolo's reaction.

Paolo took another pull, exhaling a long breath. He felt the warm air leave his lungs. Thoughts quickly flashed back to how he and Louie always had long talks about life when they were out fishing. They'd hit the VO on the way in from the outer waters and by the time they made it back to the pier things didn't seem so bad after all. That's the way it was out on the sea, a perfect place to drown all your land worries. The bay had some sort of healing power. It was hard to get upset about anything when you were surrounded by all that water and sun, hauling in fish with a good friend. And now here was Louie's kid doing the same damn thing with him.

He gazed over at Marco who was waiting impatiently for his response. Tears formed in Paolo's eyes as he gained composure. He sure hoped Marco wouldn't have to experience what his dad did in the war and how it left him. "Christ Marc' that's just horrible." He took another belt. "Whattaya think yer gonna do?"

"I, I dunno." It was a lie but he wasn't sure Paolo'd go for his taking the boat to Mexico plan. "Guess I'll just hang out on the boat for awhile." He sat up straighter on the bunk, puffing out his chest. Gotta be a man about this. He fired up another smoke.

"Uh, huh." Paolo wasn't sure what to say and changed the subject. "Look, you need to get her over to Moss Landing before another big blow comes through. I been comin' out here weekly since yer dad passed away. You know, checkin' her lines and the batteries. Yer dad woulda wanted me to. We always look after each other out here."

Marco knew that. The fishing fleet was like one big extended family. They always helped each other out. Not that many asked for help. It was something everybody just did out of respect. A guy's boat was a near sacred thing, more of a home to many than their houses on shore and a lot of guys just lived on their boats anyway.

"Thanks, Paolo."

"Hey, nuthin' to it. Look, things'll work out. Don't sweat it. I been in a lotta tough spots too. How 'bout I come back out tomorrow and we'll take a little cruise. I'll show ya how ta get 'er up an' runnin.' I mean, she's gonna be yers soon, right?"

"Yeah, yeah, she is." Marco and Paolo both knew that.

"Pretty soon you'll be makin' a livin' on 'er yerself. How 'bout roun' six in the mornin', not too early an' not too late."

"Sure, that'd be great." Marco wiped at his reddened eyes.

"I'll get us some grub and we'll take her out fer a cruise. Ya don't mind albacore an' pesto sandwiches do ya?" Paolo was happy to show him the ropes. He knew Louie would want him to anyway. Hey, it was only the right thing to do, to show the kid how to run his own boat.

"Sure, cool, great." Marco realized how lame that must've sounded, but it was all he could muster.

"Okay, now I gotta split, run a few errands b'fore dark."

They untied *Dago Red* and moved away from the boat. "You wanna row?" Marco asked.

"Nah, she's yers now, you row."

Marco pulled back towards the wharf as the sky turned pink. He couldn't quite get the technique down but figured he would with a little more practice.

Paulo climbed the stairs to the top of the wharf, turned and waved. Marco smiled and waved back then drifted away from the pier with the small wind swells. The VO had made everything seem quieter and a bit hazy, but its effect was beginning to fade.

He didn't feel like going back to the boat just yet. He opened the take-out box and ate both sandwiches then stuffed the candy bars in the coat pocket. He put the apple back in the box and set it under the seat. Who left it? Did Paolo know something he wasn't telling about it? Or did Annie or someone from the café leave it for him? It was all wild speculation. But it was free food and good too. Didn't taste like restaurant sandwiches, more like homemade with sweet pickles and a little mustard and parsley.

His tense muscles wanted to stretch. He jockeyed through the wharf towards Cowells Point aiming for the cypress trees on the end of the cliff.

It seemed like things were going to work out. Paulo would be a huge help. What a bitchen guy. Sometimes a lot of life's problems are best solved with close friends and a little alcohol, maybe sometimes a lot of alcohol. And Uncle Joe would be down to see him after work tonight. He'd have hammered out the legal issues after his meeting with the lawyer.

It was just a matter of days now, maybe even hours until they'd be heading south. And the Cove crew were probably just laying low until nightfall, before venturing to the wharf with all the boards and gear. Yeah, it was all falling into place.

The sun was lowering on the horizon as he rowed outside the huge kelp beds towards the lighthouse on the cliff at Steamer Lane. The sea was a bit choppier unlike the smoother surface on the lee side of the wharf. Marco figured the kelp beds on the Westside were actually a vast under-sea forest. They also cut down the wind bump on the surface, creating glassy conditions in the surf zone. One of the famed big wave riders of the day used to break off chunks of the brown kelp bulbs and blow across them creating a deep, hollow bellow. He claimed it was a way of calling up the big sets. Strangely enough it seemed to work.

In other areas of the bay where no kelp existed, the wind blew directly over the water causing bumpier conditions and "chopping out" the surf. The kelp beds were also home to a myriad of sea life. Fishes, abalone and seals thrived there.

As he rowed out through Indicators, an otter surfaced next to the skiff with a mussel in its mouth. Then another appeared, a mother with two newborn pups on its tummy. They lay on their backs atop a thick patch of kelp. The male chipped at the closed shell with a small stone, trying to bust in open. Marco pulled the oars aboard and watched in silence. Finally the shell was breached. The male washed out the debris and fed the tasty innards to the pups. The mother chirped her approval. Marco felt inside his coat and pulled out the bag of squished sandwiches. He pealed apart the tattered bag and dumped the crumbs from the remains of the French rolls into the water. The male lunged and gulped them down. He looked up with what Marco thought was a grinning chuckle and seemed to nod. "Eat up little friend," Marco whispered. "You've got little ones to look after now."

The otter family stared at Marco with bright gleaming eyes for about ten seconds. The male then rubbed his nose on the soft furry bellies of the pups. Then they dove out of sight. Marco wondered how long they could stay under water and thought he saw them surface farther out on the beds in the glaring orange dusk. That was so great to have helped the little innocents. He admired how close and loving they were. And they'd never have to face all the radical bullshit he was going through on land. They'd never have to step foot on it. Maybe being a human wasn't all it was cracked up to be.

As he neared Lighthouse Point he gazed at the seals on Seal Rock just off Point Surf at the Lane. They were sometimes freaky to deal with especially during mating season. Usually they were not very aggressive, oftentimes swimming directly in the kelp and surf zone as he paddled out.

One big day last winter he and Jeremy cut classes at Santa Cruz High to go check the surf. They watched a seal drop into a monstrous wind-blown set wave at Middle Peak and glide along in the tube until the wave closed out. The seal dove under and disappeared.

Another time last year during mating season Abe lost his board during a take off at Point Surf and had to swim into the cove directly in front of

Seal Rock. He was retrieving his board from the rocky cove when a seal burst out of the water growling fiercely at him. Abe thought it would attack at any moment. He squatted down, cowered like a baby and made whining sounds of fear, looking scared and sorrowful. The seal stopped growling, looked puzzled and then swam away. Abe never rode Point Surf during mating season again.

The thick kelp forest was murder at low tide if Marco's deep-set fin hit a patch as he tried to surf through it. It caused his board to lose its forward motion, stall out and sometimes even pitch him into the freeze for a long swim in. If lucky, he'd kick out, straighten off, prone in and recover. If not, his loose board might end up in the Blow Hole or smashed on the cliff.

As he rowed further outside the kelp Marco thought how great it was to spill his guts to Paolo. It was hard to open up at first but after he did, he felt better. That was something they never did in his family, never talked about how they really felt until it all came out later as angry shouts. Sitting there alone in the open boat, he began to cry. This time there was no one to see him. The floodgates burst open and he cried and gasped for air as bright tears fell into the darkening water. It felt so damn good. If he was being a puss, so be it. He was tired of keeping everything locked up. Maybe he wasn't so much like his dad, so stoic and hard. Maybe he was just being himself for the first time in his life.

He was sweating inside his dad's wool coat. He unbuttoned the front and pulled the skiff just outside the reef boils at Middle Peak. Sure as hell needed a smoke after all the tears. He smoked in the beauty of the moment as the sun dropped over the bumpy horizon. Never seen such a beautiful sunset.

Middle Peak was the reef where the biggest surfable waves would form up at Steamer Lane. The biggest, usually. On rare giant days an outside reef, Third Reef, would stand up and break. Third Reef was a huge, shifting peak that he and other Westside surfers used as a gauge for telling when the swells would be moving into Middle Peak.

They'd sit there, just outside the swirling boils which indicated the reef, and then paddle hard to get in take off position as the big sets loomed in. Middle Peak was usually best as a left-breaking tube with a steep face, but if he dropped in and rode right he had to go through a bouncy, mushed out white water section which would then form into a quarter mile long wall. If the swell direction was northwest and he managed the reef sections correctly, Marco could even surf all the way to the beach at Inside Cowells.

That's what he was a master at doing, pulling off long rides by pushing the Intruder at full speed while milking the wave tight in the tube.

And then there was the morning back in fifty-nine when he witnessed the worst wipe out he'd ever seen at the Lane. Marco sat back in the skiff, buttoned up the coat again and thought back to that morning as the horizon went from orange to dark red. The mere thought of the hairy incident chilled him.

He was just twelve years old and awoke early that bleak February morning. He'd heard the waves pounding the coastline all night long from his bedroom just a block off West Cliff Drive. He knew it had to be huge. It was back in '59 when the "foamies" were just arriving on the scene and some guys still rode balsa. Not that there were many surfers at all. Only about a dozen hung out at Cowells and even fewer at the Lane and of course Marco knew them all.

He rode his three-speed Schwinn out to the Lane and set it down next to the chain-link fence. There was a hole in the fence he climbed through. No one was around. He didn't figure there would be, too damn cold and huge, just an old black Buick rattletrap with racks on top. He recognized it. It was Jake's.

Jake was a wild, blonde-haired, little stump of a guy who drank a lot and hung out at Cowells. He was twenty-two, rarely surfed, preferring to punch guys out and hustle chicks on the beach. He always drove around with a red, eleven-foot, balsa, big wave board on top to impress the chicks but nobody had ever seen him ride it.

One time Marco and a couple other Westside gremmies saw him on the sand next to the cliff at Cowells with some babe. They were making out heavily and he had her top off. Marco and the boys tossed down big clumps of ice plant on them and ran away. Jake never knew who did it, which was good thing because he would've majorly kicked their butts.

Marco thought Jake probably passed out somewhere for the night and left his car in the dirt parking lot at the Lane. The surf was massive, eighteen to twenty feet, showing up as huge bumps on Third Reef first, then turning into Middle Peak where they sucked out into gargantuan, left tubes, with off-shore spray blowing off their tops about twenty feet in the air. Marco heard them explode on the reef, creating a melee of foam and bubbles as high as the swells themselves. He thought only a crazy person would be out on a day like that.

Then he saw him. Or rather he saw a thin, red sliver go up and over the face of the first wave of the set. Marco glanced back at the old Buick. The red, big wave board wasn't on top.

Holy shit. Jake was out there alone in freezing cold water without a wetsuit on the long, red, balsa, rhino chaser. Marco shivered from the bitter wind and the insane idea that someone was actually out there.

He climbed on top of the fence for a better view. He saw Jake go over the next wave and disappear down its back as it peaked up and hammered down blocking him from view. The next two waves were smaller and broke closer in but still blotted out any view of Jake.

The fifth wave was a monster. It stood up on the very outside tip of the reef. Marco couldn't believe it when he saw Jake suddenly appear at the top of the huge peak paddling in a frenzy shoreward. The wave sucked hard skyward, an immense amount of water swirling up its face as Jake pulled with all his might trying to penetrate downward. The wave sprang up, almost straight up and down. Jake stood up and pointed the nose of the board downward into the watery pit.

The strong off-shores blowing up the wave's face lifted his board and blew it over the top, spinning it around like a red toothpick. Jake free fell twenty-five feet down the face and disappeared in the trough as the merciless mountain of water slammed down on him. It must have felt like the whole Pacific Ocean swallowed him. Dead, he's got to be dead. That was it. Nobody could've survived that. Nobody.

The next wave was smaller and shifted inside. Marco watched as the balsa board smashed into dozens of pieces as the massive churning white water crushed it into the cliff. The pieces banged around in the foam and scattered along the high tide cliff line.

Marco searched intently for any sign of life as the set of waves waned. Nothing. Then he saw a minute splashing about eighty yards offshore. It was Jake. He was alive somehow being sucked eastward in the mighty river of a rip towards Indicators. Marco couldn't even imagine how cold he must be. The water had to be around fifty degrees or colder with a frigid wind and Jake with no wetsuit. He had to be hurting real bad. But he was alive and just treading water, bobbing along like a piece of human driftwood. He couldn't have much strength left. How long could he possibly hang on in those conditions as the current rushed him quickly into Outside Cowells?

Marco pedaled the cliffs as Jake floated around the point by the cypress trees. He lost sight of him for awhile. The river of water pushed him towards the beach at Cowells.

Marco dismounted on the edge of the cliff overlooking the beach. He watched as Jake crawled on all fours up onto the wet sand and began puking up blood. He collapsed. Two guys dragged him onto dry sand and covered him with a thick blanket.

Marco went back home, took a hot shower and slid in bed for a few hours, tossing around with thoughts of the gruesome wipe out. He rode back out to the Lane around noon but Jake's Buick was gone. And he never saw him again, ever.

The sky was turning dark purple over the slick kelp beds when Marco tossed the Pall Mall butt into the reef boils at Middle Peak and began to row back to the *Three M's*. The memory of Jake's wipe out gave way to more pressing concerns. It was flat water at sunset, nearly total glass and *Dago Red* slipped through easily. He was beginning to get the hang of the rowing technique Paolo taught him: *lift the oars, twist the blades parallel to the surface, push them forward, then sink them deep and pull hard.*

The lights from the houses along West Cliff began to pop on and he saw headlights moving across the road. The bay looked beautiful with lights from the wharf casting long gold and silver bands across the surface. He wondered how many times his dad had witnessed this exact scene while motoring in from the fishing grounds.

What a bitchen place to have grown up. A quiet little beach town with a fishing fleet and uncrowded surf. He wondered when the next swell would hit and thought about the Intruder over at Bumpsy's. He'd gotten the best rides of his life on it.

It was more like an extention of his body or a friend that was always there for him in good times and bad. He trusted the board just like his dad trusted Paolo. It never let him down and always performed flawlessly in two foot Cowells or ten foot Lane.

With other boards he'd had there was always some quirk that had to be worked out or some design flaw that made them harder to ride, but his Intruder was a magic board. And on real big days at the Lane he trusted his life to it. It was the board he'd sought after all his life. He always felt at one with it; man, board and wave in total sync.

Uncle Joe would be coming down in a bit and the boys would be showing up with all the boards and gear. Marco could always use his other team board if the swell came up before he got the Intruder back. He'd simply paddle out from the boat through the pier out to the Lane. He could surf and never be seen by the cops. They'd probably be checking out the cliffs where they knew he might turn up. The joke would be on them. He chuckled at the thought.

As *Dago Red* approached the wharf, the lights from the Dream Inn flashed on, casting bright spots on the sand at Cowells Beach. His hometown beach now looked so foreign from the water. All the years surfing the reefs of the Westside, his family, Gina, his great little room around the corner from the Cove, it all seemed an illusive twisted dream now. It was a scrapbook of his past he was about to turn the pages on.

He was feeling more akin to the creatures of the bay, the seals, otters and seabirds who never set down on land except for brief moments. He wondered what it would be like to be a seal or an otter: swimming around in search of tasty fish, snoozing on Seal Rock or sunning on top of the catwalks under the wharf with full bellies. And being able to ride big waves then dive under just before the hard thrashing. Not a bad way to go.

And how strange humans must look to them; no body hair or thick skin to stave off the cold, always rushing around on the dry land, never entering the cool, refreshing waters of the bay. Humans must seem like some weird nature experiment gone way wrong.

As he approached the tarred pilings of the wharf he realized his real world was now the ocean, too, a water world he'd loved all his life. All that mattered now was the boat, the getaway and a new life removed from the old.

He tied up to the landing and figured Uncle Joe would be there before too long. He always left the Cruz 'N' Eat around dark. Marco sat on the steps leading to the topside of the wharf and watched the nightlights from the boardwalk flicker on the smooth sea. Two seals swarmed the landing and barked at him then submerged next to the pilings. A gull sat quietly, watching him from the handrail above. Seeming uninterested, it tucked its wings close to its body.

Even with no swell, the sea moved in a quiet roll through the pilings, rising and falling every now and then. Water from the barnacles and mussels on the pilings splashed down as the sea moved through. It was a peaceful sound, lulling Marco to close his eyes. He leaned against the handrail. The dripping splash and roll became his inner world erasing all other thoughts and feelings. Drifting deeper with every swell, his mouth opened slightly, a slow breath going in and out. The swells moved and splashed…moved and splashed… as he fell into a quiet trance.

The lone gull, topside on the wharf bleated loudly, flapped its wings and launched off into the darkening sky. It squawked shrilly, mad that it had to leave its warm solace on the handrail.

Marco's limp body bolted at the sound. He yawned, watching the scowling bird flap off. He heard footsteps approaching from the wooden planks above and quickly crouched next to two skiffs stacked atop one another on the landing deck. The footsteps stopped. He knew someone was standing there, directly above. Who could it be? Were the cops on to him? The Feds? Had they somehow figured out where he was? Had someone blabbed? What would he do if it was the heat? He wouldn't be able to access the skiff; they'd surely see him. He'd be dead as squid bait.

May have to jump in and swim for it. Then hopefully make it to shore before they could nail him. Once on the beach he'd run and hide under the boardwalk or go west and hang out in the cave at Cowell's Cove. Either way it would be freezing. Still, it'd be a hell of a lot better than getting popped. He'd then climb the cliff and slink over to his mom's house. He knew how to sneak in without her hearing. He'd grab some dry clothes, maybe raid the icebox and then think up a different escape plan. Mom would never hear him. She'd most likely be passed out from red wine or brandy.

He heard the footsteps move away. A car door opened and shut. Headlights flashed on. Twin beams shot across the water out to the *Three M's*. A horn blared twice. Could it be Uncle Joe signaling or maybe just some drunk accidently hitting the horn?

Marco climbed the steps, peeked around a pile of stacked wooden fish crates and saw Uncle Joe's blue and white Chevy Nomad station wagon. He stood up and waved his hands overhead. The lights went out on the car. Uncle Joe got, pulling up his collar.

"Marco, my boy." They embraced. "Wasn't sure you were around. No sign a life out there." He nodded toward the boat.

"I'm still here."

Must be cold as blazes out there, Joe thought. "How ya gettin' along?"

"Okay."

Joe wasn't so sure about that. "Great. Hey look, let's take a ride. We gotta talk."

"You wanna go out to the boat?" Joe looked out again. It was completely uninviting, heaving slowly on the frigid bay. Marco sensed his reluctance. "I could turn on both burners. Gets real warm in there."

"Nah, forget it. Let's take a cruise. I got some grub. Ya need ta eat it before it gets cold."

"Okay."

The two double cheeseburgers went down fast. Joe made them just the way Marco liked; no lettuce, extra pickles with two slabs of cheese on each patty and light on the secret sauce.

They passed the Casino on Beach Street then crossed the San Lorenzo River driving east. The four pieces of fried chicken and fries went down a little slower. He polished them off just as they slid into the graveled parking area above the river mouth overlooking the wharf and bay. Marco sucked the straws in the chocolate shake as Joe cracked the window a few inches.

Joe squinted out trying to spot the *Three M's*. She sat in darkness, no mooring lights showing. He composed himself. Marco sucked on the double straws until air crackled.

Joe reflected on when Marco was a young boy in Little League. How fun it was to watch him hit the ball and run around the bases. And how he looked the day he was born. He thought how unkempt he looked now: unshaven and dirty, in oil-stained Levis with Louie's wool coat on. And how bad he smelled.

Marco let out a loud, rolling burp. "Sorry."

Joe took a deep breath. "Marco, you know how your Aunt Cat and I would do anything for ya?"

"Yeah, yeah, I know." He saw the serious stare on Joe's face.

"We're worried sick right now. I hate seeing ya out there on the boat when it's so damn cold out." Marco was thinking it wasn't so bad. With the stove and all. Joe took a shorter breath. "I met with Hancock, the lawyer. That bastard can really drink. Went through a quart a' Jim Beam. Lawyers are like that." He turned to get Marco's full attention. "It's like this. He said the Federal Marshall's office is stacked with warrants like yours, guys skippin' out on their draft physicals. Hundreds a warrants and only a few Marshalls. He asked about your case. They said they're lookin' for ya." He cleared his throat. "Then there's all that crap about the sex party or whatever it was. He called the local cops. They said they had a few kids in custody and are lookin' for you, too. There's a little confusion over who has jurisdiction." Marco sat transfixed on every word. Uncle Joe sighed. The few seconds seemed eternal. Joe continued. "Marco, I don't know what to tell ya. He says you gotta lay real low for awhile until he can work on it. Says he might be able to argue that you never got your notice in time because you weren't livin' at Marie's where it was delivered. You say you weren't at the party when the cops came. He might be able ta get that dropped on a technicality. For now though, ya gotta stay outta sight. If they find ya, yer fucked."

"You think he can really get it all dropped?"

"Christ, who knows? But he's good, real good and well connected over the hill. Cuts deals with the Feds all the time. Went ta law school with one a' the prosecutors." Joe cleared his throat again. "Even if he does get ya off fer now, there's still the draft ta deal with."

The words hit Marco cold. He winced. Uncle Joe did his best. Maybe the lawyer could get things taken care of, maybe not. He stared out the windshield at the lights from the wharf snaking around on the night sea.

Joe was quiet, too, and watched the muscles on Marco's face tighten with worry. "Listen, Marc, why don't ya come home with me. You could get cleaned up, have a shave and a hot shower. And wash those clothes. It'd do ya good. You could stay in the guest room like ya used to when you was a kid. Me and your Aunt Cat'll take care a ya fer awhile."

Marco didn't know what to say. God, a hot shower sounded good. He realized he hadn't bathed in a while or shaved. He must look pretty bad. He hadn't looked in a mirror for sometime.

He flashed back to when he was a just a kid. He loved going over to their house. He'd stay all weekend when Louie was on long albacore trips. Uncle Joe would take him to his little league games and cheer whenever he got a base hit. After the game, Joe would buy him some licorice and a soda at the snack bar. He and Joe would also go to the movies and get popcorn with butter on it and cokes. In the morning, Aunt Cat would make pancakes. In the evening, she'd whip up root beer floats while they watched TV or played Bingo. Those memories felt so foreign to him as he stared at his stained, smelly jeans and dirty tennies. Who the hell had he become? He wasn't sure.

"Marco, you okay?"

Okay? Of course he wasn't okay. What a stupid damn thing to ask. He looked over as tears welled. It was all coming to a head again.

"Marco, oh Marco...." Joe reached over and pulled him close. Marco couldn't hold it all in anymore. "Come here, boy."

The dam busted loose. The dam that kept him from saying how he really felt at times like these. He'd never speak up when his folks were yelling at home. He'd run in his bedroom and slam the door. When dad died he showed no tears and held it all in "like a man does." Louie always told him, "You cry and they'll laugh at you. Nobody likes a pussy or a whiner. And no son amine's no pussy." But it felt good to cry and he knew Uncle Joe was there for him without judgment.

"You go right ahead, Marc. Let 'er go."

He cried about his dad. He cried about Gina and hundreds of other things he couldn't even recall. He felt embarrassed, ashamed and uncertain about how Uncle Joe really felt. Was Joe just saying that or did he really understand? Did he actually think he was being a puss or just pretending it was okay to cry?

"It's gonna be okay, son. We'll figure it all out."

Figure what out? Just where the hell would they start: with Louie's death, with Gina, with all the other stuff? Maybe there was nothing to figure out. Maybe it was just his life and he'd have to suck it up and move on somehow. Move on and deal with it. Quit whining. Get out quick and cruise south. That's the way a real man would do it. Yeah, right. He pushed away and sat back up. "Sorry, I'm okay."

Joe studied him cautiously. "Marc, let's go ta my place. Jus' fer tonight. C'mon, whatta ya say?"

"I dunno. I don't think so."

"Goddammit, listen ta me. Ya can't go on like this. Ya gotta know I wanna help ya. We all need help sometimes." Joe thought back to the time he knocked up the gal in high school. His uncle Carl took him and the girl to San Jose and paid for the abortion. "I been in some tough spots before, too." Marco could tell by his cracked voice that he was telling the truth. "Things always work out somehow. It may not seem like it sometimes, but they always do."

Yeah, but how? Marco knew all too well that sometimes they worked out for the worst like for Lenny the Bull and Johnny Boy. He was feeling like being alone again. He didn't need any help. It was his problem and he'd work things out his own way. "I just want some time ta myself now, okay?"

Joe knew he better not push the issue too much. He didn't want to alienate Marco.

"All right, but how 'bout comin' over for a shower at least."

"Will ya take me back to the boat afterwards?"

"You bet. Anything ya want."

He could really use a shower. It might be the last one for a long time. "Okay."

They drove to Joe and Cat's place out by Natural Bridges, the northern tip of Monterey Bay. As they drove past the beach there, Marco thought about the times he and uncle Joe would explore the tide pools during minus tides. There were always tons of colored starfishes. Marco loved it when Joe would stick his finger in sea anemones and they'd quickly close up. Joe would pull his hand back and cock back a finger pretending its got bitten off. Then they'd both howl with laughter.

Caterina was playing bridge on the other side of town with her card group. Marco shaved and showered and watched " Have Gun Will Travel" on TV while Joe washed and dried his clothes. Joe made him a root beer float and warmed up some of Cat's homemade foccacia.

Joe drove him back to the pier. He bought him a carton of Camels on the way at the Midnight Drive Inn. Marco got out as a frigid gust bit him on the neck. Joe rolled down the window. "Look, ya gotta stay outta sight. I'll bring ya some more cash tamorrow aroun' sunset." Marco nodded. "Jus' keep cool till Hancock calls with more info." Joe looked out at the choppy seas where the *Three M's* bobbed. "An yer sure ya don't wanna stay with us?"

"Nah, I'm cool." Cool, what a joke. He was freezing his ass off again.

"Okay, it's your call."

The taillights from the station wagon faded off the wharf. Marco made it down the slippery stairs to the landing. It was probably around ten or so. It felt good to be cleaned up, smooth faced and shampooed with clothes and underwear that didn't stink. A crust of dirt had washed away.

It sure was great to be at Uncle Joe's again in a house where he felt wanted. It'd been awhile since he had that, about a year or so, ever since Louie and Marie started fighting. Louie wasn't around that much and Marie was always on the phone or just sitting around moping and drinking.

But Marco was mostly gone from there, too, hanging with his surf pals and riding as many waves as he could and moving up to the top of the pecking order in the water.

Home was where he kept his clothes and ate whatever he could find.

He'd come in late and be out early and never even see his dad or mom for days.

The bay air felt colder than he remembered. Being all cleaned up, he began to feel a bit removed from the sea and boat. They'd been temporarily washed off with soap and hot water. He had something to compare it to and wasn't sure which felt better.

On one hand, the boat was the way to go. He'd escape to the southlands until things blew over. On the other hand, having a nice bed to sleep in, a warm house with Uncle Joe and Aunt Cat taking care of him sounded good, too.

But how long could that last? Even if Hancock could get the charges dropped against him there was still the draft just like Uncle Joe said. He didn't have any physical ailments that could keep him out, foot problems or lung problems like other guys did.

Other local surf guys used bizarre antics to try and get out. One guy crapped in his shorts for two days prior to his physical then went in and when the doctor told him to drop his pants for a rectal exam started playing like a fag with the doctor, grabbing his cock and laughing. The doctor nearly puked and sent him home. Another guy started screaming, "Kill, kill, kill all those fuckin' gooks and anything else that moves." He then started beating on the doctors. They threw him in a straight jacket, held him for seventy-two hours then rejected him as a psycho.

Marco wasn't about to do any of that crazy stuff. Besides, he was in excellent shape, a surf star, USDA prime beef ready for the round up. The boat was the only way out, a new adventure and the *Three M's* would be the escape vehicle.

Even with those realizations he was reluctant to sit down on the dew-soaked seat of the dinghy. He cringed as the wet cold soaked through his jeans and froze his butt again. As he untied from the landing he noticed another small, cardboard box under the seat. It had his name across the top just like before.

When he'd pushed away from the dock, he drifted for a few seconds and opened the lid. Some fried chicken was wrapped in foil with a banana, a couple of sodas and two candy bars.

He wondered if one of the waitresses at the Dawn Fishers Café had dropped it off. But the chicken was homemade, definitely not restaurant style. It had mushrooms, bell peppers, onions and garlic on it, seasoned with fresh rosemary. He knew his mom wouldn't ever do anything like that and would never approve of him staying on the boat anyway. It had to be someone who knew he was on the boat, but nobody really did other than Paolo, Uncle Joe and the Cove crew.

What the hell. It was food, good food and he was glad to have it. It was late and getting colder by the minute. He slipped the dew-soaked, chilly oars into the locks and made his way back to the *Three M's*. He tried to row the way Paolo showed him but struggled.

Wonder when the guys'll show. Thought they'd be here by now with all the gear. Maybe they're hanging out in the garage for another night getting everything together. Couldn't blame 'em. The wood stove made it dry and warm even though it leaked smoke. Probably just tying up some loose ends.

He climbed aboard and wasn't a bit tired, deciding to stay up for a while just in case the boys showed up. He lit the two burners and switched on the light on the chart table. A far cry from uncle Joe's cushy digs but hey, it was sure as shit better than some cold cell at the police station or Juvie.

He poked around the closet where Paolo found the VO. A few boxes of cigars, two more bottles of VO, two boxes of 30/30 shells and a rifle case for a Winchester model 94, "the gun that won the West."

Marco had seen a lot of them in cowboy movies when the cavalry would charge down from the hills and blast the crap out of the Indian camps. The redskins would run for cover and try to hold off the charge with their bows and arrows but never really had much of a fighting chance. Bullets traveled a lot faster and farther than arrows and most of the Indians would be killed or taken prisoners. Then the Cavalry would ride off with their flag waving in the breeze as the music played a heroic song. Marco would usually be making out in the back row of the theater with Gina anyway, but always liked watching the parts where they fought the Indians.

He pulled out the rifle from the case and set it on the bunk. It was still well oiled. He wondered if Paolo had kept it that way. He knew Louie used it often to try and control the seals. Louie used to swear up a storm and get real pissed when he'd tell Marco how the seals would swim along and tear out the bellies of the salmon he'd catch while trolling. Before he could get them aboard the seals would rip the fish apart then dunk underwater and disappear.

Louie would try to blast them whenever he could draw a good bead on one of them, which wasn't too often because they were so fast. He would brag anytime he hit one. The problem had gotten so bad that a few of the guys in the fleet even had big money bets as to who could nail the most in a single day. Louie once won a hundred bucks for blasting three. The local fishermen agreed something had to be done about the seals. They were like a plague destroying the commercial catch. And their numbers were growing. They'd chew big holes in the nets, sometimes drown and it was always a hassle getting them untangled. Marco heard Louie wondering what it would be like to eat them. They lived on fish and had strong muscles, probably wouldn't be bad once marinated and barbequed. But if Louie ever got caught with one on ice the Fish and Game would fine his ass big time.

All the commercial fishermen hated the Fish and Game. They'd board any vessel at will and inspect their catches. And ever since one out of town guy got popped for smuggling pot from Mexico, things were getting a bit out of hand. All the honest guys were being hassled constantly. The Fish and Game treated them like potential criminals rather than the honest hard-workers they really were.

Louie nearly got in a fistfight with one female inspector last season when she tried to board him during a troll. She wanted him to pull up his gear and let her check out the entire boat. He swore up a blue streak and threatened her. She didn't board him but once he got back to Moss Landing a whole squad of Fish and Game officers and sheriffs searched the boat.

They didn't even find one under-sized fish or anything else that could incriminate him. He just grinned and smoked a cigar while they went through the holds and cabin. When they found the Winchester Louie just shrugged and said, "Pirates, just in case a' pirates." They were obviously peeved but couldn't charge him with anything. If he ever did pull in anything illegal he'd throw it back or fillet it up and eat it raw on the way back to the wharf.

Marco dug further in the closet. He pulled out a small bottle of extra-virgin olive oil. Deeper down he came up with a thin, flat metal box. Inside were a few copies of Playboy, Hustler and a pack of Trojan condoms. He set them on the bunk and leaned back against the hull. What was dad doing with that stuff? Then he thought about all the nights he wouldn't even come home and all the arguing. No way was his dad doing the deed with his mom. What other way was there? He had a hard time thinking about his dad on the boat spanking his monkey, but hey, if he wasn't getting any at home what the hell? But why the condoms?

Marco had thought about getting one a few months back. Intense passion with Gina was heating up fast. They'd experimented all over each other's bodies but never penetrated. There wasn't a spot on her he hadn't felt and she with him. They were real close to having it all. And then the val beat him to it. He visualized the guy pumping her hard under the wharf as she cried out. Or did she cry out? Did she actually like it and then later realize what had happened and change her feelings about it? Never know for sure. It was all over between them and he knew that she knew that. No need for any more words between them. Words would just confuse things. Better to just let her go. No time for girls anyway. Getaway time.

Not sure whether to keep the magazines. Had no interest in them. Heard about guys doing it that way. It had to be on the beach, with the sound of the waves. That was the only way. He'd choose who he wanted to do it with in his mind. He didn't need magazines.

He stared at the pack of Trojans. Might as well keep them. Never know what might come up in the future. Was there someone Louie was seeing on the boat? Or did he maybe use them with the magazine babes? It was too much to speculate. Way too weird to speculate.

His mind was jumping around like a smelt on a jig line. He'd never know the truth about any of it. But he couldn't help but wonder what his dad was doing on the boat all the times he was away.

Marco then reflected on the gentle summer days with his dad on the boat during salmon season. He'd watch Louie fillet up the fish with the sharp, thin knife. Marco liked throwing fish parts overboard for the gulls and pelicans and seals. And listening to his dad joke and talk with the other fisherman on the CB or when they came onboard to visit.

Those days seemed more like old TV reruns. He'd never again hear his dad's infectious laugh or see him waving from the cabin as he pulled in next to the wharf.

The dim cabin light made his eyes sting. He yawned and slid the Winchester back into the bag. The clock read eleven twelve. Time to bunk down. Nobody would be coming out to the boat that late. It was numbing cold outside. He turned off one burner leaving one low, just enough to keep the cabin from freezing. He flicked off the light, kicked off the tennies and pulled the wool blankets up to his neck.

The boat heaved silently over the tiny wind swells as the onshore winds made landfall. The ticking of the second hand became a focal point. After a few minutes the sound faded away into the descending black curtain of his mind and he was gone.

Marco stood atop the wharf as the fog steamed ashore, wrapped in a wool blanket with arms clenching his sides. Louie was leaning against the wooden handrail about twenty feet away staring off into the distance towards the Lane, with his back to Marco. " *Dad, dad...*" *Marco shouted to him. Louie didn't move. Marco strained towards him but his feet seemed stuck in thick tar. He pulled with all his strength, felt like he was running but couldn't move.*

Something approached in the thick mist. Slowly it appeared, the huge prow of a large, white fishing boat. It wasn't slicing through the water, merely floating in the fog at wharf level. As it neared, Marco made out a couple of the figures along its deck. They were grayish-white specters standing, staring silently at Louie. As the boat approached the wharf Marco recognized a few of them; one was uncle Theo, who died years before in an accident at sea. Another was his aunt Jane who died in car wreck on Highway 17. A shorter one stood next to Uncle Ted holding his hand. My god, it was Mary, his little sister who died as a young child from asthma. The boat slowed alongside Louie. He floated in mid air onto her deck.

Louie then turned and faced Marco with the same blank stare as the rest. He raised his arm, slowly waving goodbye. The wooden hull headed back into the thick fog as the foghorn boomed a loud blast. "Dad, Dad!" Marco screamed at Louie as the stern headed away towards the horizon. He made out her name, Neptune's Catch. She faded deeper into the bright mist. Marco bawled out loud. The foghorn blew louder, its intense droning rattling inside Marco's head. He started to shake. He couldn't stop. He was a gong inside a large metal bell, banging from side to side...

The picture of Marco and Louie with the big salmon fell from the chart table onto the cabin floor, shattering. Marco awoke panting, heart racing. He looked at the clock, three thirty-three. It was freezing. The cabin door was wide open. He was sure he closed it. He looked outside and thought he saw something, a whitish mist moving away from the wharf. It was just his eyes playing tricks, he thought, that's all, nothing more.

He slid the door shut and re-lit the stove. What a dream, his dad leaving on a ghost ship and waving goodbye. The shards from the broken picture frame glistened on the floor. He picked up the photo carefully avoiding the sharp pieces and clicked on the chart table light. Too late to clean up the glass. Have to do it in the morning. He looked at the photo in the dim light. Louie's smile seemed wider than before. It couldn't possibly have changed. It was just a photograph. Must be his mind playing games again. It's late right, too damn late to think clearly. He saw the brass plaque with the prayer the priest from Holy Cross Church hung on the cabin wall the morning the *Three M's* was christened. Marco shined a flashlight on it and read the fading verse:

God grant that I may live to fish
until my dying day
and when it comes to my last cast
I then most humbly pray
when in the Lord's safe landing net
I'm peacefully asleep
that in His mercy I be judged
as big enough to keep

He wrapped back up, hazily thinking about death. Was there an afterworld? A Heaven or Hell or a Purgatory? The dead couldn't possibly come back and visit or could they? When you're dead, you're dead, that was all there was to it. You were cold meat, chum for crabs. And dreams were just a part of your imagination, nothing more.

Ticking of the clock. He closed his eyes and thought about the dream ship, *Neptune's Catch*. Wonder if it was possible for a ghost ship to take away spirits to a spirit world after they're dead? There goes his mind again, thinking stupid thoughts.

Nah, it's all a bunch of crap. Just weird stuff that happens in dreams, but how'd the cabin door get open? And why was the stove off? And why'd he wake up at three thirty-three again? Must have stumbled out on deck in a stupor, took a piss over the rail half asleep and left the door open. Must have turned off the stove, too. And the time, three thirty-three, it was just a coincidence.

Late. Real late. Gotta get some sleep. Sleep until Paolo comes out. Six o'clock, early, real early...over...over and out.

"Ahoy, Marco…Marco, you in there?" Paolo held on to the *Three M's* starboard rail while balancing in a small rowboat. He gazed at the gold light atop Mount Loma Preita as dawn scattered across the rippled surface of the bay in the pulsing onshore breeze. Seals barked and growled under the catwalks of the wharf and gulls nesting on the landings flapped off the cold night's dew.

Marco bobbed about in a dark, silent world. Hearing a voice he rose from the deep, quiet ocean of his mind.

"Hey Marco, rise and shine."

Marco heard the thumping of the skiff on the hull next to his bunk as the light crept into the cabin, illuminating the portside wall. "Yeah, I'm here." His voice sounded cracked and gravelly. He cleared his throat. "Come aboard, Paolo." He knew Paolo wouldn't climb up on deck until he had permission.

"Aye aye, skipper." Paolo chuckled as he pulled himself on deck and tied off the skiff's line to a stern cleat. He leaned against the fish hold cover and scratched the stubble on his chin.

Marco slid open the door. "Come on in. Watch out for the glass."

"Damn cold out, fuckin' onshores."

" Want some coffee?"

"Nah, been up since five, caffeined out. Have some if ya want."

"I'm okay."

Paolo set a small white bag on the chart table. "Brought ya some sweet rolls. Know the baker downtown at Modern Bakery. Let's me have stuff just as they're comin' outta the oven. Ain't no fresher than that. I givem fish sometimes, hot sweet rolls fer salmon. Bakers an' fisherman work the same hours."

They did smell good. "That's really cool. Thanks Paolo." Marco quickly broomed the shards under a bunk.

"It ain't nuthin.' Yer dad an' me used ta have'm all the time when we's headin' out ta fish. Thought it'd be nice ta keep up the tradition. Fer the old times and the new, now that yer gonna be skipper and all. How ya getting' along?"

"Ah, better now, ever since our talk. And a nice little row out to the point an' back."

"Yeah, I know what ya mean. I took a little row over to Capitola and back one day when I had a lot ta think about. And when I got back it was all figured out."

Capitola and back. That was over 10 miles. Must have taken all day. No wonder his arms were so big. "I always feel better after a good surf session, too."

"Somethin' about bein' on the water's good for the soul. Fishin's the same way."

"Maybe I will have some coffee, ta go with the rolls." Marco fired up the sauce pan as Paolo poked around the cabin's electricals. What a bitchen' guy. No wonder he and Louie got along so well. Not only was he a good bullshitter and fisher, he was strong as a whale and dependable, too.

Paolo pulled out a few fuses and dried them with his tee shirt. "Ya gotta keep these babies dry or yer fucked. Nuthin'll ever work. Mind if I fire up the diesel?"

"No, go ahead and check her out. Be my guest. You want some coffee?"

"Ah fuck, I guess so." He looked at his shaking hands from all the coffee he'd already had, but coffee and sweet rolls were a match made in heaven he'd never turn down.

"Just show me what's what?"

"That's exactly why I'm here, Marc." Paolo knew Louie would be thrilled to know he was teaching the youngin the ropes. "Then we'll take'er out for a cruise."

"Bitchen." Marco poured the cups and they nibbled on the pastries. Paolo instructed Marco how to fire up the deisel and let it warm up for awhile. He showed Marco how to check the oil levels and activate the bilge pumps. He made Marco take out and clean off all the fuses since she'd been sitting at moor for awhile. They always had to be dry. A boat with faulty electrics was a disaster waiting to happen. The batteries were about half charged.

They tied off the two skiffs at different lengths to the mooring line and headed off northwest beyond the wharf. As they moved farther away from the wharf Marco began to understand why his dad loved the sea so much. Motoring away from the wharf was like witnessing the whole rotten picture of his life in the rear view mirror.

The steaming fog bank hovered outside in the far distance. As the coastline moved further from sight, Marco sensed the serene peace of being out on the bay as the *Three M's* chugged seaward. The buildings and houses became tiny, toy structures. And the cars moving along the cliff were like ants themselves until they finally faded from sight. Paolo told him that cars disappeared when they were about two miles offshore.

The rolling hills and green pasturelands of the north coast became the dominant images. And the sky and clouds. The dark gray horizon was a constantly undulating line disappearing in the fog.

"It's just a matter of heading where you want to end up," Paolo said. " Hawaii's southwest, Indonesia and Australia farther south. Japan, the Orient and Russia, northwest. Alaska, straight north and dead south, Mexico." Marco was impressed. Paolo added, "The entire planet's just one huge waterway and if you had the right boat and enough fuel you could go anywhere. And never be seen again." Was he reading Marco's thoughts or what? Marco was surprised by that last comment. Must be an infinite amount of the virgin reefs and point breaks in the world. Wild.

The diesel smell from the overhead dual exhaust pipes made Marco a little queasy. Paolo sensed it. "Hey, not to worry. It'll pass once ya develop yer sea legs." Marco was glad he didn't eat much for breakfast. The roll of the boat was testing his stomach. It was like standing on a big wide surfboard that was constantly dipping and shifting from side to side. He wondered if he'd get used to it. He'd heard about the guys who'd go out on a charter, hang on to the rail and heave their guts out until they finally got back to the wharf. "Just chummin' the fish," Louie would say.

Paolo wanted him to go inside the cabin and learn about the autopilot, the fathometer and the CB radio but Marco needed more time to adjust to the movement.

"Watch this." Paolo steered the *Three M's* in a giant circle southeast, running with the swells rather than against them. The ride became a lot smoother and the wind seemed almost non-existent, blowing against their backs.

Marco regained his constitution and went inside the cabin where Paulo showed him how to chart a course with the parallel rulers. He also taught him how to use the radio direction finder to get the boat's position and how each lighthouse had different signals and durations. "But if ya ever get caught out in the dense fog, it's a process called, 'dead reckoning.' Ya keep track of yer compass bearing, speed and distance traveled, listen fer fog horns, keep yer eyes peeled and hopefully find the way back in. And if yer underway at night someone'd sure as shit better be on the lookout fer other boats, 'specially if yer in or crossing the shippin' lanes."

"Hey, how 'bout showin' me how to draw a course on the chart?" Marco asked. "Say to Mexico, just fer fun. It'd be a cool learning exercise."

"Great idea. Been down there a bunch, once with yer dad and on some other boats too. Glad you thoughta that." He pulled out the charts, drew a course along the lee of the Channel Islands just inside the shipping lanes, then down to San Diego and across the border to the international port of Ensenada. "Otherwise ya gotta go way off shore ta avoid the traffic. That's cool too depending on the weather. If its foggy on the coast yer better off outside. Ain't nuthin' ta run into out there. But if it's blowin' hard and no fog, it's a nicer ride inside. Ya gotta keep yer eyes wide open though. Lots a boats go agroun' huggin' the coast."

"What about fuel?"

"Good question." Paolo was happy to see Marco so interested. "*Three M's* holds six hundred gallons a fuel and at a speed of six to seven knots she'd reach the border in two to three days. At twenty-five cents a gallon, it'd take two hundred and forty bucks to fill 'er up."

No sweat, Marco thought. He still had the two hundred bucks uncle Joe gave him. Not quite enough for all the fuel. They'd have to hit the turkey's cars for the rest of it. And uncle Joe would probably throw in some more, too. They'd have plenty.

Marco was feeling more at ease. It all was going to happen. He steered the boat back along the coast toward the northern tip of the bay. He loved the way the sun scattered over the choppy seas and the air, the pure, sweet-smelling sea air. The wheel felt good in his hands and he began to daydream about how it would be cruising south on the open sea eating fresh fish they'd troll for on the way down and eventually pulling into all those great surf spots in Mexico. He loved the way the *Three M's* glided down the swells with the wind off her stern. She felt heavy and stable like the true storm-rider she was, slow and steady and sure.

Louie once told him about the day he got caught out in a big storm during albacore season. The swells rose to nearly twenty feet for over twelve hours. He shut off the engines, tied off the wheel, went inside and ran with the storm. The *Three M's* was so heavy and stable she just rose and fell as the waves passed her by. When it abated, Louie cranked her up and continued to fish.

The sun was low on their backs when they made the turn at the lighthouse by the Lane and headed for the wharf. Marco was depressed to see the houses along West Cliff Drive, then the boardwalk and hills of buildings. The peaceful reverie of a day at sea was nearly over and who knew what was going to happen once they tied up to the mooring.

But everything was falling in place. He had to get a hold of Jeremy, Abe and DJ, get their stuff together and make a hit on the cars. It was starting to come down to a matter of hours until they'd make their break for the border.

Marco was quiet and pensive as he waved goodbye to Paolo as he rowed back to the pier. He watched him pull his little skiff on top of the landing and saw his wide grin as he waved back. What great guy, a true friend in the making. He wondered if he'd ever see him again.

The sky was clouding up, huge white puffs gathering, no rain in them just passing through. He followed Paolo's truck until it reached the entrance to the wharf. As the sun descended something flashed brightly on the landing, a hard glare in the darkening shadows. Could it be the glossy finish of a surfboard? Had the cove crew dropped stuff off on the landing when he was out on the bay with Paolo?

He climbed aboard *Dago Red* and made it to the wharf just as the sun hit the horizon line. Three boards were stacked on the rear of the landing next to a nest of skiffs in racks. Abe's, Jeremy's and Marco's red team board. Two duffel bags, a cardboard box and two sleeping bags leaned against one of the small boats. A note was taped to the box;

Marco,

> *Where are you? Out getting fuel? We're ready to split. Call
> us. Things are getting weird. DJ ain't going.*
> Jeremy 423-8940

Sounded urgent. What's up with DJ? Marco loaded the gear onto the skiff and tied off to the landing rail. They would have to bring the boards on later when someone could hold onto them. He couldn't row and keep them onboard too; they were too long and would slide off. He waited for total darkness to set in, then climbed the slick stairs and made the call from the phone booth outside the coffee shop.

"Hello?" It was uncle Pete's wife.

"Is Jeremy there?"

"Who's this?"

"Marco.'"

"Oh, Marco. I hear you're a very bad boy." She snickered, sounded like she was drinking. "Hold the phone."

Marco heard her walk away and the television on. Someone yelled out at her. "Who the hell is it now?"

She came back to the phone. "Marco, he's on his way in."

He heard some stirring and then a door open and close. "Marc, where ya been?" Marco told him about the day on the bay with Paolo. "We gotta get outta here. Pete's gettin' real weird. Wants us ta pay 'im for stayin' here. And he's drinkin' all the time."

"Get yer asses down here. We'll eat and figure things out."

"Shit man, DJ's ol' man flipped out when he heard we were gonna split town. He ain't goin'."

Not going, huh, what a flake. "No big deal. There'll just be more room aboard for the rest of us. Get down here as soon as you can."

Marco laid the phone on the hook and watched the people inside the restaurant. Families out for dinner on a Friday night, laughing together and having a good time in a warm place with a hot bowl of chowder or a seafood salad, with warm French bread and butter. He wished he had a family like that instead of one that fought or was silent at the dinner table. It was a lot better after dad cut out. At least it was quieter in the house but he wasn't really sure which was worse.

How were the guys going to get down to the wharf? Would they get a ride or bike it or hoof it? In any case, they'd all be together soon.

The onshore wind gusted as Marco made his way back to the landing. The cold penetrated his team jacket and felt even brisker a few feet above the sea surface as he hunched down in front of a skiff, using it as a wind block. Wished he had his dad's wool watch coat.

They'd have to get all the boards on the boat that night. Store them out of sight in the fish holds. He wondered if the cops had any idea what was going on. Hopefully that ass Willy would keep his mouth shut. And what about DJ? What a dick. Flaking out on the whole deal. Could he be trusted? Once his ol' man started to probe him for information would he blab? Hope to hell not.

He watched the lights from the boardwalk flicker on and thought about the fun times he'd had there as a kid with his dad and Uncle Joe. The cotton candy, the candied apples and salt water taffy and peeing in his pants after going on the roller coaster for the first time.

Louie and Uncle Joe knew all the guys who owned the businesses there. They always had free beers everywhere they went. They'd get hot dogs and go down on the beach and watch as Marco waded in the water or built sand castles. No matter how high he built them the ocean would always wash them away with the tide.

Marco couldn't recall the first time he went to the beach. It seemed like he was always there. He was swimming by age four, body surfing by seven and board surfing by ten. He knew all the lifeguards by name and all the other folks who hung out there: the Filipino surf casters, the ocean swimmers, the sunbathers and local drunks. They were all a part of his extended beach family.

He loved all the bonfires, fish barbecues and big family picnics with his cousins. Most of the time the young kids would dig for sand crabs along the water line and sell them as live bait to the surf casters for candy money. The fires would blaze into the night until the kids passed out from too much fun and excitement. They'd eventually be hauled off by their parents then wake up next morning in sandy bed sheets.

Some nights the cops would come down after work to check things out and end up swilling some homemade wine with the local fishers. They all knew one other, took care of each other and all their kids. He knew them all as his "uncles." Some were related to him and some weren't. They were more like uncles of the heart. It was a small town attitude that Marco knew was beginning to change forever.

The Dream Inn on the cliff overlooking Cowells and the new university up in the foothills signaled the beginnings of the end. Uncle Joe and Louie always talked about how the town was starting to go to hell. A lot more people would be coming into town with the university. A lot of people who "lived in their heads" with no real life experience to draw from," Uncle Joe would say. They'd bring in their influence and not give a damn about how the locals felt.

Uncle Joe and other businessmen would talk about what happened to Berkeley and Davis when the university gained control. Their influence grew slowly then gained more power, opening businesses that catered exclusively to students. As they grew in size they became rulers of the towns, swaying the student vote and taking over the city councils, changing the cities forever and running a lot of locals out.

And they talked down anything to do with the military, which really pissed off the local veterans. World War II had only been over for twenty years and Louie, like a lot of former servicemen, was still reeling from its effects.

One of Louie's best friends in high school died on the battleship, *Arizona*, during the Japanese surprise bombing of Pearl Harbor. Louie got real fidgety around Germans too, ever since he got torpedoed in the North Atlantic and set adrift in the lifeboat. His eyes would glaze as he became transported back to that god-awful place in time. The thought of some transplanted university, anti-military types running the city was a real sacrilege to Louie and local veterans who once wore the uniform in combat.

War wounds healed slowly among the veterans, especially those who were in the real tough campaigns with disabilities and major injuries like Uncle Bobo.

Uncle Bobo was stationed in Pearl Harbor on the battleship, *USS West Virginia*, December 6th, 1941. Marco heard the story one afternoon during the annual Veterans Day celebration on the wharf. Bobo was lying back in his hammock on a Saturday morning with a mug of coffee, listening to the news on the radio about how President Roosevelt was talking to the Emperor of Japan trying to broker a peace deal.

Next morning Sunday the 7th, Seaman Bobo was hoisting the American flag off the fantail for the 8AM muster. Suddenly, the sky was filled with Jap Zeroes, torpedo bombers, high-level bombers, and dive-bombers. The *USS West Virginia* was struck hard by three torpedoes almost instantly. She listed to her side, water pouring in with the force of a river.

More torpedoes hit the sinking hull, followed by bombs dropped from high above. Uncle Bobo was blown off the fantail into the ignited water caused by explosions of massive oil spills from the gaping holes in the side of the ship. He grabbed onto a fifty-five gallon drum and floated in the blazing water until he was pulled to safety. The last image he remembered before he passed out was seeing the American flag still waving off the fantail amidst the smoke and fire.

He was burned severely on the upper third of his body. His hair never grew back and the scars on his face were horrible. Now he just sits around on various benches on the wharf and mostly stares out at the bay or babbles to seagulls and empty bait boxes. Marco winced at the thought.

The next day after the attack on Pearl, President Roosevelt declared war on Japan and called the Japanese sneak attack "a day which will live in infamy." That was the very day Louie and scores of other local fisherman signed up to go into battle against the Japs and Germans. And they hated Mussolini. They were proud Italian Americans and couldn't believe that the leader of their native country sided with Hitler. The news about Uncle Bobo enraged them into action.

Marco learned to both fear and revere the vets. He knew how their moods could change radically from moment to moment. Another local fisherman, Julio, was captured during the Battle of the Phillipines on the Bataan Peninsula. He was one of seventy-five thousand Filipino and American soldiers who were forced to march 100 kilometers north to Camp O'Donell and Camp Cabaatuan prison camps. They were beaten randomly and denied food for days. Those who lagged were executed by a variety of means: shot to death, beheaded or bayoneted. Julio watched his best friend die when they used the "sun treatment" on him. They sat him hand-cuffed in the hot sun without food or water until he begged for mercy, then they laughingly watched him die.

Julio was then sent by sea upon a Japanese "Hell Ship " to work as a slave laborer in a steel factory just east of Tokyo. On the Hell Ship he was literally crammed with other POW's in the humid hold of the ship. Many perished on the voyage to Japan. After the war when he was finally released and sent home he never talked to anybody.

He rarely left his little house just a block from the wharf or ever fished again, just dug around in his garden. He finally succumbed to a rare blood disease caused by his war injuries. On his deathbed his last words were, "I'm glad it's finally over." People wondered if he was talking about his life or the haunting memories of the war, or both.

And of course none of the university intellectuals ever went to war. That's what pissed off Louie the most. They had no idea what it was like taking in hostile fire or trying to keep your buddy alive when he was shot to shit. They kept a far distance from it all and had no respect for those who did serve, spewing their anti-war rhetoric. But like Louie always said, " If an enemy ever attacked us, those university bastards would kiss our asses."

And it seemed to the vets that the rising anti-war movement was quickly becoming an anti-veteran movement. He once heard a vet say, "Those university pricks don't understand a damn thing. Nobody loves freedom and liberty more than a person in uniform because they're willing to put their lives on the line every day for it."

The Santa Cruz Marco knew as a kid would soon no longer exist. The writing was clearly on the pilings. From the landing deck he watched car lights pull into the parking lot at the Dream Inn, tourists and out-of-towners swooping into his beach. He figured there was no use fighting it anymore.

He and the other Westside gremmies would throw rocks at their cars and flip them off when they went to the beach. It worked for awhile but now there were just too many to control, too many of them coming in. He was beginning to understand how old Chief's ancestors, the Ohlones felt when the Spaniards first arrived and overpowered them. But god, it was great to have grown up here before the crowds, to have ridden all those classic waves and hang out on empty beaches.

The beach was the place he had his first sip of wine at seven, his first cigarette at eleven. He'd smoked ever since. He saw his first naked babe through a peek hole under the boardwalk when he was nine and watched a couple do the wild thing in the cave at the cove at Cowells the same year. At ten he could swim around the wharf when he was in the fifth grade at Bay View Elementary.

Whenever he had things on his mind to figure out he'd walk along the beach to the river mouth and by the time he returned have it all worked out. Except for the night Gina got screwed by the val. Things had gotten weirder ever since. That was definitely a turning point.

The dark image of the *Three M's* heaved up and down slowly, his new home, his hideaway, his get away vehicle. She was a quiet, serene island, a safe haven from all the crazy stuff that was coming down on land.

Scanning the shore he watched the boardwalk maintenance man George, take down the American flag from the pole next to the casino. He couldn't really see him, it was getting too dark, but he knew George was there.

George was a local guy, a Korean War vet who lost his left leg in a firefight on the assault of Pork Chop Hill. He nearly bled to death and froze in the snow there. It was a miracle he survived at all. The boardwalk gave him a life-long job when he finally made it home with his wooden leg. He'd always raise the flag at dawn and take it down at sunset. He was a little late tonight. The sun had set a while ago.

He pulled four shot-up guys into a foxhole just before a grenade took his leg off. He was awarded the Silver Star for bravery. He was a local hero like a few other local vets who performed selfless deeds in World War Two and Korea.

Marco would see them, the maimed ones, wearing their medals and riding in the beds of pickup trucks down Pacific Avenue during the annual Veterans Day parade. The other vets who weren't wounded would march down the street with brass bands blaring.

Louie would ride in an open rowboat that hung from a hoist on a big, flatbed truck with other navy veterans.

Afterwards the entire procession would end up on the wharf for a big celebration with fresh dishes donated by the local fishers. There were fish stews, fried fish and fish dips and of course huge kettles of clam chowder. Modern Bakery gave away free French bread for dipping in the chowder. Casks of homemade red wine were cracked and everyone drank for free.

Bands would play and other local musicians playing mandolins and accordions would take stage and sing native Italian songs and American hymns. The veterans would sob and hug as memories surfaced from the battlefields and sea campaigns.

Marco was always proud to be standing next to his dad as people came up to tell him how grateful they were he had fought for the country. Louie just stood there speechless with glazed eyes as they hugged him. That was the only time his dad had little to say. He was just too choked up to talk.

Monday was going to be Veterans Day again. Three days away. Would he still be there? What would dad want him to do? Go and fight in some stupid war in Nam? Or not take part in any of it? Who knew? He'd never know now. Wish to hell dad was here to talk to about it. Some guys are signing up, some are getting drafted and some are running. It sure as hell isn't like World War Two when Hitler and Mussolini and Hirohito wanted to take over the whole planet. Back then everybody signed up. They all went and did what they had to do to stop them.

A car pulled in above the landing. Marco saw its headlights flick off and heard the doors open. Someone ran over to the handrail. A flashlight beamed on, its rays disappearing in the thin air towards the *Three M's*.

Who was it? It had to be Jeremy and Abe. The cops would have their blinking lights on and the underside of the wharf where Marco sat would be lit up with red and white flashes.

"Hey, Marco." A voice yelled out to the boat. It was Jeremy.

"Down here." Marco called up to him then climbed the stairs to the street level.

Jeremy came over as Abe pulled out Marco's Intruder from the back of the station wagon. "We got your board. Bumpsy fixed the fin an' set it on the porch. Found it tonight when we went over there to score more food and clothes."

"Bitchen." The idea of splitting town without his favorite board would've been a bummer. Now he had both the O'Neill team boards. He'd save the Intruder for the real classic places and ride the other team board at rockier point breaks or shore breaks.

Abe handed the board to him, nodded and went back for a duffel bag of clothes. Jeremy had a backpack half-filled with canned goods. "Glad to see ya, Marc."

"You too, buddy."

"We goin' out to the boat now?"

"You bet."

They loaded up the skiff and rowed out to the *Three M's* with the Intruder in tow. Marco slid open the fish hold and lowered the board in. They went back and towed the other boards out. Marco stashed the food and clothes in cupboards while they secured the boards in the hold.

"Home sweet boat," Marco said as they bent through the cabin door. The chart light was on and a lantern rocked slowly above their heads in the cabin. Abe and Jeremy gazed about with different stares. Jeremy seemed relieved while Abe had a slight morose gaze.

"Take any bunk ya want. Mine's this one." He pointed to the one closest to the chart table and wheel.

Abe was sniffing the dank smell of the air as he slid his guitar case on a bunk. Marco picked up on it. "She'll smell better when we start cookin' in here and hit the open ocean."

Abe nodded. "Yeah, okay." His skepticism was obvious.

"Hey, it's gonna be a real adventure. You guys hungry?"

"Not really. We had pizza about an hour ago."

"Okay, how'bout a drink."

Abe was silent. "Hey sure, why not," Jeremy chimed in. Marco pulled out the half-empty bottle of VO. "Christ, where'd you get that?"

"My ol' man's. Had it onboard."

"Wild," was all Jeremy said. Abe plopped on the bunk and watched as Jeremy and Marco took snorts.

"You want one?" Marco handed him the bottle.

"Nah, not yet."

"C'mon Abe, just a sip for good luck."

"In a little while."

"Okay. Hey, tell me what's botherin' ya."

Abe sat up and surveyed the inside of the cabin for a few seconds. "I dunno, I guess its Willy. Willy and Karie. And now DJ ain't goin."

"Yeah, what's up with DJ?"

"It's his ol' man," Jeremy added. " Totally blew up when he heard the plan. Said we were stupid asses to try something like that. Said he had some ideas of his own for getting DJ out of the draft. DJ had no choice. His ol' man would've really laid into him if he argued."

What a puss Marco thought, just like a pot smoker flaking out at the last moment. He took another belt. "Ya know what? We really don't need 'im. We'll do just fine and there'll be more room on board. And one less guy in the surf." Jeremy and Abe stared at each other. "If he ain't goin', he ain't goin that's all there is to it."

"You sure we'll be alright?" Jeremy asked. "Thought we needed four guys to keep the boat goin' all the time."

"Nah, it'll be a snap. We'll all just stand two-hour watches. No sweat."

"Yeah." Jeremy replied. "Just seems a little weird, that's all."

"Hey look, there's nuthin' we can do 'bout any of it. We'll be long gone within a day or so." Marco gazed cautiously at them checking for their physical responses.

In silence they all thought about the possibilities. Was Willy in a cell at juvie or what? Were they interrogating him about the plan to split town. So far it didn't look like he blabbed, at least not yet. And Karie was still at her aunt's or was she? Would they put her in juvie, too?

"We just gotta think 'bout ourselves now." Marco added, "And we'll be outta here soon." Abe and Jeremy listened close. "Hey, all we gotta do is just hit the cars, get some fuel and head for the high seas. We'll be in Mexico in a few days."

Marco changed the subject by telling them about his day on the bay with Paolo, how he'd set the course on the chart for them. All they had to do was just steer the boat south and run with the swells. He handed Jeremy the bottle, pulled out the charts, set them on the table and explained the route south. He hoped it would appease them. They seemed a bit more relieved but he couldn't be sure.

"We'll just need a little more money. A withdrawal from the great bank of Cowells Beach." Marco thought he was being funny but neither of them laughed.

"Yeah? Just how're we gonna do that?" Abe was grilling him.

"Easy. I been thinkin' it out."

"This I gotta hear. Me an' Abe ain't sure about it. The whole thing seems a little out there."

Marco had a hunch they'd been talking things out before they got on the boat. "No sweat. You guys will hit the cars while I paddle into the crowd and keep 'em distracted. It'll be short and sweet. Then we'll meet up back at the boat and head out. Easy as pie."

"Easy, huh? What if somebody sees us?" Abe was unmoved.

"One of you will keep an eye out while the other one makes the hit. Hey, I'll be the guy in the water they'll be talkin' to. I'm the only one they'll see. I'm takin' the biggest chance. They'll never see you guys at all."

"Hmm." Jeremy wasn't sure. "Whatttaya think Abe?"

"I dunno. We might be able to pull it off, but it's gotta be fast."

"Of course it does. It don't take too long ta open a car door and empty a wallet bro. 'Specially if if it ain't locked ta start with. Scope out the ones that ain't locked first. Remember last summer when we hit that car at the Lane? In and out in less than a minute. Same thing again, 'cept this time we'll hit a few more for more money. It'll all take about ten minutes. Then we're out of town." Marco knew this was the moment of truth. "Look, I'll be the only one they'd be able to ID once they put it all together, if they put it all together. I got the most ta lose and I'm totally confident we can do it."

"Yeah, I guess so." Jeremy wasn't going to let Marco think he wasn't behind him.

"He is takin' the biggest risk, bro."

"Aw fuck, I guess so." Abe was resigned to go along.

"Hey, we'll be outta here before anybody knows what hit 'em. Once you guys signal me that you made the hit, I'll paddle to the beach an' then sprint through the wharf to the boat. You guys'll hoof it over to the wharf an' we'll meet up."

"Then what?" Abe wanted all the answers.

"Well, we'll lay low 'til nightfall, buy some food and beer then leave just before dawn."

Marco held up the bottle. "Let's drink to our success." He upended it and handed it to Abe. "Or you wanna stay here an' maybe go to jail or get drafted?"

"Aw shit." Abe took the bottle and gulped a hefty swig then coughed.

"Take it easy bro. This is sippin' whiskey." Marco chuckled uneasily.

Abe didn't want just a sip he wanted the numbing effect. "Fuck that."

Jeremy pulled another sip too, a big belt.

Abe grabbed it. "Okay man. Let's do this thing." He pulled another big gulp and winced as the hot liquor hit his chest. Marco saw his eyes water. He wondered if it was from the whiskey or something else.

"Sounds okay." Jeremy assured Abe. "Hey, 'an we'll be together for a great adventure in Mexico."

Marco knew the VO was changing the mood. "Then we'll head over to Moss Landing, fuel up and bust out. It'll be two days to the border." He knew it might take a little longer but wasn't saying so. "Then we'll pull into a nice point break and surf, surf, surf."

Abe cracked a reluctant smile. Marco and Jeremy shook hands on it.

Jeremy yawned. "Shit man, I'm beat. Hated sleeping on that goddam cement garage floor."

Marco saw the VO glow in his eyes.

"These bunks are great." Marco assured them, "Slept like dead seal last night." He was making another joke. Nobody laughed. He patted Abe on the knee. "C'mon bro, let's get some shut eye. You'll feel better 'bout things in the morning. The *Three M's'll* rock ya ta sleep like a baby."

"Yeah…okay." Abe slid his guitar case under the bottom bunk and lay down as Marco turned off the lantern.

"Hey Marc," Jeremy added. " How long to Matachen Bay once we hit the border?"

" I dunno, another day or so. And I'll bet there's lotsa unridden point breaks along the way."

"Cool."

They all listened as the lantern swayed, each in their own deep thoughts as the whiskey took full effect numbing their brains. Marco hoped his sales job had them convinced and confident.

Once they got used to life on the boat it would work all out. And the VO would help smooth things too. As soon as they were able to surf in warmer water away from the crowds the whole journey would start to take on epic proportions.

Marco envisioned trolling south and reeling in a big tuna or Dorado from the stern of the *Three M's.* They'd fillet it up, fire the stove and eat fresh fish as they cruised along the coast. And drink plenty of cold brews. In his mind he saw the way the sky would look at night when he was on watch: a dark blue apron of shimmering stars under a full moon. He imagined the lights from the barges and cruise ships as they made their way north and south in the shipping lanes, as the *Three M's* hugged the coast just inside the lanes.

The small blue flame hissed on the stove as the *Three M's* pulled on her mooring lines, creaking gently on her stays. The fog buoy began its usual evening groan and before long, they were all gliding away into quiet harbors.

Dawn broke silver gray. Low cumulus bumped up against the bay foothills. Marco listened at low volume to the weather report on KDON as Abe and Jeremy slept. Farther up the coast a big storm was moving in from Oregon. Huge waves, twenty to twenty-six feet had washed two tourists off the cliff near Point Arena. A guy from the coast guard station in Monterey was being interviewed. He was predicting giant surf in the bay by Sunday morning and warning people to keep clear of the cliffs and beaches. Marco laughed at that. He knew just the opposite would happen. Out-of-towners hearing the news would flock to the cliffs and beaches to get a close glimpse of the big waves. He wondered how many might be swept out with the outgoing surges.

Twenty-four hours. Then all hell was going to break loose in the bay. It took about that long for the swells to reach Monterey Bay from Point Arena, maybe even less. If the actual storm front backed off and it didn't rain hard or get real windy, it could mean giant, clean waves at the Lane for the final heats of the Nor Cal Championships. The best local waves were created by storms just north of the border. They'd dump all their rain and wind in Oregon and northern California sending clean, open-ocean swells pumping down the coast.

It would be the pits not to compete in those conditions. It might just be the biggest, most perfect waves of the season. But how could he compete? He wasn't even in the contest. He would've had to surf through all the elimination heats today to make the final cut. And the law would surely be snooping around to see if he showed. Everybody knew he'd be one of the main contenders for the crown. It sucked that he wouldn't be able to make the scene. He'd surfed all these years to get there, paid huge dues in the water to finally go for the big prize and now not be able to give it a shot.

Marco quietly slid open the cabin door and went out on deck. He could tell by the sky that the conditions were going to change, but it didn't look like rain, the clouds too broken-up and disjoined. A pelican took flight off the fish hold lid. The bitter air hit him. He pulled up the collar on his jacket and checked the mooring line, as wind scattered across the choppy surface. Four gulls huddled in a tight pack against the lee-side of the boat, bobbing alongside in the ruffled water. It was a bright morning, sun pockets glaring off the surface. But colder than hell.

He pulled out Louie's navy binoculars scanning the beach. Not a soul. Too early and too damn cold, even for the usual bums going through trashcans looking for bottles and aluminum cans to turn in for wine money. He peered through the wharf to the cliffs at the Lane. A large group had assembled but he couldn't make anybody out. He knew the contest would be getting underway around eight, starting with the elimination heats and going into the quarterfinals and semifinals; then Sunday the final heats made up of the six highest-ranking competitors in each division.

It would be potential suicide to show up and surf in the contest but the idea gnawed at him. He couldn't risk the whole Mexico trip just to surf in a contest. He grumbled to himself as he envisioned everyone on the cliff in their club jackets, laughing and hooting it up.

But this day was money day. It was time to collect for the trip; that was the important thing. After all, he and Abe and Jeremy would be surfing more empty waves in warm water than all those idiots in the contest. They'd have to stay in town and deal with the crowds and cold water long after the contest was over. They'd all be envious of Marco and the boys once word got back where they were and what they were doing. Marco would have the last laugh on all of them.

He returned to the cabin, rubbing his cold hands over the stove flame. He turned on both burners for more heat. The interior of the cabin wasn't cold or warm, just kind of clammy. He switched off the radio and boiled water for coffee. Steam glazed the portholes and front cabin windshield. He made sure the fuse box cover was secured. Dry fuses were a top priority. It was always a good idea to check the fuses weekly Paolo had said or any time there was a big rain event. Without electricity the *Three M's* would be nothing more than a big chunk of driftwood, floating along aimlessly at sea.

Jeremy stirred in his bunk. "Hey Jere,' it's morning."

Jeremy's legs slid over the top bunk. He flopped onto the floor gazing half-eyed at Abe, still curled up in his wool blanket. "Yo, bro." He fumbled for his glasses. They fogged up as soon as he slipped them on. "Man, it's steamy in here."

Marco cracked the door. Hot mist escaped.

"Yeah, but it's freezin' out there."

"Lesser a' two evils, I guess," Jeremy added.

That was quite a profound statement. Marco thought it sort of summarized their lives in general. They lit smokes as the coffee pot perked.

"Looks like a big swell comin' in."

"Yeah?"

"Probably hit tamorrow some time."

"Hmmm…that gonna keep us from splittin'? "

"Nah, all we gotta do is jus' make it ta Moss Landing. The swell will be aft. It'll help push us across. We'll fuel up there and wait for it to pass. No big deal."

"Cool. Coffee smells good."

The pot stopped percolating. A constant, thin steam rose from the spout. " She's done."

Marco pulled two mugs from the bin and filled them.

"Got any sugar or cream?"

'Hmm, let's see.' Marco realized he'd have to get a lot more familiar with where everything was stored. He fumbled through a few drawers. 'Here you go.' He pulled out a little red and white tin can of concentrated milk and packets of sugar from the Dawn Fishers Café. He poked a hole in the can with an ice pick.

Jeremy looked at the can with trepidation. Marco picked up on it. "Hey, we'll get some a the real stuff when we get some cash. Like my ol' man used say, "any port in a storm."

Jeremy nodded, poured the thick, yellowish-white liquid in the mug and shook a packet of sugar in. "Yeah, okay."

"Hey, beggars can't be choosers." Marco snickered then realized maybe that wasn't the smartest thing to say. He sure didn't want Jeremy to feel bummed about their situation. "We'll get some cream tonight."

Jeremy blew into his cup. Abe woke and stared at the steam-coated porthole next to his bunk. The light changed from bright to diffused grey every few seconds as clouds came in and blotted the sun. He cleared his throat. It felt scratchy as if he were coming down with something.

"Good mornin' mate. How 'bout a hot cup a coffee?"

Abe swung over and stood up. He yawned and checked that his guitar was under the bunk. "Got any hot chocolate?"

Another question Marco couldn't answer. "Let me check." He rummaged through the bin again and came up with a tin of instant chocolate. He opened it. Rock hard.

"Sorry, bro. We'll get some. Sure ya don't want coffee? It'll get yer motor movin.'"

"Nah, it makes my stomach sick." His stomach was already upset for other reasons.

"Okay." Marco searched the cabinet. "Hey, how 'bout some chicken noodle soup? "

"I dunno, let me think about it." Abe sat back down and tied his sneakers.

"Think I'll just play for a while."

Marco pulled out a can and held it up. He read the label. "Just like home made." He opened the can, added water and set it on the stove.

The nylon strings filled the cabin with a mellow sound. Abe stopped every few minutes to re-tune. He tried to finger-pick a slow classical piece, pausing from time to time to find the correct finger positions. Marco heated up the soup and poured it into a mug. Jeremy went through bins and cupboards getting familiar with the lay out. A string popped. "Shit." Abe muttered, "Goddam nylon strings. Can't keep 'em tuned. Always break. Shoulda got a steel string."

Marco thought he seemed a lot more animated than usual. He figured it was about a lot more than just popping a string. He changed the subject. "Hey, here's some crackers, some canned sardines." Marco set a jar of peanut butter on the chart table, too. "Eat up guys, then we'll go make a withdrawal. A big withdrawal, from the Bank at Cowell's Beach…valley branch." Jeremy nodded tentatively in silence.

Abe blew on the hot soup and yawned. Marco could see he and Jeremy were in deep thought and didn't want to risk saying anything stupid that might upset them more. It was going to be a very daring stunt to pull off and Marco wondered if it would all really go as smooth as he made it out. "Hey, how 'bout some tunes." He turned the radio back on. The music was a nice diversion from the intensity in the air. They sipped from the mugs and finished half the peanut butter and crackers. Nobody wanted any of the sardines.

"Never had soup, peanut butter and coffee together before," Jeremy added with an uneasy laugh. "Not half bad."

"Served only on the finest cruise ships headed for Mexico." Marco was adding anything he could to lighten things up. Nobody laughed. "An' pretty soon it'll be barbequed fish and cold cervesas."

"Now that sounds good." Jeremy was perking up. The coffee was working. Abe was silent and pensive, shifting uneasily in his bunk.

The row to the wharf was a little choppy but not too bad. The wind was settling down about to change direction with the slight warming of the morning. Marco thought it might even go offshore by noon.

Marco wore his wetsuit jacket but kept his shoes and levis on until they made it to the landing. Marco's red team board was in tow. It would be the board to ride on the smaller waves at Cowells. The Intruder had more of a speed shape for bigger, more lined up waves.

They pulled the skiff up onto the landing. Marco would give them about a fifteen-minute start before he'd begin the paddle through the wharf over to the break area at Outside Cowell's. Abe would signal from atop the shale stairs by the bathrooms when it was time for action. Marco would hold court with the vals in the water. He figured he'd talk about the contest at the Lane and suggest the kooks start their own surf club. He chuckled to himself about the idea of a "San Jose Surf Club." Might as well call it "Kooks Anonymous." He'd then discuss board designs and competition teams. They'd watch him rip up the waves for inspiration.

Marco peeled off his jeans and shoes and set them in the skiff. The side wind coming through the wharf in the shadows made his bare legs shiver. It was a lot colder in the shade, not that it was much warmer in the sun, and as soon he plunged in with his board it would be freezing.

Hell with it. Soon he wouldn't need a wetsuit in the warm water in Mexico.

Abe and Jeremy hustled off the wharf and made their way to the cliff overlooking the point at Cowells. Twenty minutes passed by in a blur of disjoined thoughts as Marco waited for the signal. He saw Abe wave his arms as planned. Jeremy must be busting into the cars.

He set the team board on the heaving surface and carefully laid down on it. The frigid sea swept up his bare legs. His hands stung from the cold as he stroked through the pilings towards the take off spot at Outside Cowells. That's where all the vals would be hanging out, trying to snake each other for the best set waves. He pumped hard trying to get the blood moving and build up body heat inside the wetsuit jacket. That was always the plan: to get the body heat stoked up as soon as possible and keep it stoked. Movement was the key. Once he stopped, the intense cold would swarm all over. "Cold water builds character." That's what the mid-fifties, pre-wetsuit surfers used to say. If that was true his character was definitely getting built up with every stroke.

The side shore wind abated. A brief period of glass coated the surface. It wouldn't stay that way for long. Not with a big swell coming down the coast from the north. Who knew? A big wind might accompany the swells or maybe it might switch to off shore. He'd know by next dawn for sure.

The stinging in his hands gave way to a workable numbness. It was only a matter of time anyway. The cold always won in the end. It was simply a matter of how many waves he could get until he lost the battle and one wipe out was all it took to take him out quick. Once water flooded his jacket, it was curtains. His legs and chest would totally freeze, his muscles would cramp and his feet would lose all sense of feeling. His hands would turn into purple stumps.

As he paddled toward the cypress point at Cowells, Marco saw the crowds lining the cliffs at the Lane. He heard the bullhorn blaring, signaling the beginning and ending of the heats. One blast at the start and two blasts at the end. He saw contestants in bright colored jerseys scratching for waves in the distance and started getting pissed. He should be there kicking ass and knocking guys out of the tournament. It took all his reserve to calm down and stay focused on the job at hand.

He paddled into the take off spot and sat up on his board in the middle of the crowd. He yelled. "Hey guys, what's up? Any good ones out here?" The crowd saw his red board with the big competition team logo on it and knew he was a hot team rider. They gazed at him with envy, a real surf star in their midst. They became nearly mesmerized and couldn't believe he was surfing with them. Marco railed on about the contest and what it was like being on a surf team. Things they all wished they could do but would never achieve.

Marco stroked into a few waves weaving through the pack, tip riding and pulling off stylish, slash-back turns. The vals ate it up and tried to copy his moves on waves they caught. As long as he was right there surfing with them, they'd never think about paddling in. About ten minutes later Abe waved his arms over his head.

Marco saw the gesture, and to keep the vals even more off guard, invited them to paddle to the beach for a little coaching on the sand. It would keep them from going to their cars a little longer. He caught the first wave of the next set, a nice four-footer and rode it all the way into the cove, perched for twelve seconds on the tip of the inside section. The vals hooted at his ride. He rode it all the way to the beach.

He sprinted across the beach with board underarm. He hoofed through the wharf out of sight then paddled hard for the landing. He never looked back, just pressed hard for the public landing and the skiff. Stupid valley turkeys, bought the whole bullshit session, hook, line and sinker.

Marco struggled up the rusted metal stairs onto the landing, bare legs throbbing. It was hard hoisting up the board with cramped, stiff fingers. He pulled on his Levis but couldn't button the top button. His fingers were too numb and stiff. He couldn't tie his black tennies either. His hands were a whitish/purple/red color. He briskly opened and closed them trying to get the blood flowing. He stood shivering, glancing out from under the wharf at guys riding waves at the Lane in the distance.

Jeremy burst down the stairway. "Jeesus, Marc. We hit pay dirt." Jeremy could hardly talk from the run back to the wharf. "We got over five hundred."

Marco couldn't believe it. It was way more than he thought they'd get. "Oh man! Hey where's Abe?"

"Felt like he was gonna puke or something. Left him at the bathroom at the wharf entrance. He'll be right here." Jeremy wiped the dirty sweat from his lenses.

"I can't believe it, five hundred?"

"Scary as hell though. Check it out." He showed Marco five, one hundred dollar bills and some other denominations. "It all came from one car. There was a brick of pot in there, too."

"A drug dealer." Marco laughed. "It don't get any better than this."

"Whattaya mean."

"We ripped off a doper, bro. He'd never report it to the cops. Perfect, damn perfect."

"Was hairy as hell, man. Suppose the guy walked up on me. Maybe he had a gun in there, too."

"No sweat, bro. It's the perfect crime."

Crime. The word hit Jeremy hard. "I dunno man, I guess so."

"Hey, we ripped off a rip off. Stoked."

"Guess so." Jeremy was breathing hard and fast, obviously shaken.

"We'll be stylin' for sure. Thanks ta you and Abe. Hey, you guys get all the biggest set waves at the first point we surf."

"Yeah…cool." Jeremy kept looking at the stairs halfway expecting someone to follow him. "God, I can't wait to get going South."

They stood on the landing, each in their own moment of introspection waiting for Abe.

"Soon as Abe gets here we'll high tail it to the boat." Adrenaline surged through Marco. "Fuck, we pulled it off big time!"

Jeremy helped Marco get his shoes on and pull off the wetsuit jacket. Wet cornstarch stuck to his arms and chest. Marco got into a tee shirt, a hooded sweatshirt and pulled on Louie's wool watch coat but he still shivered.

Abe took careful steps down the wet stairs. He looked jittery and was sweating. Marco sensed his nervousness. "Hey Bro. It was quite a score."

"Yeah?" His eyes were wide and fearful.

"You okay? "

"Yeah."

Marco knew he was lying. "Lets get back ta the boat and have some lunch. We'll have tuna on crackers, potato chips, an' I got some candy bars."

Abe was silent on the row back to the *Three M's*, clenching and unclenching his fists. Jeremy counted the loot as the skiff chattered over the mottled surface. "Fifty-one, fifty-four… shit man, we got five hundred fifty-four bucks."

"Pay dirt! We'll get more food from Beach Liquors later and head on out tomorrow morn. Man, we're almost outta here. It's only a few hours now."

"Hey Marc, how long's the trip to Moss Landing?" Jeremy asked.

"I dunno, a couple a hours I guess."

"Why don't we just take off now, get our food over there?"

"Nah, I wanna make sure the boat's ready. I gotta check the oil and generator."

"I still don't see why we can't do all that in Moss Landing."

"Look, just keep yer cool. I wanna get outta here as much as anyone. I just don't want anything ta go wrong on the way over there." Marco realized Jeremy was nervous about hanging around after the hit on the cars and Abe was quiet as crab bait. "Look, I'm freezin' my ass off. I was the guy in the water. My balls are sucked up inta my stomach. I need ta thaw out a little."

"Yeah, okay." It was a reluctant agreement. Marco could feel Jeremy's nervousness and Abe's silence was deafening.

"I just need a little time ta get things ready. That water was freezin'." Marco looked out through the wharf at the Lane. It looked like the swell was beginning to pick up. "I'm not quite done here, yet." Jeremy nodded. Abe began to bite his nails.

The afternoon flew by. Abe and Jeremy went through all the bins and storage lockers figuring out what was where. After Marco thawed he made lunch and checked the oil level and the generator, flicked off and on all the circuits making sure they worked. He also tested the running lights, especially the dome light on the compass for cruising at night, and the radios. The bilges were pumped and trolling gear fastened tight. Everything on deck was dogged down or stored below. The sun descended into thick dark mist.

Marco switched on the light over the chart table. "Okay guys, let's hit the store and get some beer too." No argument from anyone. Abe and Jeremy nodded walked out on deck and lowered the dinghy.

The sea rose and fell as the skiff approached the wharf landing at nightfall. Surges increased in size and consistency. With two hundred in cash, Jeremy and Abe set out to get food at Beach Liquors in front of the wharf. Jeremy would try to nab a few six packs of half-quarts by bribing one of the wharf drunks. Old Chief was the prime target. He was going to tip him twenty bucks just to blow his mind. Shouldn't be a problem at all.

Abe brought his guitar case. He wanted to get as many sets of nylon strings as he could from his music teacher who lived a stone's throw from the beach. Hard to tell where in Mexico they'd be able to find any. Time to stock up now. And Marco knew Abe would be a bear to live with without his guitar to play. Best to satiate everybody.

This was the last time they'd be able to get any strings for a long while. Marco chuckled to himself as he thought about how Abe plucked that guitar a lot more than he probably played with his own dick. The damn thing was like his pet or something.

Jeremy and Abe ascended the stairs to the top of the wharf and disappeared. Marco tied off the skiff and stayed below to make sure it didn't crunch into the pilings with each swell. The cold on-shores gusted periodically. The weather predictions were going to be accurate with the surf rising overnight. He felt it in his bones. He nearly tripped over a small brown take-out box just like the other ones he'd found with the food. A white envelope was taped to the lid. It had his name on it. He opened the box first: a whole baked chicken with aromatic herbs, two bananas, an apple and three chocolate bars. He set it on the bottom stair, opened the envelope and read as he ate a chocolate bar:

Marco,

> *I'm a friend of your fathers. Paolo told me you're on the boat. I want to help you. I knew your father well. He always*

talked about you. Loved you very much. Please call me. You can trust me. Hope you like the food.
                        Emma 423-6702

Emma? Who the hell's Emma. His dad never said anything about any Emma. Was she a waitress or what? He wasn't sure whether to call or not. She did leave him food. And if Paolo knew her she must be cool. So how come Paolo never said anything about her before? Maybe it was a set up. Maybe somebody heard Paolo talking and called the cops. But what about the food and how come there wasn't a letter with the other boxes? Why was this Emma writing to him now? Was she another family secret coming to light? Maybe that's why Paolo didn't say anything. Maybe he was just protecting Louie. Marco could understand that. Paolo wasn't the kind of guy to blab out secrets about his dad. Or was it some sort of set up to nab him? Ain't buying it.

It was too risky, especially now. The guys would be back before too long and they'd be set to split town. Can't let anything get in the way. They'd have everything they needed. Why chance it all now?

Marco pulled a drumstick off. He shredded it off the bone. Good, damn good. The woman could definitely cook. He tore off the other drumstick and a wing, too. After gouging the meat he tossed the bones overboard. He watched them disappear below the landing as they sloshed against a tarred piling. A new type of chum for the pile perches, smelt and crabs.

He'd power the chicken down with Abe and Jeremy when they returned. Nothing like home-cooked food and he knew they'd be stoked. Wonder if Emma was a real person who'd want to help out? Maybe she was dad's best woman friend. Louie was popular with the waitresses and he always tipped them well. Maybe she was one of them, just a friend who wanted to support him during trying times. Or was she something more? Is that why Louie had the condoms? It was all wild speculation and was getting complicated the more he thought about it. Screw it all. No time to take any stupid chances. He sure as hell didn't want to be baited and fooled like a dumb salmon, snatching wildly at something that could hook him in the jaw.

He heard a clanking sound above. A short, hunched-over woman made her way down the stairs with a dull flashlight. She wore a dark blue, wool watch cap pulled down over her ears and brow with a baseball cap, a faded Giants logo on it. She was clad in denim overalls with a black wool sweater and high rubber boots. She had to be around four-foot six or seven. It was Rosie.

Rosie lived down the block from his mom's house in " Little Italy" Louie called it, the fishing neighborhood. Some of the old time locals called it "La Barranca" which meant "the hill" in Italian. She could be seen pulling her little red wagon along the cliffs down to the wharf twice a day. She hauled a wooden bait box, an empty five gallon white plastic bucket with a few burlap sacks and a half-gallon water jug. She kept to herself and lived in the basement of her house, a little stucco place just off West Cliff Drive, a few blocks from the wharf. She would constantly mumble to herself as she hobbled along. People just left her alone. She lived in her own world anyway ever since her husband Franco died in the war.

He was in the second wave to hit Omaha Beach at Normandy and machine-gunned down by the Krauts before he had a chance to emerge from the surf. A landing craft ran over his corpse as it unloaded a squad on the beachhead during the final successful assault. He floated around with the hundreds of other carcasses for two days until he was finally fished out. Then the news reached Rosie.

She was found five days later alone in her house when her sister went over to check on her. The back door was open and two cats bolted out as her sister entered. The cupboards were banging in the breeze, food cartons shredded open and scattered about, a broken jar of biscotti cookies in the sink.

Rosie's sister found her sitting in a rocker across from the sofa holding Frank's three-piece wedding suit. There was a framed picture of the two of them outside Holy Cross church on their wedding day along with a form letter from the President and some war medals.

Rosie was in her bathrobe rocking slowly and mumbling incoherently, staring at the wall. Two empty brandy bottles sat on the coffee table. Her feet were bare and bleeding. Later at the hospital the doctor who examined her said he found tiny scratches and teeth marks on her toes. The feral cats were eating her.

After her release from the hospital with a two-month stay in a sanatarium, neighbors brought her home-cooked dishes for a few weeks. Then people just stopped coming by, even her sister. She received a widow's pension from the government every month and took to crabbing every day on the wharf.

Rosie slowly, deliberately took each step down to the landing, a burlap sack in one hand. Marco stood statue-like as she crossed the wet timbered planks. She looked up at him at the last second. "You move," She muttered in a far off, otherworldly voice. "Rosie check trap."

A yellow braided nylon rope was tied off to the wooden rail. It disappeared beneath the landing, swinging around underwater as swells moved shoreward.

"Sure, Rosie." It was the first time he'd ever been up close to her. Of course he'd seen her all his life along the cliffs but never really paid much attention. She was more like a ghost or nonentity, someone you drive by all the time but never really see.

She looked old with deep-etched eyes, silver hair and wrinkled face but in reality was probably in her mid-forties. She kept her traps in the water all year, never pulling them out except to check the catch and re-bait them. And she never ate crabs, hated the taste, just fed them to the cats in the neighborhood and tilled the shells in her garden. Marco didn't know what to say next, just spouted out, "How's the crabbin?"

She sneered at him and hoisted the net. "Crabs tell all."

That was way out there. "Crabs tell all." What the hell did that mean? She showed a wide smirking smile. She looked him up and down while pulling up the trap line. It broke water, the three-foot wide, flat metal basket with bright green kelp hair and seawater streaming off. She swung it onto the landing with a steady hand. Marco was amazed at how strong she was for such a little woman.

"Rosie see..." She pulled one big crab from the tangles with her stout fingers. "Big one dead." The second crab was smaller, squirming around erratically trying to get untangled from the web. Rosie pulled it off quickly with a sharp twist. "Father and son... father dead, son hurt, only one claw." The crab opened and closed its remaining claw warning Rosie to keep her distance. "Maybe him survive, maybe not." She looked up at Marco then tossed the two crabs in the burlap sack. She stuck some fish parts in the strands of the trap and lowered it over again. It swayed side to side flatly as it sunk below. Rosie whispered something Marco couldn't quite make out. She turned and looked at him. She had one bright blue eye and one black eye. Marco felt she was both looking at him and through him at the same time. "Maybe him survive." She started mumbling to herself again, slowly ascending the wet stairs, holding onto the handrail with her left hand, gripping the burlap sack with her right. Marco heard the wagon wheels roll and clank away towards the end of the wharf where she had other traps to check.

A wave swept under the landing causing the skiff to swing into a piling scraping off a section of small barnacles. Marco pulled the skiff alongside the stairs and hopped in figuring he could control its movement better aboard. He'd drop the oars and pull away from the wharf a bit until the guys returned.

That Rosie was nuts, crabs telling her things and all. That was way over the top. No wonder everybody kept away from her. He caught a whiff of his own breath, pretty bad, and the new stubble on his chin itched. When would he get another shave or hot shower? Hard to tell.

Hey, once in Mexico it wouldn't matter. Might even grow a beard. The ocean was almost as warm as a bathtub down there. They could always bathe in the fresh water streams or creeks that flowed into the ocean. That's the way a lot of Mexicans did it. And he saw locals catching Dorado and other great fighting fish right off the beach. The remnants of their beach fires were always strewn with fish bones and clam and mussel shells.

He imagined devouring Dorado on the beach, swilling it down with ice-cold Mexican beer or a few shots of tequila. Good tequila, the brands sold only in Mexico. The cove crew always brushed their teeth with tequila every morning in San Blas. It was a daily ritual.

Soon they'd unchain from the mooring, fuel up in Moss Landing and head out. They'd ride the southerly swells down the coast. Marco imagined the *Three M's* as a wide, heavy surfboard rising and dipping over the open ocean swells.

Lights flickered on atop the wharf, along Beach Street and the Boardwalk as if they were in total sync. He wondered if somebody planned it that way or was it just coincidence? The lights became gold and silver streamers snaking on the dark surface.

He loved the view from the water. It was a quiet and peaceful world removed from the clatter and hassles of town. Except for the occasional shrill of a gull or the splashing of a seal or otter it was pure serenity.

No wonder dad preferred it to home. No yelling wife, no weird home life just the slow heaving of the *Three M's* as she rose and fell on the rolling sea.

He spied Jeremy on top of the wharf hoofing it back with paper bags. Was Jeremy able to score some brewskis, too? He hoped so. The VO was okay but there's nothing like suckin' on a cold beer. Marco wished he'd grabbed a few bottles of Louie's homemade wine before he split his mom's. There were several untapped kegs in the cellar and racks of bottles along the east wall. Dad and the other fisherman liked to hang out in the cool cellar, drinking and laughing, and afterwards, Marco and his cousins would sneak under the house and drink from their half-empty glasses.

Marco pulled *Dago Red* alongside the landing again. Jeremy stumbled down the slick stairs. A can of corn fell out, rolled down and plunked in the water, dropping out of sight. "Hey bro, that was your serving." Marco joked.

"Marc,' you ain't gonna believe it." Jeremy set the bags on the wet timber floor.

"Abe's bailin' man. He ain't goin'"

"What?"

"Yeah, he ain't goin,' said we were nuts."

Marco then realized why Abe took his guitar off the boat with him. He wasn't planning on coming back. The whole bullshit story about needing more strings was just a big lie.

"Fuck him, man. The cops'll nail his ass soon."

Jeremy handed down the bags between swells as the skiff rose and fell. Marco saw the fear and concern in his eyes. "Marc, what're we gonna do?'

Marco hid his anger. "We'll go it alone…we don't need 'im."

Jeremy hopped down into the skiff. Marco pushed off with an oar. Jeremy's eyes burned, as he fought back tears. He was breathing hard and quick again. Marco wasn't sure what to say, feeling queasy in the stomach himself. In silence they rowed back out. Marco remembered the box of food, changing the subject. "Hey Jere, have some chicken, home-made."

Jeremy looked at the box nervously. "Where'd you get it?"

"A friend, a friend a my dad's brought it."

Jeremy stared at the chicken and fruit and candy bars. "Maybe later."

Marco knew why he wasn't hungry. "It's good chicken man. I had a little. Look Jere, I know we can do this by ourselves." Jeremy was quiet and still. "My dad an' Paolo used ta go out on trips all the time by themselves. No big deal. Believe me, we can handle it."

Jeremy surveyed the wharf and the shoreline. He buried his hands in his pockets.

"I'm cold."

Marco sensed he was a lot more than just cold. "I'll make us somethin' warm ta eat. We'll heat up the chicken. Did ya get some cocoa mix?" Jeremy nodded. "Great, we'll have hot chocolate. An' we'll spike it with a little sippin' whiskey, just ta warm up our innards." Jeremy stared blank-eyed at the wharf again. "Wait'll you taste that chicken. It's great." Marco wasn't sure how convincing he was or even if Jeremy was listening at all.

They pulled *Dago Red* to the starboard side and tied off. It would be out of sight from the wharf in case anybody was snooping around.

In the cabin Marco boiled water, made cocoa and set the chicken in a pan covered with foil. The smell of chicken grease and herbs filled the cabin, masking the diesel smell and stale salt odors from the bilge. Jeremy lay back on the bunk and listened to the transistor radio. Jefferson Airplane was singing, *"It's No Secret."* Marco felt the demons swarming through his thoughts.

Marco uncorked the VO, pouring hefty shots in mugs. "Ya know Jere. You're the only guy I knew I could depend on. Abe and D.J. an' Willy, they ain't got what it takes." Jeremy sat up and listened while searching Marco's eyes.

"I can't believe it's just you and me." Jeremy had obviously been thinking about his options. "You sure we can pull this off? Don't bullshit me."

"Hey, you can never bullshit a bullshitter, right? You think I'd do something like this if I didn't know I could do it?"

Jeremy wasn't certain about anything but he trusted Marco's word. He was his best friend. "Naw. I guess not." He thought about what a stint in juvie might be like or being placed in a foster home. Escape from it all was his best option. His only option.

"Hey, I may be dumb, but I ain't stupid." Marco was trying to lighten things up. "I know what the hell I'm doin'."

"Yeah?" He continued searching Marco's eyes for any quaver.

"Definitely." Marco was acting steely. "Look, Paolo went over it all with me. He even drew out the course for us." Marco produced the charts again with the course sketched in red. "See, same damn trip he took with my ol' man when they cruised ta Ensenada." Marco moved his finger along the route. "Stay inside the shipping lanes, turn south at Point Conception, then straight down ta the border."

Jeremy composed himself taking a swig from the mug. He looked over the charts. It seemed like a good plan. "Could we put in at Ensenada, once we hit the border ?"

"We may wanna just bag it farther south, find a nice point break and surf our brains out."

"Maybe. We might need ta get more food first."

"Sure, whatever you want, bro." Marco was reluctant to pull in at Ensenada. It might just be a little too close to the border. What if the Feds were on their trail by then? Once the *Three M's* disappeared from her mooring in Santa Cruz it would only be a short while before they were onto them. Better to high tail it farther south. "Yeah, we'll cross that bridge when we get to it."

"'Member how drunk Willy got in Hussongs?" Jeremy leaned back against a bulkhead smiling at the memory.

"Hussongs," was the most popular bar in Ensenada. It was a rite of passage to go there whenever they were on a surf trip south of the border. They served margaritas "straight up" with fresh-squeezed lime and ice in a salt-rimmed glass. No frills, just a handmade drink with a strong shot of tequila, a drunken surf dog's delight. "Sure do, puked all the way back ta the van." They laid Willy down on his wetsuit on the sidewalk until he couldn't puke anymore, just dry heave. They wrestled him in the van and took off south for Mazatlan for a day's surf at Cannon's, then on southward to the epic sand bar point at San Blas.

"Maybe we could go there again."

"Maybe. Hey, let's eat. I'm starvin.'"

"Guess so." Marco was glad to see Jeremy regain his appetite. It was a good sign.

The VO warmed their insides muting the intensity of the situation. They gorged the chicken, ate the fruit, split the candy bars then chugged a few more belts of whiskey.

They retired to the bunks all numbed out, listening to the radio, smoking a couple cigs and pumping each other up about the trip. A little before midnight they crashed out.

It was set. First thing in the morning they were out of there. Arivaderchi Surf City. See you later, a lot later and be sure not to write.

A fat halibut cruised the sandy bottom scrounging for food. The large swells twenty-six feet above churned up the silty scum from the bottom into a powdery haze. The halibut searched blindly smacking into a large engine block and chain. It ascended a few feet of kelp coated links then dove back down resuming its bottom search. A couple yards up the galvanized chain two Jack Smelt nibbled at light green kelp strands stuck between the links. A school of anchovies floated back and forth farther up the steel line as the surges moved shoreward, then receded. On the surface a gull swam intently around the red mooring float attempting to snag anything edible just below the wind chop.

The *Three M's* pulled hard against her mooring lines. The strong galvanized cleats on her rail held taut against the surges. Overnight hail had hammered away the patches of gull and pelican splats on the deck, creating a thin, whitish glaze. The boat listed lightly from stem to stern in the passing swells.

Marco heard the tugging, felt the boat rise and fall. Big swells had hit the bay overnight just like the weather report predicted. He still felt hazy from the whiskey. The empty VO bottle rolled around under his bunk. Just how big was the surf? He sat up, placed his hand over his mouth and smelled his breath… randy, with a slight VO finish. The clock read 7:40.

He slid open the hatch and went out on deck. Bright as hell. High, puffy clouds dissipating south with a freezing offshore blowing. Which was worse he contemplated: cold, windy and clear, or cold, foggy and wet? It was a toss-up. Through Louie's navy watch glasses he scanned the Lane through the pier. Medium tide swells formed on the outside reefs between Middle Peak, and Third Reef was showing. Had to be between fifteen and eighteen feet, biggest swells of the season. He watched a big left-breaking peak reel off and spit. It was huge and hollow and mean.

He spied the contest people getting ready on the cliff to start the final heats. Surf photographers were jockeying for the best shooting positions and spectators unfolded chairs. He knew that some contestants wouldn't even paddle out in those conditions. They'd drop out of the contest altogether fearing for their lives. It was a day for just the ballsiest surfers. No spineless jellyfish or wannabes need apply. He knew that meant the field in the Men's division, his division, would be down to only four or five of the top dogs.

"Hey Jere, get up." He yelled down into the cabin. Jeremy tossed around and sat up.

"Time ta split, bro."

As Jeremy stood up and yawned, powerful feelings raged through Marco…biggest damn day of the year, biggest contest of the year, biggest prize…"God dammit." He knew he might even win it if he was given the chance. He could definitely handle the intensity. Instead, he was hiding away on a boat ready to leave it all behind at the moment of his greatest challenge. Hell, he was like a lame bilge rat hobbling away from a big chunk of cheese for fear it might get caught in a steel trap. That just wouldn't do. He couldn't run away from who he truly was inside, one of the rulers of the Lane. And he was going to prove it one more time.

He fired up the engine, unhooked from the mooring and moved the *Three M's* past the end of the wharf. Marco turned the wheel towards the kelp beds outside the Lane instead of east towards Moss Landing.

"Marc,' whattaya doin'?" Jeremy was surprised.

"A slight change a plans."

"Whattaya mean?"

"Here take the wheel." Jeremy grabbed the spoked wooden wheel. " Keep her headed outside the beds towards Seal Rock. Jeremy pulled back on the throttle. The *Three M's* slowed way down. "What the hell you doin'?"

"Goin' for it."

"Goin' for what?" Jeremy was frantic.

"The prize…just one wave, then we're off."

"What the fuck you talkin' about?"

"Look, I'm gonna ride one wave in the finals, take it all the way down through Indicators and pull out before the bowl at Outside Cowells. Then you'll pick me up and we'll head over ta Moss Landing."

"You're outta yer mind. What if you wipe out and lose yer board and have to swim in. You'd get popped for sure. Then what about me?"

"I ain't gonna lose it bro. I'm gonna rip it up. Just one wave to prove to 'em I woulda been the champ…just like I did at Casino's."

"Jessus Christ." Jeremy couldn't believe his ears. He was livid, breathing short and fast but knew there was no talking Marco out of it. He watched in total fear as Marco got into his red baggies and wetsuit jacket. He pulled the Intruder out of the fish hold.

"Just drop me off outside Middle Peak then pull a big circle around and pick me up at outside Cowells. Trust me."

"Aw, fuck." Jeremy's eyes watered.

They moved out in silence past the massive kelp beds to where the big swells were forming up. Marco saw that the four contestants in the Men's final were paddling out from Point Surf where they'd jumped off the cliff in between sets and were pulling for the outside reef. He knew them all. "Okay bro, see you inside."

Jeremy was crying as Marco jumped off onto his board and sprinted over to the peak. He knew he'd have to get used to the cold water quickly. It bit hard on his bare legs, had to be around fifty degrees, maybe even in the high forties and the off shores were bone chilling.

Marco met up with the group at the outside boils where the biggest waves would form. "Hey fellas, great day for a contest, huh?"

The other contestants were shocked to see him. One of them yelled, "What the hell you doin' here. You aint even in the contest." They knew Marco would've had to surf through all the elimination heats like they did to actually qualify for the finals.

"I'm here to win." He laughed a cryptic laugh and paddled outside as a big set moved in. The others paddled shoreward trying to jockey for the best take off positions as the set approached. It was a four-wave set, every wave looming over fifteen feet. They all picked up waves and rode into the inside reef vying for the longest rides and highest possible scores.

Marco was alone on the outside. He saw Jeremy moving the *Three M's* in a big arc towards the point at Cowells. He flashed back to the morning when he saw Jake take the horrifying wipe out exactly in about the same spot he now was sitting. The bells from the Oblates of St. Josephs on the point began to chime. It was an eerie sound that made goose bumps rise on his back inside his wetsuit. His gut twisted. The chiming seemed like a warning somehow just like it was for the Ohlones whenever they heard it toll.

What was he doing? Maybe he was crazy. What if he did end up like Jake maybe drowned or at least captured after a long swim in. Was any of it really worth it?

Uncontrollable shivering enveloped his legs and arms. Maybe he should just paddle down to Cowells, play it safe, meet up with Jeremy and get the hell out of there for good. That would be the smart thing to do, the sane thing to do. What would he prove anyway? Would anybody on the cliffs really care what he did? He wasn't in the contest anyway. It was all just a crazy idea and he was jeopardizing everything for one moment of glory. Just get out of there. Leave the damn contest behind. Get out of town. Get on with life, but what kind of life? As those thoughts raced through his head he hadn't kept his eyes seaward.

A monster wave was forming on Third Reef. A bigger wave than he'd seen all morning, all season. It was a single wave making its way into the bay, not in a set. Marco had heard the stories of giant waves coming out of nowhere before. "Rogue waves" the fishermen called them. They were something all fishermen feared who dared go out on stormy days. They could easily get washed overboard or even capsize if the wave broke directly on the boat. Somehow in the open ocean a set of waves could form into one big swell if all the conditions were right.

The image of Jake tumbling down the face of the huge wall that morning in '59 emblazoned in his mind. No, banish that thought. That was Jake's fate not his. It wasn't going to happen to him.

He paddled hard to get further outside as the swell started to froth at Third Reef. He knew that meant it was gaining in power and size beginning to rise higher as it felt the deep rocky reef. The huge peak moved directly at him. Marco had never seen a wave like this one. It had to be a solid twenty-five footer maybe bigger, way bigger, at least twice the size of the wave he rode at Casinos.

The off shore winds pushed hard against its face creating a bumpy steep wall. Marco sprinted out and realized he'd never been out so far, definitely in an area of the Lane where he'd never seen a wave break before. But this was a wave like no other.

It picked up more speed as it turned for shore. Marco knew it was going break soon, steaming along directly in his path. Could he get over it in time? He pulled with all his might. The loud chimes from St. Josephs rang through him rattling his core. He sprinted like a man possessed as adrenaline surged through him. The shivering suddenly stopped and he even felt hot inside his wetsuit. His vision cleared and the whole scene seemed brighter than before. Then it came to him in a flash. He wasn't going to paddle over this monster to safety and he wasn't going down like Jake the loser. He was Marco, Marco the great.

The wave perched up higher as it felt the outside reef, water rising rapidly up its face. Marco spun around and pulled like an Olympian shoreward as the wave sucked him skyward. The wind blew hard against his body as he dug his arms deep into the steep wave. Stand up. Stand up quick. No, paddle more. Make sure you get your momentum going down before you stand up. Make sure you don't get blown off and fall into the void. Don't pull a Jake. Set the rail, set the goddamn rail. He pulled in as hard as he could. He had to stand up now or it would be too late.

He took two more mighty pulls then jumped to his feet as the swell sucked out. He pressed down hard on the board against the wind blowing up the face making sure it tracked downward. A huge plume of spray blew off the top as he descended into the pit. He took a deep breath as spray blasted his eyes. He was streaking downward at full speed, blind. It was so steep he wasn't sure he could keep the board tracking but kept pushing hard. He brushed the salt spray from his stinging eyes.

He cranked a deep, sweeping turn at the bottom and felt his fin give way for a second then track back in as it gashed a slot in the wave's face. With outstretched arms, he aimed the Intruder for the middle of the elongating wall, skimming so fast the rails of the board seemed to slice the air.

He heard the crowd on the cliff cheering wildly as he streaked along past the Blowhole. The other contestants, caught inside were ditching their boards and diving under as he rode past on the giant grey-green swell. Their boards would for sure be pulverized on the cliff.

The wave lined up all the way through Indicators dropping down to around ten or twelve feet in height. He pulled over the top as it closed out near the point at Cowells. Spray enveloped him again. He took a long breath and freefell over the back of the swell smacking down on the deck of the board. His chin slammed against the hard fiberglass. Had he knocked out a few teeth? No, they were intact. His jaw and face burned. He saw stars. He felt his nose. Numb. Then he tasted it. The blood. He wiped the warm red stuff from his mouth and chin. Was his nose broken? Was he bleeding somewhere else? He sat atop the board and scanned for the boat and Jeremy.

He waved his arms overhead. Jeremy chugged along outside the kelp forest then headed toward him. He did it. Pulled it off and kicked ass. Even though it kicked his ass real hard, too.

He made it over to the boat. Jeremy pulled him and the Intruder aboard. He shivered and trembled in the crisp air, legs going purple. Jeremy's eyes were wild with fear and relief. "Bro, you did it. Yer bleeding pretty bad."

"Yeah...yeah... let's get the hell outta here."

Jeremy aimed the *Three M's* for the deep water and slid open the throttle. The boat rose and pushed over the on-coming swells as they set the course southeast for Moss Landing. Bright glare from the winter sun sparkled on the surface. Marco, still in his wetsuit, wrapped up in a wool blanket on deck and dabbed at blood with a towel as the Lane and the wharf disappeared in the big rolling swells that pushed them toward Moss landing.

Clouds began to reform on the horizon. The going became bumpy as the winds on the outer bay kicked up. A misty haze descended on the surface blotting out the stacks at Moss Landing. The following seas were pushing them southeast and at least the wind was at their backs.

Marco sat in the cabin in his dry clothes rubbing his frozen legs under a wool blanket, sipping on a new bottle of VO. It burned his mouth from the cuts inside. He dabbed at his nose with a towel. The bleeding nearly stopped as his nose swelled shut. His face was numb. It hurt to open his mouth. Dad would be proud. Dad would be real proud. He looked off the stern. Santa Cruz had faded away in the thickening mist. He wondered if he'd ever see it again or if it was now truly lost in the fog of his past. Blood occasionally dripped on his bare feet.

Jeremy was silent at the wheel, sick to his stomach from the erratic movement of the broken-up sea, eyes weepy and red, smiling an insane smile.

I t was a slow passage across the bay with the high swells and wind but the *Three M's* never faltered. Her heavy weight and wide beam handled the conditions well. Marco took the wheel, held back on the throttle and coasted across at five knots.

Jeremy's stomach continued to cramp. He'd puked a few times, staring blank eyed into the mist, secretly praying they'd hit Moss Landing soon. Marco assured him he'd get his sea legs before too long.

It was mid afternoon, mist breaking up, when they saw the stacks at Moss Landing. They passed the mile buoy with its green light. The harbor was just east from the entrance to the Monterey Canyon. The canyon plunged to a depth of three thousand fathoms right off the continental shelf. It always bothered Marco that it was so deep so close to land. It just didn't seem right somehow.

During salmon season his dad and some of the other boys would troll along the steep canyon walls just off the shelf and hook into some bizarre species of fish that weren't local to the bay. The theory was that the deep-water fish would cruise into the canyon at night and surface in the shallower waters of the bay. Marco heard it was so wide that The Grand Canyon, which spanned many southwestern states, could fit easily within it.

They motored into the mouth of the harbor as broken clouds massed together. Waning sunlight on the surface turned the water to molten metal. The sun disappeared behind a dark gray mass of clouds, as the on-shores shattered the surface.

Marco slowed the *Three M's* and maneuvered through the red and green channel markers that guided them in. He remembered what Louie always said, "Red, right, return," which meant you always keep the red lights on your right, starboard side whenever entering a harbor.

The fuel dock at Woodward's Marine was empty. Two large drag boats were docked on the end ties. Albacore season was over by mid-October and the only boats still going out were the bottom fishers. Marco knew his dad always loved this place. No arrogant "yachties" like in the Santa Cruz Small Craft Harbor, just hard-working fishers trying to support their families and keep their boats in business.

A ghost town of a harbor, Moss Landing was loaded with abandoned and decrepit wooden buildings, now havens for rats and derelicts. They used to house the booming canning industry during the sardine era. By the mid-fifties it all but died out. Now the fishing fleet was only ten percent of what it was. The huge purse seiners, the ships that trapped all the sardines, were just about non-existent. The only two remaining canneries General Fish and the Santa Cruz Cannery barely survived. Santa Cruz Cannery bought only whole fish, which was still profitable because Moss Landing was gaining reputation as an albacore and salmon harbor. The only fish still being processed there were anchovies, mackerel, salmon, squid and albies.

A rough and tumble-looking guy in his forties wearing a black Greek fisherman's hat came out from Woodward's and spit in the water. Jeremy jumped onto the dock and looped a line from the bow around a cleat. Marco slipped her in reverse and nudged alongside then cut the motor. He threw the stern line over and tied her off. He nodded to the dockhand. "Fill'er up."

The dockhand gazed curiously at the boat and Marco. He surveyed the tie-off job on the cleats. "Ain't cha gonna put out yer bumpers?"

Marco realized he forgot to lay the rubber bumpers along the rail before tying her off. He climbed aboard, flipped them over and retied her.

"You want me to fill'er ?" The dockhand saw Marco's beat-to-shit face.

"Sure." It hurt to talk. Marco's jaw was seizing up.

"Okay, if you say so." He pulled the diesel nozzle over to the boat and unscrewed the bronze tank cap with a spanner wrench then proceeded to pump the diesel. "Haven't seen Louie in a while." He obviously knew the boat.

Marco realized the news hadn't crossed the bay yet. "He's gone."

"Gone?"

"Yeah, passed away."

" Hadn't heard." He continued to scan the boat.

"I'm his son, Marco."

"Yeah?"

"Yeah."

"Didn't know he had a son. Always came over here with Paolo or Emma."

"Emma?"

"Yeah, they'd hang out for the weekend. How come you don't know that, if yer Louie's kid?"

"Sure, sure I knew that."

"Wasn't she yer mom?"

"Umm yeah, yes she was."

"Louie never said nuthin' 'bout a son. 'Corse he never said much anyway, 'less he was drinkin'."

"Yeah. Hey, there's a shot a me an' dad in the cabin on a troll together. Where can we get some food?"

"No stores roun' here. Closest ones in Castroville or Watsonville. We got candy bars, chips and that kinda stuff inside. Where ya headin'?"

"South."

As he filled the diesel tanks on board, the dockhand scanned the deck. Marco's wetsuit was drying out on the cabin roof. Jeremy and Marco walked up the gangway to the main dock.

"Why's that guy asking so many questions?" Jeremy was glad to be off the boat for awhile.

"Just bein' friendly I guess. I dunno. He knew my dad."

"Marc,' who's Emma?"

"Oh, just a fiend a my dad's. She gave us the chicken and stuff."

"Uh huh."

"Look, we got enough food ta make it ta the border." Marco winced with pain. "We'll put in at Ensenada like you wanted, okay? We'll stay the night here so you can rest and get yer constitution back."

"Great." Jeremy was nauseous and thirsty. A night's sleep in the harbor sounded good. "This place is kinda creepy."

They gazed at the abandoned buildings, heard groaning and creaking sounds as wind swells pushed against the pilings underneath. Stacks of sun-bleached wooden fish crates piled up everywhere. The place stunk of fish carcasses. A whiff of diesel hit them every few minutes.

"All done," the dockhand yelled. "Ya need ice?"

"Nah." Marco paid him in cash. "Can we leave her here for the night?"

"Ya havta tie off over there on the end a' E dock. Ya want a receipt?"

"Nah."

"Suit yerself."

They moved the *Three M's* over to the end tie and put out bumpers. The on-shores gained in intensity. The fogbank was blowing in. Alongside the harbor jetty, big swells pounded the beach. Lights popped on in the cabins of three workboats. They heard occasional laughing. The muted sound of ship to shore radios and CB's crackled from time to time. Gulls squawked in the riggings and harbor seals swam alongside.

They climbed back aboard. Jeremy sipped two mugs of water and hit the bunk hard. Marco lay awake pondering things to come. Emma. Who was she really? Would he ever know? Maybe he should've called her. And what was going to happen next? They'd leave at first light and be at sea for a couple of days until they hit the border. Would the swell die down or stay big for awhile? Have to check the weather reports in the morning. Didn't matter much. They were leaving anyway, south to the border, south to freedom. His nose throbbed big time. He didn't dare touch it.

Marco closed his eyes, feeling totally done in. The big wave ride, the contest, Gina and Vickie, the Cove crew, none of it mattered anymore. They were all awash in the shadows of his recent past. His jaw burned too, probably dislocated. The only thing that mattered now was escape. Escape and a good night's sleep.

Marco rode on the back of a seal, clutching its thick fir. They darted through warm green water, swooshing around bright coral outcrops diving down to white rock reefs. The sun on the surface was a shimmering gold ball. The warm water tickled Marco's scalp as it flowed through his short hair. The water turned from green into brighter shades of blue. The seal banked toward the surface scattering a herd of salmon. The seal lunged at them, tearing out the firm, pinkish-orange belly meat. It gobbled away with abandon bursting through the surface with a big salmon flapping wildly in its jaws. A loud shot. A sharp pain in the neck. Another shot.

Blood pulsed from under the seal's front fin, a perfect heart shot. Writhing in pain and gasping for air it belched and choked violently, sinking motionless toward the bottom. Marco jumped off its back swimming frantically for the surface. He pulled with all his might toward the shimmering light but he was too deep. He blew out all his air and scratched wildly upward. His strength gave out. At the last second he burst through the surface, arms flailing around in the cold, dark blue water. He saw a trolling boat motoring out of sight in the distance. Two fishermen cheered on the stern, one waving a Winchester 30/30, the other swigging from a whiskey bottle.

Marco lay on his back treading water as the sky turned dark grey. A swell formed on the horizon, a huge black wave blocking out the sky. As it approached, Marco tried to swim away but it was right on him now. It peaked up, becoming a steep wall, sucking out and pulling Marco up its face. He felt himself moving skyward. He was at the top of the seething peak as it threw all its strength outward, downward. Marco freefell into a black, swirling pit ...

Marco awoke with a shudder. A dream, just another weird-ass dream. The small clock on the chart table read four forty-four. Not yet dawn. Images of the dying seal and the gigantic black wave began to dissipate. Get up, check the radio and find out what the weather's doing. Was the swell still big? Is it raining outside? How cold is it? He delicately felt his nose. It was swelled shut and still throbbed with a vengeance. Was it busted? He'd have to wait to see. Maybe in a few days. His jaw was totally locked. Even moving it slightly sent a shooting pain up the left side of his face. He had a pulsing headache.

He pulled on Louie's wool coat, turned on the propane, lighting both burners. The *Three M's* groaned on her ties as she squished against her rubber bumpers. The cabin windows were frosted with droplets on the outside, steamed up on the interior as the burners pumped out heat.

Marco fumbled with the dial on the AM radio until he found KDON. After they played *"Feelin' Groovy," "Satisfaction"* and *"Paperback Writer"* the road report and weather forecast came on: thick fog in the morning, then a day of high clouds with occassional rain, wind from the south around twenty knots. They talked about trees going down on power lines in the mountains and beach erosion overnight. A drunk had collided with a jack-knifed semi on highway seventeen with no fatalities causing lanes in both directions to be closed until further notice. " Stay tuned for more news and traffic."

That meant it would be fairly clear and windy at sea after the fog lifted. And cold as all holybejessus on the open ocean. They'd leave at dawn though with no wind in the fog. It might be a little rough for awhile when the winds came up but would definitely get smoother further south, hopefully. At least the wind would be from the aft. Jeremy would have to stomach it for a bit longer. The following seas would push the *Three M's* directly from her stern making for a smoother ride.

Marco put water on for coffee and went out on deck. Dew dripped off everything. The entire fleet was covered in a shiny glaze. A CB radio crackled on in one of the other boats. Otherwise, it was dead silent. Dense fog shrouded the abandoned wood shacks and buildings along the harbor. A mangy feral cat appeared from a hole in one of the buildings, running behind a stack of boxes with a rat squirming in its mouth. The dock creaked.

The last morning in the bay. The fog was thick enough to cut with a knife. Moss Landing was known to many fishermen and surfers as the home of the "pea-soup fog." There'd be weeks of heavy fog all day and all night. But when the salmon bite was on in the southern part of the bay, it was better to berth in Moss Landing and be out on the troll earlier rather than having to cruise down from the Santa Cruz harbor. The northern tip of the bay where Santa Cruz sat had much better weather, sunnier days, warmer temperatures and great surf beaks. In the south county a small group of surfers rode the sand bars at Manresa and Rio Del Mar. Those areas were referred to as "the beaches."

They had six hundred gallons of diesel on board now and enough food to make it easily to Mexico, not to mention all the fish they'd grab on the way down. If they cruised at eight knots all the way they'd make the border in two to three days.

They'd keep the CB radio set on channel sixteen, the coast guard emergency channel for updates and stay about four to five miles off shore skirting along the thirty to forty fathom line. They'd be able to know approximately where they were using the compass, fathommeter and radio direction finder just like Paolo showed him. Once underway they'd fasten a pole off the stern and pull a hoochie jig. Who knows what they might snag into?

It was November 11th, Veterans Day, always a sacred day for local fishermen. Many had served overseas. He knew that back in Surf City there'd be the big parade and fish fry on the wharf, the annual event Louie never missed. There'd be a lot of tearful stories and hugging and crying and wine drinking, a lot of wine drinking.

But Marco had made up his mind. He'd never serve in the military, not in this stupid war, no way. Go get shot up for what? Nobody was attacking us. No enemy was trying to do a beach landing at Cowells. It was one thing to go fight for your country and other thing altogether to go get mixed up in some bullshit conflict so far from home.

The kettle in the cabin was steaming hard. He stirred in a scoop of instant and poured in canned milk with a spoon of sugar. Clock read five-fifty and first light was showing eastward. Time to raise Jeremy.

Jeremy rolled out and yawned. "Man, I died last night."

"Sure did. Howdaya feel?" It hurt to talk but Marco wasn't about to let Jeremy know how injured he was.

"Not bad bro, not bad at all, a little thirsty." His stomach felt tight but Jeremy wasn't going to complain either.

"Good, have a cup and we'll shove off."

"Maybe some cocoa." He wasn't going to take any chances with acidic coffee.

Jeremy stirred a hot mug as Marco fired up the diesel and checked all the electronics. The red compass light flashed on. Marco pulled out the chart for Monterey Bay and set it under the chart table light.

Jeremy sipped his cup then went dockside to unhook the lines. Two cars drove down the dirt road into the harbor lot, one with flashing red lights.

"Marco, come quick."

Marco peered out the cabin door. A loud speaker screeched on. "Stay where you are. This is the Monterey Sheriff's Department. We want to ask you some questions." The dockhand in the Greek fisherman's hat was pointing at them with four uniformed men.

"Cast off, cast off, Jere'."

Jeremy threw the lines on deck and hopped aboard. Marco slowly brought up the power and pulled away from the dock.

"Return to the dock immediately." The loud speaker crackled. "A Coast Guard boat from Monterey is already at the harbor entrance. Do not try to depart, turn around now!"

Marco gunned it, aiming straight for the open ocean. Maybe it was just bullshit about the Coast Guard boat at the harbor entrance. Maybe they were trying to bluff them into going back. Hell with it. Marco pushed the brass throttle lever forward to top speed and lurched out the harbor entrance. He didn't see any boat in the thick fog. A weak spotlight scanned the water about forty yards away. Shit, it was the Coast Guard.

He cranked the wheel to port, turned off the running lights and skimmed out into the fog.

"We know you're out here," a muffled voice in a bullhorn demanded. "Don't try to escape. Cut your engine and turn on all your running lights."

"Jesus Marc,' whatta we gonna do?"

"Keep cool, bro. They won't find us in the fog." The sound of the shore break was loud. Marco knew they were just outside the surf line, a dangerous place to be if a big set rolled in.

"You can't get away. Move further out. Turn on your lights. That is an order."

The goddam dockhand called in on them, the prick. It was only a matter of time now.

As the Coast Guard craft approached in the dense mist Lenny the Bull's words echoed in Marco's memory. "Don't ever let 'em take you in, no matter what." Lenny's tortured face appeared in Marco's mind. "Listen, Jere'. Our only chance is to go in through the surf."

"What?"

"Not in the boat, on our boards."

Jeremy heard the waves thrashing the beach. "No way man, it's gotta be ten feet or bigger. Can't even see the beach." His glasses slid off his face when he bent down, shattering on the deck. He started to sob, sucking back his tears. "Can't see a damn thing in all this fog."

A spotlight was scanning the thick mist. "Hold your position and turn on your lights. We're going to board you. Do not try to resist. We are heavily armed."

" Marco….you gotta get outta here. You can do it bro." Jeremy's eyes watered but he was gaining control. "You and the Intruder."

"What?"

"Yeah man, just like you did at Casinos and the Lane. Don't let these bastards take you down. They're a buncha fuckin' kooks man. You're a goddam livin' legend bro." He was sucking back tears and livid. "I aint goin' man…I'm fuckin' blind. I'll stall 'em, tell 'em yer in the cabin, buy ya some time."

"Fuck, I can't leave you Jere."

"Hey man, I'm dead meat. You can do this. Jeesus Christ man, yesterday you rode the biggest fuckin' wave that ever broke at the Lane. Goddamit listen to me. Get the fuck outta here."

"Aw shit, I love you man. Like no other." Marco eyes were wild, filling with tears. He saw the dull beam from the search boat panning the area.

"Get the fuck outta here…now!" Jeremy was smiling huge and proud and laughing with tears streaming down.

Marco stripped down and stretched on his wetsuit jacket. It was the fastest he'd ever suited up in his life. He pulled the Intruder from the hold and balanced it on the splash rail. "Jere,' you'll be okay… I love you, bro."

" Fuckin'-A right man!" Jeremy pumped his arms overhead in a jesture of support and victory. "Marco…Marco…Marco the great!"

Marco jumped overboard scraping his left foot on the barnacled splash rail. He found the balance point and hurriedly stroked into the fog. Jeremy throttled the *Three M's* straight into the fog toward the outer bay just east of where the spotlight was flashing as a further diversion from their position.

Marco paddled toward the beach rose up and slid down the backs of a set of dark swells as they formed up and moved past him shoreward. He was out of sight from the boat in the heavy fog and could only imagine the scene. Armed Coast Guardsmen in dark blue uniforms interceding and boarding the *Three M's*. They might even have Jeremy in cuffs by now or would shortly. Marco knew he'd be really freaked out. It would take them a few moments to figure out Marco wasn't onboard hiding somewhere. Soon they'd know he went overboard. Then they'd be heading back to Monterey to impound the *Three M's* and take Jeremy into custody or maybe hand him over to the local cops at Moss Landing harbor.

Marco knew they'd be searching for him but it would be hard in the fog. He'd have to get to the beach and hide out for awhile then figure something else out. He'd stash away in the abandoned cannery buildings then hoof it down the beach to the highway and hitch a ride somewhere. Maybe one of the fishermen who knew his dad in the harbor would give him clothes and a ride south on one of their boats.

A set was forming up outside. He saw large dark lumps moving in. Should he try for the first one or wait for one of the last ones in the set? If he waited, a big close out wave might dust him. If he took off and ate it on the first wave he'd lose the board and have to dive under all the other waves in the set. He decided to wait. He rose over the first wave. Not too big, maybe ten foot or so. The sound was loud and ominous as it exploded on the sandy reef behind him. Next wave about the same maybe a little bigger.

He realized there was no logical take-off spot, just lined up, closed out walls pounding down on the bars. He'd have to paddle in hard on the take off, make the drop, straighten-off and prone in. That is if he didn't spin out on the take off, lose it all and end up in the awful churning. It didn't seem to matter much which wave he rode. The third wave was around the same size as the others around ten foot or so.

Hell with it, go for it, got to get to the beach quick. He took half a dozen strong strokes and stood as the wave rose up. Too steep. He air-dropped down off the Intruder. It flipped over at the bottom. He dove under alongside it. The punishing lip came down hard. He grabbed a full breath as it beat against him, smashing him down onto the sandbar toward the beach. His nose filled with water and started bleeding again.

It was deeper than he imagined. Swimming hard for the surface it felt like his lungs would pop. He exhaled all his air as he scrambled to get up. The surface was covered with bubbles and foam. He gulped down another breath just before the next wave broke. Luckily, it unleashed its power further out. He held his breath one more time, submerging as eight feet of dense sandy foam hit him. He tumbled underwater towards the shore.

Marco flailed to the surface in neck-deep water stuck in a strong side shore current streaming southward parallel to the beach. He fought with all his might to swim across the rip. The freezing water flooded his wetsuit jacket. The rip settled into a still, deep hole. Marco dog-paddled onto the sand. His gut throbbed from the beating. He was shivering.

Crawling up the steep, wet beach he turned and watched another set blast away on the bar. Just like Jake. He heard muted sirens in the fog and knew they were after him. Where was his board? He stood up and squinted down the beach. Gone. Did it get sucked out with the rip or was it still getting pummeled in the shore break. Too late to worry about it now, gotta go hide.

He limped up the beach toward the dunes. His nose bled. He sucked in the blood and kept going. Maybe there was a shallow cave or bushes or someone close by who'd help him.

The abandoned cannery buildings were too far away to access in a hurry, another forty or fifty yards across the dunes. His legs froze as he hobbled on his scraped ankle. His jaw was on fire. He found an indentation in the dunes next to a clump of wind-torn bushes, huddled into it and closed his eyes. The salt water stung them. They watered.

Dirty wet sand caked his legs and hands. He'd rest a moment then sprint up the beach and go hide in one of the cannery buildings. He panted hard to catch his breath, then coughed twice. The shore break hammered away at the beach as another set unleashed its power.

The dark fog was giving way to a lighter gray, as muted sun broke off in the distance. Sandpipers shrilled at his intrusion. Marco hunched down, pressing under the bushes. He hummed an old sea shanty he and his dad used to sing together, something like, "Way hey, blow the man down..." Dad would make up dirty verses to the melody. Marco laughed uneasily as he remembered one then started to cough violently, spitting up seawater.

The searchlight from a squad car panned the beach. The dark grayish fog was dissipating but still blanketed the dunes. Four county sheriffs and two Watsonville cops trudged from the jetty southward in a line up the dunes, their flashlights tiny yellow beams barely penetrating the mist.

When they found Marco he was still humming the shanty, shaking from the cold and coughing. "Hey fellas... surf's up."

Marco gazed out the Greyhound bus window. In the parking lot Marie and aunt Cat wept, hugging each other. Uncle Joe stood stoic and held his arm out with his palm facing Marco. He stomped out a cigar with his left foot.

Gina and her sister pulled up right next to the bus in their old Plymouth. Gina rolled down the window when she saw Marco, waved at him intensely and crying hysterically, yelled, "I'll always love you." Then her sister pulled her back in the car and drove off.

It had been five days since the cops found Marco in the fog at Moss Landing. The Greyhound bus was scheduled to leave the downtown terminal in Santa Cruz at nine sharp. Federal Marshall Jenkins accompanied his prisoner for the ride up to the Oakland Induction Center.

Marco heard Jeremy was going to a foster home in San Mateo after a month in the California Youth Authority. Willy escaped from a Youth Authority work detail and was still at large. It was rumored Abe was hiding away up in Mendocino County in a hippie commune. Karie was staying with her aunt who was adopting her. DJ's dad knew an anti-war psychiatrist who was writing up a profile on DJ claiming he was mentally unfit for military service. And the authorities said they never could locate the whereabouts of the kids' parents.

Uncle Joe's lawyer, Hancock, was able to cut a deal with the Feds to let Marco volunteer for the draft rather than face a federal prison term for evasion. Getting all the charges dropped was out of the question. He argued that Marco never got his draft notice because he wasn't living at the address it was sent to, and that he and Jeremy were just going on a fishing trip when they got popped. It was a sketchy defense but he was well connected with the prosecutor. There were so many draft evasion cases still on the books they were happy to have closed this one.

At the arraignment, Jesse, the dockhand at Woodward's Marine, testified for the prosecutor. Marco then realized he screwed up by asking Jesse to fill the diesel tanks. That was a chore boat owners always did for themselves. Then there was the matter of the wetsuit on deck and not knowing about Louie and Emma. When Marco didn't want a receipt for the gas it seemed strange to Jesse, too. Commercial boat owners always took a receipt after filling up for tax write-offs. All those things tipped Jesse that something was out of whack. That's when he decided to call the sheriffs. He didn't realize Marco was trying to evade the draft or that Louie had willed the boat to him anyway. Jesse then felt like an ass for turning him in.

The *Three M's* was impounded and chained to the Coast Guard dock in Monterey. Marco had no idea what would happen to her. Would Marie sell her and keep the money or what? She never cared much for the boat anyway.

A white pickup truck screeched to a stop in front of the Greyhound as it was pulling out onto Front Street. Paolo bolted from the cab and pounded on the accordion bus door.

"Open up, godammit."

The bus driver, a thin balding man with glasses, released the lock. The door burst open. Paulo turned sideways pushing his huge bulk to the rear. He kicked over a box of books a woman had stashed under her seat, saying "Sorry ma'am." There was no way he could bend down to pick them up, he was just too thick.

Marshall Jenkins, a skinny man with a potbelly stood as Paolo approached. With one big shove to the gut Paolo slammed him back to his seat knocking the air out of him. "Sit down shithead," was all he said. "Marco." He gave him a big bear hug and handed him a carton of Camels and a brown take-out box. "Some pastries an' barbequed albacore an' some pesto an' sour dough. Marc' you write me, you hear." Paulo fought back tears. "An' we're gonna go fishin' on yer boat, when ya get home, you can bet on that." Paolo gave the Marshall a look that scared the hell out of him. "Thought you might want this too." He handed Marco a copy of the latest *Surfer Magazine* hot off the press. The words, *"Steamer Lane Style: Rogue Surfer Tackles Rogue Wave,"* were printed in large letters below the cover photo. It was a full-page color shot of Marco slicing a stylish, deep bottom turn on the monster wave. He was arching with both arms outstretched overhead as the thick lip was pouring over. "Guess you're quite a celebrity now." Paolo took a deep breath. "You take good care, ya hear, an' don' worry none." Marco saw the sweat above his gleaming eyes. He was talking loud and fast.

Paolo hugged him again and gave the Marshall a hateful look that froze him in his seat. He turned sideways and shuffled down the aisle, wiping back tears. He looked down at the lady who had returned the books to the box under her seat. "Sorry, ma'am." He dropped a twenty into the driver's lap. "Sorry fer the hassle."

The driver nodded. "No problem."

He pushed out the accordion doors then hugged uncle Joe, aunt Cat and Marie. A light rain fell. He backed the truck out of the way and chugged down Front Street toward the wharf with empty crab pots and floats jumping around in the rusting bed. A woman in a black scarf leaned out the passenger side window and waved as they pulled away. Marco knew it was Emma.

The Greyhound lurched, air brakes blowing hard against the curb. Blue diesel exhaust steamed onto the wet pavement. Marshall Jenkins grabbed the carton of Camels, the brown box, inspected each, then dropped them back on Marco's lap. "No smoking on the bus." Just what some prick Marshall would say.

The Greyhound moved east on Soquel Avenue turning left at the intersection onto Ocean Street in front of the Cruz N Eat. It pulled onto Highway 17 and shifted into high gear for the winding trip over the Santa Cruz Mountains towards the Bay Area and the Oakland Induction Center. Marco caught the rich essence of the fresh pesto in the box and the barbequed albacore. At least his sense of smell was coming back.

He leaned back in his seat, slid the magazine under the take-out box, wondering what had happened to the Intruder. Did some kid or a local surf-caster find it on the beach or had it floated out to sea in the rip? He hoped it was the latter. He pulled his sunglasses down over his eyes. A tear dribbled down the side of his bandaged nose into his mouth.

Marco closed his watering eyes and imagined himself on the Intruder, knee paddling out the mouth of the bay on a hot, glassy morning, into the light-blue bubbly water, where the churning schools of "albies" surfaced at dawn. He sat up on the board, red baggies dangling below and spread his arms out wide, embracing the warm solar heat, blinded by the bright glare.

The notherlies kicked up, gusting hard against his back. He rose and fell with the rolling, open-ocean. White-capped swells pushed him steadily southward down the long California coast towards the warmer waters off Mexico.

ABOUT THE AUTHOR

Thomas Hansen Hickenbottom is a 4th generation central California coastal native and former professional surfer. He grew up in Santa Cruz California during the tumultuous Vietnam Draft era. He was a sponsored Team rider for O'neill in the late 1960's. He represented the Santa Cruz surfing community in contests up and down the California coast for 3 decades. Mr. Hickenbottom was raised within the commercial fishing and surfing cultures of the late 1960's. His deep involvement within these 2 cultures form the back drop for *Local Tribes*. Mr. Hickenbottom was drafted into the army in the spring of 1967 and has deep insights into the tough choices many young men throughout America had to make during that era. His personal life experiences add a great deal to the formation of *Local Tribes*.

CPSIA information can be obtained at www.ICGtesting.com
Printed in the USA
LVOW08s2210131213

365263LV00003B/557/P